S0-AZR-324

Inheritance

Inheritance

Jane Lazarre

Hamilton Stone Editions
Maplewood, New Jersey

Copyright 2011
By Jane Lazarre

Library of Congress Cataloging-in-Publication Data

Lazarre, Jane.
Inheritance : a novel / by Jane Lazarre.
p. cm.
ISBN 978-0-9801786-8-5 (alk. paper)
1. Racially mixed people--Fiction. 2. Interracial marriage--Fiction. 3.
African American families--Fiction. 4. Whites--United States--Fiction.
5. Identity (Psychology)--Fiction. 6. East (U.S.)--Fiction. 7. United
States--Race relations--Fiction. 8. Domestic fiction. I. Title.
PS3562.A975I54 2011
813'.54--dc22

2011016725

Hamilton Stone Editions
P.O. Box 43
Maplewood, NJ 07040
Hstone@hamiltonstone.org
www.hamiltonstone.org

This is a work of fiction. Names, places, characters, and incidents are
the product of the author's imagination unless when explicitly stated,
or are used fictitiously. Any resemblance to actual persons, living or
dead, is entirely coincidental.

Several chapters have appeared in on line and print journals. I am
appreciative to the following editors and journals:
    Hamilton Stone Literary Journal, "The Arctic Circle," excerpt from
the novel, *Inheritance.* Spring, 2004. On line.
    Persimmon Tree, Fall, 2006. Editor, Nan Gefin: Excerpt from
Inheritance, A Novel. On line.
    Salt River Review, Volume 12, Fall, 2009. Ed. Lynda Schor.
Excerpt from a novel, *Inheritance.* On line.
    Lilith, Summer, 2009, volume 34, No. 2 : "*1919: At the Connecticut
Shore,* excerpt from a novel, *Inheritance.* Print.

For Adam and Khary,
and for Aiyana and Simeon,
who will inherit it all, the stories, the warning
and the grandeur.

Praise for Previous Work

For *The Mother Knot*
"A wholly original and important book --- I cannot imagine a woman who would not be moved, or a man who not be enlightened.

Adrienne Rich

For *On Loving Men*
"A very contemporary document. Meditative, often lyrical …. Compassionate and honest."

The New York Times Book Review

For *Some Kind of Innocence*
" …a perfect matching of subject and form …the dignity, spareness, the fairness and compassion for everyone in the story make it a delight to read … Lazarre takes chances which few of today's fiction writers, more mannered and strategic, would."

Philip Lopate

For *The Powers of Charlotte, a novel.*
"A beautifully written tour de force of a novel in the spirit of Doris Lessing and Margaret Atwood."

American Book Review

For *Worlds Beyond My Control, a novel.*
". . . a special sort of literary adventure. It has the rich, dense texture of life itself."

Lynn Sharon Schwartz

For *Beyond the Whiteness of Whiteness, Memoir of a White Mother of Black Sons*
"An important affirmation of a white woman's love of her black sons. Jane Lazarre, warrior mom, has crossed over."

Alice Walker

For *Wet Earth and Dreams, A Narrative of Grief and Recovery*
" Jane Lazarre has always been one of our bravest writers. She once again makes an art of raw, fierce honesty, as she moves through pain, loss, illness . . . . Inspired by the urgent desire to know and be known, she has created an intensely gripping and profoundly moving work."
Jessica Benjamin, author of *The Bonds of Love*

For *Some Place Quite Unkown*
" . . . as intimate and urgent as a poem. Lazarre's enraptured and lyrical prose probes, with rigor and dazzling artistry, the deepest places of a woman's heart. A powerful and original work."
Jaime Manrique, author of *Our lives are the Rivers,* and other works

Works by Jane Lazarre

Inheritance, a novel

Some Place Quite Unknown, a novel

Bodies of Water (Poems)

Wet Earth and Dreams: A Narrative of Grief and Recovery

Beyond the Whiteness of Whiteness: Memoir of a White Mother

of Black Sons

Worlds Beyond My Control, a novel

The Powers of Charlotte, a novel

Some Kind of Innocence, a novel

On Loving Men, essays

The Mother Knot, a memoir

"Some months after, dragged to the gibbet at the tail of a mule, the black met his voiceless end. The body was burned to ashes; but for many days the head, that hive of subtlety, fixed on a pole in the Plaza, met, unabashed, the gaze of the whites …."
Herman Melville, *Benito Cereno*

"But the man on the floor had not moved. He just lay there with his eyes open and empty of everything save consciousness, and with something, a shadow, about his mouth. For a long moment he looked up at them with peaceful and unfathomable and unbearable eyes. Then his face, body, all, seemed to collapse, to fall in upon itself, and from out the slashed garments about his hips and loins the pent black blood seemed to rush like a released breath."
William Faulkner, *Light in August*

"Until once again it was slavery, slavery, slavery. And – inescapably – race, race, race. Until once again, due to our obsession, we were, as it were, insane. Which to the Negroes, to Lyman, made us perfectly comprehensible and trustworthy – sane. Not just another dangerous batch of well-intentioned, Christian white folks."
Russell Banks, *Cloudsplitter*

Inheritance

Cast of Characters

The Family of Samuel Waterman
Enslaved on the Summerly Plantation:
Ruth: mother of the first Samuel
Samuel: son of Ruth
Little Samuel: son born to Louisa and Samuel
Mr. Henry: (called Old Henry by the whites) a slave on the plantation; an abolitionist leader
Samuel Waterman: grandson to the first Samuel, son of "little Samuel"
Belle Waterman: wife of Samuel
Ruth Hughes: daughter of Samuel and Belle

The Family of Louisa Summers
Louisa Summers: daughter of slave owner
John Summers: Louisa's father, owner of Summerly plantation
Charles Summers: Louisa's brother
Harriet: aunt to Louisa, her dead mother's older sister
Emma: aunt to Louisa, her dead mother's younger sister

The Family of Hannah Sokolov
Hannah Sokolov: maternal great-grandmother of Samantha, grandmother of Maya Reed
Maya Reed: deceased – mother of Samantha, first wife of Jake
Corinne Robinson – second wife of Jake
Michael: Hannah's husband
Rena, Ascher, Sophie: Hannah's and Michael's children
May and Aaron: sister and brother-in-law of Hannah

The Family of Samantha Reed
Samantha Reed: daughter of Jake and Maya, granddaughter of Ami Reed, great-granddaughter of Hannah Sokolov
Ami Reed: grandmother to Samantha, mother of Jake
Jake Reed: son of Ami, father of Samantha
Jacob Reed: deceased – father of Jake, husband of Ami

Prologue:
Inheritance,
a work in progress

If you could see me as I write these words you might see a white woman – not young, but not old either, perhaps at the very edge of the approach to middle-age. You would see a face the color of sand.

But you cannot see my face. I have only my voice to tell you the story of my – of our – inheritance. And it has not always been easy for me to face my history – its complexities of color and race. But I have never forgotten the dream. Like my great grandmother, Hannah Sokolov, I wander over an icy expanse, lost and alone, afraid of losing all definition as I merge with the whiteness. My body seems to be horribly permeable – I can't see through the sleet – I am lost. Finally, my desire for escape pushes me into a violent awakening, I turn on the light, realize I've been dreaming the dream again, remember where I am and, I suppose, who I am. I cross my tan arms over my chest, taking pleasure in how they contrast with my white cotton nightgown. I pull my legs out from the soft white quilt and mark their color, too. I breathe. And each time I attempt to return to sleep, I wonder what part of the dream is made from words I read and reread in Louisa's journal, what part comes from Hannah's remembered images, what part from Myami's, and where I must face that it is mine now, as well.

The dream was handed down through four generations when it finally came to me, first dreamed by Louisa Summers, daughter

15

of a slave owner, mother of a slave, and I have come to love that young white Louisa in a way, although she was dead long before I was born. Her journal belongs to me now, and I have read it many times. Sometimes I speak her words out loud so I can hear her thoughts in my own voice speaking about color and difference and the changes in consciousness wrought by intimacy, crisis, and grief. I love her vulnerable frightened spirit, her increasing bravery, and her desire to understand. Yet, I am unable to overcome my rage at her prolonged innocence. It persists alongside the love. For what if she had been more brave, able to act sooner, before it was too late?

Yet, how can I condemn her for a need to deny the worst dangers, to resist the lessons of history that speak clearly of human capacities for cruelty we persist in calling "unimaginable?" Often, when I read about the violence people do to each other, or see it depicted in film, I want to close my eyes, put away the newspaper or book. I want to forget it all, escape its brutal reality. No one has ever hit me or beat me, yet I seem to feel the beating across a man's back, raising scar tissue as thick as rope, almost as if it were my back being broken by a slaver's whip. I am the enslaved woman on the auction block, stripped to the waist, my body examined by terrifying white men, their fingers probing, eyes evaluating, voices counting dollars as they confer about the strength of my muscles, the capacity of my womb for breeding the children they will rip from my arms. Yet, I have never been humiliated in such an extreme way.

Am I deceiving myself? Do I resist knowing because the victims are too close to being me, or because they are too far away, threatening to interfere with the comforts and pleasures of my daily life? By forcing myself to confront the violence of my history as an American woman, am I presuming too much? By avoiding it, would I be blinding myself to the shapes and colors of reality as I am blinded in the white dream? Between the intrusive presumption and the disconnected blindness, is there a place for an honest witness to stand?

My grandmother, Ami Reed, had the dream only once, and the day she told it to me we were walking on the beach where I am walking now. I had just turned seventeen and we had come for our usual summer vacation near the shore. She had finally completed the memoir I had asked her to write, and when she pulled it out of her knapsack and handed it to me, we embraced for a long time, the thick bound manuscript nearly crushed between us. I ran my fingers through her white hair and tried once again to separate the idea of whiteness and all its intricate layers of denial and cruelty from the faces and bodies of the white people I love and the three white women whose stories flow into mine.

The dream comes back irregularly, and lately there is a faint sound, like an echo, just before I wake. I like to imagine that echo is the sound of all their voices, a force that connects us over space and time. And although I suppose it is more likely an aspect of my own consciousness, I believe the voice inside my head whispering of recognition and relationship reflects not only the conflicts and complexities of my personal history, but the desire for empathy and the beginning of imagination as well.

Samantha Reed, Orient, Long Island

Part One:

*New York State
Summer, 1988*

Chapter 1

My mother drowned in the ocean, caught in a rip tide in the early morning when she went swimming alone, as my father and the local residents of the southern Italian village had warned her not to do, and from then on I could never swim in salt water, even the most calm, preferring lakes to even the shallowest of bays. When my grandmother, Ami Reed, would take me for vacations to the North Fork of Long Island, where the bay is so shallow at low tide even a small child can walk a mile into water reaching only to her knees, I would often get a dryness in my throat and a clenching in my stomach. The feel of the salt and the knowledge of tides reminded me of the ocean at the edge of Montauk where my grandmother, my father, and I had stood for long moments, watching a frigid wind carry the white ash of what remained of my mother's body away, some of it drifting into the water below, some into the sky, floating, as if it might never fall to earth again. My grandmother, a writer with an almost religious faith in the power of words, read a poem, and we all went to lunch at a restaurant where they tried, unsuccessfully, to convince me to eat my favorite dessert of chocolate chip ice cream covered with hot fudge.

From then on I preferred the lake near our cottage, just an hour up the Taconic, where I could fully relax, where I could swim and float, then open my eyes to see land circling all around me, a frame of security that enabled me to close my eyes again and let the water carry me along, surrendering to its gentle currents and pulls, its unsalty feel. Often, when I floated this way, I would imagine that I had gone with my parents on their doomed Italian trip, as I had begged them to allow me to do. I was sure

20

I could have somehow stopped my mother from doing something so stupid as swimming alone in the early morning. And when I read the A.A. Milne poem about James, James, Morrison, Morrison, Weatherbee George DuPree, who took great care of his Mother, though he was only three, I felt faint with anger and regret. For although that young boy had failed to prevent his mother from disappearing forever when she went down to the end of the town without him to watch over her, surely I, a precocious girl of five (everyone said and I believed) might have succeeded where he had failed. I was born reliable, and organized, I am told my mother said of me. Even at two, as other children threw their things around the room, I loved putting things away. I take care of my possessions and, when I am able, of people, with an assiduous attention, at times an oppressive vigilance, as if orderly habits, environments and disciplines of all sorts could protect you – much like a soft quilt on a freezing cold night – from life's incredible chaos, always threatening both from outside and from within. It is in this spirit that I look back on my sixteenth year as a turning point, its events, even now, giving me a perspective – a form to hold all the overlapping stories that have shaped my life ever since.

Even under the large oaks and graceful birches, the air felt hot and still. The breeze off the lake didn't pick up until well after dark, and during the day the water was bath-warm and stagnant. I had been swimming with a group of girls I liked well enough; they had left me at the bottom of the hill that led from the lake to the road, then to another steep hill, and finally to the downward slope that led to our small house. The black tar seemed to emit visible heat rays as I trudged up and down.

A map of the village would look like a wheel, several spokes emanating from a central "colony store" where teenagers infamously hung out. When my mother was young, for she had spent her childhood summers here too, boys drinking beer and smoking Luckies or Kools rolled up the sleeves of tight t-shirts to reveal muscular shoulders, while girls sat on the railing, leaning over just enough to expose whatever cleavage they had. Now all of them smoked marijuana. The boys' bodies were hidden under enormous t-shirts and loose shorts, the girls' cleavage exposed by tight halters ending above belly buttons decorated with tiny diamonds or gold rings. As a child, I had been content to spend a month in the country where the lake and a day camp provided pleasure and friends. But increasingly I preferred solitude and even loneliness to the discomforts of white social life. I was sick, I told my father that summer, of being treated with that mixture of careful politeness and hostility by the white kids – you can smell the feelings, they're so strong – and yes, even in this famously progressive village which was in reality as racially conscious as any other part of the country, as likely to form color lines, especially when kids got old enough to date. It's totally isolating, I told him, knowing perfectly well, even if I hadn't yet formed the right words, that as a black girl, my sexuality was both highly exaggerated and completely ignored. Finally, Jake, my father, asked me if I would prefer to rent out the house in the summer, or even sell it once and for all.

I didn't want to cause any upset in the already precarious relations between my father and my great-grandmother, for whom the cottage at the lake, belonging forever in her mind to her favorite granddaughter, was her only true home; nor did I seek any change as dramatic and irreversible as the selling of the house, which would feel like a new version of the old death to my father, I thought. I was unhappy in the all-white community, though I had known it since my birth, and was vowing to somehow make this my last summer there, but the house evoked my mother for me as much as it did for the rest of the family. I loved the calm, quiet lake even when it was murky, the dark nights filled with cricket sounds, reading stories in the slowly cooling evenings with my grandmother, my father, and my old great-grandmother, Hannah, as we lounged on the small porch.

After returning from my swim and in spite of my damp bathing suit and hair, I felt unusually hot and breathless. By the time I reached the top of the second hill, which felt like a mountain, its black tar burning in the sun, I thought I might faint. I dragged my towel behind me on the gravel and left it in a heap on the grass, lacking even the energy to hang it on the line as I would normally do, and I pushed the screen door open without wiping my feet – both of these actions, I noted vaguely at the time, a sign that something was wrong. My great-grandmother was sitting reading in a rocking chair in the small living room, and she looked up only for a moment when I walked in. Finally inside the shaded, screened-in porch, I collapsed on the day bed and fell asleep.

I slept better on the porch that summer than in the room I shared with Greatgram at the back of the house. Each night, I would try to sleep while she sat at her narrow vanity table, staring at the collection of photographs of her children, her grandchildren, her sister May, a brown-tinted one of my mother on her sixteenth birthday (which I stared at for long hours myself, secretly, when I was alone in the room), and one of herself: a dark-haired young woman with a rounded figure, a long fitted jacket buttoned up to her chin, her skirt falling just above her ankles revealing high black boots. Her eyes were dark and large, and even at ninety-four a trace of the beauty she had been famous for as a young and middle-aged woman could sometimes be seen. Now, her hair was white and bushy with yellowed ends and streaks. She'd comb it straight back, revealing an unusually smooth forehead for one so old, and the yellowish white contrasted with her black eyes and olive skin. In the city, she cut her hair every three weeks and gave herself a perm, followed by a "blueing" which resulted in an acrid smell permeating the house for hours and a head full of tight, purple curls. She looked much older then, I thought, and was glad she'd left her chemicals and rollers at home, saying that in the country where mostly we stayed to ourselves, she could give her hair a rest.

She wore long dresses she called "pinafores" with buttons from the square neck to the narrow ruffle at the skirt's edge. Short sleeves revealed heavy arms, loose flesh hanging, wrinkled and deeply tanned by the summer sun. One dress was pink with tiny purple flowers, another gray with tiny blue flowers; the third, my favorite, was a navy blue with no pattern, except that the buttons on that one were round silver flowers Hannah had taken from her button box to replace the plain white ones that remained on the other two.

Each of the flowered dresses was worn for three days, the blue one on Sunday when she accompanied my father and me, and my father's mother, whenever she was staying with us, to a nearby diner for a special Sunday dinner of hamburgers, French fries and malteds. If the night was cool, Hannah would wrap a thin cotton shawl across her shoulders, white to match her summer sandals. After dinner, singing Nat King Cole songs at the wheel of his old beige Dodge, my father would take us all to the lake where we would watch the sunset and slap mosquitoes off our faces and arms. Hannah loved the lake. Dressed in a black swim suit whose skirt reached her knees, she'd wade in and splash her face, arms, and chest with fresh water. She would not go anywhere near salt water – it made her sick, she said, a preference I did not question since it converged conveniently with my own. When the red sun had sunk beneath the horizon, we would drive home in the dark listening to my father's slightly off key *Mona Lisa, Mona Lisa, men have named you* . . . the phrase repeated over and over because he didn't know any more words. Before bed, we would eat the delicious chocolate sweet called Sour Milk Cake that Hannah baked every Thursday afternoon.

At night, as she undressed in the narrow bedroom illuminated only by a candle, I watched her roll down her thick, beige knee high stockings held up by thin, pale blue garters, the hose, as she called them, not for looks but to support her old veiny legs which felt unsteady when she walked. Looking into the round mirror near the window, she unbuttoned each round silver button with breathtaking care until she could take the dress off her shoulders like you would take off a coat, exposing the pinkish tan corset she always wore, its laces and stays across her torso holding her in but loosened in the informal summer days. She'd worn a corset like this since her teenage years, she said, so by now she'd feel naked without it, as if she were going to sleep; and there was a nakedness to her without the corset, as I saw her in the mornings, her old woman's body hanging and curving without shapely restraint. As soon as the corset and underwear were removed, she blew out the candle and put on her loose, cotton nightgown in the dark, her body visible only in silhouette.

I took pleasure, that summer, in deriding my great grandmother's habits, since I blamed her, in part, for the confusions that seemed to be drowning me. (I pictured myself drowning like my mother, gasping for breath in the depths of the sea.) But I admired her eye for color and pattern, the carefully chosen beige cotton sheet matched with the blue comforter, its neat lines of white leaf patterns bordering the sides, or the pale yellow sheet used on alternate weeks with the dark red comforter, the same white leaf pattern looking brighter against the red; the lace doilies on her bedside table, a clean one each week, one a circle, one a star, one a long rectangle that hung over the sides; and most of all, the three small drawings of a bay at different times of day framed in black wood, matted on pale green and hung in an even line on the wall near her bed. When I asked why she took these three drawings wherever she went despite her expressed dislike for the ocean and the bay, she said she didn't know. She liked the pale colors, she guessed. And I believed her, until that summer when she remembered an old story as a result of the arrival of my father's new "friend" and the book by Ruth Hughes.

Hannah bought it during one of her aimless afternoons strolling through a bookstore. It was a best seller, and though she was a slow and unconfident reader, she often read deep into troubled nights or during slow, inactive afternoons, her mouth opening and closing, as if novels and stories were food. I had noticed the glossy illustration on the cover of a black man and a white woman, both in nineteenth-century clothes, with the insert of a photograph of a contemporary black woman, the writer herself. I had seen Hannah reading it for weeks; it lay on her bedside table where she took it up in the middle of many nights when she thought I was asleep, her reading glasses at the end of her nose, her mouth moving fast.

Damp from sweat and in the deepest, dreamless cycle of sleep on the porch bed, I awakened to my father's loud, welcoming shout and an unfamiliar female voice saying, "Jake! Hey Sugar," and I would always remember the oddness of hearing someone call my father the name I had always been called. I sat up, bathing suit dry now and skin itching. I tried to pull my fingers through my still damp hair but was stopped by the tangles, and in this position, hands on head, I stared at my father who was out in the yard at the foot of the hill embracing a woman in a wide-brimmed, black straw hat, its crown encircled by a band of tiny pink roses. She wore a white dress, sleeveless and cut low at the neck. A long scarf, the same pale pink as the roses, draped over her shoulders all the way down to her waist. She kissed Jake on the mouth and almost tripped. Then, holding onto his arm and returning a delighted smile, she bent down to remove shiny black sandals with high narrow heels. She came through the porch door behind him, barefoot and holding his hand.

"This is Corinne Robinson, Sugar," my father said. He rubbed his chin and cheek, rough with a day's growth of beard, and pulled me up from the day bed where I had remained staring at the elegant apparition who had come in from our scraggly lawn, seemingly cool in the awful heat and acting as if she were enchanted by the little cottage with its worn wooden furniture and multiple patterns covering pillows, a couch and an old area rug. My father held my shoulders and gently pushed me in front of him. "And this – this is my treasure, the beautiful Princess Samantha. But we who know her well call her Sam."

I was still reeling from the shock of the smile I had seen on my father's face moments before – a smile for this beautiful stranger that up to that moment had belonged to me alone. Miss Corinne Robinson curtsied, and her large hat toppled off her head. I looked down and saw pink roses made of silk surrounded by tiny green silk leaves and vines, then up to tight black curls that shone in the afternoon sun. Skin the color of the bark of a maple tree glistened with what was in reality perspiration but which, to me, seemed like some sort of magic powdery star dust visible at the edge of sharp cheek bones and across a wide forehead. When her hat fell onto the floor, mid-curtsey, Corinne laughed loudly at herself.

"Well, so much for my planned elegant entrance, Princess Samantha," she said with a bow of her head. "May I call you Sam?"

I nodded, transfixed, not knowing whether to be enraged at my father or join him in falling in love. Then I looked around to see my great-grandmother peering at us from the darkened living room where she had remained, holding her book.

"And you must be Mrs. Sokolov," Corinne said, walking toward the old woman. "I'm so pleased to meet you," she added, holding out both her hands.

My father looked nervous. This was no simple meeting of two women, one old and white, living her last days comfortably thanks to the generosity of her grandson-in-law who possessed an unusual sense of family obligation; and one in her late thirties, beautiful, obviously charming, and black. A Negro, as Hannah said when she was being polite; "a colored girl," as she once referred to someone's maid until Jake corrected her in an angry but controlled tone. "That's what we used to say," Hannah had tried to explain, a half-hearted apology. "We don't say that now," Jake responded, emphasizing the we. Then he leaned forward on both elbows at the table where we all sat eating dinner and added, "We've discussed this many times, Hannah, over and over, and I don't want to discuss it again. I am black. And my daughter, your great-granddaughter, is black." Hannah looked straight at him, then at me, and finally down at the table again. Slowly, she removed her napkin from under her fork, delicately wiped her mouth, and excused herself. I never heard her raise the subject with him again.

When Corinne reached for Hannah's hands, my great-grandmother allowed them to be taken with a strange submissive air. A look of joyful surprise passed over her face, but it quickly turned into distress, and she withdrew her hands. "Pleased to meet you," she said. Later that evening when Jake and Corinne went for a walk around the lake and we were in bed, Hannah said abruptly, more to herself than to me, "I know you say you're black, Samantha, like your father always insists, but your skin is the color of mine, and your hair curls in the same way mine did when I was young."

I stared at the ceiling, hoping she was half in, half out of the present, as she often seemed to be, or inhabiting past and present at once. I turned toward the wall, fixing my eyes on the patterns of light and shadow cast by Hannah's green-shaded bedside lamp.

She remained silent for a while, perhaps respecting the turned back, more likely struggling to remember what she wanted to say, what she had said before, what new piece of information she might impart to me. If she repeated herself frequently, she was also aware at times that she did so, and she was embarrassed by this evidence of her mental slippage in her old age. Soon she began talking again, almost as if I weren't there, retelling stories about the five significant women in her life: her mother Rena, her sister May, her daughters Sophie and Rena, and her grand-daughter, Maya, my mother, who had been named for her great-aunt and godmother, May. I listened to the stories, filled with information I already knew, but I stared at the wall, ruthlessly keeping my eyes from Hannah's face, believing I knew perfectly well where she was headed. Each woman represented something lost, or something that still had the power to enrage Hannah even after so many years. This would lead to more current anxieties and expectations of disaster. She'd warned me for years that if my father married again, I'd be exiled to an orphanage, banished by a cruel stepmother to the care of callous municipal administrators or, worse, Catholic nuns. Now, she was afraid of her own banishment again. She was perfectly aware that Maya, her own Sophie's child, had been the only relative who loved her enough to give her a home in her old age. Asher and Sophie, her favorite children, were dead, and her daughter Rena would never consider taking her in. The only person between Hannah and poverty and loneliness, or what was to her the intolerable ugliness of an old age home, was my father, Jake Reed, a relative by marriage, a black man – or a half Negro as she called him behind his back, insisting this was her way of paying respect to his white mother and my grandmother, Ami

28

Reed. Once I had heard her refer to him as a schwartza when she was talking on the phone. "A schwartza but a good man," she had said. When I asked what it meant, Hannah replied, "Nothing. Dark skin, that's all."

She talked about her mother for a while, how she had always preferred May, then how May, and not Hannah herself, could make their father smile. As she retold the old history, holding a small photograph of her parents set into a round, elaborately designed silver frame, Hannah's voice broke, and I nearly went to her but forced myself to remain staring at the wall. She talked about her daughters, looking at a photograph of them taken when they were girls. Rena, the daughter she could never forgive for loving her father best, and Sophie, Hannah's baby, with whom she had lived for years until Sophie became ill and Maya took on the responsibility for Hannah's care. Rena had always been, as I knew her, a bitter, cold old woman, and Hannah could be her match – except for a streak of vulnerability that, when it was ascendant, rendered her child-like and dependent so that even as a small child I wanted to care for her, stroke her, cheer her up.

"Try to go to sleep, Greatgram," I finally turned to whisper, but her face was registering fast-moving emotions now, as it had when she was introduced to Corinne. She'd taken the book from the table and was tapping it angrily with her palm as she spoke. "Your father," she said. "He might marry this woman, Corinne. And you'll have to be prepared, Sammala, for . . . ." She stopped herself, began again. "There are no halves in this. Jewish mothers have Jewish children. So that makes you a good Jewish girl. Like your mother, and like me."

"I don't need to hear all this again, Greatgram," I shouted. "I don't want to hear who you think I am." I got out of bed and stomped outside, slamming the screen door at the end of the room. I sat on the back lawn for a long time, pulling up tufts of grass and throwing them as far as I could see in the moonlight. A good Jewish girl. A good Jewish white girl. The words rang in my head so loud I had to cover my ears. I was angry at my father for putting up with Hannah, not yet able to distinguish between anger at him and anger in his behalf. I was furious at

29

Hannah for what I saw as pure hypocrisy, taking sustenance and solace from people for whom she really had nothing but contempt. I was angry at my dead Grandma Sophie, a smart but compliant woman who always began and never completed family stories, leaving me with long fragments that never seemed to end. And I was angry at Ami, my father's mother who I called Myami, a name that expressed the depth of my love, but who always insisted race didn't matter at all, making me feel invisible, like I was hidden behind a mask I could neither claim nor remove. I hated them all that night, lying on the warm grass and gazing every so often toward the front of the house where, I supposed, my father and Corinne would be sleeping together in his bed, and I hated this beautiful stranger with her promising warmth, too. But more than any of them, that night, I hated my mother for leaving me with it all.

I had a vague memory of her, or perhaps I had made it up – she is standing in the middle of the room, her hands on her hips, her chin raised in defiance – she must be arguing with my father, and I always think, or remember, or imagine, she is defending me against some infraction or disobedience he thinks is important. I think I hear her say – she's only a child – and then – a passionate and exuberant child. My mother's voice is fiery hot in this memory, and I am clinging to her – I can almost feel my head pushing into her waist – I am defiant along with her, and feeling somehow proud.

But I was alone on the grass, unprotected and ashamed, feeling I had not been good enough to keep her, or smart enough to save her. Yet, if she had lived, I might have been furious at her for being white at some point, because that seemed to be the cause of the anger I reserved for myself that night. Twice, I scratched my skin so fiercely I drew blood.

The whole problem, I realized, had little to do with skin color, because I didn't look dramatically different from Hannah, and she was right about our hair looking a lot alike, mine almost as dark as my great-grandmother's had been. But there was enough of my father, and his father, Jacob Reed, in me to make a difference. I remembered my grandfather's gentle teasing, his ready smile, his long silences, his skin as rich and dark as Corinne's, and I felt comforted when I could see his features in my own. I could pass for a dark-skinned Italian girl if I'd ever wanted to, but it was the last thing I wanted. If I was ever mistaken for any kind of white among white people, I was quick to set them straight. Black people, who were accustomed to seeing all sorts of varieties and mixtures appear over the generations, could always see what I saw when I looked in the mirror or made my way through the world. Neither straight hair, nor fair skin, nor hazel eyes could ever fool them completely, and I'd seen people much lighter than myself walk into a room full of black people, trailing whispers – mmm, hmm – meaning – yeah, she's black – nodding their heads and raising their eyebrows, completely unbothered by the finer ambiguities of cultural identity. In this atmosphere, I felt safe, seeing that as long as I proved my belonging to them, I could belong.

I returned to the room somewhat calmed by the coolness and darkness of the night, as well as by the memory of my grandfather. The light was still on, and I grabbed a Band-Aid from the dresser to cover the scratches on my arm.

"What did you do?" Hannah asked.

"Thorns," I said. I stood still and looked down at my bare feet, then at her. She was sitting up in bed, her old gnarled fingers laced in her lap.

"Please, ketsela," she said. "Sit here. I'm sorry I hurt your feelings." She sighed deeply. "I know I was wrong. Your father – he's been better to me than my own flesh and blood. And he won't let anything bad happen to you." She frowned at her own words, as if hating to relinquish her angry beliefs.

I looked up, curious about the altered mood and tone.

"I've been sitting here thinking," Hannah said. "Remembering things I haven't thought about in so many years you can't even imagine such a long time at your age. I'm ninety-four years old, Samantha. I make mistakes. I want to tell you a story about something that happened long ago – when your own grandma Sophie was only a baby – long before your Mama was even born."

She began with the parts I had heard before – how much she missed her sister when she moved to Norwalk, Connecticut from the Lower East Side of New York City. She skipped over intervening years, as she'd always done before, and spoke of the difficult times after her husband's early death from a heart attack. There was little money, because it turned out Michael had invested heavily and lost equally heavily in the stock market. Asher and Sophie were still teenagers, and, with the help of Rena and her new husband, Hannah and her two youngest were settled in the Bronx where they lived on a moderate sum saved from the sale of the Connecticut house and a small income Hannah earned as a private hairdresser. Clients came to her house – she had told me that part before, but this time she explained where she had learned to cut hair in layers, an almost magical technique that made thin hair look thick and thick hair look shapely instead of wild.

"Her name was Belle," Hannah said. At the foot of her bed, my back against the wall, I stroked the silky edges of embroidery on the summer sheets, relinquishing my anger as soon as Hannah began telling parts of the story never told before. "Belle means beautiful in French," she said. "Names are important, Samantha, and I'm going to tell you about yours."

For the next hour, I was enraptured as a part of my great-grandmother's life I had never known before took shape and sound. I could see the young woman who loved the sea emerge in a kind of shadow within the face of an old woman who had come to dislike it "and all its crawling, slimy creatures." She lifted her arm to straighten the framed drawings above her bed, reached over to adjust the lace doily that draped under her bedside lamp, and confessed her old habit of "rearranging." She no longer did it in her mind, she said, had not even thought about it in maybe fifty years or more. But she remembered it tonight when I stormed out of the room and out of some old opaque darkness she found herself trying to rearrange the day, changing the words she had said.

"Just like when I was young I used to rearrange things I saw – streets, rooms – to make them more beautiful." She sighed deeply, murmuring *vey is mir*, as she did whenever her troubles made her feel old.

"When your mother married a colored man – I mean a Negro – we used to call them schwartzas – blacks – that was wrong – now it's not wrong – so – when your mother married him, I was terribly upset. It was natural, I think. People want their families to be like them. Not different. It wasn't until you were born that I accepted Maya's marriage – and when they invited me to live with them after Sophie died – you can imagine, Samantha, what a relief it was, so I wanted to help with your care, and, well – have an influence on you."

Make me white, I thought, looking up angrily, but Hannah was looking across the room, and she kept staring past my shoulder for all the time it took her to tell the main parts of the story – about a fish store; a long walk with a man named Samuel around the loading dock at the edge of Long Island Sound in Norwalk, Connecticut; about the time Belle, Samuel's wife, cut her hair. In halting words, she told how she once loved to walk on the Sound beach, even in winter; about Belle's unborn child and an oyster she tasted only one time in her life; about a story she had heard during that time that went all the way back to slavery.

"She was pregnant – Belle –" Hannah whispered. "This writer, this Ruth Hughes who wrote this book – " she touched the glossy cover in a kind of caress – " she must be the child."

She didn't tell the story in sequence, but moved from one association to the next, every so often repeating the refrain – "Oh, how I admired him...." And then she'd say the words again in a different rhythm – "How I . . . admired him . . . " After the last time she said it, she remained silent for a while, then finally looked at me and said, "I found a picture of the Arctic Circle in one of Michael's books when we left Norwalk. I remembered something Samuel had told me about a strange dream, and I started dreaming something like it myself. By that time, we had moved to another town, and soon not much was left except the dream. I remembered the two of them, of course, and some of what happened, but - - I forgot - - I must have forgot what I felt.

The dream came back about ten times in my life. Sometimes I'm walking. Sometimes I'm falling, and always the ice is shining so bright – but it's so hard, like a rock – and everything's white. I'm falling, I fall, but I never die, or break apart. I just get up and keep walking over the ice – it's safe somehow, not frightening, even though I think I might never see another person again. That's when I wake up. I'm always freezing, or so hot I have to pour cold water on my face and neck. I don't know why, but the dream always makes me hot or cold. Very cold. Or hot."

"Everything white?" I whispered, all the summer thoughts rushing through my mind, the white kids my mother would have belonged to, Corinne's dark brown skin, the vague reassurances I cherished in the story of my father's parents, Myami and my grandfather and their life together. "And she was pregnant? When you . . . when . . . ."

But Hannah spoke right over me, as if once interrupted she might lose it all once and for all. "After we moved, I never heard from Samuel or Belle again. When Maya married your father, I thought about them, and some of it came back to me, the things I learned from Samuel, the times he told me about his life, and about slavery. Every now and then, in the past years with everyone talking first about civil rights, then about racism, I remember other things – terrible things about what was done to people, killings, and – things as bad as the Holocaust, Sammala – terrible, terrible things. Then I remember . . . ." She stopped herself, unfolded her hands and touched her forehead, closed her own eyes with her fingers. "And other things, things you're too young to hear about. And then I have the dream, and the whole thing fades away again. It's as if they go to some faraway part of my mind. I haven't thought about them in a long time. Then, this summer, I go to the bookstore in our neighborhood, you know, and I find this book." It was in her lap now, her hands folded over it. "And it seems to be the same story. All the pieces are the same – so it must be the same people – I never knew all the names, or I forgot them too, but I knew his name of course. Samuel. And Belle. It's written by their daughter, this Ruth Hughes. And then she comes. Corinne Robinson, and . . . her hair, and around the mouth, she reminds me a little of Belle, I think. His wife."

My face felt tight. I swallowed saliva.

"That's the story, Samantha." Hannah sighed. "But you're too young to understand about such forgetting. It must seem strange to you. But I'm talking of something that happened almost sixty years ago. More than half a century – can you imagine how long a century is, day after day?" The lines on her face seemed to deepen, her skin to fade to an even paler shade of tan. "Now I can see him again, just as clearly as I saw him all those years ago. I told my children about them – how Negro people were slaves, like us. Like the Jews. And how some of them were brave – like him, and his father. How much they wanted to be free. I must have thought about him fondly when Maya called you Samantha, after the story her Mama, my Sophie, had told her about him. Maybe I even thought about him when my Maya married your father, a black man, Jake."

I could not make sense of it all, but I understood something of what Samuel and Belle had meant to Hannah and, suddenly, to myself. The connection, some pattern as intricate as a genetic family tree, and the fact that I had no idea how to name it, or follow it, caused me to feel a hunger as strong as I sometimes felt in the morning when I'd fallen asleep and missed dinner the night before. I wanted nothing more, in that moment, than to leave the room, go to the kitchen, and eat.

"Yes, I can see it must have been quite a business," Hannah was saying, "for his father and his people to escape from slavery just like the Jews – and for the Samuel I knew to make a life for himself at those times. I'd forgotten about telling my children a little about him, but Sophie remembered how I used him as an example of how important it was to try to be independent and free." She picked up a photograph of May and stared at it. I thought her face looked angry, as if her sister's photograph were resurrecting something long forgotten – something she wanted to forget. "She was so free, and she was the one they loved best," was all she said, and then, "my mother's favorite and my father's too. With all his harsh words, and how he could bury himself for days in his Bible and Talmud, May could always make him smile.

He'd talk to me about his studies and try to interest me in his interpretations, but you know what, Samantha? He never really looked at me. He'd talk looking down at his books. I'd pay close attention, telling myself it was a kind of love. But if he really wanted me to understand, he would have educated me, no? I suppose the truth was hardly anyone would listen to him, so he had to talk to one of his children, and he didn't have a son so he chose me, only because I was older and more able to understand. I tried to give him the answers or questions he wanted, but maybe what I really wanted – oh, it didn't matter what I said anyway. He didn't want to listen, only to talk. It's a crazy thing, Sammala. He was a cruel man in many ways, a cold man and a selfish man, like my husband. Maybe even a not so intelligent man. I don't know – that's what your great-grandfather, my Michael, believed. But I adored him, and only tonight remembering the look on that man Samuel's face when he looked at me, when we talked, I think I didn't only want to make my Papa smile, like May could. I don't know but maybe at the real bottom I wanted him to look at me, to act like he was talking – not just talking – talking to me."

She put May's photograph down so abruptly it fell onto the floor. I got off the bed, replaced it on the table, and stood there silently, not knowing what to say.

"That's enough now," Hannah barely whispered. "Don't be angry at your old Greatgram." She took my hand, brought it to her lips and kissed each finger separately, then the palm, then the knuckles. "Go to sleep, ketsela," she said.

I crawled into bed, welcoming the blankness of the wall again. Hannah's old endearment echoed in my brain, and as though in a hollow tunnel of sound, behind it came Samuel and Samantha, then my father's voice calling me Sugar, then the roll of the ocean carrying my mother's ashes away.

Part Two:

Norwalk, Connecticut
1919 – 1920

Chapter 2

The autumn of 1919 was unusually mild, as if the weather were joining in the celebration of the end of the war. She was tempted to take off her hat and feel the cool breeze in her hair, but a married Jewish woman, even one who was not Orthodox, not even religious enough to be kosher, could not be seen on the street with her head bare, at least not if she were of a certain class. She was tempted to run, although that would have been difficult in her high boots and long skirt.

She had left the children with her sister May, who was visiting from New York, and who, having married her first cousin and been warned about severe birth defects resulting from inbreeding, had had no children of her own. Marriages, they had been taught since they were old enough to understand the search for a husband to be the most significant effort of their lives, must be made with men from the same "family" only in the broadest sense – certainly Jewish, preferably from the same city or town, a *landsman*. Still, marriage with blood kin of any but the most distant sort was prohibited, and prohibitions increased outward from the circle of the most desirable husbands too: from a *landsman* to a Jew from anywhere in Russia or Poland, to a Jew from almost anywhere in the world – all these were allowed. Beyond the world of Jewish men, prohibition approached the level of taboo. Christians; Moslems; Indians and Chinese with their strange religions, incomprehensible customs, and repugnant appearance; and others too inconceivable even to mention – all were forbidden. Michael, on the other hand, was desirable in every way: Jewish, of course; not only from Latvia, from

Rezekne, too; older than Hannah by ten years; and a dentist – an educated professional man; a husband, it was decided, who would provide.

Hannah's children's faces filled her thoughts as she walked into the central part of town, the youngest still a baby, the eldest of her three only six, one born dead and another lost in between, yet Michael pressing her already to a fourth. He had lost two younger brothers in the war; she'd lost one – David – her favorite – to influenza the previous year. Jewish families must increase, Michael told her. And despite her exhaustion and the way her body changes made her feel old before her time, she couldn't help but agree. She'd been sorry when her husband decided to leave New York and buy the house in Norwalk, Connecticut, despite the clear step up from Stanton Street, despite the yard where the children could play more safely than in the streets of lower Manhattan. He was an American, he had told her, a professional, and it was time he bought a house. But she'd felt at home in the neighborhood of Jews, most of them still speaking Yiddish and Russian more comfortably than English. She'd wept when she had to leave her best friends – her brother-in-law Aaron and her sister May.

She made a right turn. She'd walk to the harbor, she decided, since the late fall weather was mild and the nearness of water was the only thing she loved about her new home. From the docks there are paths to a narrow beach, she'd been told, and a channel called the Sound that led directly to the open sea. She'd ask the clerk to pack the fish in ice, and then she'd take her time, walking slowly, letting the colors and shapes penetrate her, anticipating the calm she always felt when she was near the water. She'd allow herself this daily, solitary pleasure for as long as she could, while May was still here.

Chapter 3

Belle. The name means beautiful, and though something deep within her has always believed she is not, she feels she is suited to her name in the eyes of Samuel, since it is he who renamed her the French word he'd learned in one of his books when they married more than ten years before. Her birth name no longer matters to her. She has come to think of herself as Belle. When she imagines herself at the center of one of the stories she is always making up in her mind, Belle is the name of the central character. When she talks to herself out loud, as she often does when she's alone, especially if she's distressed about something, which she often is, it is Belle she calls herself. The meaning of her name has taken root, even as the word has lost connotation as the most familiar words do, retaining only a singular character, uniquely referential. Belle no longer evokes the idea of beauty to her any more than it reminds her of something that rings. Belle is herself. When she hears the name, she looks up.

And she does so in the moment when a white woman wearing a nicely cut, dark brown suit and peering at her through large eyes from under the wide brim of a hat enters the market saying, "Belle? Are you Belle?" in a hesitant voice, not a tone the black woman is used to hearing in a white mouth.

"Yes, Ma'am?" she inquires softly, moving from the barrel where she has been shelling shrimp for frying to the cutting table next to the tubs filled with whole and filleted fish, large greenish-brown crabs, and oysters still locked in their hard, ridged shells. She washes her hands in a nearby sink and dries them on the thick white apron that reaches to her knees while she waits for the white lady to speak.

Hannah is struck by something in the colored woman's face which is made even more striking by the white scarf framing her forehead, covering all of her hair and tied at the base of her dark neck. The woman's eyes are narrow and set far apart on either side of a broad nose. Her lips are full and nearly form a circle when closed. They look soft and unusually smooth to Hannah, who suddenly realizes she is staring impolitely, making the colored woman uncomfortable. She has the feeling she has seen this woman somewhere before.

"I was told to ask for you if Mr. Burns wasn't here. I want something fresh, packed in ice as I have a long walk home," she says, looking forward to the Sound, but thinking, why am I so struck by her face?

It is not that Hannah thinks Belle is beautiful or plain, kind or harsh looking, angry or welcoming. That her face is noticeable at all is what causes the lingering discomfort that is making Hannah behave oddly, with neither politeness nor authority. She never noticed the faces of the schwartzas in New York. They may walk by her, or be cleaning a yard – once her own yard the week they first moved here – but all she retains is an impression of color, never a specific shade but a general brown, and certainly nothing specific enough about their features to enable her easily to tell them apart. But this woman's face is a face – not simply generic human features dominated by a background of brown skin. A face.

"Belle?" It's a man's voice this time, and Hannah turns quickly from the woman who seems to be looking at her with concern to the man who has just entered. He holds a pail in one hand and what looks like a narrow rounded knife in the other. She pulls back, looking at the knife, backs into a glass showcase, becomes keenly aware of a sharp pain between her eyes. She is having trouble breathing.

"I'll go get Mr. Burns," she hears the woman named Belle say. Then, "No – you get him. Don't touch her, Samuel. I'll see to her."

She is helped to a chair, straight-backed and supportive. She smiles at Belle and accepts the glass of water she is handing her, then helping her to raise to her lips. It was the knife, its long, rusty curve; a light from somewhere in the room had glistened across its edge.

Mr. Burns, who owns the fish market, is leaning toward her solicitously. "You must not move, Mrs. Sokolov. We will see you home." He looks at her in a way she is accustomed to being looked at – especially by men. She is considered beautiful, strikingly so, and though she doesn't feel it inside herself, she acknowledges it, and in moments such as this one, when she sees the look, she knows it must be true. Just now, however, the power of her facial features and coloring is an annoyance, something she must overcome to be left alone to do what she wants.

"No!" She almost shouts the word. "Excuse me – it's only that – I'm fine – I thought – "

She looks at the hand where the knife had been, the long, graceful brown fingers, and up at the face, brown, of course, like the hand, several shades lighter than the brown face of the woman named Belle with the striking features. He too stares at her for a moment, then quickly looks away. His hair is a cap of black woolly curls. It frames a broad forehead, black, black eyes, full and shapely lips, a large chin and angular jaw- bone. Never has she noticed in such detail the particulars of Negro faces. She looks into his eyes for what seems like a long moment before she feels Belle's eyes on her.

"Samuel," Belle says, and she says it low, almost a whisper so only he will hear. But Hannah sees the colored woman's lips move, hears his name – *Samuel* – and before a strange flash of heat can betray her she looks down and sips her water again.
Samuel places his hand on his wife's shoulder and turns them both away, an authoritative gesture, yet almost unbearably gentle, a gentleness that reminds Hannah instantly of May's husband, Aaron, the way he touches May. But Aaron's touch is tentative and timid. This man's gentleness is controlled, insistent, and Belle leans into his arm. They leave the room. Hannah is left alone with Mr. Burns to whom she insists she is all right now, would like a piece of his freshest fish – snapper would be fine –

enough for four adults, two small children, and packed in ice please, because she has a long walk home. No. She'll be fine walking. The air will do her good.

The road she has traced on Michael's map of the town takes her to the harbor, but there is still some afternoon light and the fishing boats have not yet come in. She can relax her shoulders from their stiffness and allow herself to cry. Images crash through her mind with a ferocity she has always known at times like this – when many painful moments, separated by years, return to her consciousness at one time, each individual painful memory feeding into the next like tributaries flooding a river, as if the passing of time is an illusion, as if there is only one terror, one panic, one fury, one essential hateful thing made of all its parts.

Her mother is holding May in one arm, slapping Hannah's face with her free hand, calling her a bad girl, and she can never remember the bad thing she did. "A pretty face isn't enough to get you through a long life, Hannahla," her mother would say, her contemptuous tone undermining the pleasure of the pet name, the tone, Hannah knew, meant to remind her that this beauty she supposedly possessed came from her father's side. She looked like his older sister who had died when she was a young woman, not more than a girl. "A wanton girl," Hannah's father said whenever her name came up, "who thought she could do without God." May resembles their mother whose coloring and longer features are visible now in little Asher's face. Now in her thirties, Hannah can see more than ever – how her mother and her sister look so much alike. She has always been the more beautiful one, she can admit that to herself in private moments because the admission involves no simple self-congratulation or pride; any good feeling is laced with guilt: that she was prettier than May; that her father thought her looks were the mark of betrayal and sin; that she made her mother angry, or worse, jealous of her own child.

Then there is the small room with a locked door, all the way at the end of the narrow apartment, and she is banging on it with her fists, feeling the hard wood with its flaking green paint that comes off on her knuckles; and again, she can't remember the bad thing she has done. She remembers her father's harsh voice telling her she can't come out, and the rough feel of his coarse gabardine jacket as she holds his arm and is given to her bridegroom under the chuppah, the world vague from beneath the white veil covering her face too closely so she feels she cannot breathe.

She remembers the births, three alive and one dead in six years, and the blood and pain are nothing compared to the anxiety when they placed each baby in her arms; the desire, once during the early weeks with Asher, the second and most irritable, to cover his face with a pillow to stop the unending, accusatory screams; and the tool the doctor used the time she could not go through it again and Aaron had found her someone in New York, the sharp edge glistening like a knife from a light in the room, just as the knife had glistened in the colored man's hand, in both instances the last thing she saw before she lost time. Michael had never known. The one she lost naturally between the first two was bad enough. It haunted her each year its birthday might have been. But for that other one, haunting was too mild a word. It sat in her skull, screamed into her sleep, clutched her throat taking her breath away as it had just now, in the fish store.

That man's black eyes – a blackness as dark as the black dreams she has repeatedly and fears so much she sometimes keeps herself awake all night to avoid them. But the blackness of his eyes was somehow the opposite of her dream and, set in the warm brown of his face, his gaze calmed her, as if he wanted more than anything in the world to help her, to enable her to recover herself and relax.

The river that surrounds the harbor is calm. The few fishing boats already docked rock on gentle waves caused by the wakes of boats coming in. She finds the path to the Sound and stands still, transfixed by the dark blue-green waves crested with lines of shimmering white foam, gathering thicker and thicker until they reach the shore, almost to the edge of several large, brown boulders. She turns on the narrow stretch of rocky beach and watches the sea grass move in the light wind, the tall brown cat-tails behind them, the dark trunks of trees leading back to the harbor. She loves every kind of vegetation that grows near the water, loves them in every season, even in the dead of winter. Browns fade to shades of gray and pale ocher. Branches, some in full autumn color, some already bare, separate into slender V shapes, smaller and smaller until they seem as fragile and delicate as the grasses. The layered patterns of color and shape echo within her, as if she herself, or her mind, or her memory, is a tunnel. She does not know why, but layers always echo within her – layers of fabric in her rooms – white doilies on the backs of flowered chairs – on her clothing – a red shawl over a black coat over a brown dress – all the colors visible at once, their even patterns closing over all the ugliness of the world like a beautiful curtain, or a veil. Layers of color are like music, she sometimes feels, many instruments playing at once, harmonic, then dissonant, seeming to play behind each other, each different in its tone. Everywhere, she is infatuated by echoes and layers, but especially here, by the sea.

She feels calmer now and becomes aware that the afternoon light is fading. The ice in which the fish is packed has begun to melt through her shopping bag, and she hurries home where May has made a potato kugel, a tsimmes of stewed carrots with raisins and sugar, and baked challah to go along with the fish. The children are washed, fed, and ready for a game and a story when she comes home, and she wonders how she will manage it all when May has to return with Aaron to the drugstore in New York and she is alone again.

At night, when Michael lifts her white cotton gown up to her shoulders and enters her, she imagines the water she saw that afternoon, prays she will not conceive a baby, and tries to suppress her anger that he takes her so possessively when she knows he spends time each week, when he travels to New York to do his research, with the woman named Manya. Hannah has seen the pale blue envelope with the return address bearing the name, and May's eyebrows raised in a way that indicates lack of surprise told her that Michael does not trouble to hide his liaison.

Recently, Manya even visited them in Norwalk, and Hannah was expected to serve her dinner, after which Michael, Manya and other friends retired to his study, closing the door. There, she knows, they discuss medicine, music, literature, unfamiliar worlds to her, even many of their words beyond her comprehension. All she knows of medicine is what to do when a child has a fever. All she knows of literature are the stories she tells them before bed, most of them stories her mother told long ago to her. All she knows of music are the layers of sound that echo through the tunnel of her mind. She closes her eyes to banish the feelings and images and sees dark black eyes in a brown face. Startled, she moves abruptly and lets out a cry that Michael mistakes for passion.

"You'd better start eating less of that sweet bread and potatoes," he says with an unpleasant smile as he rolls off her and grabs the rounded flesh of her belly somewhat roughly in his fist. He looks at her large breasts, no longer firm after nursing three infants. She is humiliated by his disapproving stare. His fingers dig into her flesh, and she cringes. He lowers her gown over her body, kisses her cheek, and turns from her to sleep.

She dreams the black dream. This time she is near the water at night. Only one fishing boat is docked and she can hardly see its outline in the heavy darkness. As always before, she is afraid, yet alongside the fear is an unexpected comfort, as if something in her wants the darkness as well as fearing it, yet she knows she must keep walking, careful of the water's edge. She wants to shout to the people around her – there is something they must see – but at that moment she realizes she's wearing only her corset and her underwear. Now she's terrified of being seen, and she wakes, caught in the blankets wrapped too tightly around her. She sits up, throws her bare feet onto the floor to cool them, and thinks, I was trying to wrap a black cloak around myself on a cold night near the bay. For an instant she sees an image of her sex exposed, just beneath the corset's edge at her hips. But by the time she dresses, goes downstairs to cook the family breakfast and feed the baby, only six months old and off her breasts that have become so swollen and infected she had to give up the nursing she loved, she remembers only the desire for darkness and the pressing danger of too many people crowding her on the dock.

Chapter 4

A few weeks later, the temperature has dropped and a feel of winter is in the air. The afternoon is windy, but the sun is bright, so this time, heading for the fish market, she pushes the wicker carriage, its curved canopy protecting the baby from the wind, while the two older children trail behind. She believes they will flourish and, at the same time, calm down in the crisp air, and the mixture of sun and wind must indeed be hypnotic, because their usual activity is diminished. Just as in New York, war veterans huddle near the buildings for shelter from the wind. Some of them are begging. Some are missing limbs. Their scarred faces and wild eyes attest to the horrors of the battlefields from which they have recently returned. The specter of such vast human damage quiets the children too. Asher stares, and Hannah has to push his head forward more than once. Rena is unusually obedient, even her big mouth silenced by the vision of extreme adult pain. They walk quietly, holding hands, their cheeks and foreheads turning rosy beneath their woolen tams. Hannah tries to look ahead of her, like her children appalled and frightened by the ruined lives. In order to focus her thoughts on something else, so she won't waste the blessing of the beautiful day, she begins to play her old game, the secret one she's played ever since she can remember.

She turns the printing factory, a tall red brick rectangle of a building at the crossroads of South Main and Wall Streets, onto its side so the rectangle becomes horizontal. Stretching down the block is a line of trees, their leaves a chaos of red and brown, but she turns one into gold, another into a cool, pale green, and, liking the haphazard mixture of colors, she extends the trees around the horizontal red and now – it is clearer and clearer in her mind's eye – the red leaves seem to shadow the lighter red

48

brick while the gold contrasts with it, reflecting the sun. The road itself is dark gray, almost black, and it winds around the back of the building in a way Hannah likes, so she leaves it be. The rearranging game is one of the strongest pleasures she knows. At home, she sometimes makes her fantasies real, changing the placement of couches and chairs in her rooms, moving a rug from a hallway to the parlor, a glass vase from a mantle to a shelf, dragging a corner table down the hallway to another room. She alters their interiors with such frequency that Michael often teases her when he comes in from work, pretending he's arrived in the wrong house by mistake. On the streets, it's always more challenging because she has to keep all the changes in her head at once or else lose the pleasure of seeing the colors harmonize, the curves and lines and shadows take a more graceful shape within an imagined frame.

She passes shops and apartment buildings, their heights reaching three or four stories at times, reminding her of home. She prefers these urban buildings to her house, further south on Main, where trees and gardens replace brick sidewalks, and back yards lead to other houses instead of the railroad tracks she loves because they remind her of the possibility of going home. She turns on Water Street, urging the dallying children to hurry. She rushes past the German markets selling sausage, cabbages, and dark, delicious bread, but she doesn't stop – because even if they are Americans, the Germans – and sometimes others who fraternize with them as well – are still tainted as enemies, their shops vandalized; the previous week two German shopkeepers were beaten up by an angry group of teenage boys whose fathers had been killed in the war. Hannah is eager to reach the fisheries and oyster saloons that crowd the entrance to the harbor and the docks. She has chicken for tonight, plans a fricassee with dumplings and onions, Aaron's favorite, but for some reason she's decided she'd better order Friday's fish two days in advance.

This time the white woman's face is flushed, from the wind, Belle guesses, and she has three children in tow. Notwithstanding the story of Samuel's white grandmother and the wealthy white family in Norwalk who ran a Railroad stop before the War, the one where Samuel's father arrived after he made his way by schooner from Baltimore, then by foot and by train, and notwithstanding what she's heard of white "abolitionists" or even of the great John Brown, Belle herself had never known anyone white worth liking or trusting.

She was raised in the South where Black Codes came right close on the heels of slavery, restricting her every move and access. Whatever opportunity she might have carved out of the scant possibilities – to become a teacher maybe, in the school for colored children – was wiped away when her mother died and she'd had to leave school before mastering reading to work in her uncle's café. By the time she decided to leave the tiny, ugly town in North Carolina for the North, all she really knew was house cleaning, and no white person she'd ever met seemed to comprehend the limits of what one colored woman with two hands could do in a day. When she married Samuel and started being Belle, she felt new born. That he was much older than she intensified the sense of safety she felt whenever she was near him. His reading and writing excited her since she had always loved stories, and now she could learn more and more of them. Listening to him read to her out loud on quiet nights when they sat by the fire or lay next to each other in bed remains one of the strongest pleasures she has ever known. At times she feels a surging hope when she listens that she might somehow find her own voice in his. His astonishing comfort with whites – as if he never questions he is as good as them – fills her with awe and respect, even though she never stops nagging him about the dangers.

She hopes the child finally growing within her after so many years of trying will inherit her father's strength and bravery, but she'll teach her – or him if that's the case – to be cautious, too. The stories about the first Samuel and his mother, Ruth, are touching, and Belle has to be grateful for what the white woman did or she'd never have her Samuel. But Belle herself has never so much as spoken to any white person worth knowing past a formal *yes ma'am* or a nodding hello.

Now, here is this dark-haired, tawny skinned woman,

beautiful for someone white, who people tell her is a "Jew," and Belle has little idea what that means. Her tone is respectful for a white person, so Belle smiles at the two older children, compliments the baby's looks, and asks after Hannah's health.

"I'm fine," Hannah replies, and adds, "thank you," although she knows as soon as the words are out that it is an odd politeness to offer a colored gal. "I was walking this way, so I thought I'd order fish for Friday," she says.

"Well, it's only Wednesday – I don't know what the fresh catch is likely to be – but we'll have plenty of shrimp and oysters for certain . . . . " Belle pauses, sees the frown on the white woman's face, and quickly adds, "Ma'am?"

Hannah is always surprised when people don't realize she's Jewish, or that even the least religious Jews follow strict dietary laws, not merely out of respect for the ancient prohibitions but for reasons of cleanliness and health. Her surprise turns to annoyance, her annoyance to anger. "We don't eat shellfish," she says and turns away from the woman called Belle, pretending to adjust the children's clothing, unbutton a coat, remove a hat. The narrow streets and crowded shops of her old neighborhood on the lower east side of Manhattan fill her mind. There are many Jews with a range of religious convictions, some strict and orthodox, others more modern and flexible, some without much faith at all, but all of them Jews, and even the ones who have abandoned religion altogether are reluctant to eat pork, or fish that crawl in their filthy shells along the sea floor. In South Norwalk, Jews are a small community among the other immigrants and ordinary white Americans, and she feels a constant wariness that at home she'd known only when she traveled beyond her neighborhood, or listened to her parents and grandparents tell their endless stories of old-country pogroms. And the Klan is here, terrifying men in sheets who make no secret of their hatred for Jews as well as Negroes, who burn crosses to symbolize their hatred and sometimes burn houses and people as well. Anger at Norwalk, at Michael for moving them here, at his suddenly recalled rough hands and rough words a few nights before; anger at her own body, expanding after each child; anger at the Christians who turn her life into a series of frightening or at least nerve-wracking encounters; the sort of anger she tries to suppress so she will not take it out on the children or irritate Michael; old anger at things she can hardly remember – at her father's fierce rules, her mother's impatience, even at her cherished sister May; the anger she fears and hates in herself moves through her now, and when she steadies herself and turns back around to face Belle, it is she, the colored woman, at whom Hannah feels her fury. It is as if she owes Hannah something she is refusing to give that Hannah is tired of being denied. And the entire stew of feelings is mixed with the gnawing thought that she knows this woman from before.

"Whatever's freshest on Friday is what I'll take," Hannah says in an officious tone she has heard other whites use with the niggers in town. But she's never used, never thought that word before. She has always been taught to say colored, or Negro, unless she is using the Yiddish word, and she feels momentarily ashamed. But, surprisingly, the shame is followed by more anger. "And have it ready at two o'clock sharp," she says, as if the fish has always been late before. "And clean this time – last time I had to clean it again at home," as if there is nothing so dirty or incompetent as a colored woman's hands.

Chapter 5

The white voice always comes sooner or later, thinks Belle, and she has to control her mouth from sucking air between her teeth, her most characteristic gesture of contempt. Instead, she assumes an equally characteristic remoteness. The white woman, whose face she'd liked, who seemed sad and sympathetic, fades into the general atmosphere of loathsome whiteness in Belle's mind. She looks down in a flashing instant at the baby who is beginning to fuss, and the two children who are becoming impatient and putting dirty hands against the glass she's just cleaned this morning. She looks at the white woman and says quietly, as if from a great distance, "Yes, Ma'am, flounder, I expect, or snapper again?"

Beneath the shallow mask of her compliance another story forms, and Belle constructs it carefully, structuring a scene of confrontation, small gestures symbolizing the Negro woman's dignity – a lifted chin, hands wiped very slowly on a white apron, staring *how dare you* eyes. She doesn't even blink until the white woman – intimidated, ashamed, perhaps even frightened – looks away. Belle embellishes the story with additional details all afternoon and into the evening. It never actually ends – there is too much pleasure in the observation of the details of a black woman's proud anger. And that is how it feels – there is no sense of "making up" anything; rather, it is as if Belle is observing a woman named Belle. She lingers over facial expressions, hand movements, sounds and words; the white woman's clumsy excuses; the haughty disdain of the woman whose name is Belle – the word for beautiful, and for something in a graceful shape that rings, loud and melodious and free.

When Samuel returns home late that evening, after sweeping the floors of market and oyster saloon, polishing glass, wiping tables and counters down, refreshing the ice on the remaining fish and generally closing up, she is deep within her reverie. When she heats some water in the fire kettle and bathes Samuel's arms, back, chest, and thighs, she is still immersed. He can see from her face she is "writing" one of her stories, layering complicated scenes she will store in her memory, since in all the years of trying to learn, she has never been able to feel comfortable enough with writing to make it equal the stories she keeps in her head. Only in the past few months, since she was sure the baby was strong inside her, has the learning been set free in a way, and she begins to hope she might achieve the same fluency with words on a page as Samuel assures her she can. Later, when she sits in her favorite chair and stares into the fire, he kneels on the floor and leans his cheek against her slightly protruding stomach, hoping to feel the first movements of the child he hopes will be the girl Belle has agreed to name Ruth after his great-grandmother.

Belle takes a deep breath and, in a halting voice, always uncertain when she speaks the feelings she can put into her stories with surprising ease, she tells him what actually happened with the white woman in the store, the pain now considerably lessened as it is patterned thickly with the pleasures of her re-creation.

"Hannah Sokolov," he says. "Burns told me something of her the other day when she fainted. Her husband's a Jewish immigrant, but when he got to this country, to New York, he got educated. He fixes people's teeth here but he spends time in New York every week, experimenting somewhere, inventing something. She almost died with that last child and hasn't been well since."

The word *educated* overpowers the story of the actual Hannah, who by now holds little interest for Belle. It overpowers her irritation that Samuel seems to be offering some sympathetic explanation for the white woman's behavior. "Let's have a lesson," she says to her husband, her eyes shining, and Samuel takes down the Bible and the old ledger he uses to teach her to read and write.

Chapter 6

Samuel is unloading boxes of freshly caught fish from a schooner and piling them on the dock when she stops to watch the boats on her way to the narrow beach where the river widens into Long Island Sound. It is the end of November now, and the trees are almost bare. Soft piles of brown leaves gather at the sides of the roads. The wind picks up and blows them into the air around her. Many land on her coat and her dark hair, which she uncovered as soon as she came in sight of the water, any criticisms by her Orthodox neighbors not weighty enough to counter the pleasure of the damp salty wind in her hair. Thick rain clouds move across the sky; soon it will be deep winter, and after Hanukah she will be alone without help again. Weekends will no longer be lightened by the presence of May, whose formal education enables her to converse with Michael in ways Hannah can never manage.

"You were always beautiful," May reassures her, "and that's why he fell in love with you. He still loves you for it, no matter what else he does."

But when Hannah stares at herself in the mirror, she sees only her sallow, lined face, the rings under her eyes, the extra weight she still carries from the children, and she believes her sister is being kind.

She's never envied May for not having children – the children are her greatest loves, especially Sophie, the baby. Her boy, Asher, is special, too; but her first child, Rena, the one who acquainted her with the meaning of the word love more fully than she could have imagined, the one she named for her own mother – Rena seems to have gone over to her father lately. She creeps into his study in the evenings, pores over his books with him.

She's entranced with his fancy friends from the city, especially with Manya and her flaming red hair. Once, when Hannah had to slap Rena for pinching her younger brother, the child looked at her with the strangest expression, cold and unchildlike, as if something were changed between them for good, and Hannah felt her own cheeks sting, as if she had been slapped. She was the child again, back in her old home, and her mother was slapping her with one large, flat hand while holding May in the graceful curve of her other arm. She worries that between her mother's anger and her daughter's she may lose her footing altogether, but she loves all the children, can no longer imagine living without them, relishes the smell and feel of their sweet bodies cuddling into her body when she sings them her old-country Yiddish songs to put them to sleep.

But she does envy May the Normal School she attended, the teacher training she felt she had to acquire once she decided to marry Aaron, which meant she'd never have a child. She envies the ease with which May can talk to Michael about his work, and how she finds words to describe the music he plays on their new phonograph, the music called *symphonies*, and *sonatas,* sound Hannah can only take in silently and swallow, as if it were food. She envies her sister's excitement when she talks about the Suffrage Movement steadily gaining ground, how sure she is that women will vote soon, and how even women like Hannah – married to dominating men – will have rights that will have to be respected. Hannah smiles, remembering May's story of the woman from Norwalk named Elsie Hill, daughter of a Congressman. She was arrested for climbing up General Lafayette's statue in the square, during a demonstration. And she told the reporter who questioned her right after she was let out of jail, "During my years of suffrage work I've been told and retold that women's place is on a pedestal; and the first time I get on one, I'm arrested!" Well, Hannah knows how shaky a pedestal can be if she knows anything at all. She envies May for her marriage that, however barren of children, was made for love. For a moment the envy will feel like anger, but this is a feeling Hannah banishes as soon as it is aroused, for she counts on May as on no one else in the world.

Soon the months of her official convalescence will be ended, and she will have to do without her sister's support and without Aaron's gentle friendship when they return to New York. It is long past the time when he should return to his drug store, May has told her, and she would never allow him to return alone. The work of cooking, cleaning, and caring for three small children will take over her life again. There will be no more walks along the harbor, out to the Sound, alone with the water and the sky.

Samuel is counting the crates of fish, entering something in a notebook, pushing his canvas hat back from his head and, with a wrinkled white handkerchief, wiping his forehead, his cheeks, his hands. Tiny black curls are visible above his ears, under the brim of his hat, at the edge of his chin and jawbone. Hannah reaches up to straighten her own thick hair, replacing a pin that has nearly fallen out. In the moment that she stands there in that unselfconscious position, arms raised behind her head, fingers fastening the thick, loose braid more securely, eyes staring at him with frank and intense interest, he looks up and sees her.

She nods to him as if she knows him, as if he knows all the times he's invaded her thoughts since the day she met him when he carried the knife and the pail. And again, she sees the hesitant turn of his mouth, the slow, graceful lifting of his hand to the brim of his hat as he acknowledges her, this time with a long stare of open admiration. She's always been shy in this way, unable to look at people for long, but she is able to look back at him. There is no reason on earth for her to feel so ordinary with this Negro man, so comfortable with and pleased by his presence. No reason she can think of to see the distinctive, strong features set in the brown skin instead of the brown skin, as is more usual, blurring the features. There is no sense at all in doing anything but allowing such unreasonable feelings to settle and pass; no sense in doing anything but turning toward the path from the harbor to the open water where she longs to sit for a while alone, listen to the slow tide coming in, smell the seaweed and the crawling life as the salt water from the sea flows in, covering all of it for hours, until the tide recedes again. She cannot imagine why she looks around to see if anyone else is near enough to observe her, nor, even though it seems to be desolate and they are alone, she knows – should someone come by, or see them from a distance – it is dangerous to risk being seen walking side by side, let alone talking in an ordinary friendship way; yet, wondering and having no answer at all to her wondering, she walks toward him instead of turning toward the path as she had intended, and asks if he would care to walk her to the point where the river meets the edge of the sea, the spreading-out place she has learned from the people in town to call the Sound.

"It's a short walk, and it's still light," she says. "Mr. …?" She adds the word she knows he will receive as a sign of respect, so unusual as to be almost shocking. It will surprise him, communicate worlds of intention, acknowledgement, even apology for her own bad behavior in the store which he may have heard about from his wife. "How is your wife?" she asks, having suspected Belle was in the early months of carrying a child, wanting to remind him she respects not only him, despite his blackness, but his wife too, thinking the respect she conveys to the husband will somehow get back to the wife, an easy apology since she has no idea how to make the hard one.

These two have thrown her up and down and sideways in the week since she first met them in Burns's store. She says and feels things she doesn't mean to say, has no idea why she feels. She thinks of them at sudden and surprising moments. She believes she might have dreamed of them. She had no intention of speaking so impolitely to the woman, nor does she mean to be standing here in this lovely harbor where more fishing boats will soon be coming in, inviting the man to walk to the Sound with her.

"My wife is well," Samuel says. "Thank you. And it's Waterman. Samuel Waterman. And how are you feeling since that spell in the store?" – ignoring her invitation to walk.

Hannah looks down at her boots. "Fine now," she barely whispers, remembering the knife, his and the one his brought to mind. "Thank you for your help that day," she adds, looking up into the black eyes that don't seem to blink. And there is that look again, as if he has some need to understand, or see into her, rare in any man – she's only seen it in Aaron when he looks at May – unknown in a colored man looking at anyone white, let alone a white woman. He could get killed for it, she knows. He looks at her as if he is not afraid of her, not intimidated by her skin color, yet not hating her either with that constantly threatening anger she has sometimes noticed in colored people's eyes.

He doesn't cause her the embarrassment of having to ask again or having to leave without an answer to her question. Instead, after what seems to her an interminable moment of silence within which he, apparently, is annoyingly comfortable, he finally says, "It ain't – isn't – a good idea for me to walk you to the water, but we might walk around the harbor. I could – " he looks around, as if for an idea – "I could point out the freshest fish of the day coming in on the schooners – in case you plan to purchase something in the market before you return home?"

Hannah nods again, and watches Samuel watch her reach for her light veil and raise it to cover her hair, leaving only the waves around her face exposed. The thick clouds have released a steady drizzle, and the fishing boats are not due for nearly another hour; perhaps that is why the dock is deserted except for one other worker, a colored man.

They walk from boat to boat, around the wide oval of the dock and back again.

Each turn takes nearly fifteen minutes, and they do three turns in all.

"We moved here from New York about a year ago," she finds herself telling him, to break the silence and to introduce herself to him, which for some reason she feels she must do. "We live on South Main Street, but I still feel my home is at the southern end of Manhattan, not far from where the two rivers meet and flow out to sea. That's why I love this harbor. I love the water – any water – rivers, lakes, but especially the sea. This is the only part of Norwalk that reminds me of home. I used to walk to the west side docks at home and just watch the ferries moving up and down the river, up and down all afternoon – and smell the fish – oh and picture the open ocean – imagine it so vast and deep just past where I could see. I'd stare for hours at that enormous woman in the harbor as if her torch – well as if her torch was raised just for me. I know it sounds crazy – she's only a statue, but I miss her now. I do. And you? How did you come to Connecticut . . . Mr. Waterman?"

She has asked this brazenly, before she can force herself into an appropriate silence. Why is she speaking like this to this colored stranger? Why does she want to know about him? She feels her belly rumbling beneath her heavy dress and tight corset and remembers she hasn't eaten since morning. That must be the reason, then. And it must be her heavy coat and the river's humidity – because she is warm and damp under her clothes.

He takes a dry, closed oyster shell from his pocket and runs his thumb up and down the ridges as he holds it in his palm. His father's story defines him almost as much as his own. It swells him and carries him, like Belle does. During the years of his childhood and the years since his father's death, he has retold it to himself and others more than a hundred times, most likely, so by now it's hard to distinguish the original from what he's added on. When anyone colored asks about his history, this is the story he is proud to tell, much more often than he tells his mama's, who was born free to teacher parents in Connecticut. He can see his mother through his father's stories about her, just as he has always been able to better see himself when he thinks about his father's childhood as a slave in Maryland, then Virginia, and his escape just before the War.

He was always plotting and succumbing, plotting and succumbing, he often said, for as long as he could remember, until he finally made it away at seventeen. Tried once before that, but Samuel doesn't want to think about it now. He shakes his fingers, getting rid of the memory of the ridges on his daddy's back. He wants to think of his freedom, of the time his father made it and got free. Traveled on foot, in darkness, house to house – sometime many miles apart – up to Maryland where he remained a while, then in carriages, once under a heavy tarp so he could hardly breathe, another time having to pretend to be some white man's slave when he was a slave in actual fact, yet in some other way free, or almost free, or on his way to being free, so pretending to be what he still was and wasn't no more. So many masks he got real used to using them – 'cause under them was the image. Despite the fugitive law, and the catchers, despite his measurements and color seen once on a wanted poster for Runaways, the image stayed strong. Someplace where hiding was possible – escape – a bed, a window, the fake papers he had in his pocket – paid work. Then the name – kept in his head for all the months – heard from the man he called his father, who wasn't even his uncle but who had watched over him ever since they came together from the old place, the name he'd heard from his friend who ran: *Connecticut*. So when he finally got to Baltimore and the water, when he finally got onto a schooner taking him and a couple others, he could say when asked – *Connecticut*. I know a fella in Norwalk, the captain said, Norwalk's on the water, got lots of watermen working the docks, some colored too. So he came to Norwalk, worked near the water, carried big barrels of fish and swept and scrubbed the docks, always looking for the chance that came once in a while to get out on the boat to fish them in himself, to get the oysters from the beds big enough and wide enough to stop a ship, he said.

One thing he has never done is tell the story to anyone white, partly because no white person ever asked. He's intrigued that this one wants to know, but he knows too that his willingness to try, to offer a piece of the history that is so intimately woven into his being, is born of other feelings besides pride. The ins and outs of those feelings are too complicated just at the moment to figure out, so he begins to talk before he has time to obey the sensible voice telling him to refrain and return to his work.

Only the outline, he thinks, and tells her his father, also Samuel, was an oyster shucker, and sometimes a waterman when he could get the work, all over Connecticut's harbors, working on the skipjacks for years, doing anything they'd let a colored man do, as long as it was on the water he loved. "That's how he got his name," Samuel says.

"Didn't he have a name before?" she asks.

"Yeah, sure, he did, but it was the slave name, and he'd left all that behind."

She doesn't understand what a slave name is, but feels she must not interrupt again. Or he may stop, he may nod politely, touch his hat, and turn from her back to his work.

Her ignorance of many things does not include ignorance of how you're supposed to act with other races. These rules she learned as a child, as much a part of ordinary life as how to cross crowded Rivington Street. This moment, however, is not part of ordinary life. She sees this. They are not in ordinary time.

"He was a tall, thin man," the son says, looking off to a place in the distance where he can still see his father, bent over, digging for the richest oyster beds. "Could be very quiet for days on end. Then an old story would come to him and it was like you couldn't stop him from talking. Some people who known a lot of pain talk all the time, like they have to keep talking to keep the ghosts down. Some others are quiet. My daddy could be both. Either case, it's a way of getting through." He looks back at her. "He had hair a bit lighter than mine, 'good hair' like we say."

"Good hair?" she asks.

"Yeah." He looks away again, this time down at his feet. "Yes, Ma'am. Lots of people had white in them in his generation. The one that came out of slavery." But before she can ask how so much mixing happened, he keeps talking. "He was a proud man – taught himself letters when he was seventeen and had just come North. He remembered his grandmama telling him his daddy could read, so he knew he had to learn. Soon after he got himself fixed in the town, he found a colored teacher, asked her to teach him how to put the letters together into words – and she did. That was my mama – she was strong in her mind, but weak in her body. She died giving birth to me. He started teaching me when I was five, kept me at it, reading and writing every night, even when I had to stop school to work these boats with him. Books still keep me going in every way."

Hannah thinks of her clumsy writing, of how long it takes her to read when she tries to get through one of Michael's books. She feels admiration for father and son, learning so much on their own, the son talking almost as gracefully as the white men she knows.

"My daddy died when I just made twenty-one. Lived more of his life free than slave, though, and that always made him proud. He came here when he wasn't much more than a boy – on the Underground Railroad. Do you know what that is?" he asks.

His question begins Hannah's first lesson in the history of American slavery, the only knowledge of it she will possess until, almost fifty years later when a surprising and disturbing turn in family events will once again force her into the company of black people, since her granddaughter will marry one. That will be the second time she has the opportunity to learn. This time, during the lessons she will receive in the space of three short months, the learning comes to her because something inexplicable within her has drawn her to a colored man, whose face intrigues her, whose eyes compel her nearly to the point of fainting, whose wife seems oddly familiar to her, and whose story she is somehow hungry to hear.

"There's a house out on East Street," he tells her, "belonging to one of the oldest, wealthiest families in town, and the father is a sea captain who used to bring escaped slaves in secret up from Baltimore. They hid out in the basement tunnels and attic rooms of his mansion until it was safe for them to move on, further north, sometimes all the way to Canada."

Hannah's eyes are wide, her mind flooded with stories of pogroms, Jews hidden by sympathetic Christians in attics and basements until the raging Cossacks had passed through the town. He calls the flood of Negroes escaping from slavery an "exodus" and she thinks of Passover.

"My father was one of them," he says again with obvious pride. "He fought in a colored regiment in the War." Briefly and quickly, he recounts the story of a small, frightened child sold away from his grandmother, the only parent he had ever known. He describes the Chesapeake Bay as he's heard it described to him, memories carried around for over forty years. "When my father was sold, he was too young to know anything about oystering from his father, but when he worked once in Baltimore, and then up and down the Connecticut coast, he remembered his grandmama telling him that had been something his father knew, so he learned it with a special feeling. And he taught it to me." Samuel opens his palm, pulls the narrow curved knife from his pocket, gets down on one knee for leverage, and deftly pries open the crusty shell he holds in his hand.

"Hardest shell of all of them," he says, looking up at Hannah who holds back a feeling of nausea at the sight of the colorless flesh oozing from between the expanding crack. Samuel spreads the two halves wide with his fingers and shows her the tiny piece of life, a translucent silvery blue in the grey light.

"Try it," he says to her astonishment, and she recoils.

"We don't eat shellfish," she stammers, remembering her anger at Belle, this time feeling along with the nausea a strong regret.

Samuel stands up. "I forgot. I apologize," he says, and, scooping the thing up in his fingers, he sucks it into his mouth. "We'd best walk back now," he says, and extends his hand to her arm as if to steer her in a gentlemanly way. But he stops short of her actual flesh and holds only the air in his outstretched hand. There is still more than an hour of light, and as much time before she's promised May to return so she can help with dinner and be there when Michael comes home. When they stand for a moment at the loading dock – he looking away from her at the crates he will carry to Burns's Market, she away from him toward the Sound she still wants to see – she becomes aware of a great sense of guilt, as if she has sinned.

"Thank you," she says. "This has been – " but she can't think what it has been. She feels wildly exposed to this stranger, inexplicably intimate with this colored person, unforgivably aggressive with a man who is not a relative, not Jewish, not even white. Without any words, she has to count on her eyes, and she tries to return his gaze with a directness and clarity equal to his. She can manage it for a few long seconds this time before she has to look away.

He says, "No. Thank *you*. For listening to my story. For the walk." Very slightly, he bows.

"Remember me to your wife," she says – and thinks, what an odd way to put it under the circumstances, considering her behavior the last time she saw the woman called Belle, and her behavior this day with Belle's husband. The wife is not likely to have forgotten her rudeness; it is Hannah who is trying to remember if the sense of familiarity she feels means she has seen Belle somewhere before; or perhaps the first two words of the sentence are all she really means to say to him. Suffused with guilt, confused by desire, she turns quickly away from him and feels, or believes she feels, those black eyes penetrating her shoulders and her back. She reaches a hand around to straighten her veil and pull at the hem of her jacket, but she does not turn to look at him again. Instead, she plays the rearranging game and becomes so engrossed in moving shapes and altering colors that she's surprised when she finds herself at the edge of the beach, as if her feet have taken her there without her knowing it, remembering the way on their own.

Chapter 7

What in hell has he been doing, telling his history to a white woman he hardly knows, risking his life in the process. Samuel's hands become fists. He punches the hard wood of a box of fish, bloodying his knuckles. Picks out pieces of ice to ease the pain and stop the blood.

Does it have to do with the woman he's heard stories about since his childhood, the white girl whose face has remained etched in his mind as his father had described her, counting on his own never quite forgotten memory? *A narrow, bony face, a wide generous mouth, straight, long, light hair, braided and wound carelessly around her head, or clasped at the nape of her neck, large blue eyes filling up with tears as he is driven away. Looked at her only a split second because mainly he wanted his grandmama – but he saw the water streaming down her face in that second, and because of what his grandmama had told him the night before, his own tears almost came – but he fought them, couldn't allow them to drown him. Learn how to hold it all in, his grandmama had told him, that's the only way to survive.* Maybe they were his own almost-tears his father had remembered so vividly. Maybe he had created her features from imagination more than from actual memory. But he always said he remembered the feel of her body against him, her arms around him, the games she played with colored thread and clothespins, a small red ball, a dream about a winter storm that frightened her and so intrigued him he was able to recount it to his son in perfect detail. And he remembered his grandmother, Ruth, telling him the night before he was to leave, *Listen to me, Boy. That white girl who visits us is your mama. You can't never call her that. You can't even let her know you know. But you need to know it.*

It will serve you in your life. Don't never think you don't have everything in you they got in them, except their meanness, but you as good as them in every way.

Samuel hears his father's voice so clear he looks around – and remembers another piece. Happened in Cambridge, Maryland, where he got work loading at the docks while he waited for a schooner to take him North on the bay. Slave catchers were everywhere, and colored workers were wearing a kind of badge to show if they were slave or free. He wasn't free, but wasn't going back as a slave, so he watched and waited and finally managed to get a badge for himself that meant *free*. He wore it for the rest of his time there. It made him proud, he said, to be one of the free men. But then he'd think how he had to wear it – how just *being* a man wasn't enough, and how the slave men felt working there, still owned. Then he felt ashamed, and it kept going, back and forth, proud and ashamed. Samuel sees his father's mouth turn down in a particular gesture of sorrow, held in place from that old, worst memory of being driven away in a wagon, chained to the side, the gesture kept up when he wore the badge, kept even when he was free and had work he got paid for, a child he loved, and a home. But the old sorrow never left his mind, and its record never left the turn of his mouth.

Is it the old story that drives him to talk to the woman called Hannah Sokolov, a long-dead white girl who's had a place in his mind for all his life, it seems, but whose description doesn't match this dark-haired, olive-skinned white woman at all? Except that she – like this one – was white? Is it only her striking face that draws him? If you took each of her features alone, they were no more perfect or graceful than any other woman's – unless it is her eyes – something in their darkness and shape – or her mouth, so wide it's almost unnatural when she smiles. Is it simply that? A beautiful face he can't resist? Or is there something about this Hannah Sokolov that speaks to him like one of Belle's stories and draws him like a picture in the making, suggesting something wonderful and dangerous and indescribable having nothing to do with either beauty or color at all?

Her skin color is certainly lighter than his. But it's not color.

Race has always been the thing. But it's always color, even within the race, some passing, some thinking they're better than you cause they're lighter, or cause they're darker. Yet they're all black, no matter how many white grandparents, or even parents, hiding themselves in the branches of the family trees.

And if it is not color, not beauty alone, not memory, not love – for without question it is Belle he loves – then what is it? Pure animal desire of the sort whites are always thinking black men have for white women? He feels desire – he knows that – but not of a purely physical sort – although he cannot deny his body's response. There is some tie or connection he cannot place to this Jewish woman from another world whose brazenness contradicts her shyness, who has some power lying beneath her holding back, and who, like him, seems to be driven by something beyond her understanding, or her control, maybe her desire. He cannot explain it to himself, but he has read enough history and poetry to know the need for explanation would not even come up if she were black. People are drawn to each other for all sorts of reasons, suddenly and unreasonably and often inconveniently. The world is white, though, and so it must be the whiteness of the world that makes the whole thing dumbfounding. He throws the thoughts off with an actual shake of his head as he enters the store and lays down the first of the crates he must carry from the dock before he can go home to Belle. It won't happen again. That much he promises himself. He is not about to risk his life, let alone the life of his wife and their coming child.

A light but freezing rain is falling now, causing the autumn leaves to glisten as if tiny pearls line the edges of purple, deep orange, and brown. Tall grasses along the sand banks are a burnt orange in the fading light, her favorite color, the color of the rug in her parlor at home. A salty, slightly putrid smell of damp seaweed signals low tide, and she can see the mud flats beginning to emerge yards from shore. No feeling of guilt or confusion can cause her to deny this happiness – from what? she wonders. She will very likely never talk to him again. She will see him in the fish store and smile politely. But she will know. She feels a shift inside herself and knows the meaning of the rumbling hunger. Even if it is never filled, it is better to know it is there, to know she can feel it, is not dead to this sumptuous longing. It is shocking, yet even better somehow, that he is colored. That he is so completely different from herself, so foreign even though his family has been here for generations and hers has just arrived. She imagines the life crowding the shallow water and the mud below so vividly she can almost see the creatures before her eyes: tiny hermit crabs scurrying sideways; sponges and anemones that look less like creatures than like flowers opening and closing with the tides; sharp barnacles and large starfish that look hard but, like the oyster, are slimy and silky to the touch; mussels and snails and clams she is forbidden to taste. Like the river, like this water they call the Sound, she is full of noise, she can hear flowing and rippling, the slurring swoosh of the tide coming in. She can hear the crawling hermits, as if their tiny claws were tiptoeing in her ears. She can hear the undulations of the anemones. She is teeming with sound and moving life forms. *Full of herself,* she's heard women and girls say about the ones they derisively call *princesses – who does she think she is – a princess – a goyishe princess? A shikseh, to prance around like that with her nose in the air?* She stands away from the rock she's been leaning against and prances around like a shikseh princess with her nose in the air. She is full of her hunger. The sound inside her rolls into high tide with a roar.

Ordinary time seems suspended, like in the stories she has heard about war time, when only the day at hand comes to matter because death may be just around the corner. A feeling of terror fills her, then changes fast to a feeling of freedom. "Outside ordinary time," she says aloud in a tone she might use to give instructions to one of the children, just as she notices the late afternoon is fading quickly to dark, her hair and coat are becoming soaked, and she must hurry home.

Chapter 8

When Michael comes into the vestibule that evening, he hangs up his coat on the wooden hook as usual, then, also as usual, goes into the library for a quick drink. But the room does not look as usual. Hannah has been up to her rearranging again. "But never in your room," she says as she comes in rustling and skipping, obviously in a playful mood though she can see his expression of surprise threatening to become exasperation. "Don't worry, I never enter there," she says, gesturing toward the tiny back room that serves as his study. Its smallness causes him to work long hours in his office in Norwalk, and remain in New York in the laboratory for days at a time, working on a miracle drug, he calls it, that will harden weak teeth – the discovery, he assures her, that will enable him to save enough money for a new and better house, a larger study for him, a spacious nursery for the children, a sewing room, and a separate dining room instead of the large kitchen where eating and cooking must share the same space.

The knotty brown sofa that faced the window when he left that morning is off to the side of the room now. The dark orange rug that covers a part of the floor has been pulled toward the window. Several glass vases, each filled with dried grasses and leaves Hannah has gathered at the Sound, she tells him, are lined up on the windowsill.

"I can stand on the soft rug right near the window now," she says as if more to herself than to him, "and see the grasses and leaves right in front of me, then the sky outside behind them. The colors remind me of the sea."

"But it's not water, it's sky," he tells her, taking the drink she has prepared and now holds out to him. He looks at her glistening hair and touches it gently. "Have you been walking in the rain without a hat?" he asks.

"It's the colors, Michael. The blue, or gray, or even near black of the sky *reminds* me of water, and these," she points to the filled vases, "remind me of the grasses near the shore." She has turned away from him, arranging and rearranging the dry flowers and leaves. She does not seem to need his attention, nor does she respond to his question about her hair. For a minute he stares at her back, but then, going through the day's mail stacked on a sideboard, he asks about dinner, the children, Aaron and May.

Around the large wooden table in the kitchen, Rena and Asher listen attentively while their father talks of his progress with his experiments. They are proud and happy to be eating with the grownups tonight. Rena especially asks many questions, designed more to impress than out of real curiosity, but obviously appealing to her father nonetheless. They all laugh when Uncle Aaron pulls quarters out of their ears, then, with a series of knots, turns his white napkin into a mouse that jumps at them, squeaking.

"Aaron, stop," May tells him, as if he were one of the children, and, as always, she leans over to cut his meat.

"No children makes a domineering wife," says Michael, trying to mask his cruelty with a wink and a smile. Aaron smiles back, jovial and clearly unperturbed by May's ministrations or Michael's critiques. May is a *new woman*, and Aaron is a modern man who *desires* his wife to be independent and strong. Hannah has heard him say this, and amazement has silenced any response from her. He has even said it to Michael, arguing in front of the children that women and men are equal and should have equal rights. Michael had scoffed. "Some women," he said once, making Hannah's skin burn. "She's my angel," Aaron says now, and May laughs girlishly, saying only, "Eat, eat, everyone. Ess, mein kinderlech," falling into her mother's language…"yingeleh, maideleh," addressing Asher and Rena, "ess." She commands them all to eat in a harsh sounding voice, but everyone can see her fair skin flush with pleasure at her husband's words and at the way he looks at her with adoring eyes.

Before dessert, when the baby begins to cry, Hannah leaves the table and carries her upstairs, relieved to be alone. She changes Sophie's diapers and dresses her in the softest white cotton gown she can find. She wraps her in a wide pink blanket she has knitted herself and turns the gas lamp down to low. Then she holds her close as she rocks and sings – fragments of Russian ballads, Yiddish lullabies, an American song she's just learned about a "bonnie" man who is beloved but far away, somewhere across the ocean. She's heard the Scottish woman in the knitting shop singing it and learned that bonnie means beautiful. It's a lovely word, a lovely song, she thinks as she begins to sing it from memory, bending down again and again to kiss Sophie's head. *My bonnie lies over the ocean. My bonnie lies over the sea. My bonnie lies over the ocean. Oh bring back my bonnie to me.* She sings the short chorus over and over until the rhythm of the rocking and the rhythm of the singing seem to merge into one rhythm, like two instruments harmonizing in one piece of music, until she has had her fill of the exquisite hunger of the *bring back, please bring back,* and gives in to the rumbling desire that reminds her she is not empty, not nothing, a feeling something like the feeling of having the children inside her, Rena, then Asher, then Sophie who almost killed her and who, because of that, in a way she would never admit, not even to May, she loves best. She hums the tune while Sophie's eyes close, hums effortlessly, as if this new melody has always been a part of her, rocking slowly until they are both asleep.

The following day, Aaron is sitting at the kitchen table reading his newspaper while Hannah cuts vegetables for soup. Even more than with May, she feels comfortable with him when she has questions to ask that might expose her ignorance, so she interrupts his reading. "Aaron," she says, sitting down near him and wiping her hands on her apron. "I want to ask you something." He looks up and smiles.

"We're Jews, of course I know this," she says. "And we're white. But the other whites – they don't think we're the same as them. Am I right?"

"They don't think we're the same or as good." He raises his thin eyebrows and smiles conspiratorially, conveying clearly his meaning that people are crazy – so what can you do? "And yes, we're white. Of course. We're not colored, if that's what you mean, Hannahla."

"Is there such a thing? A colored Jew?" she asks.

"There is, yes. In certain countries in the north of Africa I understand there are Jews, and like the others in those places their skins are brown – so they aren't white. I knew some, a family in the old country when I was a boy. They were from a place called Morocco. And when the Russian Cossacks came for a pogrom, they didn't distinguish. White or brown, the Jews were in trouble. But they are still Jews, not black, like the colored here."

"Not all of them are black," Hannah says, more to herself than in answer to him, picturing colors, thinking of Samuel's walnut colored skin, or even Belle's – a chestnut brown it could be called. "Maybe no one is really black. Not really."

Aaron clears his throat, frowns for a moment. "No, you're right, Hannah. Well, it's not always a matter of skin color. It's also about heritage. Culture. Education. That sort of thing. We'd need a Rabbi, I suppose, to interpret for us. A *midrash* on skin color." His eyes twinkle, then he grows serious again. "The Negroes here are good people, don't misunderstand me. Some of them were brave in the war, I'm told, in the colored regiment that shipped out to France. And yes, the whites that hate them are often the same whites that hate us. But we're different from them both. We're white. But we're Jewish. That's the main thing."

She thinks about it all afternoon, unable to fix on any acceptable explanation. Even Aaron didn't really know how to explain it, she can see that, and so she had stopped bothering him. There is something huge and mysterious about the whole thing. She – they – are different from colored people. She knows that. So different that you can't really know them in the way you can know even the Irish, or even the Italians, or the ordinary white

Americans who live in the north part of town.

She thinks about it while she fixes dinner, converses with Michael and May about the children, cleans up, puts the children to bed. When she is dressed for bed herself, sitting at the edge of the mattress staring into space, she is thinking about it still. She is different from them, so different she cannot really know them. She is better than they are in a way. It can't be helped, they can't help it – it's just the way they are made. That doesn't mean they shouldn't have rights, that they shouldn't be respected. They're like strangers from another world. You should be kind to them. But never forget they're different. Never forget how different they are. She reaches over to turn off the light and pulls her cold feet under the quilt. She wants to appear to be asleep before Michael comes to bed. Samuel's being fills her as if she's always known him, as if he is closer to her than her own kin. Belle's face comes to her in dream after dream, as if she's met her some place before.

Chapter 9

Belle is tired. Tired of and tired from. She makes an *of* list and a *from* list in her head as she hangs out the clothes in the Sunday morning sun. Tired from working almost every day of her life since she was six. Tired from standing too long on feet that have always been weak in the arches. Tired from last night's wakefulness when she walked around and around the other room so as not to disturb Samuel and finally sat before the fire wrapped in a quilt, feeling a gentle fluttering from the baby and falling asleep for maybe an hour before day break. *Tired from* wasn't so bad. But *tired of* was something, and that's what awakened her in the night. Tired of Burns and his low pay for long hours of her and Samuel's work. Tired of customers calling her Belle, or gal, or nothing at all, just giving orders about fish. Tired of white people in general and their incomprehensible blindness, or cruelty, or stupidity, or whatever it is. Tired of swallowing her words or biting her tongue or trying to figure it out. Tired of one white person in particular, that Jewish woman named Hannah Sok something. Her acting human and decent one minute and white the next. Tired of a certain way she saw her look at Samuel the other day and tired of her own jealousies. She has no reason to doubt her husband's love. But doubting love is as much a part of her as the shape of her hands and as strong as them, too.

Relentless and slow, it comes upon her, and she can never stop it once it starts. Doubting everything and everyone – fear of losing everything – no, fear is too weak a word – dread is closer – a dread she wants, no longs to confess to Samuel, perhaps some night when they are lying in the dark. But she can't, she won't. The words grow wild and unruly the moment she thinks of them, and so she will touch his head instead, run her hand through his beard, across his eyes, down his nose, around his mouth.

Only once, when he was real late coming home and she started thinking of his brazenness with white people, she'd shown it to him. The terror came on like an outside thing and her skin was no match for it. It entered her and changed everything. Head, feet, stomach, throat, eyes, hands, everything ached and beat. And her chest. It started hurting like someone had punched her. She couldn't breathe. She tried to make a story. *Belle is waiting for her husband. He's later than usual but there's no reason to think he isn't safe. He's known in town. Liked, for a colored man. And he knows how to handle himself. He'll be walking through that door any minute and find her sitting by the fire.* But it didn't stick. She lost the thread. Began crying, talking to herself, no comforting words, just God, God, please, please. That sort of thing. Until she was crouched on the floor, her fist in her mouth, staring hard at the door. And she'd had just enough time to stand up when he came in. Some delay with the schooners. More crates than usual. A storm at sea. Burns insisting on everything being done all in one night. Samuel saw right away something was wrong with her. He saw her in her extremity. She had wanted to tell him about these attacks, and here he was seeing it for himself. Shameful enough to tell, but being seen in it was another thing. He looked so helpless she didn't know whether to slap him or start reassuring him. She didn't do either. Just stood there as still as she could, silent and enraged, knocked almost off her feet by the belief that she'd almost lost him and he didn't care. Because right then she believed he didn't, that no one did, that she was as alone now as she'd been as a child when they said Mama was dead and no daddy since before she was even born. Alone and enraged. Before she could stop herself she threw a pewter plate against the wall. Balled up one of her favorite cloths and threw it into the fire. Was even about to demolish a chair before Samuel stopped her. Looking at her all the time with those big, black, helpless eyes. Later, she felt she would die of shame. Felt she was a cowardly black woman. What would her mama or her ancestors think who'd had to deal with slavery, selling, killing, then war and nothing to eat, then wandering all over the country looking for each other after the War was done. And mostly never finding anyone. Now that must have been *alone*. Here she is with a home. A strong husband she loves. Now a baby coming after all those years of trying. Thinking back on that time, she felt the shame again. Tired of being ashamed. Tired of feeling disgusted with herself. Tired of never being able to hold on to the good feeling of being loved for long. Tired of the bad feelings, and the horrible dreams of messing all over herself that come periodically making her doubly ashamed. Tired of not knowing with more certainty that he'd never betray her, especially not with a white woman, especially not now with the baby coming he wants so much to be Ruth. He's not a complete fool. Tired of hating all these white people, even this one who makes Belle feel she's seen her someplace before.

She snaps Samuel's shirts straight before hanging them on the line. *Tired of* is the longer list of harder things. Except for one. Tired from the energy hating takes. But she will not ever fall apart like that again. She has sworn it to herself, silently, in the place where no outside words can distort her meaning or muddy up what she intends to do. She swears it for the second time as she stretches sheets on the line. She will not let it happen again, not before Samuel, not before any child of her own. Not before herself.

Chapter 10

Once again, Hannah heads for the Sound. The morning sun is strong despite the cold December air, and once again she takes off her veil, this time loosening rather than tightening her hairpins. Lately, she can't stand the slightest constraint. Only one more month of Aaron and May staying, so she can't let the cold keep her from the water. Since that day in November, she walks for miles and hours thinking about the two times with Samuel and today, planning how to talk to his wife next week when she goes to have her hair cut, trying to help them with a little bit of extra money with their baby coming. Hannah thinks of this friendship – as she has come to call it – as unusual, but not dangerous, as long as she is careful that no one finds out who might misunderstand, especially not Michael who would never understand her being friends with any man, let alone a nigger as he insists on calling Negroes, though she's tried to tell him it's impolite. The Klan would just as soon kill you as the colored people, she told him once. The Klan isn't my standard of judgment, he'd responded, in the condescending tone he takes with her more and more often now.

Throughout the holidays and the heavy snowstorm that kept her indoors for weeks, nearly driving her crazy with its endless whiteness and cold, she kept herself going by thinking of the time in late November with all the colors around them, and two brief encounters after that in the fish store when their eyes met in that way. She'd had the children with her one of those times, and during that moment, literally within the blinking of an eye, Belle walked in. Those sudden, momentary meetings of eyes tell whole stories, though Hannah can never explain exactly how; nevertheless, she was aware of the dangers of the mysterious transparency,

78

and as soon as Belle entered, Hannah had dropped her gaze. She felt a hard stare from Samuel's wife, and so she had turned around to the children. And there were Rena's eyes, angry and unforgiving, as if she knew every thought that had passed between her mother and the colored man. Hannah had been extra gentle, trying to adjust Rena's scarf around her neck, but Rena had jerked herself away and refused to speak to her mother for the rest of the day. *As if I have done something shameful,* Hannah thought when Rena turned her back on her mother's usual lullaby. *As if I have already committed some horrible sin.*

Finally, most of the snow melted and they haven't had another storm since. Dark patches of earth are visible along the roads. Graceful, dark brown branches of old oaks and weeping willows make intricate and beautiful patterns, so she often looks up as she walks, reluctant to take her eyes from the curves and layers of shapes against the pale silver winter sky that she loves nearly as much as the deep blue of summer, or, when there are millions of stars, the black night.

She's dreamed the black dream several times since November. Sometimes she's lost in a night without stars, or she's near water as black as the sky so you can't see where one ends and the other begins. Often she's making her way through crowds of unknown strangers. Other times she feels as alone as if there were no other person on earth but herself. A few nights ago, she was desperately searching for Rena in the blackness, calling her daughter's name loudly, and she woke, shouting, waking Michael who told her it was only a dream. *Only a dream* doesn't make much sense to Hannah. Dreams feel as real to her as waking life, as frightening and sometimes as wonderful. Last night, her mother came back to her as if she was alive as anyone. Hannah heard her voice, felt the soft caress of Rena's hand against her cheek. She'd been living in Norwalk all this time, and Hannah couldn't understand how she could have thought her mother was dead; for here she was, holding Sophie, and eating fish, but there wasn't enough to go around, a lack that was somehow Hannah's fault. All around them it was dark, but they could see in the darkness; it wasn't the frightening black darkness of the other dreams. Then Rena stood up and said she was taking the train back to New York. She walked toward the tracks behind South Main Street where a train was coming toward them. Rena climbed aboard, but just when Hannah was about to follow her, the train went underground and disappeared.

She reaches the harbor, looks around for him but he isn't there. She heads for the path to the beach, thinking about the Underground Railroad and the train in her dream. She walks along the beach for a while, feeling the goodness of being alone. No one is around for miles, wouldn't be, in this weather. She gazes up and down the shore, then out to sea, imagines for a moment what she might do if she were really alone, the only person left on earth – or, perhaps only one of two. Her shoes feel damp, but she feels brave, even daring.

Then she sees him. He is standing at the edge of the water, pitching stones across the waves. The tide is in. His stone skips three times and he smiles as she approaches. She looks behind her again, then she touches him lightly on the shoulder. He turns, still smiling, and looks directly into her eyes. Instantly, his smile fades. He looks wary and afraid. Nervously, he looks around.

"No one will be here in this weather," she says, pulling her dark red woolen shawl closer around her black coat. Then she remembers her hair is loose, and she blushes, turns from him, replaces the veil and ties it under her chin, but she sees his look. She is keenly aware of the thick dark hair hanging down her back, past her shoulders, and she feels exposed, like in one of those horrible dreams where she realizes she's naked, even though now it's only hair. She opens the red shawl and lifts it higher around her head so it covers her hair.

"I'm having it cut by your wife tomorrow," she says, embarrassed by her own words that acknowledge the loose hair and that he noticed it.

Samuel nods. "I got to be getting back," he says, and with the same gesture of hand to hat brim she's seen before, he turns away. Then he stops and, only half looking at her, he says, "I have to watch the store this afternoon. Mr. Burns is out today, and Belle is home with some painful feet, too swollen to stand."

He turns again, and within moments is hidden by brush and trees.

Hannah turns to the water. She takes off her woolen gloves, kneels and digs her fingers into the sand until she reaches the dark, wet part. She scoops up a handful, stands up and rolls the mud into a large ball between her palms, thinking about color. Black nights and black water in her dreams. Brown branches and brown earth, especially when it is moist. Her mother's dark brown hair she remembers so vividly, how Rena would let her comb it for special occasions, and now her daughter Rena has the same silky brown hair. Her own hair, thicker and wilder and so dark it's almost black. The brown of the wooden furniture she loves. The brown of – she can't say the word even in her own mind, but she cannot stop herself from picturing it, her own and the babies' when the oddest thing happened – with each one of them the same – the smell that always made her gag suddenly pleased her, a secret pleasure she added to the many crazy feelings she's been subject to since she became a mother. A pleasure in the smell that lasted until very recently, when Rena was six and Asher four. She throws the mud ball out to sea where Samuel threw his stones, thinking of brown, trees, mud, wood, his skin, and of white, the colorless ice that has always made her cringe because she fears slipping and falling on it, the snow-storms that blind you to everything in the world before they finally clear, leaving white mountains and valleys that only in the first days are kind of beautiful, reflecting light, soft to the touch, and can be sweet tasting in cups mixed with maple syrup running through its crevices and tiny holes. She loves her dark red shawl and rolls her ungloved fingers into its warmth as she heads back to the harbor and the fish store.

As promised, he is there alone. Or she feels he has promised, and when she enters, she looks at him directly, not trying to hide her acceptance of his invitation: Here I am. As usual, they talk of fish, the difficulties of getting enough catch in winter. Soon she loosens her shawl, removes her veil to reveal her now securely pinned hair, respectably twisted around her head in a braid like a crown.

"May I know more about your life, how your people came

81

to be here?" She asks the question politely but in a strong voice, feeling she doesn't have the time to dissemble, wondering where she is getting her nerve from, safely back with him in extraordinary time for an hour or so. As if he, as well as she, remembers where he left the story in November, as if he, as well as she, understands the importance and the beauty of this unexplainable secret they share.

So he begins, because despite anxiety and confusion equaling hers about what it all signifies, he can't resist it, not in the moment when the opportunity occurs. He has no special need to acquaint her with his history. He's interested in hers, but with no greater intensity than his interest in many things – how the fishing industry is growing around him; how American laws move in the direction of stated ideals, then move way back again, and how hard it is for colored people to live under them; how rage gathers and grows yet waits its turn; how stones sometimes skip three rhythmical times and sometimes sink; how much color means. He's interested in many things, passionate about only three: Belle, and the child she's carrying, and freedom. What he feels toward Hannah is nothing like that. He doesn't know what it is. When he tells her stories, it's because she asks, desires to know about him. It feels like a command. And later, when he thinks about it, he remembers the feeling of being compelled.

No, it isn't Louisa. He doubts he could be so mesmerized by someone who looked the way she was supposed to look – pale, a long pale face, thin blond hair. He never remembered his father remembering her as beautiful. This woman here was some kind of white black woman, some hybrid form that falls between, could even pass for a fair-skinned Negro passing for white – like in Louisiana, he's heard, where quadroons, octoroons, are as common as plain colored folks, and who live between the blacks and the whites, in their neighborhoods, and in their minds. Her beauty alone would not be sufficient, though. She combines it with some kind of openness, some mysterious fluidity that invites you in. When she told him she loved the water, he'd stared at her because he had just had that thought, *like some thick fluid*, almost as soon as he saw her, felt water was somehow her kin.

It's as if he already knows her, or – and this thought frightens him – as if he wants to follow her. He can't resist the extraordinary, dangerous pull.

He tells her about a place called the Summerly Plantation where his father was born and his grandfather killed, and how common that was – the killing. She listens without interrupting, trying not to cry out when he does not spare her the brutal parts. She listens respectfully, as if it's the least she can do. He tells her about Frederick Douglass and his astonishing brilliance; about the great liberator, Harriet Tubman, her fifteen different trips to the South, the more than three hundred people she led to freedom, including her old parents; about her friendship with the wild white man called John Brown, born not far from here. When he tells her about Nat Turner, she closes her eyes at his description of murdered children, but then she opens them again and waits. He describes as best he can the situation at the present time, what Jim Crow means, how the name of the demeaning minstrel figure came to be used for the Black Codes that keep the races apart.

As he talks, she realizes that even in New York she shops in different stores from Negroes, eats in different restaurants, just as she lives in a different part of town. She never thought much about it, except for a passing wave of anxiety when she senses the hostility of someone on the street or on the train. It has always seemed natural and necessary, because of the way Aaron and everyone else she knew always described it. Now, for the first time, she sees it and feels it differently, feels the humiliation, and the rage that must come close on its heels, and she almost turns away. He tells her – with softening euphemisms about "certain body parts" – about what happens at a lynching, how thousands have been killed this way since the Civil War. And still are, he adds, and tortured – blinded – burned, he says, and repeats – *certain body parts cut off and kept for souvenirs.* Still, she stands there, listening, her eyes widening, her breath shortening, yet she is silent, as if she is determined to prove something to him or herself. He tells her about his white grandmother and how common it is for Negroes to have whites far and near in their family trees, and why this is so, about the forcing, and how common it is for whites to act like they don't know about this twisting of families together for more than three hundred years.

She listens, and while she listens she looks up and down and around his face, as if she is noticing things she never noticed before, specific things about his features, his hair, as if he were posing for a drawing she was making of him.

He tells her about how long slavery lasted, how much the Hebrew Bible and the story of Exodus meant to them, how they put it in their songs.

"Sing me one," she says, somewhere between a request and a demand, but he shakes his head, no, and smiles in a kind of cynical way she doesn't understand.

A customer enters the store. Hannah stands up just in time, turns to the glass showcase and seems to be inspecting the sauces Burns has bottled for the fish. Samuel serves the woman, slices flounder fillets, counts out a dozen oysters kept on ice now that it's winter and they're scarce. He can't take money – Burns won't allow it – so he writes the amount on a piece of paper and lets the woman sign. He does this for all the regular customers, like this one, and even for the occasional stranger who enters the store, Burns trusting the white stranger more than the colored man he's known for years. Samuel says, "Good afternoon," and opens the door for her. She acknowledges neither the words nor the gesture of politeness, but smiles and says "good day" to Hannah, who has not spoken a word.

It's as if Samuel isn't there. The woman wasn't even intending to be rude. It is as if he is invisible. Hannah turns back to him, looks at him straight and long. Their time is running out.

"No singing today," he says, hardening even more the cynical expression he'd assumed before the woman came in. But even without the song, Hannah has had her second lesson. She could not say what it is in so many words, but it has something to do with the power of hatred – Nat Turner killing children – all the killings – the unpleasant, cynical smile that has something to do with singing or the song. As she begins to wrap herself in layers again, preparing to leave, she looks at him from hair to chin,

84

shoulders to feet, and this time he doesn't look so different to her. In that moment when she sees what she thinks of as his "white part" – the slightly thinner lips, the looser curls than Belle's tight black woolly hair, the slightly lighter shade of the brown of his skin – she feels a new sense of danger lurking behind this friendship that draws her out of ordinary time.

"Thank you, again," she whispers, nearly stammering, and when she turns she bumps into the glass, lets out a cry of pain. He reaches for her as he did before and again stops short of her flesh, holding air in his hand. Their eyes meet for a long moment, intensely, as they are unobserved. And for the first time in her memory, she can't unlock.

He is the one who must say, "You have to go now. You're expected, and I'm sure you have work to do before dinner." He hands her a package of flounder he's quickly wrapped so she will have something to show, should anyone have noticed her long stay in the market. "I hope you've been warmed enough to brave the walk home – Mrs. Sokolov," he tells her, pausing a moment before he addresses her by name. He has never said *Hannah*. She will never hear her name in his mouth. But he has given an explanation to her, should any be necessary for ordinary time, for the length of her stay in the store. He is afraid of the intensity of her eyes, on the verge of being completely out of control.

Chapter 11

"There was no one in the coffin, of course. But an American flag was draped over it and you were supposed to think Lincoln was inside. They had colored men in uniform marching, straight across the Washington Street Bridge, up East Avenue to the Green. It was like one of your stories, Belle. The empty coffin, I mean. No one in it really, but everyone crying anyway, because it brought to mind the real thing."

She can easily imagine the scene. Negroes only just officially freed. Everyone's poor, or almost everyone. Some people separated from everyone in their family. Everyone separated from some family – a precious child sold away years before, a beloved wife or husband, or you've been sold away yourself and want to head back to where you might've left your mama behind but don't know how to get there except starting a long, long walk, and maybe you have only one foot cause the other one was chopped off by some crazy white man who called himself your master and caught you trying to escape. The people lining the streets of a Connecticut town would be the brave ones, or the lucky ones, living in a free state for some time, but only at the behest of "good" whites since the Fugitive Laws. Now, no one can send anyone back. Jobs can be taken openly. Travel might not mean risking your life.

She pictures the blacks lining the street to watch the coffin pass, everyone stunned, not knowing whether to hope or grieve. What's next? No one knows – maybe a possibility here or there – a knowledge of oyster shucking, always able to take care of children, cook and clean house, a brother who made it out and let you know he's settled in Boston, a sister passing for white with a connection that could mean a job, a desire to walk all the way to Canada, seeing a good piece of the north on your way,

86

might as well since you got nothing to keep you here.

"I can picture it," she tells Samuel, who is looking up from a book he's reading about the history of Connecticut.

"History's not so different from the stories you make," he says. "You never know what's real and what's added on. Like all the stories I carry around with me, about my daddy's white mama and murdered daddy, and his grandmama Ruth who I can see clear as if I'd known her myself, and about Mr. Henry, the teacher and leader of the slaves. I always wondered what happened to him. Sometimes I can't tell what I remember my daddy telling me from what I remember on my own."

She's listened to his stories about his father's history for all the years she's known him, been changed herself by the stories of the courage in his father's line. The time he ran before he got away. Only about fourteen or fifteen and already feeling something inside that his own daddy must have felt – that something else somewhere else was meant for him, something far away from this, even from the girl he loved, name of Dinah, a bit younger than himself who they took into the house. She was smart, a good cook, he said. Belle pictured her with dark African skin and a beautiful nose, narrow at the very top then sloping wide to a curve like the moon. Large eyes, black as a winter midnight. Round lips he maybe kissed one time. And he knew she wasn't being taken into the house to cook, not hardly. He'd seen the master's eyes on her. After a few days he'd seen her in a better grade of cotton dress than the one she'd worn in the quarters, and her hair, Belle imagined, clean and oiled so it shone. The girl named Dinah would've met his eyes, and he would've seen the change in them. That night he decided to run. They caught him fast cause he'd gone without planning, just ran like he'd just as soon get killed. He survived the whipping, kept it all inside like his grandmama taught him. And when he healed, he told the older ones he wanted to try again, this time the right way. He waited two more years. Her Samuel had seen the scars from that whipping. They rose on his flesh like ridges of hard mud, a mud wall to remind him of all he had risked and won.

Belle is jealous at times, of his passion for his reading and his own history, and fearful, too – that she won't be enough for him. She has learned, over years, to abide the distances between them – as long as he keeps coming home to her, showing her how to be brave just because he is, looking at her in that way of his. But now she senses something else behind his memories, something dangerous and new. "Why you thinking about that story again tonight?" she asks.

"Don't know. Just thinking about how little we know about things. About everything. About how the old stories we heard as children end up influencing us all our lives. How someone can become just like some old great-grandfather he never knew, somehow his spirit handed down to one particular descendant instead of all the others. Mr. Henry wasn't even my blood relation. I know much of nothin about him, but sometime I feel more kin to him than anyone. Someone can be – well, drawn to something, or someone, and he can't figure out why." He pauses. "Like I was drawn to you that day I saw you hanging sheets in that white lady's yard when I was delivering fish. It only took a minute, and I knew."

Although she recalls the moment as well as he does, and felt, just as he did, the strong current that seemed to surround them – like sparks on a railroad track under fast moving wheels; although she is moved by his dark eyes looking into her face in the way she most loves; although she feels a rush of pleasure whenever he talks about her stories in a way that shows he understands them, and she's even started planning how to ask him to write some of them down for her while she's still practicing her spelling to be able to do it herself; although she nods, and looks down at her sewing, and remains silent for a while, she knows he is talking about something else. She has slept by his side too many years, ten in all; cried too many times when a child wouldn't come for them; taken him inside her body when she wanted him with every part of herself and when she would just as soon have been left alone; listened to his haunting memories of the child in the wagon whose daddy's body got all chopped up like they thought he couldn't feel the agonizing pain, or else, worse, like they were glad he was feeling it, wanting him in pain more than wanting him dead, and hearing her Samuel whisper in the dark – *what drives them Belle? White People. Are they people? Like us?* She has heard his stories and told him hers too many times until she feels there is nothing left about one life the other doesn't know, for her not to know now, he's been talking to that Jewish woman again. And he's scared.

When the silence has lasted so long he's putting on his spectacles, about to go back to his book, she tries to find the right words. "Samuel . . . . "

He holds his steel-rimmed glasses in one hand. His other hand closes the book and lays it on a wooden stool. He waits. But all she can say is, "Samuel," again.

He leans forward in his chair holding one end of his glasses in each hand, twisting and rubbing the wire that curves around his ears. "Some stories are so strong you can't resist em," he says. "Like they talking to something inside you didn't even know was there. Sometimes you can't figure out what it's about – the story you feel so caught by. Or it's like you'd always known it, but forgotten. Or like you never knew it before but when you come upon it, it's like you're reading about your own life. And later on, when you finish, you can't be sure why you're so drawn to it because there's nothing in the outward story that seems familiar to you."

"Be careful," is what she finally says, hearing he means *person*, not *story*. "There's Klan everywhere. Right up there in New Haven and down in Darien. Close by. And Ruth is coming. And – " It's the jolt of the reversal, perhaps – her telling him to take care, his fear, not hers, filling the room that makes her say more. She hardly ever says it because he knows, and it's a hard thing to say when you been choking on it and all the longing it brings for all your damn life, but she says it now and she looks at him hard. "I love you, Samuel."

His eyes close for a moment. They are shining with tears when he opens them and looks at her again. "You're my ground, Belle. I couldn't do without you," he says, and does not add the other truth entangling and endangering him: the way the water pulls.

89

Again, it is as if something between them happened before, but neither woman can remember it. There is something between them now, and they both know it, but neither one speaks of it. With all that going on – all the unsettling feelings moving around them, as if the air itself is saturated with something heavy, but without the shapes or colors that one of them might easily comprehend, or the words that might ease the other one in her mind – the two women stand for a moment, watching each other silently. Then they talk about hair.

"It's thick – you can see. Not as thick as yours. And not kinky – is that the word? Not really curly. But wild, and I'd like it evened out. Can you do that?"

Belle sits on a chair on wheels, an old lawyer's chair Samuel picked up at a junk yard and refinished for her so she could rest her feet from walking around the house. On this wonderful contraption, she can wheel around from fireplace to table and table to shelf when she needs something. On a lower chair, a soft green pillow at her back and a clean sheet around her to catch the falling hair, Hannah faces the fire. Behind her, Belle moves her chair to the left and right, holding the thick, wiry hair that hangs down past the white woman's shoulders.

"It *is* thick," she says, feeling it and spreading it out. She removes small, sharp scissors from the pocket of the long sweater she wears over her dress.

"Just an inch or two," Hannah says. "My husband likes it long, but the ends need trimming."

Belle lifts layers of the hair and pins them to the top of Hannah's head. Then she snips a slightly curved line around the under-layer left hanging loose. Slowly, layer by layer, ten times in all, she evens the edges and cuts the split ends of Hannah's hair.

Meanwhile, Hannah has been looking at as much of the room as she can see without moving her head. She sees the wood, chopped and piled neatly to the side of the black iron chimney tools. She sees a dark shelf to the side of the fireplace and on it some pottery dishes in lovely blue and green flowered patterns, a series of tan mixing bowls, an earthenware jug filled with wooden spoons. When she lifts her eyes she can see a shelf above the fireplace, and on it a black Bible and an old brown ledger.

Belle's eyes follow Hannah's. "Keep your head still," she says, a bit harshly, pushing it so that Hannah's eyes face the floor again.

A hand-woven, woolen rug of dark red and brown covers a small portion of the wide wooden planks of the floor. A closed door leads to what must be another room, the bedroom. It's only a closed door, normal for daytime when a visitor is in the house, but Hannah feels it is closed against her in particular, that Samuel's wife Belle doesn't want her to see in.

When Belle finishes the back, she asks, "You want the front a bit shorter?" They both feel the absence of the *Ma'am*. It goes with the unspoken thing between them, the one they know about, and somehow refers as well to the thing they don't know about but feel.

"Just a tiny bit," Hannah tells her. "I don't want anything fancy, or noticeable. Maybe just so the front and sides curl a bit more when I pull the whole thing up in a bun or a braid."

Belle gets up from the chair and walks in front of Hannah, lifts her chin up with one hand, tilting her head in the right position. "Keep still," she says, and combs a thin layer of Hannah's hair down in front of her face.

Through the veil of dark brown, Hannah can see the curves of the other woman's breasts stretching the black woolen sweater she wears over a heavy blue cotton dress. Under her breasts, her stomach has begun to protrude, a small round mountain beneath two smaller hills. Hannah wants to touch the mountain affectionately, as she might have touched May if she'd ever had a child, but she folds her hands in her lap. She sees Belle's slender, brown neck, and when her chin is lifted slightly higher by the firm hand that parts the veil and pushes each side behind an ear, she sees tiny silver earrings in the soft earlobes, and she sees the other woman's hair. She's never seen a colored person's hair up close, but heard many stories about how ugly and coarse it is, how it's greasy, and it smells. The desire to touch it is nearly overpowering. Curls as tiny and tight as the tightest woolen shawl layer thickly, pulled back into two fat braids wound around each other at the nape of Belle's neck. Perhaps some kind of grease, or oil, has been used, because, separated by a narrow part, the hair on top of Belle's head lies flat and thick and glistening until it meets the braid. The braid and the strands escaping from it look soft and pliant – the opposite of ugly or coarse. Hannah keeps her hands folded so they won't move of their own accord and reach out to touch that wonderful looking hair. Hair Samuel touches, she thinks, and shuts her eyes quickly, banishing the thought.

Belle has cut a neat line of hair from ear to ear at the level of Hannah's nose. Then she brushes it back in long, firm movements that bring Hannah's mother momentarily to mind, how each night Rena brushed her own hair, then May's, then Hannah's, tugging it into a braid that fell nearly to her waist. Finally, Belle twists all the hair into a bun and makes a sound of completion, a humming sigh. As she pins the large roll high at the back of Hannah's head, the shortened front layers wave out of the pins slightly, and a few strands curl entirely free down the sides of Hannah's face. Belle holds a hand mirror up to show Hannah, who utters a cry of pleasure. She loves the soft look framing her face, and as she touches the perfectly shaped bun, she knows she will not forget the feeling of Belle's fingers on her scalp, moving gently around her neck as she brushed and gathered the hair, combing the thick layers with strong fingers, then attaching the back with silver hairpins held ready between her teeth, finally brushing Hannah's cheeks, forehead and shoulders with a handkerchief she'd taken from her pocket when she was done.

Belle smiles at her, or at her own handiwork, a broad, satisfied smile.

"The colors in this room," Hannah says, groping for words, wanting a connection she feels deprived of, despite the efficient, gentle hands, the careful brushing, the perfect cut. "I love the dark reds and browns next to the copper kettle. I love colors." She stands and reaches for her purse, one she's made herself, knitted in thick green and blue wool and lined with black cotton. "I made this." She holds the purse out to be seen. "I love shapes and colors so much, I sometimes make up scenes in my mind that look better than the real world around me. My husband mocks me for it – I'm always changing our furniture around."

Belle is sweeping up the hair with a straw broom while the white woman talks. She tries to offer an *mm, himm* once or twice for the sake of politeness, but she wonders why white people always think you got nothing to do but listen to their stories. And the time she hasn't got for white people is reduced even smaller in the case of this particular white person who is not only playing with the only human being in the world Belle loves, but putting him in danger as well. Yet, her thoughts are interrupted by the memory of Samuel's words the night before, the knowledge that this particular white woman holds some interest for him, and despite herself, she understands how and why. She would never confess her own passionate relationship to stories, her stories made up of words, not colors and designs, but she stops sweeping and looks straight into the other woman's eyes. "I understand about shapes and colors and stories and scenes," she says. "That purse you made is real nice. It's a nice shape. The detail is fine," she adds, pointing to the tiny stitches at the edge.

Hannah opens the purse, shows Belle the black lining. It's a secret she would share only with someone who understands the importance of detail in things you make, even when it doesn't show. "It took me days to get the lining to fit just right," she says, and pulls out several coins which she gives Belle, who says, "Mmm, hmm, thank you," and puts the money into her pocket where the scissors have returned.

"We – our people, I mean – we don't believe in tempting the evil eye by wishing luck for things that haven't happened yet..." Hannah looks at the curve of Belle's stomach pushing at the cloth. "But when it happens, I'll send over some of my fish stew as a sign of best wishes. We say *mazel tov*."

Hannah looks eagerly into the face she feels she knows from someplace else. Or, perhaps it is not another time or place the face evokes, but a quality of sympathy Hannah has not known

93

for years, has almost forgotten because the desire is so painful when it goes so long unfilled. Or maybe the desire is born into you, whether you ever knew it or not. Perhaps Belle has a face that communicates the special sympathy, or would if its color, several shades darker than Hannah's own, did not preclude its articulation. She can't get rid of the uncanny feeling that there is something between them, something besides the thing they both know is between them and would never be spoken about out loud. She stares at Belle whose opaque eyes enable Hannah to overcome her own fear of looking too long. She wishes she could penetrate the hardness of those eyes, find a way to make that mouth open in uninhibited laughter.

Belle meets her stare, but there is no smile when she says, "Well, thank you. We will appreciate the fish stew." Then, as if to compromise with her own harshness with this woman who is so appealing today yet was so offensive the last time they met, as if to remind her of her rudeness and thank her for her generosity in one perfect phrase, "No shellfish though," she says.

Hannah blushes, reminded and chastened, respectful of Belle's courage and precision with words. She tries to answer with equal precision, perhaps some courage too. "Shellfish are forbidden," she says, looking straight into the other woman's eyes.

All the things she wants to say to Belle flood her mind. That she understands how prejudice can frighten and harden you. That being a woman is a blessing and a curse too. That creating scenes and arranging rooms, fixing clothes and purses and hair, making the world more shapely and comforting is the strongest happiness there is, that it somehow heals the sore parts, even if only temporarily, even if you don't know how it works. She wants to say something about the shaping, because she is coming to recognize Belle now and she feels Belle would understand. She wants to say that she understands being part of a people who have been in slavery so long they have to keep close guard of their carefully honed rituals, public and private, that remind them how hard and important it is to be free. She wants to say she understands how it feels to be hated for nothing, just for being who you are. But she senses vaguely, yet clearly enough to ensure her own reticence, that she is deeply ignorant of the extremities this other woman knows, that the tiny piece of their history she's learned from Samuel is only the slender beginning of the story of brutality and unimaginable cruelty: cutting people to bits while they're still alive; slicing off body parts in public that should be too private and sacred to name except in the safest, most intimate places; selling children away from their mothers for profit; and all of it done in memory recent enough to be heard from their own parents' mouths. These are things Hannah had never imagined, still has trouble believing. And then there is the worse feeling. Hatred of Jews has always been a huge mystery to her; something undeniable and preposterous, because Jews are not only as good as others, they are better in many ways. She has always been told this. But the way white people feel about the colored has always seemed different to her. It is not exactly hatred, except for people like the Klan and those others who support them. It is more like Aaron said, thinking about Negroes as not really ordinary people like white people are – not only less beautiful and less smart, but with different feelings, not ordinary feelings like white people have. She looks at Belle hard as she removes her apron covered with Hannah's hair, straightens the chairs in the room. She tries to see her as a *schwartza*, the way she has been trained to see, not a person with a certain skin color but a creature who *is* her skin color; whose skin color determines what she thinks, or cannot think, how she feels, or does not feel; a creature very different from Hannah, or other Jews, or anyone white.

Facing Belle in her red and brown room, surrounded by kettles and pottery and a closed bedroom door, sitting in a wooden chair with a green pillow just where your back might hurt if it wasn't there, seeing the woman's hair and her ears and her breasts up close, and knowing a baby is inside her body that Samuel put there, Hannah is rocked again by the shifting feelings she's been subject to in the past few months of knowing these two. They seem less and less different from her in the way she assumed before. And more and more different from what she's always supposed. Belle has told her she understands stories and scenes, and the way she said *shape* and *detail,* as if she were holding up a mirror that reflected them both, told Hannah who she was.

"You let us know when the time comes," Hannah says as she covers her newly cut hair with her shawl. "And thank you. Working with the hair in layers is a wonderful idea."

Belle opens the door for her and stands on the wooden step. "Be careful," she says, pointing to a crack in the wood but hearing the echo of the words she had said to her husband, this time in a different tone, cold and distant to keep her heart from breaking.

"Be careful, Mrs. Sokolov," she says, pronouncing the name just right, and Hannah hears all the layers of meaning in the words. She nods, then turns and walks away. After a few steps she turns back, perhaps to wave, perhaps only to look at Belle again, but the colored woman is already moving into the interior of her tiny house. Hannah glimpses the shelf over the fireplace with its dark ledger and Bible just before Belle shuts the door to number 20, and she proceeds down Knight Street toward home.

Chapter 12

Snow falls so fast and thick the world looks white and blurred. Hannah can barely see the road, but when she turns the corner toward the water the wind shifts, no longer pressing right into her face. She steps into a notion store and hopes the worst of the storm will pass while she inspects dozens of spools of thread, swatches of solid cotton and expensive brocade, then searches through large drawers of buttons for the small pearl ones she wants to use on the white sweater she is knitting as a going away present for May. She stays nearly half an hour, long after she's found the buttons and bought several colors of thread she doesn't really need. Then she is fortunate, because the snow has begun falling more lightly. She knew she'd let nothing keep her from the beach at the end of the path past the docks today, only one week before Aaron and May depart. She is not even looking for Samuel so much as needing to see the place where she saw him before.

She avoided the fish store in the weeks since her haircut and talk with Belle. She doesn't know how long she can pretend to Michael she's tired of fish, but she believes she can master all the disturbing feelings if she keeps away, and she wants to control them, for her own sake as well as theirs. For weeks, she's set herself a discipline of demanding housework, oiling floors, mending slip covers, cleaning out closets, embroidering sheets, baking cakes, and inventing soups. She's convinced May she's well over her crisis. Only Aaron seems to know she is struggling with something that causes deep rings to form under her eyes. She hardly sleeps for more than an hour or two at a time. When she wakes, it's always with a start, but she remembers no dreams. Yet, she cannot overcome the longing – for the thing she thought she felt in Belle that day, for the feeling she got the times Samuel gazed at her so intensely – the wanting something she can't place that is expressed in the frequent loud rumbling noises her stomach makes, loud enough, she fears at times, for others to hear, and persisting, no matter how much she eats.

And this morning she did something she never believed she would do, opened the blue envelope with Michael's name on the front and Manya's name on the back, where the letter was sealed. It was no surprise to read for herself that their "friendship" is really an adulterous love, but it was one thing to suspect, another to see the passionate words before her own eyes, and to know there was nothing she could do. Her anger was so strong she left the opened envelope on his desk. So strong she has sworn never to allow him intimacy again, stronger still because she knows she will not be able to hold to that vow, her will and strength being no match for his. So strong in Hannah that she shouted at May for trying to warn her about the weather, then laced up her boots in a fury, threw three shawls around her shoulders and head, and slammed the door. Now, as she makes her way down Water Street, past the docks and toward the path, her anger spreads from Michael to Rena – the daughter who thinks of her father as a god, the man she looks up to and adores. Hannah's rage at her daughter grows, the one she named for her own mother, yet who betrays her each day with her sullen moods and fresh mouth. She has a good mind to tell the child what kind of man her father really is. She has a good mind to concentrate her love on Asher and Sophie and let her first child go over to her father's side without any more of a fight.

She pushes the wool of the triple layered shawl up her forehead and under her chin, lets the now lighter snow wet her face.

When she sees Samuel standing near the water, snow layering his hat, collar, and boots like white velvet, she stops short and nearly screams. Her anger instantly includes him, as if he has robbed her of her place, intruded in something that was meant to be hers, and now she has no place to go at all. When he turns and sees her, he doesn't look surprised.

She walks up to where he is and stands next to him. Despite the cold, she feels hot. Despite her anger, she begins to weep.

"Things aren't always clear," he says gently, as if he would hold her if he could, touch her hair and hold her chin in his hand. "It's a strange thing. I don't rightly understand it, not completely, but part of it is plenty clear. Too clear by a mile." He looks at her, then quickly down at his boots. "I *got* to be careful. I'm going to be a father soon."

"Yes," she says, allowing herself to feel, at least for that moment, the joy of knowing he knows.

He looks at her in the way that locks her eyes; despite her anxiety and her no longer secret, dangerous wish, she cannot look away. He looks like the saddest man alive. Then he seems to clench his teeth, like he's done with something, and there is something about him that reminds her of Belle. She had wanted to penetrate the hard eyes of the woman but she had seen how futile her desire was. He looks out toward the water and begins to speak to her for what she knows will be the last time.

"My father remembered more than most children about his early years. They say shock will do this. Either you forget most everything, or you remember more than usual. Naturally, he never forgot his grandmama, Ruth. And he didn't forget the white woman named Louisa he found out was his mama the night before he was sold away. He said he could still recollect her face, and some of the games she played with him, and one special night when she was upset and told Ruth her dream. It was a dream about the world being all white, like a snowstorm had covered everything, like today, I guess, like here. But it wasn't a pure, beautiful kind of whiteness. It was blinding. My daddy didn't remember much of all she said that night, but he remembered she seemed scared, telling the dream to Ruth while she was holding him on her lap. He remembered being held too tight, like she was kind of clinging to him – that was how he described it to me all those years later. He recollected how he sort of – almost caught her fear, and how it was also kind of - you know? – kind

99

of fascinating to him. Maybe that was why he never forgot it. He must've told himself the story a hundred times by the time he told it to me, seen lots of things in it, I expect, maybe even added things to it, like Belle does with her stories about what might seem to someone else like an everyday experience – but she sees them kind of shining with something – that's the way she always says it. What stuck with my daddy was his mama's fear of that blindness in her dream – like she could somehow get lost in the white world – like she couldn't see anything – or make out anyone – like maybe she might never see anything she cared about again. The day he got here, to Norwalk, it was storming, a blizzard making everything white. He surely remembered *that* day well enough. And he got this fear that his black skin which was really light brown would be so – so – "

He stops, looks out again at the water. She is afraid he will not move or speak and she will have to push him, touch him. But he looks back at her, as though there hasn't been a break.

"– that his skin would be so clear and standing out against everything else they'd know him for a fugitive. That's when he thought about his mama's white dream, only now the blizzard was real, and it was his own skin that put him in danger, and it made him feel ashamed. But then something strange happened, something changed inside him – he described it like something changing he could actually feel, like a piece of his insides moving to some place else from where it had been before. And his voice was so deep I never forgot what he said. He said he felt like his own skin was like a badge he wore once on the docks in Maryland, a badge for free blacks so the whites would know you weren't a slave. He'd stolen his badge somehow, cause he was still a legal slave. But he was proud of who he was pretending to be, because even if he was a slave for real, he was about to be a free man now. He felt proud of where he'd got to, the courage handed down to him, as if it was a physical thing, the courage, as if he could hold it. Not ashamed of his skin. No matter what was going to happen next, he wasn't ashamed.

"But until the day he died he had a powerful distaste for winter and often said he'd move us back South if it hadn't been for race and more opportunities up here. Sometimes I don't know about that."

He pauses again but his eyes are not distant. He kicks some stones across the sand.

"Don't know?" She had been trying to hear every word, but she kept losing her focus, listening to the sound of his voice, feeling the effects of it inside her, watching the movement of his mouth, the draw of the eyes when she could watch them freely because they weren't looking at her. "Don't know?" she repeats, trying to get him to keep talking.

But he says nothing more. She has had her third lesson, but it is far too complicated for her to comprehend. He has given her a piece of knowledge handed to him across two generations, but all she will keep is the knowing without words that has haunted her and unsettled her throughout these months in so many different ways.

He removes his green woolen gloves and reaches into the pocket of his coat.

"Just try it," he says. "God will forgive you this once."

The ridged shell is hard to open but he pries it loose with his knife. Sea water spills onto his hand.

"Like this," he says, and slides the oyster into his mouth. Then he takes a second one from his pocket, opens it, dips the creature in snow, and holds it out to her.

First she tastes the snow, cold against her teeth. Then she tastes the sea as the oyster, raw, briny and smooth as silk slides over her tongue and down her throat. Right behind the sea, for an instant that would be too quick to notice except that it sends an electric current into her gums and down her throat, she tastes the edge of his finger, his body, his skin. Her eyes open wide at the new taste and the double sin.

"I'm sorry. A friendship, anything at all –between us – I done a lot of thinking in the past few months. It's like some of the old stories my father told me about his childhood in slavery. It's the same now, maybe for always. The times – the world – it's not only out there. It's inside us too, in here." He pats his chest, his forehead, his chest again. "And I know we're only talking – ah, girl."

He looks away as he lets the intimate word slip. Then he looks down, back at her, and down again. Then he seems to recover something. "Belle would be able to explain it better. You want to think it's just words, but words got real powers. They're like doors, and bridges, and roads you can walk down until there's no turning back. Some of them not meant ever to be said."

A decisive tone has come into his voice, and she feels it as coldness, a tone of prohibition she remembers in her father's voice and has heard often in Michael's, too. Flakes of snow sparkle on his black hair, and now she realizes it has left a thin veil of white on her shawl, but she pulls it more tightly around her face anyway, trying for warmth. Her mouth is still cold from the snow, hot from the sinful taste. Just as she's wishing he'd leave, he does. He turns toward the path and doesn't look around again. She sees him trip on a rock protruding from the snow and almost fall before he is out of sight.

Chapter 13

That night, after Michael has read his opened letter and looked at her over dinner with apologetic eyes that disgust her even more than his cruelty; after she has sewn the pearl buttons onto May's sweater and wrapped it in lovely pink tissue to be given to her the morning she leaves; after she has put the children to bed and been overly harsh with Rena, almost smacking her for a small infraction, she falls asleep on the couch she moved all those weeks ago to the side of the room. This night Michael doesn't bother her. In her half sleep, she burrows into the soft thick quilt someone has covered her with, only her cold forehead exposed to the night chill. All she remembers when she wakes in the dark, quiet house, so hot she throws off the quilt and unbuttons her blouse, is an enormous horse heading out of some woods just where she thought the water was, a thick forest where the harbor had been. The horse is unsaddled, unbridled, and it is galloping toward her. She is in danger of being killed.

Once she realizes she's been dreaming, she sits up. The heat in her body turns to frigid cold and she wraps the quilt around her, walks to the kitchen where she lights a candle and sits down at the table. She remembers the oyster and feels a hot longing like she's never known, like the whole world is gathered between her thighs. She sits there in her quilt and leans on the table, putting her head down on her arms and closing her eyes, then she sits up straight again, but nothing stops it. The pictures and the feelings – Belle's beautiful hair, and his face, Belle's hands pulling her hair out gently so she can cut it even, and his face, Belle's breasts pushing at the cotton of her dress and the tip of his finger on her tongue. He looks at her, into her eyes but also at every naked part of her. He leans over her and she feels her legs spreading as if of their own accord, and as the pictures grow more vivid and strong her mind, more real than the real world others live in, she leans her head back in her chair, closes her eyes, and feels the rhythmic beating begin. There is no hope of stopping it until it's done.

She jumps up, puts her fist against her mouth to muffle her shout. In a rage, she snuffs out the candle with her fingers, burning them, and washes her face in icy water. Then she returns to the living room and gathers all the sea grasses she collected and arranged, wraps them in newspaper and throws them into the trash.

The next morning at the Sound, she takes off her laced boots and runs along the icy beach in her stocking feet, as if the water that has been the mirror of her faith and desire will now cleanse her of them, as if she can fling the disruptive feelings in like stones. She feels an overpowering urge to walk into the frigid water and be done with it all. People are still dying of the influenza, and if she can't manage the courage to drown, perhaps she can bring on a chill so strong she will die of disease. Only thoughts of Sophie, Asher, and Rena make her turn and run back down the narrow beach, pull her boots back on, her shawl over her hair, and begin the long walk home. For a moment anger tightens her muscles and dries her throat – anger at Michael for his hypocrisy, at the children for keeping her alive, and at Samuel, more than anyone, at him.

She remembers the hunger, and knows she was wrong about wanting it. She would rather be empty because now she is certain the hunger will never be filled. What she thought was courage – to feel and want what was within her – was really only a deluded belief that someone – he – would fill her up at last.

For the next week, before May's departure, Hannah remains indoors, claiming an illness which is partly the truth. When May and Aaron promise to return in a few weeks, May's face looking concerned and Aaron insisting Michael come into the study with him where they close the door, Hannah tries to reassure her sister. She'll be fine. It's only a cold. She should have listened when they warned her about traipsing around in the snow.

A few weeks after this, when Michael returns from New York and tells her his invention of the medicine that will harden chipped teeth has been patented and sold to a wealthy company in Boston, that they will be moving to a larger house in a town twenty miles south so his commute will be shorter and he can come home more easily at night, she says nothing about the work such a move will mean for her, the loss of familiar neighbors who might soon have become friends, how little she cares to see him, day or night. She is relieved.

One morning, when Sophie is asleep and Asher and Rena are at school, she confronts the enormous task of packing the house. She begins with his books, hundreds of them ordered alphabetically and by subject on wooden shelves. She has bought several trunks, labeled each with shelf numbers so he will be able to arrange them easily in his new expanded space. It is a formidable task, but the burst of energy she feels is too pleasing to question. On a tall bottom shelf where the large books are kept, she comes upon a huge atlas, its maps interspersed with watercolor paintings and short descriptions of exotic places all over the world. She stops at one. A world of ice. No trees. No soil. There is something familiar about it, but the rush of emotions in the past weeks has been so unrelenting, she has almost forgotten the story of Samuel's grandmother's dream that she had tried hard to pay attention to on the beach. It comes back to her in all its detail, so she must have been listening all along. Not even water is visible in the long months of the Arctic winter. Ice covers everything. Everything that moves and crawls and grows out of control is trapped beneath the hard, smooth surface for months until the very few, short weeks of a cold, spare spring. And then the long, dark nights again, the dense snowstorms, the thick and unrelenting ice.

She walks across it in her dream that night, thick ice gleaming in the sun. Throughout her life the dream will come and go like the tides she once loved to watch in any weather, but the dream, unlike the tides, comes without regularity or predictability - and perhaps that is what she will come to dislike about the sea as her children grow up and have children and even grandchildren of their own: that its rhythms and cycles suggest a permanence to things she knows is a lie. Sometimes the night sky above the ice is black, a world of stars reflected in the white. In other versions, she is falling from a   high place and fears she will be killed by the impact of the ice, its sharpness, its hardness, but instead she gets up and walks over the white ground easily. She feels at home somehow. The world is white, and she is white too.

Part Three:

New York State
Summer and Fall, 1988

Chapter 14

I began calling my father's mother, Ami Reed, *Myami,* the summer I was six years old. It was then she began our yearly ritual of a week at the tip of the North Fork of Long Island in the village of Orient, once called Oyster Bay, where the distance between bay and sound was only a few blocks, and each offered a variety of tides, none of them as rough as the ocean. I would never set foot in the water, but she insisted I come with her, just to smell it, she said, though it was obvious she had hopes I would relent and come to love it as she did, and to eat its freshly caught fish. "Even just to hear the waves," she'd insist. So I would take long walks with her. We'd sing our favorite songs loud and in harmony. I'd try not to think of my mother and Montauk, which was fine with my grandmother, who loves to put sad and upsetting things away. She'd put them in her "True Box," as she called the place in her mind where all sorts of disturbing things were stored, kept – not forgotten, she assured me – but where they can't hurt you so much.

"Calling you Grandma would be so *boring,*" I said one day as we walked along the rocky beach on the Sound side, "and it doesn't show you're my best friend."

She told me, then, the meaning and history of her name. She had been born Amelia Katherine (after her mother) Nicola (after her father Nicholas) Marino, but had been Ami Reed ever since she started publishing her novels and married Jacob Reed, my grandfather, who had died soon after my mother. Ami Reed was how she thought of herself now, she said, adding, "Ami means friend, in French." Delighted, I had embraced her then and there, calling loudly, Myami, Myami, wanting the whole world to hear.

But the summer at the lake when I heard Hannah's story and first met Corinne, she had decided not to come with us, and I missed her company intensely. I had kept weeks of notes about lots of things, and I finally sent her a long letter, filled with explanations, complaints, and one clear demand.

I haven't told Daddy yet, I wrote, *but I'm pretty sure this will be my last summer at the lake. I'll tell you the truth, since I always have, and you always say you like it, the truth that is. I can't stand the white kids here any more. I don't care if I have known some of them all my life practically. They don't understand me or anything I feel. They all pretend race doesn't matter – that we're all the same – that's their favorite stupid line. Well, we're not all the same. You can tell that the minute we go to a dance instead of hanging around together in somebody's house. Wait til everyone starts coupling off for dates. All of a sudden, I'm the one without a boyfriend. I'm not the same as them. I'm not white. And I'm not mixed either, as you're always saying like it's some wonderful thing to be. I'm just telling you, Myami. I might be light skinned but I'm a black girl. I realized this starting last March when I took that course about slavery. I kept thinking about it, and my teacher, a really brilliant Black woman who I love, helped me see the truth of it all. And by the way, Myami, how come there is never anyone Black in your stories?*

The other thing is I don't feel well. Daddy thinks it's the heat. I think it might be partly that stupid lake which gets more and more polluted each summer. I have bad headaches. I can't sleep most nights. And I hate the mushy overcooked meat Greatgram makes so I have to eat on my own. In other words, I think I don't feel well because of everything here in this stupid place. I can't believe I used to love it. Well – I still love floating way out in the lake, I have to admit. Anyway, don't worry, Myami. I'm sure I'll be okay. I love you masses as always even though I don't think you really understand this thing about race. So that's part of why I'm writing to you today. I want to know more about your life, why you married Grandpa, someone Black, and how you felt about that, and how did Grandpa feel about having a white wife? What would my mother have felt about me, since, as I said, I am

Black you know. Since you're a writer, I want you to write something for me about all this.

In answer to this letter I had received a tentative promise and an often repeated claim. She would think about my questions, she said, and we would all talk about any future summers at the lake. She would try to write something for me, a kind of narrative about her life, although as I knew, she had never been comfortable writing about her own life directly. She might have to go into her True Box to remember things, but she would try, she said, and it would be waiting for me when I came home. But she didn't have *black* people or *white* people in her stories, she insisted. She had *people* in her stories. *That's been the story of my life, Darling,* she wrote, *the belief that people are people, and I can't change it now.*

My anger at her grew stronger when I received her letter, and I told myself it was partly about her not being with us that summer, but it was, of course, about the deeper issue – the way she made me feel like I didn't exist at times, at least not in my real skin, maybe not as dark as my father's, but still, a part of me I was sick of having ignored. Although I looked forward to whatever long thing Myami would write, I wondered if I had crossed some line this time. My grandmother acknowledged that her life contained secrets, as anyone's did, but she never put those secrets into her stories. One day the previous spring, she had taken me to an art gallery on Spring Street, an exhibit of sculpture and masks from the Ivory Coast. They were carved and painted with graceful attention to detail and symbol that made them works of art, she told me, but they were useful, too, representing fears and desires in the human spirit too dangerous for unadorned bodies to enact or ordinary voices to speak of outside of the protective boundary of ritual. Hidden in a crevice of the wood, secret messages were placed – *no longer there*, the curator's text read, *but once there, a secret connected to the work but belonging to the artist alone.*

"I wish we could read them," I said.

"But don't you see Samantha?" she had responded impatiently. "That would ruin the whole thing."

110

I nodded, wanting to please, but I hadn't seen. There were too many secrets, as far as I was concerned, starting with all the silences surrounding my mother's death, a subject that always caused my father and Myami to look around the room fast, or to leave the room altogether, as if remembering that time would bring it back with greater danger than when it actually occurred, as if knowing who she really was – as they must have known her – would be more damaging than hardly remembering her at all.

Chapter 15

First she hears unintelligible voices as if they are coming
from behind a closed door, then the lyrics of half-forgotten songs,
and she finds herself singing one or two lines over and over. Now
it's *gee but it's hard to love someone when that someone don't
love you.* And she can't think of any reason for that line to haunt
her. She's nearly seventy years old, a widow for years, certainly
not in love. Visions come and go, pass swiftly before her, then
disappear. Often she can't seem to catch her breath. Is she going
crazy? A hundred years before, there would have been no doubt
about it – a crazy woman, needing medical care. Even today,
many women would rush to a psychiatrist who very likely would
administer pills. But if this is madness, it is nothing new to her.
She's had these bouts all her life, since she was a girl. They come
and go within her, like a bad wind. Over the years, they have
become easier, if only because they are well known. Occasionally, she is defeated, thrown about by fears and anger, wandering
around nervously and aimlessly through her rooms, the neighborhood, her mind. Mostly through the years she has just kept
writing – stories and novels about women and girls who suffer
from losses and pleasures different from her own, and the writing
drags her out into the light again. She no longer fears the voices,
or the shadows that accompany them at times. Instead, she tries
to read them as closely as she would a poem. She rubs her eyes,
aching again. Perhaps she needs new glasses.

Ami Reed paces the room she loves, her workroom, with its
floor to ceiling bookshelves, its comfortable chair covered in
forest green velvet, the pile worn down in places to a threadbare
silk. There she has sat over the years, dreaming up her stories,
wrestling with their secrets, stories notable for their shape and

layers of imagery, so that, as with the intricate manifest content of certain dreams, she herself cannot divine any personal, latent meaning, nor would she wish to. She knows only that the finished story, or novel, calms and excites her at once, much like the feeling of waking from a vaguely remembered "good" dream.

The long oak table is stained with rings from coffee mugs and glasses of wine, scratched with indentations from her pens, vague notes she has written to herself when she can't wait the seconds it takes to find a piece of paper. She loves her worn desk with its visual record of her writing life, and she loves the wall covered almost completely with pictures. A guitar, drawn by Jake when he was five, the lines and perspective so perfect she thought he might end up a painter instead of the history teacher he's become. Toulouse-Lautrec's young laundress looking out a window, her wrinkled blouse and loose hair suggesting a dreamer, this print given to her by one of her favorite students, years before. Photographs of her family: Jacob reading, his glasses falling down the sloping bridge of his nose, taken a year before he died, and each time she looks at it he comes to her, as if he is somehow there, within the photograph. He has been gone more than ten years, yet she still feels him near her, hears his voice. She has never gotten over her grief, only learned to live with it. There is one of Jake as a new father, holding Samantha in the crook of his arm; and three of Sam herself: a joyful toddler, a defiant little girl, and a recent one from the previous spring in which you can see the young woman beginning to emerge. On a narrow wall near the window in a neat vertical line are twelve framed drawings she's made herself, each one symbolic of one of her books: an image taken from a dream, a sketch of a central character, a design made while listening to a piece of music that had inspired her work, a photograph of Monet whose water lilies once opened a new door in her life.

She changes the tape from Bessie Smith's blues to a particu-larly melodic Mozart quintet, hoping to get that damn line about unrequited love out of her head. Right now, all the doors feel closed. She had decided to stay away from the lake to avoid complications – Jake was bringing his intended wife, Corinne

Robinson, to meet Samantha, and between that and the old woman, he had plenty to deal with; he didn't need his mother there too. She had even relinquished her yearly summer journey with Samantha to the North Fork, the only sacrifice she minded, but the compensation would be all this time to work, she told herself, and she looked forward to becoming a hermit, lonely but productive in her comfortable home. Instead, she has the voices, the shadows, unshakable anxiety each morning, and disappointment each night.

She's accomplished nothing. Is blocked in a way she hasn't been for years. And all, she has to assume, because instead of a new work of fiction, planned for months, she is writing these endless, fruitless notes, or letters, meant for Samantha who has – well, *demanded* it, saying she wants "the truth." Well, she is a writer, she prides herself on knowing how to get at "the truth," but not so directly, not unembellished stories of her own life. She isn't a good reader of memoirs, let alone a writer of one. She keeps journals, but she has never wanted to turn those unshaped, private pages into public autobiography. Just getting her feelings out in words is enough to stem the tide of thought – and that is all she wants to do; contain the flood so as to separate it from that other more intelligent and coherent flood, the words and stories that become her work. She does not want to be a public witness to her actual life. What she wants is the sharp pleasure of creating the beautiful shapes and structures, the images and echoing phrases she can somehow imagine out of the dust and mud roads in her mind. And if occasionally she wonders why she does not destroy all the journals at once in some huge bonfire in the back yard of Jake's little cottage at the lake, it is a contradiction she can live with, at least for a few more years.

Yet here she is after all, trying to write something just as it happened, one part of her life – a central and defining part – her life as a white woman married to a black man. Her fear of focusing her life in this way begins in her throat. She swallows with effort. It tightens her chest and becomes a dull ache in her temples. Soon, it goes away, but she feels enervated, as if she has suffered a long illness and only just come back to ordinary life.

114

We met on a picket line, she writes. *Unions were just beginning to organize widely, and Lefties – like us – following the Socialists and Communists – though we never joined their Parties – were welcoming black people – Negroes, we were taught to say then – not just welcoming them, needing them, searching them out.* No sooner does she begin than the other thoughts come, an unwanted disturbing wind of thought, and become a sentence on the page: *Could it be that my white body felt it all differently from those other, darker bodies?* She erases, tries to push the feeling away. She has scoffed at the idea that it was all an illusion – the comradeship, the shared sacrifice – as people now claim, has dismissed the black writers who insist that white racism dominated that time, has criticized the ideas that threaten to destroy her own memories. They were all linked together, were fighting the same fight, interested in social justice in the same way. But the bad wind returns and circles her and she has no idea what it means, let alone how she might eventually put it into words.

On the same day as she received Sam's letter, Ami had gotten a worried phone call from her son. Samantha was acting strangely, he reported, echoing his daughter's words, and she looked tired, was probably not sleeping well. She was moody, stayed by herself in the house most evenings. It was obviously the racial thing, he told his mother, it was clear the all-white village had been a mistake for some time, he'd been a fool. This was said belligerently, as if she were responsible for the decision to keep and use the house. Several times, Jake went on, having trouble himself getting to sleep, he had gone for a glass of water and found Sam in the kitchen, standing before the open refrigerator, eating steadily – leftover chicken, pasta, chunks of cheese she pulled off with her hand, and ice cream out of the container with a large spoon. *Sam* – he emphasized the sound of her name – who had always been so meticulous, so orderly, so controlled. She left her wet towels on the floor of the porch, forgot to hang her suit on the line. He didn't know what to do with her, or for her. Corinne had made every effort to befriend not only Sam but the old lady, too.

Ami tried to calm her son's worries using stock phrases – growing pains, a passing phase. She assured him it was completely natural if Sam was upset by Corinne's arrival, however nice the woman had been.

But she can't shake her own anxieties. Sam's questions have disturbed her. She's read them over a hundred times by now, noting the quick leap to the last one, the first time Sam has asked so directly about her mother's feelings about race. Ami's fear that her letter of response was inadequate has been confirmed by Sam's silence, and so her first attempt has led to others, until now she has over fifty pages of wandering, unshaped prose, none of which she has shown to Sam, about meeting, loving and marrying Jacob Reed.

Of all the people I have known in my life, she wrote, *he was the most in tune with myself. Beneath all the superficial differences of belief – he a tolerant agnostic who allowed for all sorts of mysterious forces beyond his comprehension (a form of God, he was willing to allow); and I, a thoroughgoing atheist who feels utter disdain for the Catholicism of my childhood and a hearty dislike of all other religions, too. Even beneath the racial difference most people think of as defining in an absolute, essential way – beneath it all, he was more like me than anyone I have ever known, and this likeness, over forty years of marriage, was both comforting and erotic.*

She has crossed out the last word thinking her erotic life is surely not the thing to share with her granddaughter, and that was always the trouble about writing "the truth;" sooner or later you come upon truths that shouldn't be written. She shuffles and stacks and reshuffles her pages. Then she cannot bear to look at her work another minute. She escapes the pile of printed sheets, the desk, the room, and her apartment. The heat of the afternoon surrounds her as she steps out into the street. She puts on dark sunglasses, stuffs her hands into the deep pockets of her eggplant-colored smock, and thinks of Orient, of the peaceful bay, the Sound beach at the end of Youngs Road where, during any other summer afternoon like this, while Samantha sat reading or staring into the water, she'd be swimming, on the lookout for nothing more lethal than jellyfish, rocked by the gentle waves.

She should not have broken the summer ritual, Ami thinks, as she walks across the fields of Central Park, stopping at a line of benches facing the lake. Sam needs to get over her fears of the sea. And their time together has always been important in ways that, even for her, defy words. Rowboats slip through the still water, appearing almost stationary in the heat. For a moment, Ami sees herself and Jacob in one of the boats – vividly – as if their bodies, having once been there, were there still; as if memories were as real and present as the trees she sits beneath now, savoring what shade she can find. For a moment she relishes the thought that, like the old trees, she and Jacob are still there, rowing on the lake where they often rowed. No, she should not have relinquished her few days alone with Sam, the slow bike rides over flat curving roads, the old-fashioned ice cream parlor run by a jazz musician from the city whose conversation is as thick and sweet as his homemade hot fudge, the beach consisting entirely of smooth stones of pale lavender, coral, and bright white that forms a graceful curve around Long Island Sound. Ritual preserves memory. Predictable cycles and reliable habits get one through all sorts of dark. When Ami knows what's coming, when things are in their accustomed place, she feels safe. She is not rigid, she tells herself, certainly not repressed. But like her granddaughter, she likes things to be under control.

She rises from the bench and makes her way back toward home, distressed by all the loose ends. The letter to Sam she cannot finish, cannot even satisfactorily begin; the memories of Maya's tragic death that Sam seems to want to dig up again along with her increasing obsession with race. Well, Samantha can blame her father for that. He has always emphasized it, first as a boy, causing his mother to feel as if he were closing a door on her in particular; then as a father, insisting his daughter's complexly mixed heritage did not change the fact that she was Black. (When he speaks, she can hear the capital letter, when he writes, she can see it.) For all these years, she has insisted on their "sameness," yet now she silences his attempts to argue with platitudes she finds remarkable to her own ear. *Well, people are different, we agree to disagree.* And if she knows, for a passing moment, that she is using words to obfuscate rather than to reveal, to hide and hold her son at a distance, she knows it only for that passing moment. Then, she "forgets." She thinks the quotes even as she buries the thought. She changes the subject to something on which they can agree – the recent election, the current war, the pleasure of a new recipe. Jake obliges. He loves his mother in a deep unspoken way and he has no need to be at odds with her at this point in his life. But he calls her less often. When he does, their conversation is short, pragmatic. When important things come up in his life, she finds he tells her after the fact, as with his decision to marry Corinne. What she doesn't want at all is for Samantha to suffer from the discord between them.

She takes the next exit out of the park, stops in a corner market to purchase some salad greens for her dinner – a block of cheese, a baguette. She enters her apartment through the front room with its wall of windows facing the north, so that it's cool on summer mornings and freezing in the winter. She loves the cold, loves to wrap herself in blankets, turn the music up loud and sit in that chilly room watching the city lights, getting rid of her wandering thoughts by writing them into her journal. *Blood letting,* she has come to call it, letting the impure blood pour out until what remains in her is a purer liquid, and from within that stream she can write.

Once inside, she moves around her living room, its colors of beige, dark red and brown harmonizing with the music she quickly turns on, Ruth Brown singing *Down and Out Blues,* the wonderful sounds reminding her of the life outside her head. She counts on sound for this – low music, talk radio, even traffic noises comfort her in some way; she can hear her true voice, the one she wants to hear, only if some deeper, persistent chatter is drowned out by rhythmic sound.

She wanders back through her study, opens the beautiful wooden door she'd had made years before, enters her bedroom where she lies down on her wide bed covered with pillows and a dark red quilt. But her agitation will not be calmed. Sam's letter has set her on this path where her memories – the very ones she believed to be so reliable – are breaking – shifting – fragmenting – and among the signposts of what she thought was "the truth" of her own history, blocks and interruptions appear. Worse, none of it is clear. The feelings might be as intense as any she has known, but – and here is the heart of her anxiety – the feelings have no words. She picks up the letter from the corner table and reads it again. *How did Grandpa feel about having a white wife? What would my mother have felt?* In the deafening sound let loose by those two questions, Ami has lost her own voice. Once again she feels old fears pushing, the threat of old angers she thought she had left behind. *I don't have black people or white people in my books, only people,* she had written. Had she been a complete fool? Was some vast ignorance exposed in her work, the place she's felt most in control? She grabs the pages she has begun for Samantha, shoves them into a folder, and slams the file drawer shut. For a moment, everything tilts and spins, the room grows hazy. She lies down again. She is afraid of losing someone she loves and needs – perhaps more than anyone ought to love and need. And that person can only be her son.

He was born on a cold autumn morning, one a.m. It had taken the entire night and half the day before to deliver him. A strange word – deliver – so mild and domestic for the extraordinary transformation of pushing a human being out of your body and into the world. Your grandfather leaned over me once they let him into the room, after they'd cleaned the baby, wrapped him into a tight oval of a light blue blanket, returned him to my body again, this time on the outside. Neither of us spoke. We only stared at his face, trying to take in, I suppose, the actuality of what we had done, created a new life out of our bodies which would never seem quite so ordinary again. So here he was – Jacob Reed, Jr. – instantly "Jake."

Do you want me to describe the moment he came into existence within me, fluid of Jacob Reed permeating the interior crevices of Ami, born Marino, now Reed, until the one accidental joining out of thousands of possibilities occurred? I don't think

I remember after all these years whether his mouth or hands or sex felt different that night – more careful, or purposeful, or insistent. I only know that nine months later, that cold September morning, I looked into the face of the person who would be the great love of my life. Then I looked over at my husband, whom I loved more than anyone ever before, except perhaps my own mother, and I knew nothing would ever be the same again.

I do remember another time, perhaps a year before, when I made love to my husband full of hate. That memory hasn't faded with time, though I don't remember what he had done to ignite my rage – no doubt something to do with making me feel unwanted, or excluded – the feeling I am still most vulnerable to, even at nearly seventy years old. I remember feeling his weight on my body – crushing, suffocating – I remember digging my nails into his back, wanting to hurt. I won't say more to you, Samantha, though I remember every moment of that shocking night. For all the years after, filled with friendly, passionate, tender, dull, intrusive, loving, unwanted, weary, mechanical, and transcendent sex, it never happened again.

And why do I tell you this now? Because I want you to know that between two such moments in any life, both of them secret (until now – because you, my darling, have demanded "the truth"), stretch days and years and decades of ordinary orderly feelings. Because I want you to see that I understand how angry you are, though I do not fully understand why, and I want you to know it's okay.

She hasn't sent that piece either, just added it to her collection of notes which has expanded all summer and, now, into early fall. "For Samantha," the carefully labeled file folder reads. So far, Sam has seen none of it, but Ami takes it with her wherever she goes, making notes, adding memories. It's stuffed in her bag now, as she drives east on the Long Island Expressway out to the North Fork with a silent and pensive Hannah buckled into the seat beside her.

She had received the surprising call from the old woman the week before. "Can you drive with me to the sea?" Hannah said after a quick greeting. At first, Ami thought she had finally slipped into a pre-death confusion. But Hannah had gone on to explain, quite cogently, that she had important things to talk about with Ami, things that concerned Samantha, and she knew it sounded strange after all these years, but she wanted to do it by the sea. "And I want you to read a book first," Hannah had added, and given her the name of a memoir by a writer named Ruth Hughes. "It involves Sam," was all she would say in explanation, so, worried and intrigued, Ami has agreed to both requests. Her worries about Sam persist. Jake tells her at least once a week that she's getting fat. She must eat when she's alone, he nearly screams, because she certainly won't eat anything at meals. Ami has seen her. She wouldn't call her fat. A bit overweight, maybe, but it's a stage, Sam is fundamentally athletic, she'll come through it okay. She worries more about the dramatic change in style and habit than the pounds.

She turns on the radio to blur the intrusive, unmanageable thoughts, glances down at her new, bright red Reebok hightops that ease the chronic pain in her ankles and fill her with childish pleasure when she sees how they match the fire-engine red polish she wears on her nails. But she's distracted from this small pleasure by the pain in her eyes, from a sinus infection, she thinks, or the need for a new prescription for her reading glasses. The discomfort increases each time she tries to read the damn memoir, especially the parts that take place during slavery. She has read about the white woman who gave birth to the child of one of her father's slaves, but she has not managed to read the earlier chapters. Nor has she finished the book, so she doesn't know if Hughes ever discovered what became of any of them. The way race is emphasized disturbs her, as usual: always the inescapable, defining difference, a person's whiteness covering everything else, a grotesque Halloween mask signifying unbridgeable distances between people rather than a ritual mask meant to symbolize connection.

Before Jacob, she had never thought of herself as white. She was just herself – an ordinary woman, physically ordinary, any specialness she possessed residing in her talent, not her skin, a person who had been taught that all people were people, and race didn't matter. That so many whites were hypocrites, including some members of her family, was disappointing but neither surprising nor uncommon, and certainly not undermining of the truth of her beliefs. When she'd begun to live among black people, she'd become aware of her whiteness as some *thing,* and it has taken years for her to accustom herself to this new perspective, that what had seemed so perfectly normal to her it was not even noticeable, her skin, was a sign full of meanings, warning, history, fear, even hatred to the new family she came to love. Then it had seemed all the more important to teach her child that all people were the same, skin color a false and dangerous sign of difference. And now, here is Samantha – well, in reality only one- quarter black – insisting on her racial identity as primary, dividing her thick beautiful hair into dozens of skinny braids pulled so tight it makes Ami's head ache to look at them, dividing her grandmother from herself.

As she exits onto Old Country Road, Hannah dozing beside her, the bad wind begins blowing again through the familiar tangles of feeling and thought, and there is Bessie Smith's sultry alto again, singing about being unloved. She's forgotten to do something important, Ami feels – perhaps to pack all the necessities for the afternoon. With her free hand she checks the inside of her purse – reading glasses, wallet, house keys – all are there. The gas tank is three-quarters full. Two large bottles of water and several sandwiches wrapped in tin foil are packed in a cooler in the back seat next to two neatly folded light shawls in case a late afternoon chill kicks up off the sea.

Chapter 16

It's after one o' clock when Ami finally parks along the side of the road and slowly leads Hannah down the rocky, sloping path to the beach. The air feels more like late October than September; even the leaves seem to have begun changing color early this year. It has been evident to Ami from the moment of Hannah's request that this is to be no ordinary occasion. With one arm around the old woman's waist, her hand supporting Hannah's wrist while the older woman leans heavily against her, Ami murmurs typical encouragements for physical anxieties – "don't worry – I've got you – take it slow" – suspecting deeper concerns will find their expression before long.

Hannah takes the last step down the hill clumsily and almost falls, but once she is on the sand, she says in a tone more pleading than imperious, "Take off my shoes, Ami, it's cold, but I'll be steadier without them." Ami bends down, unties the laces, removes the worn black leather oxfords and the nylon knee-highs that leave deep crevices in the loose skin of Hannah's calves, then takes off her own shoes and socks and leaves them all in a pile at the foot of the hill. As the two women walk barefoot toward the water, Ami sees tears stream from Hannah's eyes; she hears a muffled cry.

"Are you okay?" she asks, still supporting the old woman's waist and wrist with her hands.

Hannah nods. "Just to the edge of the water," she says, and when they get there she adds, "maybe you could help me get down – I want to touch the sand with my hands."

At sixty-nine, Ami is far from as flexible herself as she might wish, and she curses a lifetime of intermittent physical neglect, the only disciplines she has mastered being the mental sort, but somehow she manages to get them both to a seated position so that each can lean forward on raised knees. They sit close together, and Ami wraps one of the shawls around their bare feet. Hannah is still crying, but the sounds have stopped. "I haven't been here since I was a young woman," she says. "Well, not here – I've never been here – but I mean by the water – the bay – or the Sound. This is the Sound, Ami. No?"

"Yes, it is." Ami looks out to sea. Fairly rough waves crash over a semi-circle of large rocks to their right, but where they sit the beach is higher and the waves break several feet farther out.

Hannah digs her fingers into the sand, forms some wet earth into a ball in her palms, and she throws it underhand into the edge of the surf. "Once I could throw it pretty far," she says. "Did you ever skip stones, Ami?"

Ami finds a flat one right next to her foot and throws it perfectly. It skips three times, which causes the cry to erupt from Hannah again.

"I thought you disliked the sea." Ami stares at Hannah, who is obviously and profoundly moved.

"Me and the sea," Hannah says sadly. "You'd need a *midrash* to understand such a long story with so many twists and turns. You know what a *midrash* is, Ami?"

But Ami is anxious to get Hannah talking about whatever she's come here to say, not to hear an explanation of the meanings of *midrash*. If the tide is coming in instead of going out – and Ami can't tell right then – they don't have long before they'll have to move up the beach, and getting the two of them to a standing position will be difficult if not, Ami suddenly fears, impossible. She pictures them rolling around or trapped on all fours, unable to stand, being swept out to sea, and the image is so ridiculous she laughs.

"Something's funny?" Hannah wipes fresh tears on her thin black sleeve.

"No – I'm sorry, dear – not you – or your memories – just something about getting old – how hard it is to move around."

"You're a spring chicken, Ami Reed," Hannah says. "And don't even think about getting old til that girl of ours is safely grown. She needs you. Take my word."

Ami feels the pressure again, first in her temples, then behind her eyes. Despite the sea breezes, her sinuses begin to clog, causing the dull pain to spread over her cheekbones, and she has to breathe out hard through her nose before she can breathe in easily again.

She looks forward to living many more years, certainly to providing her granddaughter with anything she needs that is in Ami's power to give. What her granddaughter needs, however, is not lately easy to know. She fought about it with Jake when they returned from the lake, he telling her that she remained blind to Sam's racial identity at her peril. *My peril!?* she shouted, though it had been years since she had shouted at Jake. Then she had asked in a softer and far angrier tone, *What on earth do you mean, my peril?* Samantha is the person she loves most in the world – not more than Jake, of course, but Ami has tried to contain her craving for intimacy with her son since he was a boy. The craving is always there, but her wiser self (the one who writes, she feels) has prevailed, and over years that disciplined distance has become familiar ground. She knows its hidden paths and its pitfalls. She understands its geography as if it is an adopted country and she an immigrant, but an immigrant who has lived there for many years. "Do you ever long for Sicily?" she remembers asking her parents when she was growing up. And once her father said, "It's like a dream now – I love it, but *this* is my *home.*" By *home* he meant America. By *this*, in relation to her beloved Jake, Ami means the holding back a mother must practice with her son – or so she has always been told – so as not to suffocate him as a child, cripple him as an adolescent, or alienate him as a man. So that when, with obviously suppressed rage, he told her again what he'd told her many times before, since he was almost as young as his daughter was now and, like his parents, protesting and picketing – though with different messages on his signs – that there was more to the idea of black identity than skin color or even genes, that racism was virulent and ubiquitous, in case she didn't know, she had refrained from saying any more about her views. What she wanted in the wake of her own shouts and his restrained fury was to return to their usual companionability. She cannot imagine living without his approval, because his approval has become entangled with her ability to sense his love.

She looks out at the water, reminded of ships, and for a moment the view she loves includes a shadowy vision of those evil vessels of the Middle Passage, as if hundreds of them were appearing right then on the horizon, blocking out the sky, bringing millions of suffering souls to the American experiment with its paradoxical faith in human freedom embedded in one of the worst crimes against human freedom ever known. She banishes the image. It annoys her and makes her anxious, a combination of emotions that reminds her of how she feels each time she reads another chapter of the memoir by Ruth Hughes.

"Why did you want to come here, Hannah – why – " Ami's voice cracks, and for a moment is lost. When she is able to speak again, she asks, "What about Sam?"

"Something at the lake, last month," Hannah says. "Something Samantha said. And that woman your son likes – Corinne . . . ."

"He's going to marry her, Hannah. Right after Christmas, I think."

"Well, nobody tells me," Hannah sniffs. "Anyway it's none of my business – I guess she'll want me to move out, if I live that long. So I'll go to the home, where Aaron is, which will kill me anyway. She reminds me of someone I used to know. That's why I'm telling you our Samantha needs you, Ami. Why I wanted to come all the way out here to remember things, and tell you. She needs you. You – you're important. She's a Jewish girl – but still there are things you can understand."

Because I'm white, Ami thinks coldly, as Samantha has always been in Hannah's eyes, white like Hannah herself, a whiteness she was reminded of, perhaps, by the blackness of Corinne; Ami is surprised that Hannah has ever known anyone black to be reminded of. If her own love of the sea has always differentiated her from Hannah Sokolov, there has been this far more significant difference. Ami not only married a black man but raised a black son, and on occasion she has allowed herself a private fantasy: that people might think she herself was black – or part black. She did not consciously seek to "pass" in the opposite of the traditional racial direction – although she could have, she liked to tell herself, with her deep tan skin and once dark hair. She simply neglected to assign a racial or ethnic identity to herself in certain situations unless directly asked – and even then – she had to admit she would sometimes shrug her shoulders as if to suggest she didn't know, or didn't care. Most likely no one mistook her for anything but what she was: a Mediterranean type, Jewish, Italian, or Portuguese, some mixture of southern Europe's darker inhabitants. But she enjoyed the private pretense, especially when Jacob was alive and when Jake was a child: the three of them, all the same. Samantha is Jewish, she knows, if you go by biblical law, but Ami retains her own sense of things, and her favorite sense of things involves mixtures no one can or should separate, like truth and fiction, like Jacob and herself merged in their son.

"I'm hungry all of a sudden," Hannah says, and Ami thinks she hears the old woman's stomach rumbling, then sees it's true because Hannah is holding her hands over her protruding belly, a surprised look on her face, tears filling her eyes again. The wind has picked up, and it is clear now that the tide is coming in, so Ami retrieves the sandwiches, water, and second shawl from her backpack, judging they have about an hour before they have to leave the beach or at least move to higher ground.

Hannah bites into the soft bread and cheese, pats Ami's knee as a sign of thanks for the food she can manage with her false teeth, the cool water, and the shawl which she draws around her with her free hand.

"Who does Corinne remind you of?" Ami asks

"Did you read the book?"

So Ami has to admit she's read only parts here and there. "I don't much like memoirs," she says. But Hannah seems indifferent to anything but her own need to work something out in words.

"A woman I knew long ago. My memory is bad now. I don't remember what happened yesterday half the time, then suddenly whole parts of what happened long ago come back to me. This woman, she was colored – a Negro I mean. We called them *schwartzas* – it wasn't just a word for black – it carried an insult with it."

"It did and does," Ami says, surprised to hear Hannah admit the negative connotation of the Yiddish word.

"It did and does," Hannah repeats. "Well when my Maya, my Sophie's baby girl, married one– married your son– well a half Negro at least– I don't mean to leave you out of the picture ....."

"You're not leaving me out, Hannah. Whatever my son is, I'm his mother, and so I am – well partly – somewhat – well, what he feels he is, and that's black." Her voice comes out angrily. She looks away from the old woman, toward the large rocks.

"Well, so – he's black," Hannah pats Ami's knee again, her acquiescence clearly meaning she has more important matters to discuss than Jake's or Ami's racial identity.

"When our little Maya married him I was upset, I admit it to you. I didn't want people in my own family to be so different from me. I didn't dislike colored people like some Jews do. I used to fix their hair in the Bronx – when we moved there after Michael died and I still had two kids at home – Asher and Sophie. I was the only white hairdresser who could do it. Of course most of them went to their own, but I got sort of famous for layering – so some of the colored women with straighter hair would come to me. Everyone said I could do it because my hair wasn't so different from theirs, but I knew it was more than that. When I cut it and combed it and braided it, I was picturing her hair, the woman I knew, and remembering how she'd cut mine once, and remembering her husband's hair – Samuel was his name – that I never got to touch." The sound comes from her throat again.

Ami puts down her sandwich, fascinated by the story that is opening some sort of door – not only within Hannah's memory but some place in herself as well. She presses her fingers against her eyes to quell the pain. "Yes?" Gently, she touches Hannah's hand.

"Yes – I still remembered them then – but not everything. I'd already forgotten a lot of it by then. But I'd get the picture of his face – of their faces – kind of a picture memory that passes through quickly. So by the end of the day it was probably forgotten again. And now, all these years later, I read this book, the one I gave you. I picked it up almost by accident one day, looking in the bookstore for something else. And the names are the same. And the story. And the dream. I read it twice, and that winter in Norwalk begins coming back to me, and then she – Corinne – walks into the room in Jake's little house by the lake. She was holding a hat in her hand, and her hair was thick in a circle around her head, and her skin – and *oy gevalt geschrieben* as my mother would have said, it all comes back to me. All of it. Even now, this hungry feeling, reminds me of things I thought I forgot a long time ago, things I feel ashamed to admit to this day." She digs up wet sand, forms it into a ball between her palms again, but instead of flinging it toward the water she lets it break up in her hand, staring as it sifts through her fingers. She picks up a flat stone which she slips into her pocket, then reaches up to dry her tears, leaving a trail of sand on her cheeks. Ami stops the sandy fingers before they reach Hannah's eyes and hands her a napkin from the pack.

"Samuel?" Ami asks, the tone of Hannah's phrase *I never got to touch* clearly signifying him as the center of the story.

"He worked in a fish store, and sometimes on the boats. A waterman, he was called I think, or his father was. That was his name. Samuel Waterman."

Samuel Waterman. The name of the man in the book – and the name evokes something else in her, but Ami is distracted by the unusual lucidity of Hannah's eyes. Here is a woman's half-century-old desire. This is what Ami feels certain she is witnessing, although only the smallest piece of the story has been revealed. The frame of Hannah's story, like her own, is this day, their journey to the saltwater Sound. Something about the water had been intended by Hannah to serve as a frame for her memories right from the moment when she called to ask Ami to bring her here. The frame may have been chosen for the ancient

129

and inescapable allegories of the sea, with its depths and hidden currents and cyclical tides, but the center of the story is a youthful Hannah, hungry and lucid and suddenly grieving, it seems, for someone named Samuel and a woman who cut hair.

Nothing has been said since she spoke his name. Ami sees the old face slacken, sees Hannah's mouth open, her eyes staring blankly at the sea. Once she tries to speak but can get out only one word – *forgot*. She looks very old, and then something changes, her entire face softens until for a second she is not old, not young either, not any age, just alive, and beautiful.

Slowly and hesitantly, she begins talking again about that time in her life, describing a scene here and there – a walk around the docks; watching fishing boats; a curved knife and a vague reference to some traumatic surgery in Hannah's past which Ami suspects was an illegal abortion; a long meeting in a fish store when no one was looking and she was free to stare into his eyes.

"We weren't supposed to be friends in an ordinary way with colored," she says. "Not just because people felt it was wrong. It was dangerous. There was Klan, even in New England. There was lynching."

Black bodies hanging . . . Billie Holliday's voice now, pushing the other song to a fading margin, words she has never been able to listen to without a shortening of breath. She remembers a large book of photographs Jake had bought after a museum exhibit he'd attended when he was a young teenager. Horrifying images of bloated lips and protruding eyes, of pants torn at the crotch and blood dripping, pouring, of white faces in expressions of weird ecstasy, men's faces, and women's, even children's, hands clapping, mouths opened, shouting for more. Testicles mounted on sticks, kept as souvenirs. She could not look at the horrifying images with him. *Black bodies swinging in the southern breeze, strange fruit, blood on the leaves, ain't it hard to love someone . . .*

And where was Jacob? She remembers her anger, now decades old. He hadn't helped, had taken one look at the horrific photographs and disappeared. His mouth had tightened in an expression of rage she'd only rarely seen in him, and she had turned away, wanting his mouth soft, opening to her as she kissed his lips, touched his tongue with her tongue. His shoulders had been stiff, or hunched. For a moment she had felt afraid of him, or for him. It's history, she had told him. It's over, Jacob. And Jake had been listening. She knew because she had heard his angry footstep down the hall, seen the criticism and disappointment in the turn of his lip when he left the room.

Well, she was angry too, is angry now. At Jake for his fierceness, now given to Samantha, too. And at Jacob? Now? Dead all these years? Or at the white faces ...?

Hannah's voice changes, the faraway look in her eyes is gone, but her lips still look unusually soft and sensuous when she turns to Ami and says, "It must have been that way for you too, Ami. No?"

"What? Oh – that we weren't supposed to love each other? Yes – it was. Supposed to be that way. Even illegal in most of the country. But, you know Hannah, I was one of those rebel girls from the start."

Was that it then? Even part of it? She, a rebel; he, black? After years of marriage Jacob's blackness had become invisible to her most of the time, as, she hoped, her whiteness had to him. But maybe this was another case of masks – the mask of invisibility covering colors – the bronze of his arms turning a rich oak in the curve of his neck, the way his thighs burnt purple from too much sun, colors with too much history to be merely themselves. Somehow, she had to separate her own story from the history without denying the history; the rape of black women history; the black man obsessed with white woman history; the black man estranged from the black woman. And now she is expected to start trying again – to collect all her fragments for Samantha, navigate the cross currents of conflicting stories? How could she do this? How could she do any of it?

"A rebel girl," Hannah sadly replies. "Like May. And?" She pushes Ami's shoulder gently, reclaiming her attention.

"And what?"

"And your parents? How did you – an Italian girl – a white girl – how did they...?"

So this was Hannah's real question, why she wanted Ami to take her to the Sound this day. *How did you do it?* But she cannot answer since she no longer seems to know what *it* was. She married a black man, even though it was against the law, even though in many places it was punishable just outside the law by death for the man, banishment for the woman, even though in some place she could barely hear herself, a voice cried – *it's not that I was white, Jacob, was it? but that I was Ami, who had your child, lived with you until I kissed your beloved eyelids for the last time, pressed my cheek against your bony hand, stroked your thin white curls, closer to me than my own mother, my father, my grownup child, my face the last face you saw, my skin the last skin you felt, my voice the last voice you heard, your voice the one I will carry until I die myself.*

"They didn't like it," is all Ami says. "We talked to each other, saw each other, but we never really reconciled before they died."

Hannah nods, as if this estrangement over color and love were far more understandable than the love itself. "And your name? Is that an Italian name? Sounds like *ah me* – a sigh or something. I've always wondered. What kind of name is that?"

Ami laughs. "I'd always thought of it sounding like the French word for friend – a French spelling for an English name. But you're right. I became Ami just as I became Reed. My original name –" she pauses before her well-practiced speech – "is Amelia Katherine Nicola Marino. Katherine for my mother. Nicola for my father. Amelia for a great-grandmother left in Italy and never seen again."

"So why French?"

"Oh – it wasn't that it was French. More that it meant friend, yet sounded like my original name. Being a friend, in all sorts of ways, has always been very important to me – central you could say. It's why I love it that Sam – Samantha – calls me Myami – my friend . . . but . . . ." She stops her own story, suddenly realizing the obvious about Samantha's name. "Why did Maya name her child Samantha?" she asks.

"You're right. I was surprised when she did it. Her mama,

132

my Sophie, had heard the name from me off and on. I used him as a story for my children, the part about how he and his people kept trying to be free. I was trying to give my girls a passion for freedom, so they'd be more like their Aunt May – Maya's namesake – than like me. I remembered that part of his story and – somehow – I don't know how – I forgot the rest. Or I didn't really forget it – I just changed it. You know how you can change the stories of your own life? Then believe the change? Or you don't know which version to believe? I used to rearrange rooms a lot – in reality and in my imagination – scenes, as if I was painting over a picture, making it better. So why can't you rearrange stories too? I do it all the time. *Childish foolishness*, I'd say to myself if the old feelings came back. Or *it was a very bad time for me – three little children – a bad marriage* – yes, Ami. I don't deny that. But Sophie – of all my children – she loved stories, and especially family stories. I always thought she could have been a Rabbi if they had let women then, like they do now. She'd tell stories over and over, each time making sure we got the lesson. So she told the story of Samuel, the free man, and his father, the waterman, to her daughter Maya – and I think even at Seder some years, when we'd tell the story of the Exodus, my Sophie would say in front of everyone – Remember Samuel, Mama? The Jews aren't the only ones who escaped to freedom. I'd wave her away, but she kept it up. And soon Maya picked it up, and would talk about this Samuel she of course never knew. When they spoke of him I – I don't remember – not exactly – but I think I'd get those fast picture memories – his face, the Sound, a salty oyster I tasted once, its smell. But it's all old – old stories in an old lady's mind. And that's what I'd tell them – *old stories, girls, what's the difference?* But Maya remembered it, and convinced your Jake to use the name. She made a *midrash* I guess you could say, kept up the story but added her own part, and then Jake shortened the name to Sam. She just found out, Ami. I told her the story this summer, one night in the country, the night I met Corinne. And she seemed very upset. I upset her – all the parts she doesn't know, maybe. Or I told her too much. I left out lots of details, of course – about the way they killed people in those days – so many killed, maimed, sold. Away from their own families. When he told me all those years ago I was no kid, I was in my thirties then, and I could hardly stand to listen to him. I only made myself listen because – well I don't know why. But I didn't repeat to Samantha the parts – the parts she writes about in the book. Knowing our Sammala, though – you know her, Ami. Since she knows about the book I was reading, I'm sure by now she's picked it up and read it for herself."

"Yes," Ami murmurs, still back in the part about changing stories, doubting she has the courage to change some of her own.

"And I told her about my dream about the North Pole, you know the Arctic Circle? How I saw a picture in my husband's book, and it connected up with the story Samuel told me about his grandmother's dream about blizzards and ice. How I began to dream it too, and can you believe it, Ami? I have had that dream on and off all my life, ever since then, when certain things happen. When May died I had it. When my Sophie died too. And Maya. I once told Aaron, the last time I went to see him in the home, and he seemed to get a kick out of it. No wonder you lived to be so old, Hannahla, he said. He still calls me that. When I told Samantha about the dream, and how the idea of it came not only from my Michael's book but from Samuel's story about his father, and his father's story about his own mother's dream, she looked kind of upset. I didn't say anything, but I noticed."

So Ruth Hughes was the daughter of Samuel Waterman who had known Samantha's great-grandmother more than fifty years before, the brilliant man, the writer's father, who worked in the fish store and married a woman named Belle; the woman who wrote the memoir she's been avoiding for weeks was the daughter of Samantha's namesake. Her Samantha.

But no, not hers. She sees it in an excruciating moment of loss. Just as Jake, who had *seemed* – she feels its truth as undeniably as her own existence – *who had seemed to be hers* – has turned out not to be hers, even though for years the belief, however false, has comforted and healed and transformed her. It happened long ago with Jake – the realization that although he will always belong to her in the depths of her mind, or heart, or in the place in her body he had shared – *the secret folded into the crevice of the mask meant only for the artist's eye* – at the same time he is not hers at all. He had been Maya's husband, then Samantha's father, and is soon to be Corinne's husband. Yet of course he is not theirs, either. Just as she is no one's, not completely, not the way she has always in some dark part of herself wanted to be. She should have faced that when Jacob died and she continued to live. There are parts of the grown man her son has turned into she cannot know, let alone possess. And now Samantha, named for a man whose lineage has nothing to do with her, but whose story, she feels, might somehow help them both through this odd, agitating time, Samantha also is not hers. Not hers at all. She looks back at Hannah, but the old woman is far away again, staring at the water, her mouth soft again, that odd look of agelessness.

"Imagine Ami, imagine. How after all this time that dream lasts like it's a – like a tombstone on all the buried memories. You want to think it's all like this beautiful seaweed in tangled layers, and the shellfish we can't eat, and all the other living things that go away and then come back with the tide. But in life it's different. What you waste. What you let yourself forget. What you can't get back. And when you know it, then something is over and done."

But Ami's thoughts and Hannah's poetry are lost, suddenly, in the need to pay attention to the actual tide, fast edging up toward their feet. The two women stand up, Ami helping to lift Hannah's frail body that feels heavy enough to her, and they slowly make their way back to the dune. When they reach it, however, their shoes are nowhere in sight. Ami searches the surrounding brush and under the rocks. She pulls out damp seaweed laced with mud, broken shells, a piece of old yellow plastic, probably part of a toy. But no black Oxfords and no red Reeboks. No white athletic socks. Only one torn knee-high stocking, Hannah's, shredded on a thorny bush.

"Who would want to steal old ladies' shoes?" Hannah's face and tone are caught between a laugh and a cry.

"Some prank," Ami mutters, furious about her missing red

Reeboks. "Stay here. I'll see if they threw them up on the road."
As she makes her way up the hill, searches the shrubbery and
behind the rocks, contemplates then rejects the idea of searching
at the edge of the deepening sea – the shoes would be ruined then
anyway – she coughs and sniffles, her clogged sinuses making
it difficult to breathe or to talk, even to mutter to herself. She
gives up hope and shoes and returns to the beach where she puts
her arm firmly around Hannah again, guiding them both back to
the car where they realize, cursing and chuckling, they will have
to drive back to the city barefoot. But her laugh feels bitter in
her throat. She is as uncertain of herself for a moment as her
adolescent granddaughter. Something is threatening, as if from
some cavernous part of her brain as overlain with seaweed as the
crevice under the rock where she had searched for their shoes.

Chapter 17

For days afterwards, fragments of the two songs – *strange fruit hanging from, gee but it's hard to love* – persisting. For many nights in a row, dreams waking her, nightmares born of Ruth Hughes's memoir, which she still has only read in part, her imagination too vivid, she tells herself, to endure the horrific detail. Often, she gets out of bed, turns on the light, grabs her glasses and the pad she always keeps by her bed, and writes a possible letter to Ruth Hughes. After three attempts she decides against it. Why should the woman be willing to see her? Why would she be interested in some white person's memories that suggest an attraction whose mutuality is at best the fantasy of an old woman's mind, at worst an encounter hinting at betrayal, at least in thought, a moment best left buried for good. *I used him*, Hannah had said of Samuel. If she writes to his daughter, how would she, Ami Reed, be using him now? For weeks, images of the day at the Sound intrude into other thoughts, prevent her from concentrating – the incoming tide, Hannah's face turning young, their bare feet going home, Jake's fascination with lynching, testicles mounted on sticks, white people's faces, Jacob's mouth – as if that day, with its recurring images of closed doors and unintelligible sound, was itself a door opening, and pouring out, like a powerful desert wind coming off mountains and sweeping toward the coast, an endless gale of words.

She writes them down – memories, thoughts, partial letters, even dreams – all collected in new notebooks, each entry designated only by the date of her writing. Because she's become so engrossed – and for other reasons as well, but she does not think of these, practiced in keeping one thing separate from another – she does not visit Jake, Corinne, and Samantha for several weeks. Perhaps it has been almost a month – more. She calls. She makes excuses. Her work. They are glad to hear she is working. She is not feeling well – maybe a flu. No, don't worry, she is fine, she is taking it easy. She will be fine. At night, often during the day as well, she opens the current notebook, ignores the IBM Selectric she still uses, and with the old black pens she used for all her early books, she writes.

The most recent entry describes a late night call from Samantha. Ami had been close to sleep when the phone rang, and it was immediately clear in Sam's voice that she not only had read the memoir by Ruth Hughes but many other books, or parts of books, articles and stories, histories and autobiographies about slavery. Jake had told her about it with some anxiety, describing Sam's notebook, full of descriptions, and even illustrations, drawn and pasted in, of the atrocities and tortures common to the slave system in the United States. Samantha's List of Terrible Things, he had called it, having heard some of it read aloud while he and Corinne sat in fearful silence, knowing the history, not knowing how – or if – to protect.

It was close to midnight, and Samantha's voice was loud and enraged in her grandmother's ear.

"Between 1620 and 1865!" she shouted. "Way over two hundred years! I read it in a history book, Myami – not in some cheap novel – and the book was quoting *documents!* A fifteen year old girl, one year younger than me, made to strip naked and flogged to death by a slave trader because she refused to dance on the deck of a slave ship!" Her voice went low, so low Ami couldn't tell if she were trying not to cry or crying already. Then she spoke again. "You should see these cartoons, Myami. They depict black people with enormous asses, faces that look like apes – there's so much about sex in this stuff – I mean the racism and sex are all mixed up. Did you know you were breaking the law against so called *inter-marriage* when you married Grandpa? Do you know even my parents were breaking the law in some states when they got married? Do you *know* what Grandpa lived

138

through in his life? Do you think about it now? Did you think about it then? That he could have been *lynched* in plenty of places for marrying you?!"

Ami did know, and was glad her granddaughter was not in the room to see the anger she felt must surely be visible on her face. Did she dare to think it had been easy for them in the '50s and '60s, even possible to blind themselves to the open poisonous hatred, the dangers of simply speaking out? *There was one day*, she would write, during a demonstration – she could not even remember what it was for – *when we were dragged into police vans, and as I was shoved against the wall of the van, thrown really, my arm broke. It stayed broken all that day and overnight until we could be bailed out and I could get to a hospital. Can you imagine the pain*, she wanted to scream through the phone. *Of course it's hard for you*, she would write later, retelling the story more calmly in more careful words, *of course it is important to understand, but do you understand* – wanting to scream again – *what it was like for me ....*

Her thoughts were stopped, her voice silenced – fortunately, she thought – by Sam who had not paused long for an answer.

"And did you know slaves were forbidden to read? By law? And they think between fifteen and sixty *million* were taken out of Africa and between eight and twelve million – *million*, Myami, died in the Middle Passage. I read a memoir by someone who had visited the slave castles in Ghana, just a year ago. The floors are nine inches higher than the ground. And you know why? Because there are layers and layers of human skin, dried blood and bone, hair and shit packed down in those dungeons where people died waiting to be shipped across the ocean. Did you know that even the patterns of fish migrations changed over the time the slave ships were riding? And why? Because there was so much blood and flesh in the ocean all the sharks started following the boats, and that changed everything else about where fish swam!"

She had paused for so long Ami spoke – "Samantha?" thinking, *death in the ocean,* but knowing enough not to make a link out loud.

139

"I'm here," Sam answered, her voice now filled with enraged contempt. "I read some white observer, in the West Indies in the 1800s I think, who described a naked woman being whipped nearly to death, then *flayed* alive. You know what *flayed* means, Myami?" And in case she did not, or had not formed the picture vividly enough, "It means layers of flesh being sliced off – like you flay a fish – like you see them do it in the fish store when you ask for a fillet of *sole*, or *salmon?* Why doesn't anyone know about this stuff? I mean why don't most people know, because obviously some people do know – these writers, people who actually saw it all, or who have studied it. It's in *books*!" A deep sighing breath, a moment of silence, then, "Shit!! Why doesn't anyone ever admit it happened? Maybe then we could understand why everything is such a fucking mess in this country now!"

At several moments during the recitation of the list of terrible things, Ami had wanted to shout for her to stop, but at the end she'd only said, "Samantha, Samantha my darling," and she wished Sam's other grandmother were here, Maya's mother Sophie, who loved stories, especially stories about freedom, even stories that contained terrible things, who might have been a Rabbi, "if they had let women in those days," Hannah had said.

Another long silence passed between them after that, nearly a full two minutes. Ami held the phone tightly to her ear, whispering *God* and *Jesus, Mary, and Joseph,* trying to make sure Sam didn't click off. Finally she heard Sam sigh again. "I wanted to let you know what I've been doing. I'm reading all this stuff. I'm even taking a kind of independent study with one of my teachers – the brilliant black woman I wrote you about. She knows so much."

Ami felt short of breath – the familiar shame, the old childish terror of being shut out. When her granddaughter added, "and where have you been, by the way, Myami? I haven't seen you in weeks," she breathed deeply, in and out.

But Samantha returned to her real subject before Ami could respond. "It's horrible, I know, Myami. But at least I know. At least I know why I'm so angry all the time. It's not just the horrific terrible things but that *no one talks about them.* No one seems to want to remember."

The dangerous obvious link was almost into words, words Ami very much wanted to delay. Quickly, she said, "I'm trying, Sam dear. We must – I know – but – "

"Write to me about my mother, Myami. Describe her. I want to find out about her. I want to know."

Anger threatened, pure and defensive – *it's not my fault, Samantha* – she wanted to shout. But what is not her fault? History? Silence? Her own ignorance? Or that old terror keeping her company for so many years, not her fault after all?

And, afraid of her own fear, of changing stories, of opening true boxes and being shut out, of the spoken demand and the unspoken one too, Ami promised, "I will."

Part Four:

Saint Elizabeth, Maryland,
Western Shore of the Chesapeake Bay
About 1845 - 1851

Chapter 18

On the western shore of Maryland, near the point where the Potomac River meets the Chesapeake Bay, the shoreline is smooth and easy to navigate, unlike the labyrinthine inlets, marshes, and countless tributaries common to the eastern shore. As a child, Louisa Summers was grateful for this geography as it enabled her love of the water to be more easily satisfied, since her father and aunts deemed it safe for her to run down to the shore-line that came right onto the edge of the land near their house. There would come a time when, like the slaves seeking the North, she would appreciate the value of those complex thickets that create such fine hiding places on the eastern shore. But when she was a young girl, feeling free and unencumbered, any morning or afternoon in any weather might find her walking the shoreline or standing still, staring out toward the water as if she were trying to witness in each moment the infinitesimal retreat or incursion of the tide.

Now, she walks the narrow strip of sand at flood tide, or the broader expanse of seaweed-laden beach at the ebb, and she tries to separate her passion for him from his skin color and his situation: that he had been her father's slave. Now, in enforced and welcomed isolation, she tries to allow all the terrible memories to settle and sink down. She stops as she walks only to make notes in her journal and hopes that the two activities – the writing and the walking – will give her the courage, or at least the clarity, to know what she must do.

One thing she is sure memory cannot distort or alter: it was not when she saw him in the barn stacking tobacco, his muscles straining, sweat glistening on his brown forehead and shoulders, and she felt transfixed by the dark beauty of his skin, almost as if she had never noticed it before, that her passion first changed a childhood love into something else. For she had loved him since childhood when they played together, then later when they read aloud to each other in secret the books he was forbidden to read. Perhaps it is impossible to pinpoint the moment when friendship turned to love; yet, compelled by a need to understand what others might leave vague, and although she is aware that at times her compulsive efforts at clarification detract from rather than enhance meaning, she can't help wondering, trying to figure it all out. Perhaps it was when she was ten and witnessed a whipping for the first time.

They had all been called to the yard. Even the youngest. They all heard her father's words, intoned like he was a preacher and they were all in church, words about the absolute importance of obedience, about God's natural order and the crime of running off being a sin against God, words about how it was a lesson for all of them, even the slave-children, and, she couldn't help feeling, for her brother and herself. A female slave was hung from a large post by her wrists. She was stripped to her waist, and the flesh of her back was opened with repeated strokes of the cowhide. Brine was poured over her to intensify the pain.Louisa has never forgotten the smell of her blood and the sound of her anguish.The woman was almost old, probably near forty, someone close to Samuel, and Louisa saw tears fill his eyes, saw him wipe them away roughly as if he were angry at his own eyes, saw him watch until the woman was nearly dead. She can't say if she began to love him that day, or came to hate her own family and her place in it, or if both feelings were born in the same moment, one following the other, like twins.

Perhaps she had already come to love him only didn't know it when he helped her understand the words she had difficulty pronouncing, warning her that he could get a bad punishment for reading, so she should never tell.

Or most likely it was that more recent time after all, coming upon him at dusk when all colors can seem muted to shades of tinted gray. He was staring out at the sky as it darkened, and when she passed, their eyes met in a new way, the way that makes the soul feel stripped bare. Her body changed from fluidity to focus, and all her muscles tightened, as though water from the swift, wide stream of the bay were rushing into one of the many narrow tributaries that edge through the land. No words passed between them, and the silence where ordinary words might have been aroused a compulsion far stronger than any attempt to contain it could be.

Later, in the barn, where she went long after dark in response to a quick glance from him, one she could not be sure of but hoped was real, she learned a hungry, sinful need for words, heard them whispered in the dark, the naming of her body parts – *your lips, your feet, your ...* just loud enough for her to hear. And then she whispered back, enchanted at first by the fun of it and then deeply and seriously aroused. All the parts hidden and degraded, or exposed and degraded, made sacred again with erotic, affectionate words. The next morning she could not say them aloud to herself, nor even write them down in her journal, but was content with the shorthand that brought the images to mind: *Our eyes met. We said words. Color faded to gray.*

Chapter 19

Their lives are filled with prohibitions of the strictest kind in order to preserve the dangerous way they live and have lived for many generations, over two hundred years. The increasing presence of militia is everywhere it seems – in town, on some of the roads, especially the least traveled. It is illegal for slaves to read or write. The men must avoid looking directly into the eyes of white men and never directly at white women. White mothers and sisters are aware that some of the slave children reflect the features of their own families even if their color leans more toward all the shades of brown, from a tan light enough to be called white to nearly black. But they must pretend to ignore these similarities and learn to breathe sighs of relief when such children are sold away. White boys who are too sensitive or fearful as young children must be trained to a toughness and entitled authority based on skin color they can no more question than their right to own large tracts of land, or to amass fortunes without work, or to satisfy their sexual desires when and where they please, from the marriage bed to the slave quarter. If the mothers and sisters and sons do not manage these distortions of vision and knowledge which must come to seem not like distortions but like unquestionable truth, there will be no land, no income generated, no home protected, no world maintained or fathers recreated, generation after generation, to maintain it. Everything, in short, will fall apart. Nevertheless, more and more people are aware of and repelled by the stranglehold of color difference made into the foundation of a way of life. One of these unadaptable souls is Louisa's Aunt Emma, one of two of her mother's unmarried sisters who live at Summerly and are therefore beholden to the generosity of their brother-in-law,

Louisa's father. Whenever she can, Emma attempts to teach Louisa that human slavery is a great sin and hints of her liaisons with other whites who believe as she does. When they are alone, she sings Louisa the spirituals the Negroes sing, and whispers to her the true and subversive meanings of the songs. Then Louisa, a careless and passionate girl, tries to sing the songs to Ruthie who cares for her, puts her to bed at night, lets her follow along when she does the housework during the day. But Ruthie shushes her and will not join in the song.

What matters is not simple color difference, but what color, or the hint of it in a family or a body, has come to mean over the past two hundred and thirty years, and the meanings of color have been drummed into her since she can remember. She tries to think his color is like any other part of him, that she loves his color as she loves the shape of his hands, the line of his jaw, his narrow chin. She holds onto this belief if only for the defensive comfort that she is different from most of the others in her family and her town. Anyway, in the dark it is the opposite feeling that envelops her. Color disappears. It is the inexplicable, entirely unlikely way they seem to be the same that drives her to continue on their reckless path.

And Samuel? What drives him, despite his mother's suspicions of what they are up to after it has gone on for some weeks? Ruth is terrified and enraged, and she makes no secret of it to either of them, two fools, she calls them, having raised them both. But her warnings to the white girl she raised are muted and careful; her real anxiety is for her son who's acting crazy as he's had a tendency to do since he was small – claiming once at only six years old that death might not be so bad as this life, here. He reminds her of his father, she tells him, like the father's ways of thinking have been handed down to the son even though Samuel had been a baby when his daddy was sold, *I have to think of myself as free, even though I'm a slave,* Samuel had said to her once, and she had stared at him; they were almost exactly his daddy's words. *I fear for you,* she'd said, as if she could hear the dangerous thoughts rambling around in his mind. One night when he is only getting up from the table, ready to carry his dish to the pump outside, she slaps his face, hard. *What?!* he shouts. Her look is harder than her slap - *don't risk your life and mine too just for some white skin.* He bows his head, walks silently outside and sits down on the wooden bench next to his mama's shack. It is not that she's white, he thinks, but that she's free.

He gets up and punches the wooden bench, bruising his knuckles, walks to a narrow path behind the quarter where he can pace unseen. How can he be sure, living in the midst of centuries of association of whiteness with freedom, if in some part of himself he doesn't make the degrading identification? Her whiteness and her freedom feel tangled up, each one wrapped around the other, separating then twisting again, like weeds, or vines. What he feels when he sees her, likes her, then desires her, is that she is Louisa, his childhood friend and foolish comrade. In his world, weakness of any kind is hidden – driven down by absolute necessity, buried so far back even memory's gone, the lessons learned in earliest childhood – he remembers slaps for crying, for wanting, and words along with the slaps – *I'm saving your life boy – you hear?* He came to understand the rightness of the slap, the truth of the words. But she is free to be weak, and there is something more than pure delight he feels in her childish expression of all she feels – something meaner, harder, a kind of vengeance on those he loves, has always loved most of all. He is excited by her innocence, even though he knows it is ruthless, just as when they were children, teaching the younger slaves to read, he had been aroused by her bravery, even though he knew it was rash.

"I just know it's the right thing to do," she had told him, hands on hips, chin pointed defiantly upward. Pacing behind his Mama's shack, he laughs bitterly as he had then. "And you think this whole world's just waitin for you to tell em what's right?"

"Yes I do," she had said.

"You believe you know, but you don't," he told her in later years, and they both knew he meant she was white. Once, when they were sixteen and just noticing the hints that their feelings were taking on a dangerous dimension, she had been begging him to tell her why he liked her, demanding that he describe her virtues and her strengths, since he'd known her all her life and was her best and secret friend, she said. And she turned her mouth down in a sorrowful pout when he refused. It was the first time he felt like kissing that mouth.

He denies it vehemently when his mother accuses Louisa of manipulation. "She ain't so innocent, you listen to me," Ruth had told him once. "Not like you think. More like – can't say it right – more like she know how to get what she wants . . . from you. I know that girl. Been knowing her. She crave love since her mama died. Do near anything to get it." For all the training his mother has worked hard to instill in him so he just might survive the brutality he encounters every day, for all his knowledge, second nature now, of how word and gesture can be used as mask, he will not believe that Louisa is indifferent to everything but her own need for love. He wants to believe she is genuine, wants to believe there is someone, something, out there that does not want to control him. And she is in a way who he wants her to be; she loves him fervently and without regard to the dangers it requires her to share. Only she needs him desperately too, to blunt her sorrows and for other reasons so laced with irony that they remain far from her awareness. She needs him for a mirror, and for a wall.

They were both misfits from the start, outsiders even in their small worlds. "I'm a slave, Louisa," he told her one night, "and that means I don't belong nowhere – not really. I know that. Anyways – I always felt different from everyone else, even from my own Mama." He paused and rested his chin on her head. "Maybe if I'd gotten to know my daddy – I think of him every night, picture him escaping, making it through the woods, onto a steamer, getting all the way to Philadelphia, then Canada – free. Maybe if he stayed I might've been *like* somebody, would've looked over at him and felt *kin* in those ways that go deep, but that ain't my blessing. Never wanted to bring danger to the people I love, but I can't get used to all the lies. I get real angry, and that's the most dangerous thing of all."

He breathed so deeply, once in and then out, she felt the cycle of that one breath would never end. Then he whispered, "There's *gotta* be somethin else for me – some place in this world."

Hearing a new determination in his tone, she pulled away and stared at him. He glanced at her but quickly shifted his gaze to the ceiling, pulling her face against his chest so she couldn't see his eyes. He held her but she felt his absence, and the distance between them stretched wider so she leaned more closely against him, clutched the worn cotton of his shirt in her hands.

"You have that faith?" she asked.

"Not faith," he answered, looking at her with surprise. "It's more – I don't expect nothin good, not much anyway. So I think, there must be something better, a little better than what I know. Here."

She felt her anxiety building. In that moment of loneliness, for she belonged nowhere if not with him, Louisa felt the threat – that she was nothing. There was nothing for her, or to her. She pushed herself into his chest, as if she might find a way to penetrate the boundaries of his flesh, and she forced her mind to focus on those other moments, when she seems to see herself mirrored, safe in a companionship more profound than any she has ever known.

She will long for that sameness for the rest of her life, the interior place glimpsed by someone else at last, but she will never find it again. When the worst is finished and she is alone again, she will sit and think of it all, reliving the violence so horrible she will dare to remember only with opened eyes, for the minute she closes them she sees the image too clearly – his broken limbs, the raw and bloody lines across his back, his sex cut off – and at last his blessed faint and death. She will turn to another view of the room as if in this way she might change the image, might see his face when it all began, and feel beautifully exposed again, even to herself, as never before.

The back of the barn. A room of hay and wood, piled high nearly to the windows in places, where they dared to acknowledge their love for each other and to confirm it with their bodies in the dark. Samuel, ordinarily a man of very few words, could talk so long about the ongoing struggle for freedom, the stories

151

of escapes and rebellions, the analysis of the slave system he was mastering with his secret studies, that she'd have to put her finger on his lips to remind him of how little time they had. When it came to words of the heart he had little vocabulary. He said almost nothing to her in those long, life-changing months to explain why he risked so much just to love her; never exclaimed, like the lovers she read about in books, that he found her beautiful, or wonderful, so special in some particular way she took his breath away. There was only the soft listing of her body parts in the dim light – *your eyes, your mouth, your shoulders* – the whispered list she came to crave accompanying his fingers and his eyes. His eyes spoke of his feelings, so she learned to trust his eyes. No gesture of embarrassment or timidity broke the purity of his steady and immodest gaze. It amazed and enthralled and terrified her – the enormity of their double sin. Then she would look down, or away, unable for all her easy words to claim, as he could, a passion as deep as was implicit in that unbroken gaze. Shyly, she responded with a list of her own, naming his beloved parts, and once, when she thought he'd come to trust her enough to understand her meaning, she even allowed herself to say, *your skin, your skin,* wanting, perhaps, in her own small way to counter the vicious hatreds he lived with every day; or needing, she later feared, to erase what she shared with those hatreds with a daring claim, for when she said it, he grew still, so still she could almost see in contrast the individual stalks of hay move behind him. He placed his hand on her hand and stopped its movement as it crept along his arm, laid the fingers of his other hand on her mouth. He held her closely so she couldn't see his face, but she felt his chest and shoulders stiffen and she knew somehow she had gone too far.

Only years later will she understand what she could not have understood in that moment when he pulled her to him but was really pulling away: how rare was Samuel's imagination to create an act of love – that tender list – so perfectly healing of the wounds caused by the hatreds that had become habitual and everyday; how defiant and generous his heart to be able to love anyone white; how the list defined a strict and final limit to what could be said aloud.

The gift of compassion and a love of justice are rare but not unknown in her fellow whites, she has always been told, and she tries to remember hating slavery even when she was a small child. What were the roots of this hatred? Was she somehow inexplicably good when others were, equally mysteriously, bad? Was it a case of sensitivity, a gift of empathy that became, in some fortunate whites, a capacity to see evil for what it was and dare to embrace struggle against it as a way of life? Of course there were many whites, most, she thought, who, even if they hated slavery, still believed blacks were inferior beings. Was she like that, even with some small hidden part of herself? Could any white person not be? And how could you be sure of anything, she was already beginning to ask in her teens, when your own memory could betray you and your eyes could be blind to what was right before them even while you thought you were seeing everything that was there to be seen – like the time Samuel had whispered the word she'd been trying to sound out in her book, and she'd realized: he could read.

Secretly, they had begun to teach the other Negro children, whenever her father was gone on some journey that took at least a whole day. By the time they were nine years old Samuel could read better than she could, and so he helped her plan her lessons. It was plain that someone must be teaching him, but she had no idea who the teacher might be. During the spring they were twelve, she might have come to know, but that was when ingrained assumptions prevented her from seeing what was before her eyes.

They had been alone in the kitchen, Ruthie – who was still *Ruthie* – having left the day's food in mid-preparation to go retrieve the laundry from the line before it dried completely and made ironing more difficult. Samuel was stacking large sacks of corn he had carried in from the fields. Louisa's older brother Charles had gone away with their father on business, and she was reading at the table, practicing her lessons as her father had instructed, at the same time planning how she would teach two younger slave children if she could figure out how to get them alone. Then it came to her. At the next low tide when they were all supposed to be digging for clams, she would teach them, without books or writing, by practicing spelling words out loud and then writing them with a long stick in the wet sand. She would write the words over and over, until she was sure they remembered. In the end, all the evidence would be destroyed and she would be a help to Samuel and whoever was teaching him. She began to write short sentences to use in her lessons: *Get up. Lie down. Never tell a lie.* But she couldn't remember if the spelling of *lie* down and tell a *lie* was different or the same. Since they were alone, she stopped her writing and told Samuel about her plan and her spelling confusion. His approval thrilled her. He glanced through the screen door and then ran out to old Henry who was moving stacked tobacco from a loaded wagon to the barn. Louisa remained staring through the doorway, noticing how the grass and trees and people were blurred in an interesting way by the pattern of the screen. She saw old Henry, a slave she'd known all her life and never much liked. He was hard-looking and unfriendly, though he was always obedient, and not danger-ous, her father said. He was talking to Samuel about something, probably the tobacco or the corn that still remained to be moved from the fields to the house. A few moments later, Samuel ran back and told Louisa the two words were spelled the same.

Later, when she learned who and what Henry really was, the memory of Samuel running out to ask him about spelling seemed so obvious she would be amazed by how reality could be hidden, then revealed through later knowledge, just as when Samuel opened the door, the other people in the yard and the yard itself assumed a clarity that had been blurred by the screen. And there were worse self-deceptions. She remembered seeing the capital S for Summerly – a half circle beneath it to distinguish it from other slaveholding families whose names began with S – darkly indented on arms and shoulders, yet she had failed to wonder what the mark was doing there, then accepted the partial explanation – *it shows they belong to us* – without questioning how it got to be part of the flesh, let alone the concept of *belong.*

By the time she knew it on Samuel's arm as intimately as she knew the scar from a childhood fall on her own, she would be learning about even more horrifying tortures, enacted regularly but seen differently, because performed on a body she had come to love.

Chapter 20

When Samuel and Louisa had been meeting secretly for nearly a year, he was caught teaching a group of five young slaves to read. It was the second time he had been caught and warned, so Louisa's father called for a severe punishment – a whipping and a week under the iron mask. Louisa saw Samuel outside the tobacco barn, his entire face covered in iron, only his eyes visible through the narrow slits. Long iron rods surrounded the collar enclosing his neck. His mouth, the origin and location of his crime, was completely covered. Inside, an iron gag shackled his tongue, preventing him from swallowing food or even his own saliva that dripped down through holes in the plate. When she saw him she turned away, not wanting to add humiliation to his pain.

The night it was taken off, the two of them sat in the barn in silence for hours holding each other, her head on his chest, his arms surrounding her like a mother's arms while he stroked and massaged her shoulders and spine. Finger by finger, inch by inch of her spine, neck to waist, she felt the pressure of his hands and sank into a sleep so deep and peaceful she was ashamed, when she woke, to have slept through his hours of pain.

"I'm sorry," she whispered, but he smiled and nodded in a way that made her know it made him feel better to watch her sleep, and although he had never done so before, he allowed her to change positions and pull his head onto her chest, returning the maternal embrace. He kept his mouth slightly opened, his tongue raw, layers of skin burnt off by the heat of the metal so long imprisoning it; any contact of tongue and the roof of his mouth caused searing pain. His feelings came to her through the silence, in a very slight pressure of his fingers on her back, and she thought she saw his eyes glisten briefly with tears – though it must have been the moonlight coming through a broken slat in the ceiling because he told her he never cried. As she sat there holding him, one of her oldest and most frightening memories began to push everything else out of her mind. It was a memory she had always tried to obliterate with activity or talk; once or twice she had actually run across the yard, as if she could somehow outrace the thought and leave it behind.

She was young – perhaps ten – when she first heard of a thing called a *scold's bridle*, used on her great-grandmother in England as a punishment for some impudence. She must have overheard the story as her Aunt Emma was telling it to someone, Emma being the only one in the household who would have taken pride enough in this history to break the secrecy to which everyone else assigned it. Louisa asked her father about the incident, innocent of the implications and the inevitable consequences, and he vehemently denied it had occurred. "Mind your business, Louisa, and stop eavesdropping, especially on your Aunt Emma who's a known liar from way back," he warned.

But Louisa persisted, always attracted to minding business other than what was called "her own," and one late afternoon when she thought she was safe – it was in the library where she spent much of her free time – she asked Emma, the person in the world she trusted the most. Emma drew the child to her, and Louisa felt the softness of her aunt's breasts beneath the green cotton of her dress, felt her head kissed, her light wispy bangs drawn away from her eyes where they were always falling. Then Emma gently pushed her away, keeping her hands on her niece's arms, and told her the truth. "Your great-grandmother, my grandmother, was a brave and intelligent woman," she said. "She studied books all the time like you do, religion and philosophy, during a time in England when reading was looked down on for women. Some families wouldn't allow it at all. But she had a fiery temper and instead of reading quietly or keeping a secret journal like many others, she spoke her feelings – to family, servants, and once – the time she was punished – to some of the villagers. I don't know what she said, but she was made to wear that scold's bridle in public for days. The story is that her mouth and tongue were permanently injured, and from that time on she lisped, so she spoke little, out of shame – for all of it. I'm named for her," Emma said with a sad smile. "It must have been my mother's one act of rebellion. Now we use a version of that horrible iron mask here, on our slaves."

Louisa had suppressed the last piece of information until now, when she realized the iron mask he had been forced to wear was the same one her aunt had described being used on the first Emma two generations before. The two images linked, one in her imagination in response to a terrible story, one as she had seen it in all its horrible reality – a jagged edge along the right side that she had thought might be cutting his cheek – a glistening in the sun where the forehead curved so it looked almost beautiful – and the two images were permanently connected so that for the rest of her life she would never be able to see one without the other.

Her father did overhear Emma that day. He burst into the room and threatened her with the mask if she persisted with her lies, and as the brother-in-law of an unmarried woman, he'd have the authority to carry out his threat. For Louisa, there was more than threat. Pulling her roughly by the arm, he dragged her upstairs for a punishment. The pain from her father's belt, until then used only on her brother Charles, was nothing compared to the humiliation of having been forced to stand half naked before him, her dress pulled up and her bodice opened, the newly forming maturity of her narrow chest exposed to him. He looked at her for a long moment, his eyes shifting from her throat to her waist, from one small breast to the other. Then he slapped his daughter's face, turned her around and laid his belt three times on her bare back and buttocks, all the while muttering, "I love you, Louisa, that's the cause of me doing this. You got to be taught respect – you have no mother to teach you – and you're all I got now she's gone." When the beating was over and Louisa turned around, there was a kind of smile on his lips, and the worst part, the part she would say to no one in the world, she felt a flash of heat on her cheeks and between her thighs, and she answered his smile with a small one of her own. That sort of beating occurred twice more in her girlhood, and each time the terrible smile, the flash of heat, the shame.

"Sometimes I can't help wondering," Samuel said after he'd held her silently for nearly an hour, not long after the iron mask, when he could talk again. "Here is my one and only life. And here is me, a slave, just acting like I'm a man putting me in danger. And in love with you – one of the most dangerous things I could do. Your father would kill me if he ever found out, if my Mama doesn't kill me first." He shook his head quickly, looking off into the distance. "If there *be* any place on this earth where I can make the life I feel meant for, I promise you Louisa, I'm gonna find it."

Louisa ignored his terrifying warning and imagined he was trying to mitigate a sense of helplessness with improbable hope, an effort she could recognize in herself, so instead of attending to his words and their meaning, she began to think about her own feelings – how she is subject to terrible fears, how if she is left alone the fears get twisted up with anger. If she didn't press her fist into her mouth, she might scream. She has thrown books across the room, ripped her clothes from the drawers and flung them onto the floor. Several times she has found herself – as though she had passed out for a few minutes – crouched on the floor trying to find some better part of herself, as if it has been lost somewhere.

By then she'd no longer be angry or frightened. It would have become a terrible emptiness that felt like a thing and a blankness all at once.

She did not recount for Samuel the details of these extremities that embarrassed and confused her, but she tried to describe the emptiness, because it seemed very much like the powerlessness he was wrestling with beneath his rage. Believing her understanding would ease his mind, she continued to talk, pushing on, blind to the irritated, impatient way he was looking at her, trying only to ease her own mind. "I sometimes feel completely out of control," she said. "When I was a child they called the bouts

159

'tantrums' and I was punished for them by being hit, or sent to my room behind a locked door. After the beating or during the punishment I'd get a feeling of being – well, *nothing* – like I'm worth nothing. It's worse than a feeling of being all alone, forever. It's like that, except there's no *me* there to feel alone, like there's nothing in the world and I'm nothing in it, like. . . ."

It was a hard thing to convey in words, and she feared Samuel might not understand. She began to lose the thread of the connection she thought she'd seen between her experience and his words. Angry herself that he refused to see how they were alike, she was surprised when he interrupted her in an angry voice.

"One, I ain't never felt like nothing," he said. "Two, if I ever lost control that way, I'd be dead. My Mama taught me from the time I could understand words I better never do what you call lose control. And she said I was something *good*, a *good* boy, a *good* son, *good*, somehow, in spite of all the ways I was meant to feel bad by the people around me and – and how my life is here. I can't say how she figured out how to teach me all that at once, but she did." He paused and stroked Louisa's hair, as if apologizing for his anger. But then he continued in a more disturbing, cynical tone. "And three, I never thought I was worthless. I know exactly what my worth is in dollars and cents. What I been trying to tell you is I'm trapped. In the wrong life. Trapped. You white, Louisa, so you can't understand."

If she could have read his mind, she would have read the very thought she feared, that he had risked his life long enough in these secret meetings. She could not read his mind, but she could read its hints in a tightening of his lips, an abrupt closing of his eyes, a shake of his head. It was time for him to get control of something he'd been succumbing to for too long. She was afraid of losing him, and the fear triggered the other knowing – what to say to protect herself from that.

"But this *is* your life," she said, "here with me, and I – I couldn't do without you." She knew he would see her selfishness, and she made her voice a little childish, pouting her lips, for it was always this childishness that drew him in again, as if he was

160

the one who had to worry about her safety, as if there were some force that could destroy her, and the only one who could protect her was himself.

But there was no reassurance that day. As he rose to leave, he said, "Yeah, it's my life. I know that for certain. But that don't make it the one I'm meant for, or that suits any part of me." He did not explain further. He seemed to know the pain he had caused her and wanted her to know she had caused him pain. What she knew for certain was that she had failed him, but she would not begin to understand how until she had endured a small portion of what he had known since he was old enough to know anything at all.

Chapter 21

"My father was the one came to Mr. Henry's aid right after he was sold here," Samuel said one night at the end of summer when she asked how Henry and Samuel's mother had become such close friends. Henry was frequently a central character in the stories Samuel told her about life in the slave quarters. Often in the evenings, if Louisa walked across the large front yard down by the quarters, she'd see Henry and Ruth gossiping, she assumed, sitting silently, side by side.

"Mr. Henry was as low as a man can be the way he tells it, sold away from everyone he loved. Didn't care if he lived nor died, he told me, was lower than a bug on the ground, he said, lower than the bottom of a freshly dug grave."

The barn was hot, so they had ventured out one at a time and walked separately to the bay. Once there, hidden by the lush summer trees, they came close and whispered through the night. Mostly, he whispered while she listened hungrily to his story, nearly holding her breath with the pleasure of being trusted enough to be told.

"When I was a little boy, long after my daddy'd been sold away, Mr. Henry started teaching me about the people working against slavery. Not just the people up north but the ones right here, and not just colored – some whites, too. Boat captains on the Chesapeake who take slaves into hiding and ferry them up to Baltimore, then put 'em in touch with others can get 'em to a free state, Pennsylvania, then Connecticut, or even Ohio or Michigan, hoping for Canada some day. Taught me about the Underground Railroad that ain't really a railroad but a long train of houses and people who see clear the great sin we live in down here. He read to me from pamphlets, newspapers, and the Bible. And he told me stories he heard from others – friends – family lost for years, strangers passing through, slaves who'd actually escaped, got *free*, then came back to save others, to show 'em where to run. He's the one taught me to read, though my Mama didn't like it since it's against the law and you risk your life learning it. But I was excited by the chance like Mr. Henry was excited giving it to me. I studied in secret, at night, whenever I could, and talked about it all with my teacher, about ways of escaping and the dangers of life in the North."

"That day in the kitchen," she said, realizing that Samuel had been asking old Henry, whom he called Mr. Henry, about whether there was a spelling difference between lie down and tell a lie. "Henry – Mr. Henry – he was the one who taught you."

But Samuel didn't remember the day. What had been a charged moment for her had been ordinary, even trivial to him. There was no change in Mr. Henry's character to cause him to pause now, as she was doing, marveling at how the actual images of memory could alter suddenly when new knowledge was grasped.

"One day after the lesson," Samuel continued, "Mr. Henry said he had a special story for me. Then he told me about how my daddy was an expert oyster shucker and one time even worked as a waterman, harvesting on the bay, even though mostly that wasn't work done by colored. One time he was hired out for three weeks for some work on the eastern shore because they needed a man who seemed to know the water. Some white waterman had got sick or died and they was worried about their catch and the money they might lose more than about one colored man working the boats. Daddy was taught how to catch the crabs in nets when they ran ashore during the low tide, where to find the beds of oysters and clams buried in mud, how to pry the dark blue mussel shells loose from the rocks. He was the fastest harvester on the work crew, and he was so good at it cause he loved it so much, like Mr. Henry told it, loved the low tides especially where you can see the mud trying to keep all that life down inside it – all the plants and tiny animals comin' into view when the waters pull back. He loved all the faces of the water itself, even its storms. Water can be harnessed, but only for a time, he told Mr. Henry once. Water runs, my daddy said."

Samuel paused, looking out at the dark bay. She dared not break the silence for she knew what he was thinking.

"One night my daddy told Mr. Henry he wanted him to taste something. He pulled near a dozen oysters from his pockets and took out a kind of curved, flat knife. Then he opened the tough shells and out came the slimiest creature Mr. Henry had ever seen. But in his mouth it tasted like a king's feast, carrying the salt and the briny taste from the sea, Mr. Henry said, or maybe it was just my daddy's pleasure that was catching. That's exactly what Mr. Henry told me. I still hear his words like he was speaking right now. When the story was finished and our lesson in reading done, we walked down to the shore in the dark. It was ebb tide, and we walked way out onto the mud banks and kneeled down. I was so scared we'd be caught, but we was dressed in dark clothes, and Mr. Henry told me not to worry. All white folks can see is skin color on niggers and they wouldn't never be able to tell us from the mud, he said. His joke calmed my nerves, so we dug down into that mud and raked up as many oysters as we could fill our pockets with. Then we went back to the quarter and sat down at Mama's table where Mr. Henry proceeded to teach me what he had learned from my daddy. I never forgot it, still practice it all the time, trying to become a real good shucker like I hear my daddy was."

From deep in his front pocket Samuel took a partly opened oyster. He spread the two halves of the shell a crack and let the remaining sea water drip onto his tongue. Then, as if suddenly remembering Louisa was there, he held the creature out for her. She had eaten oysters grilled, fried and baked, but never one raw. She was scared she'd be disgusted, but she opened her mouth, shut her eyes tight and tasted one of the loveliest, smoothest things she'd ever had on her tongue.

Mr. Henry became a different person for Louisa after that night. She had seen him only as one of her father's slaves, an old man less strong than he once had been, but still looking more like fifty than the sixty years Samuel said he had passed. She had never really looked at him, just called him old Henry like everyone else did and found it odd because he didn't look as old as some of the others. She remembered his way of smiling that seemed closer to a frown and how for that reason she'd never liked him much, maybe was even a little bit afraid of him – although her father said he was a good boy and she had nothing to fear. It was confusing and interesting to change her mind's picture of him, to see a teacher, a carrier of stories, a leader of the slaves not only on their plantation, Samuel told her, but of many others in the county, someone who was obviously revered. But it was because he had trusted her with this story that she found the courage to tell him the terrifying news – news that would be wonderful if it weren't a disaster: she was carrying their child.

Chapter 22

Several weeks later, four Summerly slaves, three men and one woman, were caught trying to escape. They began in a narrow tributary and got as far as the bay at Yorktown when a skipjack captain spotted them and brought them back for the reward. The whippings were severe but not lethal, since they were four strong workers and John Summers did not want to sacrifice them for their usefulness. As a result of this incident, however, sentries around the Summerly plantation were increased. Whippings for small infractions became common. Waves of fear, always rolling through two hundred acres, rolled higher and stronger, and even the men kept their eyes down and refrained from whatever illegal activity or simple disobedience they might have been involved in during less dangerous times. They feared the whites and they feared each other, especially the more recently purchased slaves who were not yet well known, or the older, broken ones who might accidentally or intentionally betray. Samuel couldn't risk running during a time like this, although when he told his mother about the disastrous outcome of his year long love for Louisa, Ruth had set aside her rage, as he knew she would, and began making inquiries into networks and plans for escape. But the period of lock down lasted for many months, and then, when Louisa was six months into carrying the baby, first her Aunt Harriet and then her father discovered her.

They confined her to a room at the back of the house where she was attended by Ruth. So far, all they knew was that she was pregnant. They tried to pry the father's name from her, cajoling and threatening, so a wedding could be quickly arranged, but she refused to speak.

For another three months secret inquiries about escape plans were intensified through complex networks; oral messages were sent out in whispers repeated as carefully as military codes; but the increased security had not diminished, and sometimes it was impossible to get anything through.

Louisa knew nothing of these efforts and frustrations but appealed to fate to save Samuel and herself. Many mixed children were born looking white, and some of them retained their white appearance for life. She had heard of slaves escaping to the North, some from this plantation, who hoped to pass for white up there, start new lives as white people, and she assumed some of them did, the ones who weren't caught and never returned, because she remembered being confused about their color when she was a child, seeing they looked white yet were slaves. If her child was born that way, he might be given to another family to raise, at worst sent to an orphanage; or if she was twice blessed, if the child looked white and was allowed to remain with her, both of them might be sent to some distant place to live, perhaps to some relative up North who might believe, or agree to believe, a story about a husband, tragically killed in his youth, the young wife needing a new beginning in a city far away from home.

But Samuel wasn't white when he was born. His hair was thick, black and curling in a line across the crown of his head, and his skin was a medium caramel color brown. They were outraged, of course, but not shocked. This reversal of the usual way mixtures happened occurred now and then all over the South, occurred a year before to a neighbor family. The male slave was sold to Alabama, the child to Texas, the daughter sent away – no one knew exactly where and no one asked. Some similar arrangement must be made, so they questioned, threatened, demanded, then beat her until the bleeding intensified so much she was feverish for weeks. Still, she refused to betray Samuel, though they came every day for six in a row to demand his name. Ruth stood by silently, watching her, never taking her eyes from Louisa's eyes until they were alone in the room again. Then she turned away, dusting surfaces, washing Louisa with gentle strokes of a soft cloth, never saying a word that might assuage her guilt or tell her what to do.

Finally, they lined up all the young men and threatened to beat them all until someone confessed. When the beatings were about to commence, Louisa's father announced it was his intention to beat not only the young men but the mothers, first a son, then his mother. Samuel stepped forward after the first lash on the back of the first son. He was praying he might be sold, knowing he would more likely be killed.

And he was killed, brutally and without mercy. She stood in the yard, her back against the side of the barn, gripping its boards so as not to fall down. Mr. Henry watched from start to finish, but at one point, he turned Ruth around, pressed her face to his chest so she could not see. Louisa, watching them, turned her own face away because she knew what would happen next, and in those moments that seemed like years she thought about how Samuel loved his mother with all his heart, perhaps more than anyone else in the world, perhaps more than Ruth herself even knew. When he spoke of her caresses, her stories and songs, even the harsh beatings she administered when she felt his rebellious spirit demanded a hard discipline in the name of safety, his face turned soft in a way Louisa never saw it otherwise. She was jealous, yet she did not so much begrudge him this love and care, in a world so bereft of tenderness, as his descriptions made her long for her own mother as she had not done in years. Louisa turned away from his final agony, from the dismembering of the body she loved in the light and the dark, piece by beautiful piece, and she tried not to name them in her mind.

She wanted nothing more than to rush into Ruthie's arms, as she'd done so many times as a child. She had always wanted to be included in Samuel's mother's love for him, but she understood that her skin meant it would never come to be. Henry and Ruthie were together, and she was alone, and as she prayed that Samuel had died quickly, she knew that if she only had a weapon deadly enough, she would kill her father, her brother, and everything and everyone they loved, perhaps even her brother's small children. How could she swear she would not descend into such desperate revenge? Then she heard Samuel's voice trying to help her understand Nat Turner. Not only the men and women, he had said, and it wasn't even pure rage, Louisa, he had said in a strange calm tone. It was practical. He even cared for one of those children. But he knew what the children would grow up to be. She would never forget the coldness that came over her when she heard those words. A vague awareness began within her, a question she never asked before and could not yet articulate. *How do they live with this – in this way, how do we . . .?*

Her father could at times be kind. His eyes twinkled when he joked and teased, his face softened when he kissed her forehead after she played the piano or read a poem to him out loud; what enabled him to *also do this?* And he'd committed actions of equal violence before. She witnessed some herself, like the beating of Samuel's aunt, heard stories of others, an old male slave's foot chopped off at the ankle when he was caught trying to run, a favorite kitchen slave's child sold away when he reached the age of maximum financial return: seven years. She had heard the woman's cries but only for a moment. A whip had been raised by some white hand nearby, and Louisa had walked away with the others, trying to forget the low, agonizing sound. It came back now, laced with questions: *how? how?* and behind that, *why?* She recalled Samuel's cold tone, and the same coldness seeped through her now, a cold hatred that took the place of wild anger and filled her with a determination which – though she might lose it temporarily at times – would never finally desert her again.

When she turned around to see them throw him into a sack, toss the sack onto a wagon to be scattered somewhere far away so no decent burial could be provided, all the joints of her body tightened, as if they were being strangled by wild weed, making her bones ache. This is what she knew: the memory of her desire, the reality of her love, and – even then – her gratitude for the life of her son, little Samuel, who would be cared for by his grandmother but who, perhaps, she could manage to see occasionally, from time to time even to touch. It would take more time before she had the capacity to wonder how she could have given desire such free reign, how dared to consummate such love. What arrogance or blindness enabled her to deceive herself as to which of them would pay the ultimate price?

A sense of shame spread within her. She only knew she must find the courage to leave this place and join the fight against slavery, though she had no idea how. She was still weak from a pregnancy complicated by the beatings, and the violence she witnessed made old childish fears gigantic again. She felt them rolling in like bay water at the start of a storm. She would have to face the fears down this time, if she were to have any hope of saving her child.

Now, the prison room to which her father consigned her through the last months of her pregnancy, where Ruthie attended her labor and Samuel's birth, became her chosen home. It was an added-on room at the back of the house, two hallways and a storage room away from the rooms where the family lived, on the ground floor, far from the family bedrooms upstairs. A place that felt like the banishment to which they sentenced her, but which she craved. A place with its own door she could slip out of unnoticed at night. She retained only necessary furnishings – a bed, a quilt, a table, a straight-backed chair, a supply of candles. She allowed herself a collection of books, notebooks, a bottle of ink and a box of pens. She was frightened of the dark, so she vowed to blow out her candles early, especially on long winter nights. She was frightened of loneliness, so she vowed to remain alone for days at a time, allowing herself to venture out only one night a week to visit Samuel in secret in Ruthie's cabin, or for an occasional family event, to keep up appearances.

Since the birth of little Samuel made clear the full nature of Louisa's crime, Emma had been forbidden to see her, but twice, before she left Summerly once and for all, she managed a secret visit. The first time, she held her niece as if she were still a small child, rocking her and kissing her head while she hummed the old songs. The second time, she sat across from her at the table and told her she was leaving, that she wasn't certain where she was going but somehow she would let Louisa know. "I'll find a way to send for you," she promised her terrified niece. "But in the meantime, Louisa,"– Emma paused, looked out of a sad and honest face, drawn with fatigue and fears of her own, "in the meantime, you must face it, Louisa. Your childhood is over. You must make yourself strong."

And so, knowing no other way than to dive into the worst of it without delay, Louisa swore to learn to live in solitude, hoping her family would think she was searching her soul for repentance and looking to God for guidance. In reality, she would be writing her thoughts and attending to her dreams, reading whatever materials she would somehow convince Henry to give her. And when her words were exhausted, or her eyes could no longer retain any more of a printed page, she would stare. She would pace the room, and only at night, when she was certain she could be alone, would she allow herself the respite of the beach along the bay. There, she walked along the tidemark and tried to see it as a symbol, a reminder that everything, even the sea, had a boundary, a place where it goes no further and another cycle begins. She became two women – one overtaken by panic, weeping perhaps, wringing her hands, but the other watching, keeping very still, getting strong.

Chapter 23

Are these vows, these notes from my reading, this record,
leading me to some decision, or are they just words, as impotent
as my written attempt when I was a girl to bring my mother's
face out of vague shadows with ever more extensive phrases and
descriptive words? Only her voice remains vivid after all these
years, so that when I close my eyes I can still hear her sing a
lullaby, a saddening and irresistible sound. Since Samuel's
death, old images and traces of memory of her come to me
suddenly. This new loss opens the scar of the old one. I dream
of one and some sign of the other intrudes. I cry for one, the one
I lost so recently, and my tears are increased like the level of the
bay when a storm brews far out to sea. Just so, this grief of
Samuel's loss is as great as any loss could be, but its strength is
made even greater by the old storm whose exact nature is by now
invisible, yet whose impact has influenced everything in my life.

I know nothing will ever change me in this regard. I was
fortunate once in my life to have had a feeling of closeness to
another soul that made us seem almost like one. I have yearned
for that feeling forever, I think, but now I must be comforted by
the blessing of what Samuel has left behind. When I look into my
son's dark eyes I will forever comprehend both the permanence
of absence and the promise of relief.

She wrote many times a day, and at the same time began
reading whatever books she could retrieve from her father's
library, works of history, philosophy and one on world religions.
She read about the transmigration of souls and reincarnation,
beliefs held by people living in eastern countries she never heard
of before, and in a place far to the south called the Amazon. The

idea gave some solace when she thought about Samuel's soul.

After several months of weekly visits to see her child and fruitless attempts to gain a soft word from Ruthie, Louisa began to ask questions of Henry, whom she tried to remember to call Mr. Henry, about the lives of the people her father owned. She had lived with them all her life, but had been blind to all but a fraction of what they endured. *How?* The question kept recurring with no hope of an answer, so she asked Mr. Henry about facts. Facts were what she needed now.

"You know the facts," he told her, his voice practiced at suppressing emotion. "Reading? That's forbidden. We ain't allowed to marry – ain't allowed to look whites directly in the eye. Can't so much as glance at white women, even if they talking *to* us – got to learn a kind of *looking–not looking*, all at the same time. And got to step aside when we meet white men on the road. We bought and sold just like the cows and pigs, even the chickens, away from each other, away from the only home we know."

He was right. She has always known these things, had watched sales in progress, yet when he said the words, when the words were said by someone she saw as an actual human being like herself, something changed, as if a veil has been removed, or a screen door opened. When she heard the human voice, saw clearly the human expression of anguish he could not banish from his eyes no matter how neutral he made his tone, she knew it all differently, knew it as if for the first time.

She had heard it, or much of it, from Samuel, and she had been able – how? – to what? Forget? Imagine it would not affect them in some magical way? Or, more selfishly, did she want to put the knowledge aside some place where it would not interrupt her happiness, the fulfillment of her own desires?

"There's more," Mr. Henry said, but when she asked what, he said only, "Think, Miss Louisa. You know everything there is to know yourself."

So she began to think carefully. She thought of the slaves who looked almost white, or were suddenly much fairer in their brown skin than their mothers, of the familiar facial features on some of the children. Then she saw one child in particular, a girl with a familiar face. Had her name been Lina? She remembered narrow braids beginning at her forehead and proceeding in neat rows to the base of her neck, a small mouth with narrow lips. She saw the girl's eyes for a flashing minute – light brown, dark lashes, and her neck – slender, almost skinny, and long, sloping into bony shoulders covered by a green cotton dress. The details of her memory made her uncomfortable, and quickly, she assigned that particular girl to the less upsetting generality of people being bought and sold, and she pondered, more abstractly, the layers of the human mind.

Another month went by when, hoping Mr. Henry had gained more confidence in her, and one night when he was alone in the cabin, she asked, "whatever became of Ruthie's husband, Samuel's daddy?"

"Sold cause your father was jealous of him," Mr. Henry said, letting her know with his eyes she was never to tell anyone what he had just told her. Then, after telling her to get back to her room before they were both discovered where they were not supposed to be, he added, "Ruth. Ruth's her name."

She nodded and obeyed, encouraged by Mr. Henry's trust, and she focused on this – a kind of approval she'd always hungered for, but especially now, and so the fragments of what he told her remained separate: the girl named Lina with the familiar face, Louisa's father jealous of the man Ruth loved; all remained unconnected, meaning obscured.

A few nights later, a large dinner party was being held at Summerly, and Ruth was working in the kitchen until late. As usual, she'd have little Samuel with her, nestled in a basket or tied in a soft fabric to a young slave girl's back. Louisa made her way to the slave quarters again, daring a second meeting in one week. She needed to find Mr. Henry alone to ask the question that lurked behind all the others. He was inside Ruth's cabin as she'd hoped. Having now learned the strict formalities required of young people toward their elders within the slave community, she sat down at the table where he was eating and said nothing.

She nodded when he looked at her, and remained silent until he finished his soup. When he pushed his plate away and wiped his mouth, he looked across at her, giving her permission to speak.

"Will she always hate me?" Louisa asked, her voice unsteady and low. "She used to love me once."

"She took care of you," Mr. Henry corrected, but Louisa detected, or imagined, a small tone of sympathy in his voice. "She blames you. That won't likely change I don't believe. I don't believe she hates you. More like she don't want you near her – scared of you – don't want you too close to the boy."

Louisa was silent again, perhaps for longer than she realized, for Mr. Henry got up from the table, indicating it was best for her to go.

She walked toward the house slowly, trying to accept what Mr. Henry told her, but it left her hopeless and adrift. Her mother, Samuel, Emma, even little Samuel in a way – all lost. Ruth was the only one left – *she tied my shoes, taught me how to wash myself, gently and thoroughly in the female places, called me Sugar, sang swing low sweet chariot to me, comin for to carry me home – home to her – I hummed it each time I went away for a day or overnight someplace with Aunt Emma, or Daddy, or Aunt Harriet, even with my own mama – as soon as we entered the gate I'd run to find her, run to her and in my head the words, the chariot brought me home, Ruthie, carried me home.* The words and the melody repeated over and over until she was back in her room. They beat in her head while she undressed, spinning and echoing until she fell into an agitated sleep.

In the morning, she awakened with the understanding that the few pieces of information she'd learned from Samuel and Emma about the fight for abolition were only a small part of what she wanted and needed to know, and Mr. Henry was the only contact close by whom she could trust. She would have to figure out some way to prove herself, to convince him that *she* was trustworthy, and brave, and if she found the right thing to do, she might even be able to prove her love to Ruthie –*Ruth,* she said to herself angrily - *Miss Ruth, Miss Ruth, Miss Ruth.*

Soon she was given her chance. One night, she was holding

Samuel in her arms and, lulled by her own soft singing, she had fallen into a light sleep along with her child. Whispering voices awakened her, but she kept her eyes closed, at first only because the cabin was warm and peaceful, the weight of the child's body against her luxurious, the low voices a melodious, hypnotic hum. When she heard the words *danger* and *abolitionist*, however, she woke fully, and listened more carefully. Mr. Henry was talking to another man, a slave Louisa did not know by name, about some abolitionist pamphlet he wanted. "Can't think how to get it," he said. "The danger is real great now. People killed for a thing like this. But it might do a lot of good."And she was shocked to learn the title of the tract.

It took a month of careful, secretive planning, but finally she was ready. On the excuse that she needed an outing after so many months of solitude, Louisa obtained her father's permission to be taken in the carriage to the shops in town. Her father's face softened when he saw her wearing her bonnet, a white lace collar, starched and ironed, lying crisply over the bodice of a bright blue dress. Standing next to him, Aunt Harriet frowned. Her eyes met Louisa's, and in that quick instant Louisa feared her aunt suspected something less frivolous than a shopping expedition. She would have to take care.

It was dusk when she returned. She carried a large package wrapped in brown paper in her arms. She climbed down from the carriage and turned to face her aunt, a house slave named Sallie, and Mr. Henry, who was in the process of hauling large bags from a wagon to the barn. He moved slowly at his task, taking as long as possible to lift the last bags from the wagon onto the ground, watching.

"Let me see that package you got there," Harriet said.

"Here? Now? It's only a bolt of light cotton to make a new set of tablecloths for the house, Aunt Harriet. Some blue and green thread to embroider the borders of the napkins." Louisa avoided everyone's eyes but her aunt's. She willed her expression to match the innocence of her words.

But Harriet grabbed the package, and began untying the string. "Sinners like you don't get to be trusted just because a bit of time has passed, Louisa." There was a tone of excitement in her voice.

She opened the paper and saw the cotton, each yard folded like an accordion over the one beneath it. Pressed into the top layer were several spools of delicate thread. These she handed to Sallie. Then she opened the cotton cloth, shook it out into the air as if she were about to hang it on a clothes line. But nothing fell out of the folds. Nothing but yards of cotton cloth. Louisa was weeping by then.

"I've been treated like a criminal for months," she said. Her sobs slurred her speech, tears streamed down her cheeks, the truth of the emotion causing the tears that gave a sense of truth to the untruthful words. "I know I've been wicked. But I can't be a prisoner forever – searched and suspected as if I weren't living in my mother's own house. She turned and ran to the back of the house, up the stairs to her room. She locked herself in.

From beneath the wide overlapping folds of her skirt, she extracted three copies of a pamphlet tied to her thigh with a strong cord.

After three more nights, when Harriet's attention had turned to other matters, Louisa made her now familiar way in the dark to Ruth's cabin. As almost always, Mr. Henry was there. When she was safely inside, she turned her back to them, lifted her skirt, and removed the pamphlets from around her leg where they had been tied again. Holding them in her hands, she looked directly at Mr. Henry, then at Miss Ruth, then back to him, and she nodded her head slightly. Without stopping to enjoy her child, she left the pamphlets on the table and returned to her room. She never explained to them how she knew about the pamphlet, nor how she'd obtained the copies, how she'd discovered the name of someone who worked in the post office who sympathized with the abolitionist cause, how she convinced him that she was an ally by sending an unsigned note with a trusted messenger, requesting three copies of what she learned was an infamous call to rebellion, risking her own safety by so doing; how when she arrived at the post office, she dared to identify herself as the writer of the note and was so greatly relieved to discover her risk had been worthy – he had obtained the writings and managed to slip them to her within the pages of a ladies' magazine subscribed to by her aunt. She understood Mr. Henry and Miss Ruth would not want to know these details. But after that, bolstered by pride in her own lies, bravery and initiative, she dared to ask Mr. Henry to lend her writings that would help her understand what she needed to know in order to educate herself. She wanted to begin with her own secret prize, Angelina Grimke's "Appeal to Christian Women of the Southern States." Hundreds of copies had been burned in Charleston, she learned, hundreds more confiscated in Richmond, but small packages of the radical appeal kept coming into southern cities and towns in response to orders, or simply sent to anonymous post office boxes, each stamped with a false address.

"It was written for the likes of me, wasn't it," she asked, adding in a softer tone, "Mr. Henry?" She had learned about the writer – daughter of a large slave plantation in South Carolina who was now a leading abolitionist, writing from the North to her Southern "sisters."

He stared at her for so long her skin blushed hot under his gaze, and she feared he would mistake the blush for the sign of a coward or even a liar. But then Miss Ruth nodded her head slightly, and she added this to her list of all she owed to Samuel's mother who helped her in every way but would never speak more than the most basic and necessary words. After this, whenever she returned one book or newspaper or pamphlet, Mr. Henry looked directly into her eyes, as he was forbidden to do. She returned his gaze, intimidated by his stoic confidence and frightened of the path she had chosen for herself. Soon another piece of writing appeared in her room in some hidden place.

Chapter 24

Throughout the many long days when she spoke to no one and communicated only with her own thoughts, she sometimes pondered the story of her mother and her aunts – Eliza, Harriet and Emma – and she tried to understand the mystery of families – how different each member can be from the other, yet in another way as alike as reflections of one person in a series of attached mirrors that alter the angle but not the contours of the face.

Eliza, weak and submissive, suddenly appeared in Louisa's memory cowering in a corner, her face a mask of obedience as her husband beat the young Charles for some small infraction, or whipped one of the slaves, and Louisa's rising anger was so mixed with guilt she felt almost split in two. Or the other image, actual memory perhaps, or else some scene Louisa embellished from stories overheard for years. She heard women whisper since she was a child – "she is too much in love with him," jealousy vying with concern. She saw her father, John Summers, approaching his wife at a large party given in their home, Louisa not much past her third birthday, for it was in that year Eliza died. She was seated on the stairs with her cousins, other children, perhaps even Samuel had been there because when they were small they were often kept together: the official children of the father; the unofficial children he had fathered with his slaves – children everyone, even the wives, knew about and never acknowledged; and the children of the other house slaves who lived in the closest contact with her family, even though they belonged to an entirely separate sphere.

As Louisa paced the circumference of her small room, pausing at the bare window where she could see the barn, unable to focus on it for long without the horrifying images pushing all else from her mind, she saw that other room, large and full of light, its sparkling aura reflected in crystal vases and a large chandelier, in mirrors, in the silver candlesticks, bowls and frames Eliza loved and placed on the surface of every table and chest. She saw her amiable and gracious father look around for her mother who was shy, moving among her guests with an appealing reticence. His eyes rested on Eliza at a moment when she seemed to be experiencing some discomfort – perhaps someone had intimidated her, asked a question she felt inadequate to answer. She pulled her fingers nervously through her light brown hair. He glided over to her, took her arm, murmured pleasant excuses and led her to the dance floor. He swung and twirled her and on her face was an expression of relief and adoration, of gratitude and even, Louisa thought now, of desire. She saw the two of them as vividly as if they were drawings in her books of kings and queens, come suddenly and magically alive.

All these years later, after all the terrible events in which she played a central part, she wondered as that picture filled her mind: what lies beneath such adulation and dependence on someone so violent, so strict and, despite instances of tenderness, so cruel? She even allowed herself the suspicion that Eliza's final illness, in a way no one could ever know for certain, might have been self-inflicted, as though a disability she must have felt for years finally caused her to succumb to disease, so that her death may have been as willed, or at least sought, as if she'd hung herself or cut her throat. More vows followed this supposition – that Louisa would not succumb, would overcome dependency and fear, and whatever mysterious vulnerability may have hastened her mother's early death, she would, like Miss Ruth and the other slaves she is coming to know differently, become strong.

Harriet, the eldest of Louisa's mother's siblings, was in all ways Eliza's opposite, although she and Eliza resembled each other more closely than either of them did Emma, who looked, they always said, like her own mother's side while the two older girls were their father's daughters through and through. Harriet's hair was dark blond, like Louisa's, and both had blue eyes, but this resemblance had provoked no affection in the aunt. Indeed, she always seemed to dislike her niece, even before the girl was proven to be a traitor and a whore. A friend to John Summers since their early school days, she was more his sister in spirit than Eliza's. Or maybe, Louisa thinks now, she was in love with her sister's husband all along. When Harriet discovered Louisa's condition, even before she reported her, she slapped her face so hard the girl fell back from the blow. Her hatred for the Negroes was reflected in her contempt for all children, who frequently ignited her anger into a violent physical rage. And she was calculating, shrewd in her personal relations and swift with numbers, which earned her a place as her brother-in-law's confidante and partner. Since she was a child Louisa had returned Harriet's hatred, and she had no desire to see any similarity between herself and this aunt. But she has taken a vow against sentimentality, and she forced herself to admit a respect for the cunning and power in Harriet she hoped to find nascent within herself.

Emma, whose quiet warmth, if not her face and figure, always evoked memories of her mother for Louisa, was the child in the middle and the true opposite of both her sisters; brave and resilient, vulnerable yet strong. How she came to possess her love of justice in this family is a mystery, but Louisa's identification with this legacy was now more than ever intensified by the knowledge of her aunt's efforts and plans. She hummed quietly the songs Emma used to sing, the ones the Negroes sang, about going home to their Lord, which Louisa now knew meant earthly freedom as well, and escaping to a better world, meaning not only heaven but the free states in the North or all the way to Canada. As Louisa hummed, she remembered the tears that sometimes fell over Emma's face when she sang, the woman's tears permitted the child's until, exhausted, she would fall asleep in her aunt's arms. Now that Emma has been banished for her evil influence, Louisa longed for her and wondered if she would ever see her again. *Emma has bequeathed to me her love of justice,* Louisa wrote in her journal, *and I have always taken pride, perhaps too much, in that. But unlike either of my aunts, I must face the fact that I have much of my mother's submissive*

nature, her passivity and fear, and if I am to carry out my plans
and be equal to the tasks ahead, I must kill this woman in me.

She expanded her daily regimen of study – newspapers, pamphlets, tracts, anything she could get from Mr. Henry whose contacts brought him weekly packets he collected in a veritable library of works he hid, – Louisa had no idea where, and of course never asked, was only thankful she had been able to convince him of her sincerity and alliance.

One week, she was given an old, torn copy of an "Appeal" by a free colored man from Massachusetts named David Walker – now dead, but his fiery words transferred from hand to hand since 1829. The pages were yellowed, some of them ripped, one torn right through, the two halves mended with a piece of thread. Many have read his words, Mr. Henry told her in a bitter tone. Fewer have benefited from his analysis, she concluded. But Samuel did, she knew, and as she opened the fragile pages she imagined his touch lingering on them and she brought them to her nose, searching for a remnant of his smell, and to her lips. She transcribed three passages into her journal to remind herself of the fury and righteousness of the whole:

Remember Americans, that we must and shall be free and
enlightened as you are, will you wait until we shall, under God,
obtain our liberty by the crushing arm of power? Will it not be
dreadful for you? I speak Americans for your good. We must and
shall be free I say, in spite of you. You may do your best to keep
us in wretchedness and misery, to enrich you and your children;
but God will deliver us from under you. And woe, woe, will be
to you if we have to obtain our freedom by fighting.

The whites have always been an unjust, jealous, unmerciful,
avaricious and blood-thirsty set of beings, always seeking after
power and authority. – We view them all over the confederacy
of Greece, where they were first known to be any thing, (in
consequence of education) we see them there, cutting each
other's throats – trying to subject each other to wretchedness

182

and misery – to effect which, they used all kinds of deceitful, unfair, and unmerciful means. We view them next in Rome, where the spirit of tyranny and deceit raged still higher. We view them in Gaul, Spain, and Britain. – In fine, we view them all over Europe, together with what were scattered about in Asia and Africa, as heathens, and we see them acting more like devils than accountable men. But some may ask, did not the blacks of Africa, and the mulattoes of Asia, go on in the same way as did the whites of Europe. I answer, no – they never were half so avaricious, deceitful and unmerciful as the whites, according to their knowledge.

I will give here a very imperfect list of the cruelties inflicted on us by the enlightened Christians of America. First, no trifling portion of them will beat us nearly to death, if they find us on our knees praying to God. – They hinder us from going to hear the word of God – they keep us sunk in ignorance, and will not let us learn to read the word of God, nor write– If they find us with a book of any description in our hand, they will beat us nearly to death – they are so afraid we will learn to read, and enlighten our dark and benighted minds – They will not suffer us to meet together to worship the God who made us – they brand us with hot iron – they cram bolts of fire down our throats – they cut us as they do horses, bulls, or hogs –- they crop our ears and sometimes cut off bits of our tongues – they chain and hand-cuff us, and while in that miserable and wretched condition, beat us with cow-hides and clubs – they keep us half naked and starve us sometimes nearly to death under their infernal whips or lashes which some of them shall have enough of yet. They put on us fifty-sixes and chains, and make us work in that cruel situation, and in sickness, under lashes to support them and their families.

From other books in her father's library, she transcribed vicious words and sources:

The Negro is an example of an animal man in all his savagery and lawlessness and nothing consonant with humanity is to be found in his character. (found in "Lectures on the Philosophy of World History, by G. W. F. Hegel.)

And another:

I saw a black man suspended alive from a gallows by the ribs, between which, with a knife, was first made an incision, and then clenched an iron hook with a chain. In this manner he kept alive three days . . . Another Negro I have seen quartered alive . . . As for old men being broken upon the rack, and young women roasted alive chained to stakes, there can be nothing more common in this colony. (found in "Narrative of a Five Years Expedition Against the Revolted Negroes of Surinam, illustrations by William Black, by Captain John Stedman.)

Once having transcribed the passages, she read them out loud – words, written and spoken, always a necessary confirmation of reality for her. She was not able, as Samuel was, to think clearly without forming thoughts into audible words. Nor could she think words in her head and remember them well. If she did not write them or speak them, they faded. She forgot their implications, what they taught her, what they clarified about some inchoate feeling or vague perception. Even when she was alone by the bay, she sometimes talked out loud to herself – *the waves move delicately today – the color fades from the blue of mussel shells to the gray of oysters.* Otherwise, she would lose it all – the intensity, the perception, the memory of it gone like the wave itself when it breaks onto sand.

In the margin of the book, next to the description of torture, her father had written a note: *"European philosophers and even our American forefathers agree – the Negroes are between animals and men. Their feelings not the same as ours, of love or of pain."*

Did this false conviction provide a partial answer, then, to *how?* It was insufficient. She still could not imagine how so enormous a lie could take root, persist, and convince. There had to be some human depravity that welcomed it, knew it was false, yet needed its permission. She remained in furious confusion. But at least she could read the words out loud, over and over, and would never pretend she didn't know the truth. If she were half as brave as the people she is learning about, half as heroic as

184

Samuel, she would shout them from the town square, let the allies of her father shackle her and take her away. She would brand her flesh with them like Samuel's flesh was branded with the initial of her father's hateful name.

In a locked drawer under the surface of her table, she preserved one of the public advertisements for the sale of people. She took it out now, whispered the names out loud and remembered Cora, a woman Samuel called Miss Cora, who was sold at public auction when Louisa was a child. She was put in a wagon with six or seven other slaves and her daughter cried so loud Aunt Harriet began beating the child with a broomstick while someone else held her down.

There were increasing numbers of runaways, rebellions told and reported from nearby plantations and faraway states. Yet, there were three foundations that helped keep the system in place, and she was beginning to comprehend their force and their effectiveness: the belief that the Negroes were not fully human, a self-deception as cynical as it was ingenious; the prevalence of torture so common and so disturbing many of the whites actually stopped seeing what was before their eyes; and the selling away of family members which struck more terror and ensured more obedience than any other strategy employed.

Another memory with no specificity or preamble, as if it were always there: the name *Gabriel*, leader of a rebellion of the slaves. At the mention of his name, the white people would open their eyes wide, the women darting glances everywhere in gestures of anxiety, the men's faces hardening in rage. The Negroes, if they were present when the name was mentioned, remained inscrutable, no expression crossing their seemingly dispassionate faces. Then one specific time coalesced out of the general sounds and indistinct images. A dinner table crowded with white people, conversing and laughing, elegantly dressed. Miss Ruth was serving food from a large china platter. Her dark hair was pulled back under an immaculate white scarf matching an apron that covered most of her body from breast to ankle. Light blue cotton sleeves reached to her broad wrists. A hem of the same light blue touched the floor. Louisa was about fifteen and, by then, had hated the system so long it seemed like all her life to her, yet was still innocent of its worst acts and crimes. She wanted her hatred to be visible, and she allowed her eyes to meet Ruth's for an instant when the name was uttered: *Gabriel Prosser.* It was one of those glances between people in all kinds of situations that conveyed precise feeling, commentary of all kinds, when words could seem to be merely inadequate translations of thought and emotion, compared to what is transferable between two sets of eyes. In that moment of vertigo, she saw that Ruth saw her feelings, and she swore even then, with all the fervent resolve of her youth, to join the fight for abolition some day.

And yet, after all that had happened, despite her ongoing studies and to her constant shame, she was not able to speak any of her feelings out loud, but instead felt chained by her fears. It was not only her realistic fear of final separation from her child, she admitted to herself, but some more personal cowardice for which her love for little Samuel served as justification and excuse. She aspired to but could not yet claim the courage of the great William Lloyd Garrison who publicly asserted his convictions: *I do not wish to think, or to speak, or write, with moderation. No! No! Tell a man whose house is on fire to give a moderate alarm; tell him to moderately rescue his wife from the hands of the ravisher; tell the mother to gradually extricate her babe from the fire into which it has fallen; – but urge me not to use moderation in a cause like the present. I am in earnest – I will not equivocate – I will not excuse – I will not retreat a single inch – AND I WILL BE HEARD.*

Louisa wrote the fiery words of the great abolitionist into her journal. She read them out loud, memorized them, whispered them to herself when she lay awake in bed or paced her room. She gathered stories of courage as if they were medicinal herbs for a chronic illness, as if she could swallow the stories and become them, as an ailing body is said to absorb those herbs. But throughout the first year of little Samuel's infancy, at night when she was rarely able to sleep for more than two or three hours a night, she saw her Samuel's body as if before her or next to her again. She wandered the room, looked out at the barn, and saw him there. She saw him tied, and tortured, a bestial pain inflicted on him she could almost feel on her own back and limbs, across her chest, at her ankles as if her own feet were being chopped off, at her wrists . . . her sex ached as if she'd been repeatedly violated, the closest thing she can imagine to what was done to him. She cried out from his pain and wanted nothing more than to banish the image, to drink the entire bottle of sleeping draught Miss Ruth has prescribed, but she grasped the window sill, forced herself to remain standing and seeing and feeling until the images finally passed. Then she allowed herself to think: It is done. He is at peace. And she breathed deeply until the next time.

She wrote the outline of the story of Denmark Vesey, a former slave who purchased his own freedom, a vengeful and passionate man, she has read, who might have remained in his relatively secure position in Charleston, but instead organized a rebellion of six thousand people, establishing alliances as far away as Haiti. Thwarted, arrested with more than thirty others, tried, hung, then shot when the hanging did not finish the bloody job, he is not forgotten, his name is still respectfully whispered in the slave quarter at night, his story told to wide-eyed children, and that is how Samuel heard the story he had told to her. The name Denmark Vesey was still feared by whites, and she was coming to believe their terror was intensified by some buried knowledge of the rightness of his cause, which they masked with incomprehension of what they termed *his* brutality. Still, she felt the terror too, for although it was perfectly clear to her who the brutes were in this history, of which she records only a small part, she too is white. She cannot escape the skin that caused her beloved to be killed, that separates her from her child, that marks her belonging to the family whose brand fired the flesh of the woman who would, in other circumstances, in some other world, be called her mother-in-law, a figure to be respected, in some places even revered.

Whenever she was able, as soon as darkness fell, she covered

187

as much of herself as she could with a wide black shawl, left her room and walked quickly across the several acres of yard and around a long row of trees to the slave quarter, to spend an hour with her son. Each time, Louisa encountered Miss Ruth's coldness anew. A certain intimacy remained between them, since Ruth cared for Louisa from birth, and they were able, often, to read each other's expressions as if they were blood relations, but the prescribed silences of Ruth's position have been deepened now by her rage, not spent by the passing of one year. It never would be, Louisa feared. Still, Ruth was helpful to her, instructing her in baby care, allowing her to hold Samuel in her arms for as long as she managed to remain in the small cabin. Once, in the early days of Samuel's life, when Louisa's breasts were still filled with milk, Ruth risked her own safety by bringing the child to his mother so that Louisa could know the physical intimacy of his sucking once in her life. She felt the tightening in her body where Samuel had lain and the soreness between her thighs where he had emerged into the world, and from then on, whenever her breasts filled and had to be drained by hand to ease the pain, she wept, putting her quilt over her mouth so her screams wouldn't reach her father's or Harriet's ears.

When Louisa entered Ruth's cabin and said, "Good evening, Miss Ruth," she received only a silent nod in return. And always, Miss Ruth was different with her grandson than she was with Louisa and her brother, Charles, when they were infants and young toddlers. Harsher. He has to learn strict obedience, she said many times, so he can protect himself. One evening, little Samuel grabbed a shiny metal cup from the table and spilled its contents onto the floor. Ruth slapped his hand hard, and when he cried out, Louisa nearly shouted, *Don't,* before she remembered her place. "He's only one year old," she whispered instead, and she took his hand into her own, and kissed it.

Ruth left him there, cuddling into his mother's lap. "You ain't doing him no good," she said, her eyes shining with rage – as if she wanted to slap the woman more than the child. Then closed exhausted eyes and a slack mouth replaced the shining rage. She turned her back, ran her hands through her thick, dark hair and adjusted some of the pins. She sighed audibly, murmuring, *Lord, have mercy.*

Looking at the straight back and square shoulders, Louisa realized Miss Ruth might still be a beautiful woman for all her forty-five years if her face were not aged by loss and overwork. In the uncomfortable silence, her eyes glued to Ruth's back, she watched for the slightest sign of its bending and reminded herself of the details of Ruth's story as Samuel had recounted it to her. Five children, the first born when she was fifteen; the last, Samuel, when she was twenty-one, two years older than Louisa is now. The eldest caught after attempting to lead five slaves in an escape, too valuable to kill, sold as far away as possible – to a cotton grower all the way in Mississippi, it was said. The next two, also boys, each one sold for a good price as soon as he made fourteen years. That made four sons lost, including Samuel.

The next thought came fast, leaping over connection. Mr. Henry's voice – *Samuel's father sold because her father was jealous.* Four sons lost made four children, not five. A girl with a familiar face, Louisa herself not more than four years old, the older girl so short she was often taken to be the younger when they were found playing together in the yard. A girl named Lina with a long, slender neck, neat braids, a narrow mouth, a familiar face. Sounds of crying filled Louisa's ears – her own crying – she is covering her ears with her hands, pleading – *Daddy, Daddy* – but he is pushing her away, shouting at Ruth to shut the child up as a wagon full of people drives out of the yard. The girl with the familiar face is in the wagon. Louisa is hiding her face in Ruth's body, but she feels the body bending, almost falling. Someone pulls her away, and the next thing she knows Ruth is gone and it is Emma holding her. She's in Emma's arms, shouting and crying. The girl with the familiar face is gone, but Samuel's face is there, somewhere, sitting nearby, and the anguish he must have felt then suddenly raced through Louisa's body. In Ruth's cabin, staring at her turned back, Louisa almost dropped her child.

"Lina," she said in a low voice, remembering what she had not been able to remember before, wanting and not wanting Miss

Ruth to hear.

With her back still turned, Ruth said, "Melina. We called her Melina after a lady came to sing in town, then right here, in the House, come all the way from a place sound like grease. We listened out in the yard and her voice was so loud and strong we could hear it, and we got a glimpse of her too. She had black hair, and kind of light brown skin, not so different from some of ours. So when I had the baby I named her for the singer, Melina. They called her Lina, trying to make it simple like they do. He sold her. We ain't never seen nor heard tell of her again."

Now Ruth's back was comforting. Louisa was afraid she would turn around and read her face – see that she knew, now, who she, Louisa, was. But she was not ready to say the words out loud yet, not sure at all what Ruth's response would be if she did. Ruth's daughter and three sons sold. Only one child left to try to protect and now he was dead, and Louisa was to blame somehow for all of it, she was to blame. She felt Ruth's hatred so strong a cry came out with the intake of her breath. She was remembering the years of demands and unapologetic authority when she was young enough to be Miss Ruth's child, calling her Ruthie, while she was called Miss Louisa, ignorant until recently of even the small signs of respect the young Negroes afford the older ones to counter the many humiliations of daily life.They stepped aside if an older person came toward them on the path. They said Miss Ruth instead of Ruth, and never Ruthie. Ruth's coldness toward her, the absence of the old affection that used to seem so natural and sincere, was inevitable, maybe even right. She tried to imagine how she would feel in Ruth's place – grief-stricken, enraged, and, perhaps in even worse moments, relieved to be alive when so many, including her son, were gone.

Yet, Louisa was angry too. It was *not* her fault. She was *not* wholly to blame. Samuel *did* love her. She hadn't really known the truth about her father, and about Lina who they call Melina, not really, she had been too protected, too young. Resentment and remorse mixed within her, almost made her cry out again. She felt her very individuality, her being at its core, wiped out by the color of her skin. As soon as she named the feeling she knew that was how Miss Ruth felt every day, how her own son would be forced to feel, how Samuel felt, why he never spoke to her about his sister – and hers. To herself, then, she silently said the words. *The mother of a slave. The sister of a slave.* She marveled again that he had been able to love her at all, and she feared– the worst fear – that her son would not.

Miss Ruth remained standing rigidly by the window for some time, then slowly she turned around. "You believe you can save that child, or even keep him here, and I don't blame you, Louisa, cause you white. You don't know no better. But you can't keep him. He'll be sold, and I'm the one's got to prepare him for it. And then, " she paused for a long moment, breathed heavily, and added with a deadly calm, "I'll have nothing. Nothing left at all."

Louisa remembered the time she had tried to tell Samuel about feeling like nothing, and she wondered if Miss Ruth would be able to understand as he did not, if when she said *I'll have nothing,* she also meant in some way, *I'll be nothing;* if the double nothing – one from outside and the other from inside – is special to women, even women with lives as different as Miss Ruth's and her own; or whether men felt it too, but it was too frightening to them even to form the words. She did not dare ask. She touched Samuel's cheeks, kissed his lips and his fingers and, swore to herself she would prove Miss Ruth wrong. She handed him back to his grandmother. She was white, but she would understand.

When she returned to her room it was with the intention of imagining plans for future escape, but her thoughts kept returning to the yard that day long ago, Ruth's body bending, almost falling; Melina and her familiar face. She stopped pacing and lay down after a while, but only after she let the new knowledge suffuse her, head to toe, and this time what she knew came to her clearly, in words, and she spoke them out loud. *I am Louisa Summers, nineteen years old, the mother and the sister of slaves.*

Now the dark which had been her greatest comfort when Samuel was alive became her enemy again. Even with her candles softly lighting the room, the black night outside seemed threatening. She knew this feeling well, remembered it from earliest childhood when Eliza had just died and she was turning four. Now the feeling was just the same. The night itself did not scare her in any reasonable way. She feared no intruders, no sudden hurricane or ghost. Rather, it was something about the darkness itself. A darkness within, hiding frightening possibilities. Some long forgotten thought or pattern of memories, perhaps, ones she dared not coax into clarity with image or word. Or else it was not exactly either of these, not the darkness, not the lost memories, but something more diffuse, a kind of panic with no specific object, as if the entire world was dangerous, and to her especially. The darkness would swallow her. Would be inside of her, and there, inside, she would be as empty as the night sky seemed to be when no star or cloud alleviated the blackness. She required another soul to be right near her, in the room with her, for there to be any relief, and that was not to be. The aloneness was absolute, as if she did not exist at all among other living beings, as if no one knew or remembered, or cared about her existence, as if she were buried alive with her dead mother as for years she had wished to be, indulging in the paradoxical reverie that by being with her, dead, she could somehow bring her back to life.

She lit a second candle, reached for a sheet of paper and her pen in a rush, and wrote four words: *I will save Samuel.* Then she lay down and fixed her gaze on the flame. Hours later, when the first light of dawn entered the room, she knew she had slept and that she had dreamed.

She was walking to Miss Ruth's shack from the house. The night was dark, yet the very darkness she feared seemed protective, as it enabled her to visit her child. She noticed the blackness as if it were a thing - no moon, no star or cloud – and yet it seemed to have a shape, oval and finite. Then suddenly the blackness became white, frightening and blinding and without any shadow of comfort. As if the entire world had become a world of ice, and she was lost within it. She could not find the path to the shack. She felt cold. The ice was so white and so blinding she could no longer see her own hands when she held them up before her face. All she could see of herself was her black shawl and dress, and she began to tear at the cloth, ripping it to shreds, as if she was compelled to expose her nakedness to the cold.

She awakened with the sound of Miss Ruth's angry words in her mind, relieved by the gray dawn breaking through the window. She had never had this dream before, but she felt she would have it again, that like the empty darkness that had always threatened to swallow her, the whiteness that threatened to obliterate her was at once outside her and rooted within her deepest soul.

Chapter 25

She woke in a mood like the minus tides when the water is
so shallow, calm and translucent that walking over the flats in
bare feet you can see the life usually hidden from view: tiny
scurrying spiders, white shelled clams with their pulsing gray
life oozing through the slit, tightly locked oyster shells, their
succulent inhabitants protected by the hardest shields in the sea,
hundreds of tiny fish in the tide pools, and skinny brown worms
where the mud has dried in the sun. It had been some weeks since
the white dream, many days since she'd written down her
thoughts or transcribed passages from her readings. Perhaps her
mind was resting from its long preoccupations. Perhaps while it
seemed to be resting things were happening beneath her awareness, just as life goes on at the bottom under the flood tide of the
winter sea. She could not say why things seemed clearer that day
than ordinarily, but she knew what she witnessed was not new,
only that, as before, she had long been blind to something that
on that day she could see.

Walking across the yard toward the road, she came upon her
cousin's two children playing with Charles's son and daughter,
all of them between the ages of five and ten. She saw instantly,
they were playing a game with little Samuel who was not much
more than a toddler, not yet aware of the realities that would very
soon become as well-known to him as the cabin where he and
his grandmother lived. He was dressed in an old coat that dragged
on the ground behind him, and a bent straw hat, obviously cast
in some sort of theater game as an old man. Much too young to
understand what was happening and delighted, as any child might
be, to have older children (unknown to him, his cousins) playing
with him, he did as he was told. And as Louisa came closer she

194

saw what he was being told to do. He bent over and pulled down his pants. Then each child smacked his backside, laughing at him, calling him "old nigger" as they did so.

Her horror was three-fold. To see the child forced to humiliate himself for the sport of older children. To realize, also, that he was made to pretend to be an old man – an old slave – and they, the young masters, were punishing him for some infraction, and shouting "you stupid slave" as they slapped him, though not hard enough to make him cry and ruin their game. The hatred and contempt the white children had already been poisoned by was unmistakable and frightening. And third – the worst part – she knew her son would be subject to real humiliations and physical dangers all his life, not so different from the sort he was play-acting on the road.

Just as she was about to approach the children and stop the game, Miss Ruth walked up from the other direction with the same purpose. She bent down and adjusted Samuel's clothes, took off the hat and coat and picked him up, telling the others to get along. But she spoke to them politely, calling them "Master" and "Miss" as if she were not old enough to be their grandmother. The eldest boy, Charles Jr., turned on her and kicked her leg, saying, in a tone much like his father used to his slaves, "Get on with you, Ruthie, and take that baby nigger with you, only watch your manners or I'll tell my father on you." His younger cousin, still softened by his affection for Miss Ruth, who had cared for him since birth, looked frightened, but she reassured him with a pat on his back and turned away. Her only reaction to Charles Jr. was to nod her head in a gesture of obedience, and watching, Louisa knew she did it for Samuel's sake, so as not to risk being separated from him through temporary punishment or permanent sale. Horrified and helpless, she too feared the power of her father and brother, but her ignorance of Ruth's true feelings toward her was almost as disturbing as her hatred of her family of blood. Would Ruth, in such a moment, view Louisa as a silent ally, or, like Nat Turner and his followers, as another white-skinned devil whose life should be extinguished without regret? And if such hatred were the inevitable consequence of this evil system in

195

which family ties were betrayed with whips and bills of sale, in which children of five and six and ten years old felt it permissible to practice such disdainful cruelties on others, what sort of rage or terror, she wondered, must be mirrored in the whites, including herself?

These thoughts and questions plagued her. The image of her child's body exposed to the slaps of white children rooted in her mind like a devouring weed. Nothing near it could grow. It spread. A splitting headache, nausea, and a sharp persistent pain in her abdomen send her to bed, but not to rest, for along with increasing awareness, came the knowledge that at some point in the near future, her father would get rid of the child that was, to him, a family disgrace. The right moment, and the offer, would come, and Samuel would be sold.

Every morning, then again in the afternoon, before she slept, or when she woke in the middle of the night, she wrote, words now the place where she felt confident of her existence and the medium through which she was faithful to her goals. The scene she encountered on the path was like a trap door, for in the aftermath her fears for Samuel's future, Miss Ruth's furious stoicism, and her own cowardice engulfed her like an oceanic undertow ripping through the bay. She encountered in herself a weakness so fluid and unbounded it threatened to spread out into a kind of madness with no climax and no slow healing, no ebb and flow, only the relentless deeps, as if the bay had ceased its rhythmic alterations between deep and shallow waters and remained at flood tide for two full years. For all that time she lived at a constant edge of fear, except when her anxieties were suppressed by a melancholy so paralyzing she longed for death, and only Samuel's life prevented her from turning that longing into a reality. Except for him, she had little interest in anything outside herself, despair of action and transformation having replaced her hopes. She continued her studies, but half-heartedly, losing her concentration, forgetting what she learned the day before. Instead, she was morbidly fascinated by every feeling, every change in her mood, every nightmare and occasional hopeful dream. She described every tiny step in her struggle, so that, looking back, when she finally reached a break in it, it seemed she did almost nothing for two years but write about her internal life, except for the one precious evening every few weeks when the opportunity arose – the family gone for the evening, an especially heavy rain – and she was able to visit the slave quarter where, for a few moments, a half hour, once an entire evening into nearly dawn, she was with her child.

Not only her vows keep her from visiting him more often, but the strong advice of Miss Ruth who believed it would only hurt him to become attached to or even to know her as his mother. Louisa held in her anger at Ruth, because she could not argue with her wisdom, but here, too, conflicting feelings plummeted through her like chaotic rip tides – old habits of seeing the older woman as her slave, someone who should obey and not give orders, vying with the present reality of Ruth's position in Samuel's life, her knowledge of how to raise a slave who – Louisa remembered Samuel's words – must somehow also be assured he is a good child, a good boy like any other. So Louisa treated her son as a friend might, offering him moments of tenderness, then forcing herself to leave him - though everything within her wanted to take him, brave the bay and its surrounding marshes, find their way somehow to some other place.

Despite her broken down state, she was able to construct and adhere to the most elaborate system of lies to fool her white family. To them, she easily pretended she was recovering from the "madness" of her liaison with a slave by willingly submitting to the punishment of isolation and the quiet work of sewing clothes and mending bed linens for the house, it being as common for a woman to seek redemption in solitude as it was inconceivable for her to be seeking a personal transformation in intellectual discipline and confrontation with her own fears. No one noticed the long period of her depression as long as her clothes were clean and her hair fixed. No one showed any interest in what she did during the days she remained alone. No one, except a young slave who brought her food, came into her room.

One afternoon, at a formal family dinner of the sort she began to attend periodically on holidays and special occasions, her brother sat next to her at the table. With an expression of affection she had not seen in him for years, he shocked her by asking, "How are you Louisa? I mean sincerely, how are you feeling now?"

She looked into his handsome face, his wide mouth reminding her of their mother, his eyes a clear blue like their father's, but vacant somehow, as if something essential had been plucked from them, and remembered him as a boy of thirteen. He had been caught doing something prohibited, told to strip to the waist and turn his back to their father who administered five hard lashes with a leather thong. He cried that night as Aunt Emma and Miss Ruth applied salve to the cuts while Louisa, who was only five, watched from the doorway. When Samuel was beaten for his teaching, before the iron mask was lowered onto his face, it was Charles who wielded the whip, his expression one of deep hatred mixed with an awful pleasure that made Louisa remember her father's smile. It was Charles, as much as their father, from whom she separated herself now, much preferring to spend long days and nights locked in a room with its large window facing the fields and a view of the barn. It was Charles she feared might discover her visits to Miss Ruth, Charles who seemed to treat her with an attentive hatred that made her father's cold indifference seem benign. More than once, she saw him looking at little Samuel when he passed holding Miss Ruth's hand. She knew he meant to sell him, and as she listened to his brotherly tone at the table, a sharp and lucid anger replaced her depression, at least for a time.

"I'm stronger each day," Louisa said with a cunning that reminded her of Harriet. "I feel very sorry for all the grief I've brought to everyone. I am grateful my child was allowed to live." She looked down, managing the words only for Samuel's sake, protecting his life her only goal.

Charles lifted his glass and sipped his wine, but she saw hatred replace the momentary affection behind his smile, felt it in his fingers resting for a moment on her own. From observing the Negroes she learned to control and adjust her tone of voice, to convey a calm she did not feel, to remain silent when her emotions were so intense she could hear her stomach growl as if in hunger, or when her anger flared so suddenly that a piercing current cut across her forehead from temple to temple. When she felt like shouting or slapping someone's face, she learned to smile. She smiled at her brother, now.

Once, she asked Miss Ruth how you learn to keep it up over time without screaming in rage or losing yourself somewhere too far inside to find again. "You just do," Ruth said in a clipped tone that meant she had no intention of elaborating. And the silence between them covering far too much feeling to acknowledge, let alone express, stretched like something solid around them and within each of them until it was so thick, oppressive, and impenetrable that Louisa nearly ran out into the cool night, prematurely ending her precious minutes with Samuel.

After two years and two months, she'd honed a capacity for lying in public while in private writing as honestly as she could about what she observed, heard, and felt. She'd made sixty-three visits to Samuel in Miss Ruth's shack and noted each one in her journal by number, followed by one or two phrases of description: *Caressed his beloved flesh. The softness of his fingers. He laughed at a funny face I made.* Number 63 noted: *His fears are growing, and his carefulness. I asked him which toy he wanted, a clothespin doll I'd made or a small red ball I found in the yard, and instead of choosing he said warily, which do you want to give me, Miss Louisa?* Despite the obvious dangers, she kept up her journal, the only sustenance she possessed. She hid the now worn book as carefully as she hid the materials she continued to receive from Mr. Henry, and she retrieved it from its hiding place only late at night, when she saw the lights in the main house had been extinguished, or when everyone was gone from home.

Finally, she felt, or decided, a new time had begun. One by one she ripped out the pages that recorded the meticulous and incremental steps of her inner journey, seeing in them no value for others and only a record of shame for herself. Reading them over, she was amazed by the blessing of the passing of time, how even misery included its own routine, how routine somehow got you through. While she learned to present a mask to her family that would ensure her privacy; while she learned to endure a distance from her beloved child marked not only by a few acres of land but by social relations so powerful and strict she could not even reveal herself to him as his mother; while between bouts of what she had come to call madness, she'd maintained a strict effort to learn what the history and contours of those social relations were and had been; she found she had learned and retained more than she supposed. She thought about burning the pages narrating her breakdown, but in the end she folded them into thirds and pasted them to the back cover of the journal, thinking perhaps she might need a reminder some day, if and when extreme loss threatened again.

Since Samuel's death, new habits had formed that seemed increasingly her own. She had become more like Samuel, she hoped – strategic, disciplined, secretive, able to contain her passions and bide her time. And sometimes she wondered if he would love her more or less if he knew her as she was now, as she was attempting to be.

Chapter 26

A night in late summer, leaves and branches very still, the breezes of early September that will chill the bay are just beginning every so often to move through the yard. Thick beds of white Queen Anne's lace are slightly bent from the heat of the sun. Yet, there is a lifting of solid heat once the sun goes down.

Louisa wore a white cotton shawl over her blue dress, the knitted pattern mirroring the Queen Anne's lace she loved to walk through near the shore. She was sitting at the table with Miss Ruth and Mr. Henry for a while, after Samuel had fallen asleep. She admired Mr. Henry above all others now, the sense of him as "old Henry," her father's churlish but competent slave, as far from her perception as her old image of Miss Ruth as an obedient servant with few feelings of her own. For nearly three years she'd been reading the materials Mr. Henry somehow kept delivering to her room, sometimes wrapped in a dinner napkin, sometimes hidden beneath a long skirt, sometimes left under a certain board in the floor. She must have asked him a thousand questions, must have wearied him almost to tears at times with her slow and painstaking mastery of the history, her desire to know every organization working for freedom now and in times past. Still, she was afraid that her weaknesses might cause him to worry that he'd placed his faith where it might not be deserved.

"I don't understand," she confessed, leaning forward on her elbows on the now cleared table, "how the slaves can keep up their hopes for escape with such powerful forces ranged against them."

Mr. Henry brought his two large and heavily creased hands together, resting them on the old wood. He looked down at them then up at Louisa for a long moment, as if he was deciding something. Slowly, he stroked his white beard then ran one palm over his thick hair, pulling it back from his large forehead.

"I come from Jones County down in North Carolina," he said. "Sold here when I was just fifteen. Left my mother, two brothers, and one half sister behind. I can still see their faces watching me the day I was led away in chains. Saw my younger brother put his arm around my mother and I moved my lips in her direction, trying to say some kind of way – I love you Mama. I think she got my meaning cause I saw her sway and nearly fall. When I come here I fell into a long despair, did my work, but didn't much care if I lived or died. It was Ruth's husband, Samuel's father, who told me – You can't stay down there much longer, friend, or you'll never come out again. And he began to teach me to read and write. When he got sold – because your father couldn't abide Ruth's love for him – I vowed to teach his son what he taught me. Now that son is dead, and his child, little Samuel here, is next in line. If I didn't believe I could live long enough to see him free, I might as well have wished my own mama dead when I last saw her standing on the path. Because her life wouldn't be worth a thing in that case. We chained together, Louisa. You understand?"

The easy fluidity of his language was far more familiar to her by now than the quick phrases and clumsy words she had grown up hearing from him, as well as from the other slaves. His words suggested a faith more brave than any she had ever witnessed; or they represented a denial of reality as any madness she had recently known. She felt proud that her son was heir to this legacy, and terrified for him, too. But her feelings also included a surprising happiness. Mr. Henry had called her Louisa, dropping the *Miss,* as if she belonged with them, too.

Then, in the following week, two events occurred that marked the end of something and signaled something new. Louisa had been collecting her mending basket from the house when she overheard her father and Harriet talking of a good offer to buy some slaves, including some children, money that would finance the purchase of needed farm implements and a team of plow horses. She heard something new in their tone, something unlike her father's indifference to human life or her brother's hatred for it – something that was neither of these but a tone more like interest, genuine and wholehearted interest in the business at hand; so she knew that sooner, rather than later, Samuel would be sold. Even though her father had sold at least one, probably more than one child of his own; even though she knew half siblings who were master and slave to each other on neighboring farms; even though she grieved, now, for the sister she would never know; she had managed to deceive herself again. She had known. And she had denied it again. She was disgusted by her capacity for blindness. She felt a rage so murderous and impotent she lost track of where she was. Everything around her became suddenly unfamiliar, and she recognized only Ruth, who, having appeared from somewhere, led her back to her room after she had begun asking foolish questions, like whose house was she in, and where was the slave Samuel – because she needed him to spell something for her. She felt Miss Ruth's hands on her body, loosening her bodice, removing her skirt and shoes, a touch that went as far back as Louisa's own life. She clung to Ruth, and whispered, "I love you, I'm sorry, I love you."

Ruth held her. She rocked her for a few minutes, laid her down gently on the bed, pulled a pillow under her neck and shoulders, another one under her head. But she never said a word, nor did she ever meet Louisa's eyes. When she left to return to her work, Louisa vomited many times, onto the floor and bed sheets, as if she were emptying the entire contents of her body – the smell dank, the taste more bitter than any she had ever known. When it was done, she lay back in a purged stupor, exhausted in body and mind, the emptiness a great relief.

Hours later, she awoke in the dark, ashamed, confused, and disgusted by the dampness and the smell, but with her memory restored. Her first thought was the recollection of the reality and manner of Samuel's death, and she was afraid to return to sleep. But neither her mind nor her body could resist the escape from consciousness, and once again she dreamed the white dream.

Two nights later, when she visited Samuel, she told Miss Ruth about the conversation she had overheard. "We must do something," she said, but Ruth didn't answer, only leaned on the table and sat down heavily in a chair. To fill the silence and assuage her own discomfort, Louisa recounted the dream as she held her child in her lap.

"This time I was walking from my room to your place here," she said, "when the black night turned into the white blindness. And this time even my dress wasn't dark. I couldn't see any part of myself, and I began calling for you and Samuel but no sound came out of my mouth. I woke as usual with my head burning, as if I had a fever."

Ruth touched Louisa's hair and face as if she were still caring for a child. Her words were harsh, but her voice soft. "You're weak, Louisa," she said, "and you'd best find some strength some place cause bad thing's comin."

Samuel's eyes were wide. He looked from Ruth to Louisa, quickly back to Ruth again. "Tell the white dream again, Miss Louisa," he begged.

Louisa's throat constricted as it did each time her son called her the name that masked their true relation, yet which he had to believe in for his own protection. "No more dreams tonight," she managed to say, her lips against his hair muffling the shakiness in her voice. She would never cry in front of Miss Ruth, risking her anger, provoking her pity and disdain, or opening up the chasm that in the last two years Louisa had learned to watch out for and hide from everyone's view, where her need for love widened and gaped. She knew now she possessed a treacherous timidity and tendency to despise herself, inherited, no doubt, from her mother; but somehow the part of her that knew it had separated from the part of her that felt it, and she knew she felt anger too, harder to face than timidity, toward the people she wanted so to please.

She had battled the voices of father, brother, aunt, and, much worse, the voices of Miss Ruth and the other slaves she had come to respect and rely on. On one side, she was accused of treachery, on the other of cowardice. In both, she was the primary cause of

Samuel's death and all the misery that had followed, not yet completed in its course. Only in these many months of continual inward searching, of digging down into the muddy bottom of her fears, had she come to see those voices were partly her own, her own complicity giving them strength and resilience. She was culpable in the events that led to Samuel's death; Louisa knew that and she would have to live with it until the day she died. But she would not forget how he looked when he held her, how his fingers moved lovingly up and down her spine, how he loved the body parts he named. She would not forget their happiness or diminish, as was the custom of even sympathetic whites when describing Negroes, the force of Samuel's own will.

The second event that signaled the end of one period and the beginning of another was a letter received from Emma, brought to Louisa secretly by the same brave soul who often brought the periodicals and pamphlets acquainting her with the world beyond the town. Emma was living in Philadelphia, she wrote, in a community of Quakers and abolitionists. She hinted she was involved in the dangerous, clandestine work of aiding slaves in their escape to northern free states and Canada. Louisa's own escape to join her – for that is what she knew instantly she must do – would have to be carefully planned and secretive as well, for somehow she must find a way to take Samuel with her. There was not a moment to waste. On the other hand, such planning would take time and the quality of patience she had learned to admire in Miss Ruth and Mr. Henry. *A disciplined patience is the twin of courage and the cousin of hope,* she wrote.

To resist precipitous word or action while she waited and planned, she determined to focus even more fully on her studies. She had become acquainted with herself in ways she may not have wished to know but which illuminated her weaknesses sufficiently to show her how to increase her strength. She read her materials over and over, searching for ideals on which to model her self. As often as possible, she continued her visits to Samuel and Miss Ruth, now almost always including Mr. Henry who, she was sure, could read her thoughts as she contemplated her plans. She tried to pay strict attention to his formal teachings while also observing him closely, seeking to comprehend the capacities human beings develop to resist tyranny from the outside and the treacherous alliances to those tyrannies that inevitably take root within. She forced herself to remember her father's slaps and probing hands, and her own repulsive, responsive smile. She forced herself to remember her son, then not much more than a baby, innocently capitulating with his own humiliation for the benefit of what he thought was love. He was now approaching five and was already imbued with more control of his emotions and ability to strategize than his mother possessed.

A few days before, she had seen him standing by Miss Ruth, who was hanging newly washed sheets on a line. He was handing her the clothespins from a large canvas bag when Harriet approached and accidentally knocked over the basket that held nine or ten clean, wet sheets, each one rolled up, waiting to be snapped out flat in the wind and hung on the line. When the basket tipped over, all the sheets rolled onto the dirt and would clearly require a new washing, a task that would take several hours at least. Miss Ruth sighed heavily and grimaced. Samuel put down his clothespin and watched intently while Louisa walked over, bent down, and began helping Miss Ruth pick up the sheets and shake off the dirt. Suddenly, Harriet pulled her up straight by her sleeve. "The nigger can do it, Louisa. Just because you're estranged from us doesn't make you a slave. Come back to the house," she said.

"Just because she's a slave doesn't mean she doesn't get tired," Louisa said, and she bent down to get another dirty sheet from the ground.

Harriet looked disdainfully at Louisa, at Ruth and the sheets, then at Samuel. His face was impassive, but his eyes darted from one white woman to the other and then back to his grandmother. He walked over to Louisa before Ruth could hold him back and pulled her by the skirt. "I can pick em up, Miss Louisa," he said, and gathering them into his arms, he dumped them into the basket as fast as he could. "Come on, Grandmama," he said, and pulled Miss Ruth away with one hand, dragging the basket with the other, before anyone could think to stop him. As they walked away toward the house, he looked back at Louisa with awareness well beyond his years, then at Harriet with a movement of his little chin she could interpret only as a nod of respect. He had seen the entire situation clearly and knew what had to be done. Louisa wished he had the openness and spontaneity of a child with an easier life, but she was grateful for Miss Ruth's training, that she could instill such strength in one so little and so young. She had learned to notice the distance and hardness, at least on the surface, in the slave children, but she had begun to see that some possessed a resilience that enabled a love of life to flourish in the midst of death and constant tragedy, and remembered Samuel's words about his mother. The lucky ones had been enabled to value themselves as well. Her son's character had been shaped in a way that would make it more likely for him to survive.

She watched the way white children were treated too, her own nephew and nieces. She remembered Charles when he was still sweet and open-hearted, and she saw the effects of cruelty toward children on their future efficiency as cruel masters themselves. If your only goal for children's character is that they be obedient, how better to achieve this end than with physical intimidation; just as if obedience of slaves is your primary aim, which it is and must be if the work of the plantation is to continue, you must inevitably rely on the same form of intimidation with them. But she could not help feeling pity for Charles, too, the way early softness had been beaten out of him, brutality sharply honed. And once again, she saw the terrible alternatives – her father's indifference to human pain and her brother's pleasure in it. Most of the white men, and women too, in this generation were beyond redemption, she thought. Worse, she saw their own ruin would not be limited to their individual lives. No – a cruel and vicious race of people were in the making who would continue to be blind to the reality that others, with skins darker than their own, possessed the same human feelings as themselves and therefore the same rights. This simple and evident truth would be buried by the illusion of purity and reinforced by savage greed. It was like waiting for a September hurricane, still out at sea but destined to hit land and destroy.

She heard Samuel's voice again, words he'd never actually said. *I didn't know we were waiting, Louisa,* he said with a laugh covering unutterable grief. *I thought the ruin was already here, with us right now.* She heard his voice as if he were standing right next to her, yet as if he were inside her too. As if his voice had become a part of her voice. It was a way of keeping him, she supposed, and at the same time a way of changing herself. What human gifts would be needed to counter the perpetuation of this evil? What human capacities might resist the evil now and its repetition down future generations? And what part might she play in this resistance? How, she began to ask herself daily, might she live the remainder of her life to help nourish these surely possible gifts and capacities into a blossoming, even if only within a few open and imaginative souls?

She wrote careful notes of everything she learned during her now weekly lessons with Mr. Henry. Through reverie, sketches and memories spoken out loud to herself, she focused on Emma. She transcribed short biographies into her notebook of women like Sarah and Angelina Grimke, white women from "good Southern families," whose passion for justice and vision of human equality enabled them to leave home and join the abolitionist fight at the risk of their own lives. Often her pen stopped as she wrote their stories, and she became lost in thinking, why them and not so many others?

"I stand before you as a moral being," Angelina Grimke had written, "and as a moral being I feel I owe it to the suffering slave and to the deluded master, to my country and to the world to do all that I can to overturn a system of complicated crimes, built upon broken hearts and prostrate bodies . . . of my sisters in bonds..."

Was it some individual gift of insight, or compassion, some influence that enabled them to face, and know, and act on what so many others denied? Was there some dramatic event that altered everything in its path? She recognized in their writings her very early hatred for the system into which she had been born, and she realized that if she did not yet possess their courage, she could begin to feel it on its way.

Questions of origins fascinated her as always, but she resisted the inclination to ponder the causes of the principles and bravery of such fighters and forced her mind back to the facts of history – recording dates, individuals, organizations resisting slavery since its inception in her home state and town two hundred years before. She reminded herself, through notes and lists and time lines, of Gabriel Prosser, Denmark Vesey, David Walker, and the great Harriet Tubman they called Moses. She recounted what she'd read of the recent trial of Cinque of the Amistad, with its radical assertion, written in newspaper accounts and talked about with contempt and fear, or with admiration and conviction, that Africans are human beings with hearts and minds and rights the same as Europeans or white Americans.

Let no one ever claim that these ideas were not in the journals of this time, in our conversations in parlors and around dinner tables, available to all with ears to listen, their implications thick in the very air we breathe, she wrote.

She learned of the hypocritical Colonization Societies that would send all Negroes to Africa – supposedly as an act of liberation, but reeking of a more insidious belief that the inequality of races and the inferiority of Africans could never be overcome. She learned from Emma's few letters of how women's anti-slavery societies were allied with free Negro men and women in the North to work to liberate more people from the hateful system. She learned about William Still and the Vigilance Committees that searched for escaped slaves and helped them on their way. She committed his address in Philadelphia to memory, imagined herself carrying Samuel, finding Still, finding Emma, somehow making her way to Canada, which she pictured as a land of broad fields, thick forests, newly built cities full of free thinkers from all over the world. She collected mailings which attempted to recruit white allies by describing the true realities of the slave system and read them over and over, as if she did not know the sins as intimately as she knew the rooms of her home or the path from her father's house to the slave quarter where all she loved in the world was now contained.

*Many deny these realities still, people we call "good hearted"
who nevertheless manage to close their eyes to the evil in which
so many of us thrive. I no longer call them good hearted, and
will not claim that virtue for myself until I find the strength to
pursue a path, in the words of the great William Lloyd Garrison,
"as harsh as truth, as uncompromising as justice."*

She wrote the words into her notebook and three times read
them out loud.

Chapter 27

She could look at the barn for long periods now, without the image of Samuel being tortured and killed taking on a physical reality that made it seem as if the horrific moment would last until the end of time. She remembered every moment of that day, but her body no longer responded as if it were happening right then. The image came; she knew Samuel was gone; she saw the barn again. What she would never forget, never allow to be dimmed by years, were the lessons that began for her in that moment and were still coming to consciousness even after all this time.

"As harsh as truth." She repeated the words out loud one night, watching the barn in the dark. She whispered them over and over, as if they were tattered sails she had to keep mending, strengthening with small tight stitches so they would last until she reached some long-awaited shore. She vowed to know reality for what it was without the comforting illusions by which human beings are so tempted, and she began to give up her belief in God. She was not blind to how religion could work for good as well as evil, nor did she disrespect those whose faith in one superior being seemed to inspire them spiritually and morally, to be brave and to do good. Mr. Henry was a devout Christian. He read his Bible in secret and drew from the story of Exodus not merely the courage to aid so many in their escape from bondage, but also an understanding of human frailty that enabled him to afford others less brave a certain paternal forgiveness that persuaded them, despite failures, to risk testing themselves, like the generations of ancient Hebrews, again and again. She found hours of unique peace in churches and knew ministers whose gentle temperaments saved children from harsh punishment, women from beatings, even slaves from sale. But there were other "men of God" as cruel as her father, who used passages from the Bible to justify the beating, selling and exploitation of other human beings for profit and pleasure.

The first time Samuel denied the existence of a god who would allow such cruelty as the system of slavery to go on for hundreds of years was soon after she had told him she was carrying their child. "What if there are other gods, like the ones in the stories Mama can remember old folks telling her about?" he had asked.

They had been standing in the back of the barn that night, and he whispered a tentative plan for escape that was never to be, for they would be discovered before the winter came. When she called on God's mercy and goodness to protect them, Samuel confessed. "I'm an unbeliever, Louisa. Maybe there's some spirit in this world unknown to us that enables goodness and mercy to follow us all the days of our lives," – he mocked the words – "but if there is, it don't belong to the Hebrew god of the Bible, and not even the redeemer," – the bitter tone again – "Jesus Christ."

She had been stirred by the formality and beauty of his language, even as she was frightened by what she felt then to be his blasphemy, a blasphemy that has now become her own. He described how he intended to cross one of the narrow tributaries of the Potomac that fed into the Bay, then stow away or be taken on by a sympathetic captain of one of the ships sailing up the Chesapeake. Once in Baltimore, he'd try to pass himself off as a free man, earning his keep in the shipyard until he could make his way on foot or find passage on the Railroad to Philadelphia where he'd heard some free blacks worked as oystermen, hauling daily catch for restaurants and fisheries lining the docks. He wished, he told her then, for the shallows of the eastern shore he'd been told about by Mr. Henry, who had seen that complex topography for himself when he was shipped there for several weeks of fishing and oystering after Samuel's father had been sold.

Louisa imagined the marshes, dense and silent and dark, a

blessing to a fugitive waiting for a boat to dock long enough for a swimmer to sneak aboard. And she remembered her childish love of the western shore where water and land intertwined in varieties of simple reciprocity, her pleasure in those even patterns that allowed her to play alone near the water when she was young. Samuel said he would have to wait until winter. Then, the water would overcome the land, making possible a safer hiding in the brush and among the trees. By then most of the boats for pleasure and fishing would have disappeared. He'd have to be prepared to risk snow, even floating ice, but the harsh weather would also enable him to wait more safely for the occasional conspirator who'd signed on to the dangerous work of taking runaways to Baltimore, or even as far as the Susquehanna. Eventually, he hoped to get all the way to Canada. He'd find a way to rescue his mother and his child, and then Louisa could run away to meet them in the faraway place where he'd settle them into a decent life.

She had been sitting by the window watching the barn for so long half the night has passed. A grayish blue light began to edge the horizon, yet the dome of the sky was still dark. It was a black night with no stars or moon, and the edge of light looked as if it had been painted – a swift streak between the dim gray land and the black sky. It was the sort of night that might have hidden some fugitive making his or her escape if luck and goodness allowed.

Except for little Samuel, whom she longed to claim soon, she was alone. This was her belief, her certainty, her strength. Watching the streak of light thicken bit by bit as she sat quite still leaning on her window sill, she welcomed the aloneness that once frightened her with childish terrors and vague anxieties in the dark. It was more than tolerable. It was comforting now. The voices that for so long pursued her solitude were mostly gone. In this new aloneness, with no one watching over her for good or ill, she could think of her mother and feel simple pity, for she saw Eliza as a frightened woman, her life cut short by spiritual and physical diseases generated by forces over which she had no control. Louisa possessed a realistic fear of her father and brother and took great care, therefore, in constructing her plans to escape them, but she knew an independence from them that was altogether new. And now, surprising herself with the clarity and definition of these thoughts which she somehow did not have to write down, she began to consider that her two year personal confession was perhaps not a shameful thing, but a worthy enterprise, and she was glad she had not destroyed those compromising but honest pages.

But she had little time now for the past. She knew without any doubt that her father would not shrink from including her child in his next odious plans. It was mid- November. She meant to use Samuel's lessons about the winter bay, and Mr. Henry's contacts, to escape with her son to her aunt in Philadelphia before the storms of January arrived.

On the last night of November, Louisa's father sent for her. He called her to his study and greeted her with a distant yet eager politeness, as he often did during these years when she had been through such storms of change within herself, while presenting only a cold self-containment to him. The more removed she was from him, the more genuinely cold her feelings, the more he seemed to feel comfortable in her presence. Charles stood near the door and said only her name in greeting: "Louisa."

She nodded in return. She waited. Then her father spoke. "I've completed a transaction for the selling of six slaves, including two children, for cash to purchase land. The sale has been settled outside of auction and the transference of property will take place at dawn." He smiled at her, as if expecting her relief, or pleasure, in return. Louisa's heart beat fast, for now she knew what this audience signified. This time, well schooled in the discipline that contains anguish and covers pain, she did not faint. She did not even move. She stared at him.

"Samuel is among them," he said, more distantly. "It will be better for him, and for us all. Not least," he adds, his expression softening again, "for you."

She begged only one time. "He is my child, Papa," she said in a tone almost too low to hear, compromising with her hatred

214

by using the name she hadn't used in nearly six years. Staring unflinchingly into his eyes, she made her futile, desperate plea: "Let me leave with him tonight, instead. Please."

For a moment, she thought she saw him soften again. His mouth loosened, and opened slightly, and in that instant she recalled long-buried images and half-forgotten scenes. The two of them in a small boat on the Chesapeake one summer, she sitting between his legs as he taught her to row. She remembered the feeling of his large hands covering hers as they pulled the oars together, looking around and seeing sunlight sparkle on his blond hair, shining so brightly on his spectacles she could not see his eyes for the glare. His hands on the reins of a horse the first time she learned to ride. The back of his lowered head, his rounded shoulders and the sound of his weeping as he knelt by her mother's bed when she died. Then the awful image of the beating, his cruel smile, her bare chest, and their growing estrangement since that time. The moment of rushing images passed, and when she looked up it was to receive the shock of his slap across her face. When she turned her head from the shock and the pain, she saw her brother smile.

"You're still a nigger's whore," her father said, his lips now a tight line in a clenched jaw. "Your *child*, as you call him, is my property. He's sold for good money. I was fool enough to think you'd returned to your senses, to take your place in our family again. I had brought myself to forgive you, Louisa. "

She saw the reality as clearly as the image she will always retain of Samuel's broken body being taken away like a sack of garbage. And the realism infused her with a new and sustaining calm. For a man who loved what he could control and hated what he could not, there were to be no consequences, in his mind, of the terrible events that had transformed her into a person he could no longer know. That was his invidious hope, or more likely an assumption he would not think to question. Their way of life would go on, he thought, as if an unpleasant disturbance had interfered. The offspring she had borne, her father's own grand-child, like Miss Ruth's children, one of whom was his own daughter, would be sold or kept as economics and their family's need for service dictated. The answer to *how* it all happens – such self-deception, such *belief* – still eluded her. *That* it happened, with audacious efficiency, was all she knew.

She rushed from the room and walked back and forth in the cold night, trying to clear her thoughts, one thought drowning all the others: I must take him away tonight. She ran to her room, packed a few necessities, a small blanket and the cough syrup she used to put herself to sleep during the worst nights, thinking she will have to keep Samuel quiet somehow. Then she rushed across the yard to Miss Ruth's shack. Ruth was standing in the room leaning heavily on a table as if she were about to collapse. Samuel had already been taken, of course – that is why her father called her to his study, a pretense of affection or respect. He was chained with the others in the barn where he was conceived. Louisa dropped her bag, ran outside again. Standing in the doorway of the barn, she saw him, his eyes frightened and staring, his little legs and arms shackled, his fate sealed. She stood in the yard all night, watching the barn. After a while Miss Ruth came out and wrapped a woolen blanket around her. Then she went back inside, but once Louisa looked around and saw Miss Ruth staring out her window at the yard. All night the women waited for the sound of the horses' hooves approaching, pulling the wagon that would take him away.

Chapter 28

It was a clear morning. The winter chill she had hoped would signal the time of her departure was in the air. Boats were scarce on the Chesapeake, only a few lone crabbers daring the winds to trap the few creatures not yet buried in the mud floor beneath the water where the rest would remain until spring. She thought she could smell a coming early snow.

Black, black eyes stared out helplessly as the child was bound and tied to the side of the wagon. He searched the yard until his eyes found his grandmother who looked at him squarely, unblinking, straight-backed, her hands clenched into tight fists, willing him and herself to be brave. He did not cry out. He had been prepared for this day, to exercise the control that might have been bravery, or else a terror so encompassing it found no sound or movement, but caused everything around it and within it to be still.

She was utterly still. She heard the whip crack on the horse's back, found an instant's sympathy in the eyes of the young man standing nearest Samuel who knew of her relation to him and, looking at her, blinked once slowly, as if to reassure her, or so she hoped: *I will watch over him; he will be my son;* then he quickly looked away. She was utterly still when the wind picked up and the carriage began to move, and at that moment the stillness seemed to infuse the atmosphere all around her so that although she knew the wagon moved, it seemed to stay in one place, like a large rock implanted there, and in the silent terrible stillness everything seemed to go white, like the whiteness of her dream, everything except Samuel with his tan shirt, brown hair and skin, his black eyes staring, as if refusing to relinquish something. She looked where he looked and, out of the blinding whiteness, she saw Miss Ruth's face and heard her voice, then Samuel's – *you're white, Louisa, you don't understand.* When she looked back to the road, he was gone.

Louisa would always see her father in her mind as she saw him that morning, folding his barbaric bill of sale and inserting it neatly into his breast pocket as the wagon holding Samuel pulled away. She vowed to remember him that way, obliterating horses, rowboats, and the vulnerability of his grief, until one of them was dead.

She wanted to be brave, for they were watching her – Miss Ruth, Mr. Henry, the others. She wanted to be stalwart and dignified, like them. But when she woke in her room she realized she must have fainted again, and she felt the familiar heavy weight of shame. Ruth was sitting by the bed looking at the window, a blank stare. Louisa reached for her hand and she let it be taken, let Louisa stroke her palm, her fingers, trace the edges of her nails, but all the time Ruth stared out the window at the barn, her mouth set in a tight line.

"Can we – is there – still– Mr. Henry said to hope . . . ." Louisa whispered fragments out of fast rising resignation.

"Time when hope is done," Ruth said.

In the next few days, Louisa learned one more terrible thing. When she saw her son sold and disappearing from her life, she experienced a devastation entirely new to her, yet she had seen many slaves sold, children of other mothers, husbands of wives, mothers of children left behind. And it was not only the natural feelings of maternal love that made her feel it differently when they took Samuel away. When the whiteness in her mind covered everything except his face, she had seen there was no difference between them marked by their difference in color. As if his skin did not make a difference as dramatic or significant as the other skins, as if his skin color were just that, skin color, and not a sign of a species different, however slightly, from herself. His skin color was not significantly different from hers at all, just a few shades darker, like the wet sand is darker than the dry. And in that moment of sameness, when she knew that a difference in skin shade covered a human heart and mind as close to her own as any in the world, she also knew that with all the others, the feeling of difference went as deep in her as in her father, or Harriet, or Charles. She had not escaped the perfidious barbarisms of her time. She had learned to love uncompromising justice, as Mr. Garrison said, but she had sworn as well to love his harsh truth. Even with her beloved Samuel, whom she called her husband now, she had retained a feeling of inequality that went beyond their stations in life, and therefore she had not fully appreciated the tragedy of his life.

Now she understood what he meant in the barn that day when he said – I am trapped in the wrong life. And she saw the ignorance and selfishness of her words: But this *is* your life, she had said.

Ignorant, because it implied his soul was not, like her own, essentially free, as if his life as a slave made sense in a way it never could to him unless his mind had been as shackled as his legs when he was punished for walking where he had no permission to walk, or his spirit as bounded as his neck when the iron collar was placed around it once, as if he were a wild animal, or the family dog. She grasped a truth that extended from that long ago time to mere months before, even weeks, when she'd been blinded by illusions that would never be possible for her again: that the interior constraints and anxieties all humans share, even if some are subject to extremities of fear and inhibition, belonged to another realm from the terror and imprisonment of those who are actually enslaved.

And selfish because of her inability to comprehend, as she could now, that in this life the whites had constructed here, love and freedom more often formed a tragic opposition than a natural and nourishing alliance, and that most often one could not choose a life that encompassed both. Samuel had not been denying his love for her by wanting to be some place else, but he realized, as many slaves had done before, that he would likely have to sacrifice love in order to be free. Perhaps she had not known him well enough to understand, until, face to face with her own powerlessness, she finally left childhood illusions behind. Perhaps it took years, not months, and devotion, not only passion, and extraordinary effort, not simply love and a good heart, to counter ingrained assumptions about skin color with feelings of true equality. With Miss Ruth she came closest to feeling the way she felt with her child – that they were simply two people, separated by age and experience, but kin in every other human way. And yet their experience was so vastly different, she knew Ruth would never feel the same about her.

Once more, she had the white dream, and this time though she walked through the white night as before, it was as if she could see the blackness at the edge of things. And everywhere she walked, there were crowds of people – strangers – pushing from behind her, blocking her way. She knew none of them. She seemed to be looking for her mother, and even though she knew in the dream that her mother was dead, she kept pushing through the crowds trying to find her, both frightened of and heading toward that black edge where the whiteness seemed to end. She awoke in a sweat. Had she found a way to act sooner, her child might have been saved, and time, once a good companion to her grief, seemed an enemy now: she had not acted sooner; just as Samuel's escape had been fatally delayed by events having little to do with him. She felt the weight of history, its power over and within them, and the weight of the double desolation she must now carry to have lost both mother and child. Then suddenly all of her thoughts were pushed away by a sharp, vivid memory of Samuel – how he had made her feel – a feeling that even now, with all she knew about guilt and shame, seemed to call out a truth she must never deny.

Fragments of thoughts – dark edges of memory – how she had never fit into this world, how sameness, not difference, had drawn her into that place with him, how she knew Samuel's skin was dark brown, but it was touch she was in touch with in the dark – in touch with his hands on her neck, her shoulders, her breasts, her legs pressed against his legs, the feel of his palms flat against her shoulder blades, then the backs of her thighs, as he pressed her to him, himself into her, whispering each part by its name. Her mind flooded with images far less specific than color, of all the times she knew she was somehow different, a girl who could not fit in, a woman who had learned to mask the difference, the not fitting, more adeptly than the girl, but it was still a mask, a mask so closely attached to her face it seemed to fit but it did not fit. Only when she felt him, a perfect fit inside her, did that sameness reflect the other less expressible sameness, and it was that feeling of sameness, some fragment retrieved of something lost she thought never to find, that caused her blood to race until all the world had funneled down to where her thighs parted to enable him to fit more deeply in.

Now, all of her thoughts had to be with finding her son. She had no idea to whom he was sold, whether to someone as near as Virginia or as far away as Texas, and she knew it would be nearly impossible to find out. Her father would keep the information from her. Harriet and the others would comply out of respect or fear. She would look for him and try to free him, but she knew now, that like so many other mothers, she would most likely fail. She began to comprehend the harsh truth of Miss Ruth's castigation. She had been blinded by her skin color and position into thinking she could easily have her way against history, succeed against the powerful, corrupt and systematic forces of men. Now, Miss Ruth was suffering through her final illness; its cause, no doubt, was one too many children dead or sold away.

Every day, Louisa sat by Ruth's bed waiting until she needed something. One afternoon, Ruth became agitated while dozing, tossing and turning as if from a bad dream. Louisa touched her forehead, trying to wake her, but she could not rouse her from her sleep, and when her agitation increased Louisa lay down next to her on the narrow bed and took the older woman into her arms. As she held her, trying to soothe her with soft maternal sounds, she became very aware of Ruth's body – first its frailty, the sharp protruding shoulder blades, her back, even her skull where premature age and illness had altered her hair to thin waves of nearly translucent white. She felt the fragile bones of Ruth's spine and hip, rested her finger tips on the tendons of what used to be muscular arms. She looked at the dark brown of Ruth's skin, saw her own pale hand on her, and felt how different they were again. She sighed heavily, feeling different, then the same, then different again, until she feared her truest self was as invisible to her as her body in her dream.

Chapter 29

Ruth awakened at that moment and looked up to see who was holding her. She stared into Louisa's eyes and whispered, "Who are you?"

Louisa, the young white girl answers, and says her name again several times, like repeating it will cause me to know something it don't seem like I want to know. But look like something in her face pleases me, as if my own lost one's face has returned to me like a pleasing shadow in this face, my own Melina they called Lina with eyes and a mouth like this girl's eyes and mouth, and I feel kind of relaxed as the white girl keep saying, it's Louisa, it's me, Louisa, like she wants more than anything else in the world for me to know her. And why? Because I held her and cared for her when she was a child? Because my last son, the one she killed, was her fool lover and his son my grandbaby gone too? Because she loved me for all I taught her, and for the ways she hurt my heart? Or only for these large hands with them old bony fingers, and the way my once nice thick hair used to curl around this shapely neck when the hair was pinned up and covered with a scarf? Or for the way she once heard me singing to myself about a chariot coming and she began to sing it and dance to it around and around the yard like it was a play song instead of one carrying dangerous meaning, nearly scaring the life out of me cause you never know what them white people are blind and deaf to and what they understand? She keep saying Louisa, a pretty white girl with light hair who tends me in these last days when I am nothing but all my grief and sorrow, all them leavings and dyings, mine again, mine forever, and no I don't know her, don't know who she is at all.

She closed her eyes again, whispered something muddled.

Louisa strained to hear but Ruth had returned to sleep.

Louisa traced slow fingers down Ruth's arms, noticed the sparse hairs, the various scars and blemishes, lingered on the hateful S, the raised scar of it oddly smooth, a dead and silky thing just above the tiny wrist bone, prominent in the near absence of flesh, down the long fingers with their heavy darkened knuckles, across the brittle, shapely fingernails. She held Ruth's hand and pushed at the loose skin, and finally that was all it was – skin. Then she pulled Ruth closer, and a word came to her mind that she would not allow to escape her lips. She wanted nothing more in the world than to be rocked, stroked and held, but she held the dying woman in her arms, rocking her, stroking her hair and back like she was her child.

Louisa tended Ruth every day. Each night she lay on the floor mat beside the bed and tried to sleep. She brought clear soup Ruth was less and less able or willing to eat, lifted her head to coax small spoonfuls between her dry and flaking lips. One time, just as Ruth lay back on the pillow, Louisa thought she heard the murmur, *thank you baby*, but she was not certain those were the words. She cleaned the bed linens and washed Ruth's increasingly skeletal body with warm water and comforting oils. Neither her father nor her brother would stop her now, for she had crossed over into a place where they either hardly noticed her or had ceased to care. Only Harriet watched her when she crossed the yard to the slave quarter, her eyes conveying a disappointment so fierce it merged with rage, as if something about Louisa pushed and threatened, some old identification of herself with Eliza, the weak sister, or with Emma, the good one, and without Louisa there would be a poisonous void.

Louisa turned away from her aunt's hatred quickly. Since everything had been taken from her, she had nothing left to fear.

Miss Ruth had been silent for three days. The sound of death began to rattle through her chest and throat like a sea storm making its relentless way to the shore. Soon she would die, and since no love any longer held Louisa to her father's house, she began to plan her journey to join Emma and the abolitionists in Philadelphia.

Chapter 30

In the late afternoon after the morning they buried Ruth, the day before she would leave her childhood home for the last time, Louisa walked down to the shore of the bay. Mr. Henry was there, and they exchanged a long look of sorrow and friendship. Her eyes filled up with tears, and she heard him make a soft sound. It was ebb tide, and cold, and thinking of how Samuel dreamed of waiting in this weather for the flood tide that might take him to freedom, almost losing her practiced calm, she knelt down to pay close attention to the swarming life in the tide pools, the abandoned and broken shells that lay half buried in the mud.

"She told him," Mr. Henry said.

Louisa stood up and looked around at him. Her mouth opened. She held her breath.

"Told him who you are, the day before they came for him. She knew they was comin so she told him five things," Mr. Henry said, watching the sky as it reflected and was reflected by the colors of the water, from shimmering turquoise to dark steel gray. "Told him not to forget the name of the place where he was born, his grandmama's name and my name. That's three. She told him his daddy was murdered and even that they chopped him up in pieces before he died. Four. And she told him who his mama was."

It was as if the flood tide had come suddenly, before you had the chance to adjust to the changes in the water's depth and speed, carrying the danger of drowning along with the promise of escape. Miss Ruth had not cared to give Louisa the comfort this knowledge would have brought. It was her grandson's life she valued, not the white woman who had birthed him and gotten his father killed. But as he grew, he would observe the whites around him enforcing and reinforcing the strict and sadistic divisions between themselves and the Negroes they kept enslaved, and he would have one way of being certain deep in his bones of their hypocrisy, the full extent of their lies about purity and their terror of great retaliation for great sin. Samuel's memory of her would fade with the years, Louisa knew. But now, knowing what he knew, she thought he might recall the color of her hair, or the shape of her chin, or a phrase of melody from a song she hummed putting him to sleep in her lap. Perhaps he would fuse her face with the faces of many other women he would know, or love, or lose. Ruth had given her a gift even if she hadn't meant to, and she had armored Samuel, hoping he would develop a combination of clarity and bravery that might enable him to escape the lies, and maybe even the land itself, and find a new life far from what they all knew as home. He would have to find a way to balance himself between the knowledge of sameness and the equally real knowledge of difference, each side encased in feelings of love and hate as thick and encrusted as the oyster shells his father knew how to pry open to get at the delicious pulsing flesh within. Between the two – the safety of the shell and the attraction of the raw flesh – he, like herself, his mother, would have to find the capacity to imagine his own freedom, and out of that unlikely and brilliant inspiration, to form the will to act.

"Thank you," she tried to say to Mr. Henry, but there was so much thanks to be given it came out as a low cry. She swallowed and said it again, this time clearly, and hoped he knew it was for everything. Then, for a swift second, he did what he had never done before. He laid his hand on her shoulder and left it there for a long moment, flesh against flesh, heart to heart.

Weakened knees bent, and she pretended to observe a scurrying hermit crab, to pull an oyster from its bed, to collect a perfect scallop shell. She thought of Samuel again, not of his broken body but of their perfect fit, of his sullen bravery and sacred hope. She tried to imagine his spirit somewhere, perhaps reborn, as she recalled some eastern religions held, in one of the broad-winged geese or wild swans she sometimes saw flying over the water at dawn.

Part Five:

New York State and
Norwalk, Connecticut
Winter and Spring, 1989

Chapter 31

For months after the day at the ocean she had spent with Hannah, and the night of Samantha's list of terrible things, Ami continues to write. There is no shape, no careful separation of chapters, no arc of slowly accumulating awareness in the series of notebooks piled on her desk. The story she is writing emerges and grows, sometimes in fragments, sometimes in isolated scenes, occasionally in sequences that approximate her notion of a story and seem worthy of the name. It is nothing like the organized memoir she had planned in response to Samantha's need. Time periods and tones of voice collide as they come to her or come out of her, some odd combination of personal memory and historical notes she barely understands. She writes through most of the winter. Then in early March, Ami Reed receives the call from her son telling her that Hannah Sokolov is dead.

Chapter 32

It would be a relief. There was no denying it. And close on the heels of the relief, guilt; nor was it hard to see where that came from. Maya had been dead for more than ten years, his father for longer, and he missed them both; will do so, he realized, until he was dead himself. Whenever Sam does something wonderful, reaches a new stage in her development, or when he is anxious about her unhappiness and anger, as he had been since the summer, he was permeated with regret.

Jake glanced into the mirror, checked Sam's face. She leaned against his mother in the back seat, but she stared out the side window with that expression of bereft rage he'd learned to dread in the past months. As for his mother, whose eye he'd caught in the mirror, she returned a look of coldness he knew was a cover for pain. Their last argument, the night of Hannah's death, was a bad one, worse because Corinne was part of it, even worse because Sam was there too. Just when he had allowed himself to hope for harmony, discord and conflict reigned.

Their fight wasn't about race, except that lately everything was.

His mother arrived soon after she learned of Hannah's death, wrapping her love, as usual, in layers of efficiency and decision. "Well, it's done," she said. "Let's make the calls. The funeral home. Aaron – he'll know a rabbi." Sam was curled up in a large armchair eating a thick sandwich. Ami took one look at her, then anxiously at Jake. "And then we'll go out to dinner," Ami added. She seemed confused, uncomfortable with her own gestures and words – yet they were so typical of her, he could

229

have written the script before she spoke. So something was wrong, and he didn't know what it was.

Then Corinne spoke vehemently. "No," she said, standing in the middle of the room. "We shouldn't do that. We shouldn't go out. We should stay here. Talk. The *shiva* the Jews do? I know it's supposed to come after the funeral, but we can do a version of it tonight. Not on boxes, or covering mirrors. I don't mean that. But we can eat here – I'll cook something. And you can tell me about her, Sam. You can tell us . . . ."

Sam looked up from her plate and interrupted Corinne, "I don't think you want to hear what's on my mind. But if you – " her voice was raised now – "but if you do, I've been reading the book Greatgram gave me, the one she was reading over and over all summer? It's about this white girl who has a baby with one of her father's slaves. And then of course, he was killed – but tortured horribly first, *cut up into pieces.*" She was breathless – almost screaming – then almost in a whisper, "what the fuck was she trying to do? What are white women always trying to do with black men?" She looked at his mother and then at him. Everyone looked down.

Ami whispered, "It's not always the main thing, Sam. It's not always what matters."

And Corinne again, "It's a different time, Ami. People are trying to reclaim ..."

But his mother had cut her off, "Claim what!?" She shouted the words. Her anger filled the room. She clutched the back of a chair, slapped it hard.

Corinne, in a soft tone that was far more intimidating than a shout, "Do not ever shout at me, Ami, do not raise your voice to me. Here. *In my home.*"

And they all looked at him. *Why didn't he speak up for pity sake* - he read his mother's thought. And, *This is the first moment when you have to decide – there will be many others –* Corinne's. And the most difficult of all, Sam's silent question, the one she'd been begging him to answer for months, something inarticulate, without even the hope of words. All he could see in her face was – *Daddy?*

His own thought? The problem was – his problem – he had not felt torn. With all of his being he wanted to embrace his mother, despite his own anger, to silence his wife, despite his love for her.

His mother faced him, stony, hurt. "Well – you give me a list of what you want me to do." She said it softly this time. "And I'll do it from home." She went to the closet to get her coat, her defeat far more painful for him than her anger had been.

Then, Sam's explosion—"Sure Myami. Just walk out! What you always do in one way or another."

"Walk out?" Ami asked, genuinely and profoundly confused. "On you?" She held one hand to her head.

"Not literally, Myami," Sam said, a half hearted attempt at retraction that didn't work. "You just don't face things, Myami. You always kind of script everything, like you're writing one of your books. As if no one can tell the difference." She finished with a snort, loud and snide.

It was obvious to him, and he hoped to his mother, that Sam wanted nothing more than to run into her arms, be given the words she longed for to release her from the knots of anger and pain she'd been sunk in, but what those words were he had no idea. He wished Sam would run into her grandmother's arms, balance it all again. Instead she stood up, her fists clenched at her sides.

"Sam's right, don't walk out." Corinne's words were meant kindly, he hoped, a plea rather than a command. She had her arm around Sam.

So Ami replaced her coat on the hanger, took a seat on the couch, her hands folded tightly in her lap. They talked, uncomfortably, for a while, about Hannah's life, but only as they had known her, her old age, the way her feelings about race had seemed to harden with the years, how difficult she could be, how it was okay and natural for Sam – for all of them – to feel some measure of relief. She'd had a good life, a long life. No one mentioned Sam's namesake, or his father or grandfather again, the three Samuels, that other family suddenly and uncomfortably connected to their own. No one answered Sam's earlier

231

questions, or talked about her mother, or her new stepmother who was in the process of redecorating their home, replacing old wallpaper with clean coats of paint, buying a new couch, hanging two of her favorite paintings, adding some of her family photographs to the shelf where there were at least a half dozen of Sam at different ages, including one in her mother's arms.

Ami kept her voice low. Jake saw her try to smile – he saw how hard she tried. And when she finally did leave, before dinner, she made an excuse and this time Corinne accepted it. She wrote down some names of people she promised to call when she got home. She embraced Sam, kissed Corinne's cheek, and put one arm around him as she brushed his cheek with her own. Her one armed embrace, Jake had called it since he was a child, her attempt to keep up appearances when she was angry or hurt.

Everything was coming to a head, he thought as he drove carefully over the slippery icy roads, keeping the windshield wipers on fast. His mother's long-standing denials, his daughter's defensive certainties, his wife's presence inevitably altering accommodations that had been in place for years – all of it filtered through the silence in the car like pollution in stifling air. He could smell it. And it went far back in him, long before Corinne.

He remembered the first time he was called a nigger, when he was five and his parents had taken him on a vacation to Fire Island, a small community close to the city, famous for its progressive climate and lack of cars. Should have been famous for its lack of black people, he thought bitterly, recalling the little girl who had hurled the epithet at him. That day, when his father walked him back to complain to the parents of the girl, Jake had learned the absurdity of the idea of being "mixed." He was a black boy with an Italian mother, and in that moment he understood the meaning of *blackness* more clearly than he could ever explain it to anyone white, including his mother, though he loved her as much as anyone on earth. She comforted him that day, praised Jacob for the action he had taken. But she had been

232

the one who had chosen the house on that particular island. Just as he had chosen to keep Maya's house on the lake after she died, Sam's future feelings obscured by his grief. He regretted it now, and he blamed himself more than he blamed his mother. He, of all people, should have known.

Halves, quarters, eighths, paint tanks full of whiteness or genetic drops of blackness – that sort of thinking missed the point. You can't divide it up. Nor is skin color a sign of any-thing. Anyone who knows any American history knew that, or should. As long as there is racism – and as far as he could see, it was as ubiquitous and virulent as ever – as long as there is history – there would be a significance to black identity that is cultural, political, spiritual – that is *national*, and Jake, for one, hoped was indestructible. Ralph Ellison's preacher's sermon and all the controversy that still raged around the ideas packed so densely within it were important and provocative, but it was James Baldwin's astonishing sentence that turned Jake from a student searching through tangles of historical confusion into a teacher who understood something, at least, of what he was meant to convey. *The world is white no longer, and it will never be white again.* It was whiteness all people needed to understand now, whiteness black Americans had grappled and wrestled with for four hundred years. A lie, Baldwin called it, yet a brutal historical truth as real as the wheels under the car in which he was now seated next to his new wife, on the way – *at last*, he allowed himself to think – to the funeral of the grandmother of his first wife.

He felt satisfied to have provided a home for Hannah Sokolov long after many people would have deemed their obli-gation fulfilled. He could have sent her to the institution where her brother-in-law Aaron still lived, but her physical surround-ings were the key to life for her, she'd told him – and told him only once. "May I continue to live with you, Jake? My physical surroundings are the key to life for me. I'll die in a nursing home." It was a few days after Maya's funeral and he'd been staring out a window, wondering how he'd manage with a grieving six-year-old girl to comfort and raise. And thinking of his mother's busy life, his own teaching job, and even, he

233

supposed, of Sam's Jewish heritage, he said yes. He put his arms around Maya's grandmother and kissed her white hair. She said, "thank you," in a low but sturdy voice, and it had been hard, from that moment on.

She'd been a practical help, there was no denying that. But he had to keep a constant watch for the racism layered into all of her views – what constituted a "good" neighborhood, a "dangerous" man, a "beautiful" face. Once, the year before when Sam had begun proclaiming her blackness in a voice so angry he wept privately at the depth of pain that must have given rise to such fury, he heard Hannah whispering to Sam when she thought no one could hear – "Don't worry, *ketsela,* you're a good Jewish girl. Look at your face – just like your Mama. Look at your skin." She had no idea, it seemed, how profoundly uncomforting her words were, how perfectly wrong if her aim was to ease the child's conflicts. He had to exert all of his own control not to send her off to the nursing home in what must surely be her last days, but he said to Sam, "She's an old woman, don't let her upset you." Then, after the summer, something had changed. He saw Hannah looking through some of his books on African American history. When he asked politely what she was doing, she replaced the book quickly and looked down, shyly. "Nothing," she said and walked away. Soon after that, she asked his mother to take her to the Sound, and he had heard some of the story Hannah had told Ami that day. All of this only made him angrier – at the endless years and decades and centuries of ignorance, at realizations that come far too late.

He was mistaken to allow her such intimate access to his daughter. He shook his head. She's dead now – *at last.*

There was not much traffic on the Long Island Expressway, but the late March blizzard continued to beat against the window faster than the wipers could clean, and he drove slowly hoping for a quick, informal funeral at the grave. The funeral home should have delivered Hannah's body by the early morning. The coffin would have been lowered, already in the grave. There would be a few words, appropriate prayers said by the Rabbi Aaron had recommended. Then the coffin would be covered

234

with earth and it would be done, his burden lifted, his new life with Corinne unencumbered.

And there was the guilt. He took a long breath. His new life. His new wife. He'd never stopped feeling responsible for Maya's death, for not stopping her from taking the lethal swim. Even now, the knowledge that he might have prevented the tragedy clouded the deep happiness he was experiencing for the first time in years. He heard Corinne's voice in his head. *Thick clouds are part of adult happiness. What a foolish man you'd be,* she said to him when he confessed the sadness edging the joy of their approaching wedding day, *if your happiness didn't include a bittersweet taste, as if the past could disappear without a trace.*

Sam, he hoped, would heal and flourish under the care of her new stepmother. Her spirit might even be cleansed, if he was lucky, by the impending ritual, her mood lifted by the chance at long last to have her own room.

He felt Corinne's hand on his thigh, and he reached down to cover it with his own. She reminded him of Maya in only one way – the strength of his love – because the two women were of completely different characters. Maya was the most undefended, open person Jake had ever known – too open, he'd often thought – while Corinne was careful and self-contained. He was in love with her firm boundaries as much as with her physical elegance. And if occasionally he found himself missing the way Maya rushed headlong into experience, other people's as well as her own, he felt an exquisite peace in Corinne's love, a familiarity and belonging he had never before known. Some shallow observer might see race in this, he knew, but that wasn't it. Not at bottom. Corinne was a solitary soul, and he loved her need for solitude. Even her sometimes month-long absences when she traveled the world with her bird-watching group pleased him. He missed her, but he also marveled at her passion for finding exotic birds to observe, nothing material to show for it, only the knowledge that she had seen something rare and beautiful hardly anyone ever got to see. There was a place inside himself Jake never shared, a place Maya always wanted to dive into, heedlessly, like she dove into the early morning sea. She felt he was holding back, but he wasn't, just being himself as he always felt himself to be. Corinne, with her shadows and silences, allowed him to breathe deeply, as he'd done in the past only when alone. Her hand rested on his thigh again. She must have sensed his discomfort, or seen it in his face, and she was always pulled out of the comfort of herself by a need to offer love. Who else but such a person would have accepted the task of caring for a former wife's old grandmother, a white woman, full of old racial attitudes, ignorant and offensive. He allowed himself to think his two wives would have liked each other, that if Maya's spirit were anywhere around, it was grateful to the woman who agreed to care for her grandmother whom she'd taken in herself when no one else in the family would consider doing so. It was Corinne who'd been in the house, alone with Hannah, when she died. She died in Corinne's arms.

He glanced into the mirror again and this time missed his mother's eyes. She was looking out the window, her gaze following her granddaughter's. She rested her lips on Samantha's head, brushed short dark curls back from her forehead in repetitive, rhythmical strokes of her hand.

Jake turned off the expressway onto the smaller, local road. They passed a series of huge cemeteries, one after another, tombstones stretching to the horizon, it seemed. Compared to the countless dead, their life within the small car felt unbearably fragile to him. He cherished each woman in his life: the young wife of his youth who died believing she could single-handedly stop race from mattering in her child's life; Corinne, with whom he shared the early stages of an intimacy he believed would expand over a lifetime; his daughter, whose current crisis, he hoped, would pass, if only he, with Corinne's help, could direct her confusion and anger toward – something – he can't think yet what; and his mother – he felt a wash of guilt for his behavior in the past couple of days: not supporting her although he knew what she was feeling, not calling her to make up. She had always been ruthless in her commitment to him, sometimes ignored even her husband's needs if her son's desires interfered.

Or so he often thought. He had criticized her over the years for overpowering his father with her demands for order, causing Jacob obvious sadness with her need for secrecy, and anxiety when he was forced to witness, helplessly, her bouts of despair. As often in the past, he wished his father were here now. He could use a heavy dose of his lighthearted perspective. A black man raised deep in Jim Crow years of a legally segregated South, whose own father walked out forever when he was a child of two, leaving a mother who was severely depressed and permanently hospitalized by the time he was seven – destroyed by racism, poverty and a sensitive nature, he'd always said bitterly. He attributed the goodness of his life to a devoted aunt and uncle; the good fortune of an easy going, resilient nature; and a belief, given to him by his aunt, that only work and an absence of self-pity would get a black person anywhere in this harsh, unjust, and deceptive nation. How did a heart that had suffered so many losses and disappointments remain so light, both in its weight and in its luminosity? Jake wondered this often, still found it profoundly unsettling when he recalled the doctors diagnosing the heart attack that killed Jacob Reed as having something to do with heavily burdened arteries. Did his father retain the heaviness within himself somehow, for all their sakes, until his body could no longer manage the weight?

It's nice poetry, son, Jacob would have said, but my clogged arteries aren't a metaphor for our life. Give yourself a break, Sugar.

A married man, a professional, a senior member of the faculty of a large community college, still called Sugar by his father when he was a grown man.

As they came to a stop in the parking lot in front of the office, his eyes welled up with tears. He pulled up next to his cousin Nicky's car, waved to Rena, a mean and critical woman, Hannah's only surviving child, and to Aaron, looking ancient and amiable in the back seat. Yes, he thought, turning off the ignition, it would definitely be a relief. He met Corinne's eyes for a moment before turning to his mother and daughter. He smiled at one – and hoped she knew he was apologizing, wanting all to be peaceful again – and he winked at the other – trying to convey the reassurance his father would have given him, as if his resolve and faith might sweep away the sorrow in his daughter's eyes.

It was time to go in, make sure all was ready, and pulling up the thick hood of his gray down jacket, he sighed into its muffling layers and stepped out of the car just as his cousin Nicky, smiling broadly, stepped in.

Chapter 33

"Hey, Princess, how's my bellissima cousin?"

But even Nicky can't penetrate this fucking realm, I thought. *The other realm*, I'd begun to call it, the one beneath the orderly habits and self-controls me and Myami seemed to love so much. Did she teach me this as a way of coping with the chaotic feelings my mother's death left in its wake? Or was I born with it – a kind of survival kit for terrible times? Lately, my feelings were constantly jutting up through those habits. I would think I was going to be quiet, and there they were, a torrent of angry words I didn't mean to say, like the ones I hurled at Myami the day my great-grandmother died. Or, I'd be thinking I would wait until dinner to eat, and I'd find myself in front of the refrigerator, shoving food into my mouth by the handful or spoonful. I attempted a smile at Nicky, who played basketball every week and watched his diet like a hawk, figuring he had actually noticed how much weight I've gained despite his "bellissima."

Of Greatgram's original family, only Aunt Rena remained who, in my opinion, was nothing less than a racist bitch. Her disdain for Myami and my father was so obvious it made me even angrier at my great-grandmother, even though I couldn't deny loving her, too, and I knew I would miss her very much in a way. That morning, I'd claimed the drawings of the bay framed in pale green and the old bedside collection of photographs as well. These objects were not only beautiful in the unique way Hannah's objects were always made beautiful, they emanated all the feelings of the summer night when I first heard the story of Samuel and Belle. I felt as if I'd discovered forgotten members of my own family, though I knew it wasn't true, when I found out about my name. I had kept the story of that night to myself, even after I read the book, and although I felt Myami somehow knew about it, we hadn't spoken of it in all these months. She had looked at me a few times in that way of hers – when you know she has something on her mind to say. But she would never ask. Respect for privacy, she called it, but my anger was enflamed. I had fantasies of sneaking into her workroom one night, reading her personal journals, invading the part of her world Ami shared with no one, maybe not even my grandfather when he was alive. She had said no more about the promised memoir I had asked for, and we hadn't spoken since the showdown at our house the day Hannah died.

The four of us sat in the car; Nicky in the driver's seat greeting Corinne, whose discomfort, now that my father was gone, I could almost smell; Myami getting her boots back on (Jake kept the car as hot as a tropical desert, she complained), folding and refolding her soft woolen scarf; and me, of the four of us the only mourner (I guessed I'd be called) who was actually related to the person we had come to bury in the winter ground.

It was a perfect scene, I think now, remembering that day – the heavy snow gathering in high drifts, lining the branches of trees like thick white down; the ice on the paths, accumulating on the car windows – all of it like the bleak, vast, horrible whiteness of Hannah's dream.

Then suddenly summer, and warm blue waters, not winter ice, filled my head. A drowning, not a burial. And my mother's face. It had followed me all the way from the city. I saw it clearly in the thick fog of snow as, leaning against Myami, I stared out the window while the old childhood poem about James James Morrison Morrison resounded in my head. *Don't go blaming him*, he had told all his relations. *If someone went down to the end of the town, well what could anyone do?* My eyes filled with old tears, the kind I had known for what seemed like my whole life, tears with an ineluctable specificity so I could never mistake them for ordinary tears, the worst longing:

never again, never never again. Then the tears spread over my face and everyone noticed instantly, since all three of them were taking turns staring at me, observing me as I'd been observed throughout my life at every occasion that could possibly bring my mother to mind. To my surprise, it was my grandmother who spoke, and what she said was even more surprising.

"What happened at the lake? You've been upset since then. It isn't only Hannah's death. What did she say that disturbed you so?"

Nicky looked down, but I was cornered between Corinne's and Ami's eyes. Trapped, I lashed out.

"It's *not* just that. It's *not* just Greatgram! Though I did love her, Myami, even if you hated her, and I know you did."

"No," Myami said softly. "Not in the end, Sam. We had – a kind of date, you know. Last September. I told you, we went to the beach together – after all those years of her hating it. She was – she told me a story – about a long-forgotten piece of her life – the part you've been reading something about in the book she gave you. Well, she's not in the book of course, but it's about that time she lived through. Well, I've been reading it too. When people do that – when you hear them tell their stories? It's hard to hate them when they do that. Don't you think that's true? I didn't hate Hannah. Sometimes I hated what she did to you."

"So why haven't you mentioned it all this time?" I demanded.

"You were – are – going through a lot. I didn't want – to intrude, I suppose." She looked down into her lap.

My anger was growing and spreading so wide I was scared of it myself, but I regained control enough to say, "Well, yeah, she was always telling me all that stuff about being Jewish and white, and I'm like *hello!? I'm black!! Like my daddy! My daddy's black! My mother was Jewish – I know, I know – but she's dead.* But it wasn't just that – it's you, Myami, you too. You never told me – helped me – you use all that stuff about intruding as an excuse. And you're the one who's always been saying I'm *mixed race.* More like mixed up."

"I'd never use that word," Myami said. "I may have said culturally mixed, but not – I'd never say that . . . ." Her cheeks paled and her eyes looked narrow. Frightened, I saw my grand-mother was getting old.

"Whatever," I said, caressing her wrinkled fingers, twisting the loose gold wedding band, sorry for my outbursts and accusations. I thought of all our summers at the bay, the many peaceful hours I had spent in her comfortable, lovely apartment, a relief from the heavy pressures of my home, all I had learned from her throughout my life. But I understood how angry her sense of *privacy* made me, how much I hated that word – *intrusive* – an excuse, I felt, for cowardice. I hated how much she kept to herself. How hard it was, at times, to know what she really felt about things.

After a long pause during which she seemed to be contemplating something infinitely demanding, she finally looked up at me.

"And your mother?" she asked, surprising me once more.

"What about her?!" I heard myself shouting again. "No one *talks* about her. You guys took *all* the pictures down, except for one, and that one of Greatgram's, and in that one she's sixteen! I don't even know who she was! Maybe she was a fucking racist, like Aunt Rena! Sometimes I don't even know who *I* fucking am! My mother named me for some black guy named Samuel who it turns out Greatgram was half in love with. Did you know that?" I stopped suddenly. *A waterman who cleaned and swept the docks when he longed to be on those skipjacks, out at sea, and his father somehow finding the guts to run - leaving who knows what and who behind, and his grandfather's body, cut into pieces like hunks of meat.* Pieces of the book filling the car like smoke, invading me. "I don't even think Daddy knows."

Corinne had been looking toward the office door from where my father, hopefully, would soon emerge, but now she turned around abruptly to look at me. "She – your great-grandmother – was talking about someone named Samuel just before she died. After she fell, and I ran to her and saw she was going? I called 911 – you know all this, Sam – but it took them about fifteen minutes – remember, I told you? And in that time she mumbled something about Samuel, and she kept calling me Belle. Do you

242

know who these people are?"

I told Corinne that part of the story as Hannah had told it to me. "She was half in love with him," I said again.

"Maybe more than half," Myami said, and added some detail she had learned the day at the beach.

"Write it all down, Sam," Nicky said, reaching across the back of the seat to take my hand. "It will be useful to you someday."

Finally, we saw my father coming toward the cars. He stopped to talk to Rena and her daughter first, then opened the back door and slid in next to me.

"I have to go back in," he said, rolling his eyes, a bitter laugh erupting at some absurdity he was about to impart. "They think they got the wrong day. The Rabbi's here, and so is the coffin – but they don't think the grave is . . . dug . . . ." He swallowed the word, glancing at me quickly. I instantly recognized my father's reluctance to utter any word that evoked the physical facts of death, scared he would cause me to think about the cliff and the white slivers of bone and ash. Beseechingly, he looked at his mother.

"Well, if it isn't . . . ready," she said, finding the best substitute for *dug*, then we'll wait. We're certainly not coming back again."

My father nodded, pulled his hood up again, stopped at the other car, and then entered the large doors of the office a second time.

"Sam," Nicky repeated in the vigorously focused tone I had loved ever since I could remember. "Write it all down."

Of everyone in the family, at least the white family, I felt most comfortable with him. He never seemed embarrassed to talk about anything. And he knew everything about black history, which he always called *American* history, smiling ironically. He taught it in a college, like my father, and suddenly I wondered why, how he'd gotten so interested in it as a white man. He'd always been Nicky, my white Italian cousin who knew all about African American history and understood things about race few white people even guessed at. Now, it seemed odd, some mystery to uncover, just like everything else that year – layers and layers of stories I'd only just begun to notice and needed to understand. My mother's life, Myami's, Nicky's – three white people I loved who had tied their lives up with black people. Then I thought of Louisa, the white girl in Hannah's – no – Samuel's story, described in Ruth Hughes's book. I looked hard at Nicky, and didn't respond.

"Write it all down – what Hannah told you. It will be important some day. I feel this for certain." He repeated this once more, and Corinne nodded her agreement.

It was a phrase of his – *I feel this for certain,* and a tone he had whenever he talked about the ideas he studied and taught, ideas that always seemed as if they were new and fresh to him, as if he'd just learned about them and understood their importance for the first time. "But you've taught this stuff – Frederick Douglass' life – his book about his life – so many times," I had asked him once. "Doesn't it ever get boring?" He'd looked away and said, kind of dreamily, "Every time a new student understands it – sees what really happened in this country – it's as if I'm learning it for the first time."

The women, too – Belle and what she might have experienced as a child, the white woman's sister, the girl who was sold away. So mixed hadn't helped. Mixed meant nothing. And the grandmother Ruth who had lost everything. And Ruth the writer who was writing it all down.

Nicky turned away from me and checked out the office, lookng for my father, then back at us. Myami looked at him for a long moment and whispered something into his ear.

"Did Greatgram say anything else I should remember?" I asked Corinne.

"She said – and, remember – she was barely whispering – it was right before she died, and I had to lean close to hear – but I think she said – something needs rearranging, Belle. Do you know what she meant, Sam?"

I did not have to answer because at that moment my father knocked furiously on the windows, motioning us to get out, shouting that everything was finally ready – they'd dug . . . the grave was ready. It was all in place. He opened a large umbrella for Corinne, and kept one for himself. Nicky rushed over to help Aaron, who had to be pushed in a wheelchair, and Rena's daughter took her mother's arm. Myami and Corinne led the procession down the icy road, heads bent together in conversation beneath their umbrella, and I hoped they were making up, at least for now. I was pressed so closely against my father's side that I felt almost carried along, as if I were skip-sliding across the icy paths to the block of graves where Hannah would be buried near her daughter Sophie, her son Asher, and her husband Michael.

The idea of burial made me feel suffocated, and for the first time I thanked god, or whoever, that my mother had been cremated when her body was found – *not stuffed in a box, not eaten by sharks* – her ashes thrown into the wind from the edge of a cliff overlooking the Atlantic Ocean where it beat against the southern Long Island coast.

Either way, this day, like the one long ago, was full of death. It moved inside me like a prowling animal and suddenly it screeched, loud and high, like a monkey I'd seen once in a zoo. I felt entirely distant from them all, as if I were being swept away by all the frightened and angry feelings I'd had since the summer, swept away like white ash of bone in a high wind. Everything seemed to be swirling around – Corinne with her elegant clothes, her daring hats, and her comforting understanding, but also the way she had shout-spoken to Myami, a tone that had split all that thick humidity of unspoken adult feeling like a coming storm but also made me feel a little scared. So far, she hadn't used that tone with me, and I had a pretty good idea how I would react when she did.

"Myami!!" I called desperately, and she came quickly to my other side so I was walking between them, my arms clutching their arms, my daddy on my right, Myami on my left, just like when the three of us trudged up the cliff to throw my Mama into the sky, into the wind, into the sea, children ripped from mothers' arms, a girl called Lina, the sound of shouting, of crying, louder and louder, the thunder of waves crashing, of wagon wheels rolling, enormous white snowflakes piercing the small circle of the black umbrella Daddy held against the wind. I wanted to vomit, or pee, right into the snow. I pictured my hot pee melting the ice. I opened my eyes wide, tightened my vaginal muscles, holding my urine in.

And suddenly it is there, the narrow box made of white pine, and there is a tiny canopy too small to cover all of us. Our feet are submerged in deep wet snow, and the Rabbi begins speaking loudly, trying to be heard over the wind. I see his mouth moving but I hear nothing. Inside my head I am seeing Samuel, Ruth Hughes's great-grandfather, murdered, cut into pieces like a piece of beef. I am seeing his son on the water, hauling shellfish, going out on the skipjacks whenever the white people will let him. I am seeing his son, the third Samuel, with the dark eyes and heavy brows his daughter describes so lovingly, and he is gazing at a white woman, a tan skinned Jewish woman, but white, my great-grandmother, Hannah Sokolov. I'm seeing the dry white bones of Hannah's granddaughter Maya fly into the sky, spread out thin in the wind, like birds, like snow.

Daddy and Myami hold on tight. Aaron's wheelchair looks dangerously tilted for a moment, but Nicky clutches the handles, steadying it and himself against it. Rena, her daughter, and two kids I hardly know, her grandchildren I think, stand in a semi-circle on one side of the grave. Rena's heavy black shawl is drawn up to her nose, and for a moment her dark eyes fall on me and I see the rage in them, and then I see white as Myami places a large, white handkerchief over my entire face to wipe off the wet snow.

When I shake my face free, I see the pine coffin again at the bottom of the grave, but the bottom of the grave has become the sky which is not normal and faraway and blue, but up close, and beneath me, and a sickly pale yellow, like pee, or white pine. Before I realize it is my own voice, I hear the screams, and I am yelling, "Mama! Mama!" and I know I have to get into that box. Daddy is trying to lift me into his arms, but I am too heavy, or I am pulling away, and I hear him say, "Let's get her out of here!"

246

And I can't have that, can't have getting out of here, I know that much. "No!" I yell at him, and for some reason I run to Nicky and clutch his arm.

Slowly, my father walks toward us. Everything stops. Everyone is looking at me. My father steadies the wheelchair and I feel Nicky's hands pressing gently against my arms. Uncle Aaron whispers, "Take it easy, *ketsela* – your old Greatgram is at peace now." I want to tell him it isn't Greatgram, so I yell, "Mama, Mama."

Kneeling in the snow before me, my father grips my shoulders and looks up into my face. "It's not your Mama, Sugar. It's old Greatgram. Remember? It's old Greatgram. Not your Mama." His voice breaks, as if he is about to cry, but that cannot be true.

Then I see Nicky moving slowly toward the Rabbi, whispering. I see the Rabbi's shocked look, then his eyebrows lifting, his head nodding. Snow falls off his thick, uneven beard, as if his beard is an unpruned hedge shaken by the wind. Then Nicky moves to the two gravediggers who are leaning on their shovels, their faces nearly hidden by large black waterproof hoods. *She'll never be satisfied unless she sees.* I hear these words as if Nicky has shouted them into my ear. One man nods. The other takes some money from Nicky and puts it into his pocket and then, shockingly, the two of them jump into the grave where I want to be.

There is a loud rustling, a low hum of moans, cries, and Yiddish words. I feel Daddy's arm holding me, his fingers gripping the cloth of my coat. He holds me against him so tightly I feel as if my feet are floating just above the icy ground. There is nothing in the world I want as much as what I am finally going to see. Nails are extracted. The snow-covered pine lid is lifted. I have never felt so focused, so clear, so terrified and ecstatic at once. Then I feel dizzy, as if I am looking up at the sky and at the same time looking down. I look down.

And there is Greatgram, her tiny body wrapped in a white cloth as if she were a baby, her face looking much as it did in life – gaunt, pale, heavily lined. Her eyes are closed. A thin white

247

braid lies gracefully on her shoulder. Only her mouth looks different – fuller, looser, younger. I whisper, "Greatgram."

Nicky nods. The lid comes down fast. I hear nails hammered in. The Rabbi's mouth moves again, and this time I hear Hebrew words I don't understand. I feel surprisingly alert. I look around.

Rena was swaying, pulling her black scarf off her face where it had apparently been covering her eyes. Aaron was crying silently. I looked past them. Corinne looked worried, but Ami's face looked alive with energy, a look I had seen before when, if I promised to be silent, I had been allowed to read in the study while my grandmother worked. Our eyes met.

Aaron spoke to us all then, in his old man's voice, very soft, but I had no trouble hearing his words. "Jake goes first," he said. "He's been our savior. Hannah's savior. Her guardian angel."

My father looked at me, and I whispered, "I'm okay, Daddy."

He left my side and dug the huge shovel into the frozen earth, then spilled the dirt onto the coffin. I heard pebbles and ice clatter over the wood. Then Rena, helped by her grandson, took her turn. Wet brown mud laced with frozen ice, three shovels in all when the last had been given to Aaron who poured his share of earth into the grave. He remained looking down, and I thought I could imagine a small piece of what Aaron must be seeing. A beautiful young Hannah I knew only from photographs, the sister-in-law he'd pitied and loved, whom he called Hannahla, little Hannah, as if she were still the cousin he had known all his life, the sister of his own beloved May, dead for twenty years. A woman who had endured a loveless marriage and been somehow involved with a black man named Samuel. The mother of Rena, Asher and Sophie, my grandmother, who listened to her mother's story, and – who knows – maybe even guessed her secret. She cherished freedom and so appreciated its hardships that she gave the name of the man in her mother's story to me. I heard these thoughts as if he were speaking them out loud, I was sure of it, and I also heard my own voice, silent in my own head, introducing myself like we do at Passover – *I am Samantha, daughter of Jacob and Maya Reed.*

But it was unfinished. Something else needed to be said.

Aaron remained there, looking down, until finally Nicky turned the wheelchair around and began the procession back to the cars. "How you doin, *Bellissima*," he paused to ask me, and Aaron motioned for me to sit in the space his thin body left on the seat. I sat down and was pushed back over the now slushy paths. The snow had turned to rain, and it soaked my face. Something had changed. I felt it everywhere – in my head, which felt clear; in my body, which felt light, my muscles loose as they hadn't been in months; in the sky that seemed far away again, normal again. Something had changed like the snow had turned to rain, but it wasn't over. Something wasn't over. I let sweet old Uncle Aaron hold my mittened hand in his, but I tried not to look at his pale face. With some surprise I saw Myami walking ahead of us, talking to Rena with genuine interest. When my eyes rested on my father's rich brown skin, I thought of earth and felt comforted

Chapter 34

Long after your father's birth – when he was grown up and married, not long before your birth. A beautiful day in late August. We were in Orient, Long Island that summer. You know how I had fallen in love with that place. The flat, peaceful roads between salt ponds and grasslands, easy to bike, and in the early morning you'd see those gorgeous swans gliding across the water, knowing they could be vicious but in awe of their beauty anyway. And the Causeway! A point where the distance between bay and sound is only the width of two cars and two narrow stretches of beach. The water changes color with the light and tides, silver in a morning mist as if to welcome the rain, aqua turning to sapphire in the afternoon sun, and at twilight, as a stripe of rose across the sky fades to purple, a shimmering navy blue. Jacob and I are driving home from the nearby town, home being a lovely house we've rented for a month, and as we reach the Causeway, I ask him to slow down, don't stop, just go slow. There are no other cars in sight. He moves at fifteen, maybe ten miles an hour, so I can keep the moment longer, between water and sky, and I look out, as if to breathe in and swallow the dimming light. That night it was a dusky blue, and you could just make out the start of a light rain. I looked at him, and I saw how he loved me. We were far from young – if you were soon to be born, we were into our fifties then, but it still thrilled me, in part because it had become so rare, to see him look at me that way. Outside, the vast sky, stars fading in the darkening evening, the water on each side, the rain – all of it seeming infinite and formless – and I am safe inside with him, bounded by the road, the car, the window frame.

The rain had turned into a light mist so every few minutes she turned the windshield wipers on, creating a soft background percussion to the melodic jazz, an unknown piece on the radio she kept low. April had been full of rain. Unlike most New Yorkers, Ami was pleased by the damp gray mist parting only just before sunset when wide stripes of pink appeared in the sky, while beyond the Hudson River, New Jersey lights were coming on. Then she would stack her papers, close her notebook, and walk along Riverside Drive fifteen blocks downtown to the Boat Basin where she stood with the other West Siders appreciating the golden-edged pink rays fading into twilight.

How could she ever complete the true story Samantha wanted? She could not. But as the feelings came to her, she wrote them down, hoping her memories might convey something for which she might never find adequate words. The thing that had pressed her since the summer was still pressing. Even as the April downpours washed pollution away, or thinned it at least, she frequently felt as if she couldn't breathe. Even after she had finally written her letter to Ruth Hughes and received her answer, even now as she made the hour-long drive to Norwalk, finally on her way to meet the woman, an ache in her right temple spread down to her eyes.

She had not told any of them. Something had made her know she had to come on her own. She'd tell them all about it tomorrow, she promised herself. For now, she needed secrecy. She was after something she didn't yet understand, and that always felt risky to her, more so since their last visit a few weeks before. The last thing she wanted was to appear – to them – to Jake – out of control.

The misty rain continued, and so did the low jazz – a sax, she thought, although she wasn't good at distinguishing among brass instruments, an ignorance that had always embarrassed her, except with Jacob, and he always told her gently – *that's a sax, or that's a trumpet, Ami, can't you hear the difference?*

There was never any criticism in his question; rather, he was inquisitive, surprised. And there was another memory about

251

Jacob and cars, his infuriating silence just when she wanted to talk. He bore her silences happily, since talk had never been necessary to him, but each time she got into a car with him for a long drive, no matter how many years of experience should have taught her to know what to expect, she hoped for intimate conversation, imagined each of them telling stories of recent life or long ago memory, stimulated by the forced companionship and the rhythm of the movement of the car. And each time she'd be disappointed, annoyed by his failure to respond perfectly, unsettled by his difference, and she'd have to take care not to let loose a barrage of small criticisms about his driving, which could be too fast, or his drinking, which could be excessive at times, when what she really wanted were his words.

Her rambling thoughts had turned into writing thoughts; she would put that piece down for Sam.

She was used to being silent in cars, having to think to herself. She could thank Jacob for that among the many other gifts a long marriage provided, some rooted in the incomparable intimacies of sharing all the bodily aspects of daily and nightly life; some in the love of what she could only call Jacob's soul; and some, ironically, in the very deprivations she had suffered most in loving him.

She pulled into a parking lot near a gas station, went in to buy a bottle of water. When she returned to her car, she clicked off the radio and rifled through the tapes in the glove compartment. The Bessie Smith was there, a Billie Holiday that did not include "Strange Fruit," a collection of arias from several operas sung in the thrilling soprano of Kathleen Battle, and a Ray Charles album of Classics: "Georgia," "America the Beautiful," "Cryin Time," – but none of them seemed appealing. "I'll drive in silence," she said aloud to Jacob, suddenly afraid that buried in his silences was some part of him she never knew, that maybe he had not known himself. Perhaps, he hid from himself in his silences as she had learned to hide (she had known this for months, ever since becoming immersed in her long letter to Samantha, her *Midrash*, she had begin to call it) in words.

Traffic was heavy on the Merritt Parkway due to the seemingly endless construction and reconstruction of roads. It would take another hour to get to Norwalk. However, her appointment with Hughes wasn't until three and it was only noon. She wanted the chance to walk the streets Hannah had walked, to see the docks and oyster markets before she entered the house, part of which, Ruth Hughes had written in her letter of invitation, had once been the home of Samuel and Belle.

She'd read most of the memoir now, though she'd flipped quickly through several chapters, including the section where the first Samuel was killed. And she'd written a section in her *Midrash*, dated the morning after the day at Hannah's grave, describing her own parents' funerals – first her mother's, then her father's, their faces, unlike Hannah's, transformed by the embalmer so they looked almost unfamiliar in their elaborate coffins bought by Ami's older sister. She hadn't tried to describe the bodies in any detail. She wrote, instead, about the small comfort cremation gave her, Maya's, Jacob's, eventually her own; the process complete, the spirit, if any, free to merge with the earth, not trapped in a box.

Despite some obvious improvement in Sam's mood since the macabre scene at Hannah's grave, she did not want to dwell on death, as Hughes had dwelt on the sordid details of the murder of the first Samuel in the town called Saint Elizabeth on the western shore of Chesapeake Bay. She still couldn't see the point of it. Or maybe she just couldn't bear it. It was too overwhelming, like the newsreels of Holocaust survivors and mountains of skeletal corpses, repeated over and over since the long-ago end of the war, in films and exhibitions and museums, so no one could ever forget. Thinking of it all, she felt impatient, then an anger that always made her feel ashamed.

Since the day after the funeral, Sam had been pressing her to write to Ruth Hughes. "A fellow writer, Myami," she insisted. "She'll see you for that reason – she'll believe you."

She'd resisted, but finally she had called her nephew Nicky and asked him to dinner, telling him frankly she needed his help. She found herself confiding in him – as she could not in her son – that there was something frightening to her about digging up all this past history, and she found she could listen, as if she were an interested student, without feeling as if her very life lay in the balance of what he had to say.

They sat at her table sipping wine and eating her carefully prepared food in companionable seriousness as he talked to her in his most patient and pedagogical voice about the denial of the dark and sorrowful center of American history. How from the earliest days of European settlement, through the short, hopeful period of Reconstruction after the Civil War, and from the days of Black Codes, Jim Crow, and legal segregation right up to their present lives, right here in New York City, right in her famously multi-cultural neighborhood, ideas about skin color defined opportunity and infected every institution of their lives.

She knew it; then why did she feel reminded, as if she had forgotten? And why had he become so involved with this history, she wanted to know. How had he escaped, without the benefit of a black family like her own, the ingrained racism of his parents, grandparents, and siblings?

He didn't have a clear answer. He had always felt connected to black people, he said, perhaps initially through his uncle Jacob, but through others too – the only black kid in his high school who was his friend; a school janitor who was so obviously gifted with kids he was made first the supervisor of the cafeteria during wild lunch periods, then an assistant coach of the basketball team; an inspiring Black Studies professor in college. He had never understood why, but he'd begun reading about slavery in his adolescence and never stopped. For years he had felt a secret and powerful shame, even though his grandparents were immigrants. The shame was for the bigotry he knew was in his family and common to all the white homes in which he was welcomed and could be comfortable – except that sooner or later the language about "niggers" would begin. There was a time when he came to loathe his own skin, he told her. Then he read a biography and a novel about John Brown, and despite the controversial violence – "I know all about the callousness and wild killing in Kansas," he told her – he had felt, well, almost redeemed. He was a white man but he understood, Nicky had said. He had actually wept when he discovered the great, mad Osawatomie, and he'd hung his portrait over his desk, where it remained to this day.

He had followed her into the kitchen carrying plates and glasses, setting out dishes for coffee and pie. Didn't she know from Jake how many writers had worked their whole lives to understand this thing we call whiteness, he asked. Didn't she talk to Jake about his work? And, getting back to her point about it all being frightening, if people didn't remember and face up to the history, how did she expect anything to change? "It's the same as with personal history – with what's going on with Sam," he had said. "You're a writer, Aunt Ami. You must know that."

She had talked about it all with Jacob, many times, so many times she could not remember one conversation from another, which argument had been about what from one year to the next. She only remembered they had always made up, declaring their mutual love, their love for Jacob. Now she wondered what Jacob had really felt, if he had been disappointed in her, as her son clearly was. Hoping Nicky could not see her discomfort, she'd said, yes, of course she knew, and knew about her son. But clearly not fully or sympathetically enough, she thought, and she remained troubled until the following week when they met again, this time for a walk.

"Our family were peasants in Sicily during at least two generations of Summers-Watermans," she told him, trying to hide with her tone any trace of the anger she felt.

"By the time the third Samuel was working the docks as an oysterman in Norwalk, my mother, your grandmother, was several Connecticut towns north in Waterbury, struggling to raise four children, the last one, yours truly, an accident, and always too demanding for a mother in her forties – both of which facts she must have told me hundreds of times in my life. My father was a low-paid insurance adjuster for a large corporation, for god's sake. She was a housekeeper and homemaker whose chores, she assured us, were never done. A kitchen slave, she called herself – and she was, in a way. She had heavy varicose veins that throbbed every night when she finally sat down. I used to help her pull off her elastic leg sleeves, and bring her hot rags to dull the pain. When she was sixty-nine, looking far older, I hope and believe, than I do now, she collapsed from a massive heart attack and died. They were hard-working immigrants, Nicky. It's hard to think of them as what you call privileged."

She breathed in and out slowly, patted his arm in a half-hearted apology.

He told her the story of Harriet Jacobs, who called herself Linda Brent in a narrative about her enslavement in Maryland, her escape and spiritual transformation, a memoir Ami had never read, though she'd seen it printed in various editions over the past few years. Years after her escape from slavery to relative freedom in New York, he told her, Jacobs visited the field and factory workers of England and Ireland and noted the many hardships in their lives, the injustices that constrained them generation after generation, the miserable conditions in which they lived. He took his arm from hers, clenched his fist to make the point. "But they knew where their children were, and no one came at will to beat them or rape them on pain of being sold themselves. *I would ten thousand times rather that my children should be the half starved paupers of Ireland,* Jacobs had written, *than to be the most pampered among the slaves of America.*" Nicky spoke the memorized words with strong feeling as he had done, no doubt, in his classes many times.

A few nights later, Ami tried to describe what she had been learning to Jake and Corinne, hoping to prove something to them, she noted with surprise, or to herself.

"But you sound so astonished," Jake said. "I've told you that story many times, Mom. We're talking about people being *bought* and *sold* – not merely their labor, *themselves.* We're talking about nearly three hundred years of human depravity and hatred allowed to run amok – unchecked and wild – over two hundred years of legal, savage murders and rape." His nearly forty-year-old voice was laced with the pure disappointment of a faithful and betrayed child.

Corinne had looked uncomfortable. She sat near Jake on the couch, and she leaned toward him until their shoulders touched.

"It's hard, Ami, when people . . . white people" – her voice was soft, and sad – "people you love . . . take so long to comprehend."

It was the second time Corinne had admonished her, and for the second time Ami felt her anger grow. But this time, she was silent in response. Jake was not only *not hers*, clearly, but was understood better by this woman he'd met only a few years before than he was by his mother, at least in certain ways. It was obviously true, naturally true, and yet a fierce jealousy moved through her. Or, deeper than jealousy, it was envy, she thought, not merely for Corinne's place in Jake's life, but for her place in the history that meant so much to him. She envied Corinne her blackness – yes, she would have to say this – for all the clarity and definition it gave her that Ami, slipping in and out of the borderlines as she'd been doing all her life, could never possess. It wasn't that she was incapable of knowing her son, the meaning of his work, or the source of his passions. She remembered how she and Jacob had worried at first when he married Maya – Jewish, yes, but white, a white American, and who could tell what lurked beneath the apparently unprejudiced surface of peoples' feelings? Then they had come to feel relieved because Jake was so obviously enchanted by Maya's differences from himself – her flamboyant openness, her unashamed vulnerability. Ami had been enchanted almost as much as her son.

But this woman was different, somehow closer to the very center of Jake. It was not simply that she shared his blackness, then. She shared his solidity, the self-containment and strength Ami had marveled at since he was about twelve years old, watching it develop almost suddenly out of an early childhood marked by fragility and what she had thought was dependency. Now, looking back, she saw he was only getting ready. He'd been building a beautiful wall of dark stone, not too high to cross but a cordial signal of its owner's preference, and he had assumed his boundaries and his right to privacy with a grace she had worked all her life to achieve.

Looking at her son in his now newly-decorated home, feeling the magnetic pull between him and his new wife, hearing Corinne say – *Ami, I'm sorry if I sounded harsh* – and Jake –

Sorry if I overreacted, Mom — she recalled the question Corinne had asked her on the path to Hannah's grave, right after making a gracious apology for the conflict a few nights before, and just before Sam's alarming but thankfully short-lived breakdown. Apart from Sam's name and her fascination with the story, Corinne had asked, what did the lives of the Summers and Waterman families have to do with her, Ami Reed?

Once again, she'd stayed away from them for several weeks – keeping in touch only by phone. And during that time she finally decided to write and send the letter to Ruth Hughes, explaining the twisted threads that linked their families, telling her something of Sam, asking if they could meet. Hughes had written back surprisingly quickly, saying yes, and then other questions began to surface in Ami's mind, questions she knew Samantha would want to ask. She had become interested in the Southern white girl who had grown into a brave radical, along with her Aunt Emma a speaker for the abolitionist cause, but Ruth Hughes hadn't written about Louisa's life in Philadelphia. And what was the story of Ruth's mother, the woman called Belle? Was there a fourth Samuel?

She was driving too slowly, she realized, as several cars honked at her and she moved over to the right lane. She felt heavy and exhausted, but just before the heaviness turned into the headache that began in her eyes, she decided to write it all for Samantha. Sam wanted the whole true story, she had said, and that, it seemed, was what she was going to get.

The second reason she was here, driving north on this old picturesque Connecticut highway, was remembering Samantha's "terrible list." She found herself picturing that girl on the slave ship, humiliated and terrified, the woman hung by her wrists and *flayed,* the face – as if she knew him – of a man chained in a castle on the Atlantic coast of Ghana, terrified, waiting for the slaver to take him away. Quickly, dangerously, she shut her eyes. The car veered. She heard the horns behind her and gathered herself. She turned the radio on, then off again, and remembered the moment in the car while they waited for

Jake to clarify the arrangements for Hannah's burial.

Samantha had accused Ami of failing her by insisting on the richness of her "mixedness" and by not talking enough about Maya. Ami had held to the belief that the terrible loss in Sam's early childhood could be ameliorated, even left behind, by limitless love. But what if it had been a mask – this concept of love she'd held onto since she left her own mother behind for a new life she wanted more than anything she'd ever wanted before? What if, like history, one's own past, unremembered or distorted or trivialized or denied, was inescapable after all, and formless, like the shapeless, proliferating narrative she'd been writing for Samantha for all these months? What if our shapely stories and linguistic structures were resistances to, instead of penetrations of, history's actual truths? A dangerous vertigo made her head swim. She breathed deeply and turned the radio back on.

And what if she'd been wrong to encourage Jake to minimize talk about Maya, to get rid of her clothes and jewelry and most of her possessions instead of storing them away for her daughter to go through some day? She'd been afraid the past would haunt and cripple Sam. But now it seemed Nicky and Corinne, with their insistence on recording, and Hannah, with her old memories resurfacing so close to her death, had understood something about the dangers of repression that Ami herself, for all her immersion in character, motivation, and carefully placed flashbacks, had missed. What if her work had been more a Halloween than a ritual mask, beautifully constructed but fundamentally untrue?

And what if the idea of *racial* mixedness, like a bad work of fiction, was simplistic, evasive, and, from both a biological and historical point of view, absurd?

Waves of feeling had stormed through her in the instant it took to formulate her question at the time: *And your mother?* she had asked Sam. Only much later, in her lamp-lit room, Armstrong's horn a hypnotic background to her thoughts, had she begun to formulate the insight into words. Now another word drummed in her writer's brain. She had wanted to *amelio-*

rate Samantha's tragic loss. That was the word she'd thought and written. *Ameliorate.* A version of her own original name. She'd believed Samantha's loss of her mother could be ameliorated by her own uncompromising love.

Ami took the exit to South Norwalk, crossed Main Street, and drove slowly down Washington Street to the docks where an historical museum now stood. The old stories were still coalescing, opening her to what seemed obvious now. How blind and stupid she'd been, thinking she could replace Maya with herself, or replace Jake with Samantha, and before that, perhaps, replace Jacob with Jake. She felt an old, forgotten, nauseating sense of what she thought, at first, was sin, then saw might be the opposite: a vision of what was irreplaceable and lost; what might be redeemed and repaired; the effort it would take to understand each, and with that grace to know what had to be lived through, and mourned.

She parked in front of Jeremiah Donovan's Restaurant, noting the large sign advertising *"Beer, Wine and Spirits,"* and *"Oysters Brought Fresh from the Wharf Every Day."* A plaque at the entrance read: *Established in 1889.* Hannah might have eaten here. Samuel and Belle might have passed by this very door. She entered and took a table near the back. She ordered oysters and bottled water. The staff was boisterous and friendly, the place crowded with people who looked like tourists come to visit what had become a historical district in Norwalk, and others who clearly knew the waiters as well as each other, regular patrons of the oyster saloon. Tourists, waiters, bartenders and local customers – she noticed it with a feeling of discomfort, almost a sense of doom – all were white, and she fit right in, as she would not have done if Sam had been with her. Or Jacob. Or Jake.

She tried to relish the texture and subtle taste of the oyster dipped in cocktail and horseradish sauce, but she kept thinking about what had pushed her to this journey to Norwalk, the full purpose of which she was only starting to comprehend.

She remembered a long ago summer in Fire Island when Jake had been called a nigger for the first time. He was only five years old, and she had learned something from Jacob that day when, his face set in a grim frown, he had taken his son's hand and walked him back to the house where the insult had occurred to report the injury and insist on an apology. You had to speak up, even if only one child heard you, even if no one heard at all.

On the frigid, dramatic day of Hannah's funeral, she had asked Rena as they walked back to the cars if she recalled anything from her childhood in Norwalk about a black couple named Samuel and Belle Waterman. Rena had cut angry eyes at Ami. "How did you know about them?" she asked, clearly surprised, and Ami had responded simply, "your mother once mentioned them to me." For a moment, she felt a strong sympathy for Rena – an old woman who had never reconciled with her mother. Sophie, Sam's grandmother, idealized as the good daughter, Rena, blamed as the bad one, to the end of their mother's days, none of them ever grasping the irony of the similar positions Rena and Hannah occupied as rejected elder daughters and thus the possibility, never attempted let alone achieved, of sympathy either for each other or for the inevitable emotional tangles of maternal life. Then Rena had told her of an afternoon in the town fish market when she and her brother Asher had been playing while their mother talked to the Negro man about the price of fish. "I saw the way she looked at him," Rena said. "She had the best, most brilliant husband in the world, and she was flirting shamelessly with a ... with a colored man."

Her sympathy dissolved, Ami tried to emulate the precise timbre of Jacob's tone of controlled rage, emphasizing her words with a deadly calm. "That's a racist thing to say, Rena. His color had nothing to do with it." But even as she said it, she saw how wrong she was.

All the small and large events that had pushed her to this day seemed to come to mind at once. And the final thing had been the dream. She had it once, the night she finished the Hughes memoir and remembered Hannah's story. An expanse of white. A blizzard, perhaps, like the one that had covered the northeast the week of Hannah's death, or else she was in some remote and

261

frigid country, colorless and dim. She was walking down a dirt road, its gravel and mud the only brown in the world of the dream, but then she was lost near the ocean, and she knew that if she did not walk with exquisite care she might fall in and drown. Then, still within the dream, she was watching the dream unfold, and the woman walking perilously close to the ocean was a woman of mixed race, a woman of about forty with slightly stooped shoulders, long wiry hair and a scarred face – from acne? she wondered from within the dream. The woman seemed to be well known to Ami, as if she had dreamed about her off and on for years, ever since Jake was born. The woman's feet entered the dangerous water, and Ami was screaming for Jacob who was coming toward her, but she was being sucked into the white blizzard, and the old and common nightmare feeling took over. She was screaming but he couldn't see her or hear her, no sound would come out of her mouth. She woke moaning, trying to scream, and she grabbed her pad in the dark, blind without her glasses and still half in the dream. She wrote something. In the morning, more agitated than she'd been since it all began the summer before, a sinus headache pounding in her forehead down to the bridge of her nose, she'd read her words: *not me.*

She had better try to regain some composure, she realized as she paid the check, put on her dark brown raincoat, and wound her soft black scarf around her head. She stared at the ground as she walked fast through the now heavier rain back to the car. She felt the sickening shame of which Nicky had spoken, then Corinne's anger, and Jake's, now, unexpectedly, her own. And Samantha's terrible list. All these years, wanting to belong to them so much she'd even imagined people were thinking she was black at times, wanting to be Jacob's wife, his sister and his spouse, his soul sister – that too – free of history, free to belong.

Nicky had told her she wasn't alone, it was a paradox all white people had to accept if they were anything like John Brown, freedom lovers, travelers between two worlds. Certainly, she was Italian, and Sam was part Italian, there was no doubt

262

about that. But Ami was white too, a white American, and that was different from being Italian, or Jewish, or Black, (now she saw the reason for Jake's insistence on the capital B) with their languages, and foods, and culture. Whiteness was something else. It had been a terrible thing. To deny this meant to deny the blood at the root of this nation. Only very few whites questioned their innate superiority. Even some of those who fought against slavery, who went to prison to break the segregation laws, who insisted there was no difference, *we are all the same, yellow, white, and brown, black and white together* had believed in their hearts – some of them, some of the time – just as her own parents had, as Rena Sokolov did, as even Hannah Sokolov had until, perhaps, the very last weeks of her life, that skin color made all the difference in the world. *Not me*, she had written. She didn't want to belong to that terrible list. But she couldn't imagine a place for herself, and she was filled with a fear of exclusion as old as her life. That was the part she had taught herself to control and shape in her work, choosing with a ruthless care what to pull out of that private place, her *true box*, but it had remained within her, and she kept as much as she could of it to herself. The old feelings burned again and fueled a new rage like dried wood thrown on dangerous sparks of flame. She felt ashamed of her actual skin, all it had meant and still meant. Mostly she was afraid, of the long period of grief that surely lay ahead, the hopeless sorrow she would have to go through.

She needed time now, time to find her way to the mud road through the white blindness, and she didn't have any time. She passed the Bethel AME church on her right, and then she was turning into the driveway of 20 Knight Street. In a few moments she would meet Ruth Hughes.

Chapter 35

This is a kind of memoir – a story partly known, partly imagined. I remember my mother, Belle Waterman, as clearly as if she died yesterday instead of nearly forty years ago, as if I were just twenty-eight, returning too late to see her after a ten year absence, throwing dirt on her grave first, then my father's; as if I were twenty-eight instead of nearly seventy – older than my mother got to be. Perhaps it is partly because of my advanced age that I realize no memory is pure; we all have to bring imagination to an understanding of the past – to collect the facts when we can, and then fill in the blanks.

Belle Waterman - or Carrie Johnson as she was known before she left first the town and later the name she was known by in the town - went off into the world, quite on her own, when she was only sixteen. She had no living family and no reliable friends – partly, I think, due to her own reclusive nature and partly to the hard lives and frequently early deaths of the black people in her part of the country. She bought the ticket for New York it had taken a year to save for, knowing nothing about the place, no one who lived there, only that she was going "up north." It was 1901. She passed through Delaware, Philadelphia, and Trenton, New Jersey, at each stop contemplating it as a place to begin, but she was so frightened of trying to make her way in those huge cities with no real destination in mind, she found herself literally unable to get off her seat. When the conductor told her Grand Central Station in New York was the last stop, she asked if there was a train that went further north. Sure, he said, a local making all stops between here and Ver-

mont, but she'd have to get off and onto another line.

She spent an hour finding her way through the enormous station, looking up at the blue ceiling full of stars and line drawings, finally overcoming her shyness and fear of white people enough to buy a ticket to the end of the line and be told on which track she'd find her train. Holding her worn leather suitcase in a strong arm, looking down at her feet as they moved, her strict attention driving them, as if they were not entirely a part of her, she somehow managed to find her way to the train, the car, and a seat made of tightly woven straw that scratched her thighs through the thin cotton of her dress. She had no idea where she was headed nor where she might disembark. When the train stopped at a place called Norwalk, the only other person left in the colored car got off, so she followed him. He was an old man wearing a neat black suit and a broad-brimmed black hat. White hair was visible under the brim, hair that matched a well-groomed beard reaching from ear to ear and shaved off neatly where his chin met his neck. He looked like a preacher, my mother thought, or even a doctor, she said once, realizing years later that she needed some justification apart from naked fear of white people for following a stranger to an unfamiliar place.

Standing on the platform, the man looked north and south, then seemed to think a while. My mother watched him from a polite distance, and when he started walking, she walked behind him. They walked nearly a mile (sometimes she said it was over two) until there were a lot of colored people in sight, walking down the wide main street, standing behind store counters selling things, standing in front of counters, buying. He walked into one of the stores, bought himself a bottle of cold soda and asked for two cups. Wordlessly, he filled both and handed one to my mother. She drank greedily until the soda was gone. Then the man filled her cup again. When he asked about a rooming house and was directed to one on Marshall Street, she followed him there. They walked up to the main floor desk, and he asked for two rooms for one week, then placed two dollars on the counter and handed her a key. My mother nodded her head in a sign of gratitude and respect, but said nothing. She looked at the ground, hoping the man would know the depth of her appreciation, and when she looked up at him he nodded back at her. They went up the stairs together, she a few steps behind him, and opened the doors to two rooms across the hall from each other.

For each of the next four days, my mother saw the man in the morning when she went out looking for work, and in the evening when she returned. He'd be going and returning too – but she had no idea where, of course. In the middle of the fourth day, my mother found a job cleaning house and washing clothes for a white woman on the south side of Main Street where the white people lived. When she went back to her room that night, she planned to speak to the silent man who'd helped her get settled and offer some future payment for what he'd done for her. But the desk clerk told her he'd gone that afternoon, left the payment for the three days remaining on his room to cover another three days on hers. Now she'd be able to keep the room until she got her first week's pay. She never saw the man again, nor knew who he was, where he was headed, or what his business was in Norwalk. She'd been working for the white woman two years when, hanging clothes on the line one bright afternoon, she met Samuel Waterman, my father, who was delivering fish. First she became Belle, then his helper in the fish market, and then she became Belle Waterman, Samuel's wife.

Ruth had written those pages over and over for weeks, correcting and revising, adding and subtracting adjectives, finding simpler sentence structures, picturing over and over the man her mother had told her about so many times – how she would have been lost, ending up Heaven knows where doing Lord knows what if the silent, kind stranger hadn't gotten her settled. And having spent many hours in the Norwalk Museum archives, staring at faces in high school photographs, reading through old tax ledgers and hundreds of pages of police records, Ruth knew that more Negro women were arrested for prostitution – entered as "keeping a disorderly house" – than for any other crime. It was nearly impossible to imagine her quiet but fiercely moral and occasionally explosive mother reduced to such circumstances, except that Ruth understood the impact of circumstance on life, that fortuitous or disastrous accident could have a transforming impact on human personality.

Her own life might have taken a far less fortunate turn had she not happened to meet William Hughes, Jr., a visiting teacher in a Negro school, when she was seventeen, and fallen so deeply in love she left her parents' home town and state to travel with him to Boston, where he married her and saw to it that she received the formal education her parents could not have afforded but which he insisted was a necessity for a person as intelligent as herself. Ruth communicated with Samuel and Belle through monthly letters. She sent money when she could, but she did not visit for ten years. When she returned to Norwalk with her husband and their two young children, it was to attend her parents' funerals. They had been asleep in the back room and had died together in a smoldering fire whose smoke had damaged but not destroyed the small house Samuel had built on land it had taken years for him to buy, the house in which Ruth had been raised and which now belonged to her.

Repaired and fully renovated, those two old rooms still formed the back wing of the large house she and William built around it. They had put in new windows, replaced smoke damaged walls, but left the old wide plank floors, now scraped and polished, and they had retained the original stone fireplace where Belle had cooked and warmed water for baths, on whose mantle she always kept the ledger that contained her writing lessons and, eventually, the stories she wrote.

Ruth sat in one of those rooms now, but both had been recreated as her writing place at the back of the house. She wrote in long-hand, filling dozens of legal pads before she dared transfer her words to a printed page that made them seem prematurely permanent. When she had begun gathering information and ideas into notebooks that would be the raw material of her book about her father's life, she had felt an ecstasy greater than she'd ever known. She researched his work as an oysterman. She read all the writers he'd told her about when she was a girl and with William's help added many more. Combining old family stories with an expanding knowledge of history, she recounted and imagined her grandfather's escape from slavery; the murder of her great-grandfather, the first Samuel; and the lives of her great-great-grandmother Ruth, Mr. Henry, the abolitionist leader, and Louisa Summers, her white great-grandmother who had run away to Philadelphia not long before the Civil War. Going further back was unnecessary to her conception of the book about her father's life, and she'd been glad, anyway, to skip the painful contradictions involving the slaveholder, John Summers, whose genes were a part of her heritage she wished to but could not deny.

Those contradictions, however, were nothing compared to the troubling doubts and resistances she was sunk in now, trying to write her mother's story. Her relation to her father had been straightforward: he was an intelligent, strong, and kind man whose faults always seemed forgivable to her. Telling his story had been straightforward too, an act of generosity to the world and her people, a tribute to her father and a fine legacy for her daughters. The book did well, was still doing well seven years later. Scholars, writers, and ordinary readers wrote to her, moved and educated by her work. Belle's story was different. Its plot – if you could use that word to describe a life – its themes and characters (including herself) were all layered with conflicting emotions she felt it her responsibility to describe. There was no chance of a simple telling. Ruth knew that by now. She had stayed away from home and her beloved father for ten years, returning home only to bury him, because she found it so difficult to be in her mother's presence.

Something had been wrong between them since Ruth could remember, since her infancy if she were to believe Belle's sometimes angry words. Some expectation impossible to fulfill. A too threatening similarity to her intellectual father? An inadequacy of feature, she had sometimes thought, skin too dark, or lips too wide?

"No, it ain't your lips," her mother had sighed when Ruth accused her once of being color struck. "It's your mouth." Belle had spoken so low her daughter had repeated, "my mouth?" But Belle had already turned away and could not be reached.

Her mouth then – her will, her capacities – the very things that might sustain her in her life were what her Mama seemed to hate. Or no, it wasn't hate. She had known this even as a girl. But some inexplicable coldness toward her, more upsetting because of its inexplicability; more enraging because its effects, even its existence, could always be denied.

When she told them she was traveling to Boston with her new husband who promised to send her to college, her mother had remained silent for days. "You'd be better off staying here among your own," she finally said on the evening before Ruth and William were about to depart.

Ruth walked toward Belle who had been sitting in her favorite chair, her ledger opened on her lap. "Are you saying you *want* me to stay, Mama?" she had asked.

"No, uh-uh, no. I want you to do what you want to do," Belle had responded quickly. Then she had walked into the bedroom and closed the door. Samuel followed her, and when he came out alone, he said, "She loves you, Ruth. She just don't know how to say it right. All her love of words seem to go into those stories. Something changed in her a long time ago. Ain't no changing it back." He closed the ledger and returned it to its high shelf while Ruth set her mouth tight and her mind firmly on Boston, anything to get away from the cold and impenetrable suffering she had hated since she was a small child.

The next morning, she promised herself and her father that she would come back in a few months. But William's easily expressed passion and physical warmth were a relief that went so deep and fast into her, and the coldness such a painful memory, it would be years later when Ruth finally returned. When she and William took possession of the place and the half acre of land it stood on, she had walked back and forth between the two now partly burned but still immaculate rooms and found Belle's large notebook under a stack of folded linens, all protected in a metal trunk that stood at the foot of the bed. Her parents had been buried for a week when Ruth learned, from the ledger, the story that revealed the dimensions of her mother's capacity for silence and at least some of the reason for Belle's discomfort with her own child.

A boy had been born first, and although – perhaps because – he was premature and sickly, his mother adored him. But she always felt Samuel was disappointed; he had counted on a girl he wanted to name Ruth. *For nothing makes his passion rise,* his wife wrote in her awkward but legible script, the bitter disappointment clear to the daughter who read the words, *like the story of his father's line.*

Samuel loved his son, but he was disappointed – perhaps, as Belle thought – because the boy wasn't Ruth, or because he was sickly, born too early to survive. He was dead in two months. And a year after her brother's death, she'd come, healthy and large, the "Ruth" her daddy had always wanted. There were no more after her, and when she asked about the grave at the edge of the yard behind the house – with one word cut into the stone – *Henry* – she'd been told her uncle, Belle's younger brother, was buried there. *We can't tell the girl because Samuel fears it will cause her to feel guilty or frighten her, and he wants her strong,* Belle had written.

The girl.

The last entry in the huge ledger was the day after Ruth left for Boston. *She's gone,* Belle had written, and placed her work at the bottom of the trunk, her daughter supposed, abruptly ending and preserving twenty years of work. That Ruth had a good idea of why writing her mother's story was so much harder than writing her father's in no way eased her pain or facilitated the flow and concentration of her work. She'd been writing out notes, discarding possible structures, trying out different approaches for nearly two years and was coming close to abandoning the entire effort. Perhaps she was not the one to write Belle Waterman's story, unloving and still angry daughter that she knew she was, fifty years after leaving home, forty years after her mother's death, more than twenty since her own daughters had become mothers themselves. The thought filled her with shame.

And now, out of the blue, this letter comes, from a white

woman, a writer named Ami Reed whose novels Ruth had read, who said she was connected by her son's marriage to a woman who might have tempted Ruth's father to stray. Maybe this would be the breakthrough she had been praying for, the one William assured her would come if she waited patiently enough. Maybe it was her own pathetic need to find herself innocent, finally, of causing all her mother's misery and anger. If Samuel had – well, anything at all – with the white woman while Belle was pregnant, it would have been enough to cause a lifetime of bitterness, and since the child she carried had then died, more than enough reinforcement for an angry fear of any too-encompassing love, old or new.

There was also, of course, her inveterate curiosity. True stories had always intrigued her as nothing else did – their mismatched layers and surprisingly matched patterns, their echoes and allusions to other stories, and yet their uniqueness and perfect newness, all their own. It was the thing about memoir she loved, when it became like the most luminous fiction, stretching to encompass chaos, sacrificing everything, even a beautiful shape, to come closer to life itself. And isn't that the point? she asked out loud as, rising from her seat in the old part of the house, and stretching her aching arms, lifting and rolling her shoulders, she went into the modern kitchen to set out the coffee cake she'd made that morning and boil water for tea, just as she saw a car turn into her driveway and an olive-skinned woman in a dark raincoat walk toward her door.

Chapter 36

The black woman's hair is divided into dozens of twisted locks, all of them gathered and tucked under a bright blue band forming a loose bun. Gray hair frames her face and weaves in and out of the twists, an intricate web through the black. Her eyes are narrow, shifting in the light between almond brown and dark hazel. Her nose is broad and flat, its nostrils flaring wide above her mouth. Her skin is a rich maple brown. She is smiling in welcome, holding out a hand to the woman standing in her doorway. "Good afternoon, Ms. Reed," she says. "Come in out of the rain. You must be chilled. Let's have some tea."

"Oh please, call me Ami – that is if you don't mind?" and Ami takes the hand, admiring the short, neatly clipped nails, the narrow wedding ring of tiny diamonds, a heavy amber bracelet surrounding a thick wrist. Gratefully, she accepts help getting out of her damp coat and scarf and follows Ruth Hughes down the wide foyer, through a large dining room, its forest green walls setting off dark wood antiques – a long narrow table; a hutch whose shelves overflow with pewter pitchers; goblets and plates; a tall chest covered with family photographs framed in silver.

"Yes, of course. It will be Ami, then. And I'm Ruth." The white woman looks youthful for someone their age, but wrinkles gather around her mouth, and between her dark eyes what Ruth's daughter used to call "worry lines," deep cracks in an otherwise smooth forehead. And Ruth has noticed her guest's hands – long tapered fingers and manicured nails, perfectly rounded and polished in a rich bright red. Her hair is a sort of whitish tan, previously brown, Ruth imagines, its short waves

272

pulled back from the forehead in a nicely layered cut that makes Ruth think of her mother. As she offers tea and cake, seating herself and her guest at a square, light oak table in the kitchen, she wonders about this Ami Reed whose books she has admired; whose story about the woman named Hannah Sokolov she is eager to hear; whose hair is shining, just now, in a few streaks of sunlight trying to come through the large window, at last, after days of rain. Before their visit is over it may be possible to walk across the lawn without drenching their feet. Within minutes she will know if this is a white woman with whom she would want to walk across her lawn – but she likes the woman already, is attracted to the way her broad smile is complicated by those worry lines.

"I was very interested in your letter," Ruth says, looking into her steaming tea. "Oh – I'm sorry – I've been so immersed in my work lately, I've forgotten about normal conversation. How was your drive? Would you like something more than cake?"

But Ami, never entirely comfortable with small talk herself, is relieved by Ruth's plunge into the real subject of their meeting. Something about the woman feels instantly familiar to her, and she knows it is that they are both writers. (In the moment of familiarity, she recalls feeling left out of a local SNCC organization when she tried being an activist in the early seventies, yearning for comrades, yet excluded because she was white.) She is drawn to Ruth's face, finding it beautiful despite the many age lines and wrinkles. Yes, she thinks, something about them is similar, two women nearing seventy, becoming writers when it was still such a difficult thing for women who were also mothers to do.

"Your daughters?" she asks, pointing to a photograph of two young women on a nearby shelf. It's out of place among white bowls and tall glasses, as if it had been left there by mistake.

"Oh – I was looking at their faces this morning, drinking coffee and wondering if I could see my mother's face in either of theirs. I'm trying to write my mother's story now, and having a lot of trouble with it. You know how it is –"

"Belle Waterman," says Ami, remembering Hannah's de-

273

scription more vividly than the brief one in Ruth's memoir. And she relates the story of the haircut that left so lasting an impression on Hannah. The silence between them when Ami finishes is thick with sensation. Ruth's eyes are wide, and her fascination is reflected by Ami's tone when she says, "It took place in this very house."

"Not in this house, exactly," Ruth says, eyes narrow again. "Back there – in the old part – where my study is now – the part my father built. Survived storms, fire, all these years – would you like to see it?"

They walk back through the dining room, through a short narrow hallway and into a square room, old wooden beams exposed beneath a triangular ceiling. Sparks are jumping and shimmering in the old stone fireplace. A large archway that may once have been a door opens into a smaller room whose back wall has been cut almost entirely into a large window that looks out on a neat lawn and garden. Through the curved space formed by the arch Ami can see a pair of tall wooden file cabinets; built-in shelves filled with neatly arranged books; a large work table, bare except for a computer and a box of disks. In the larger room where they are standing, a work table is stacked with books, files, and papers. More are piled high on the floor and on a green brocade couch, leaving no room to sit down.

Ami tries to picture those other women, more than seventy years before: one white and probably guilt-ridden; the other black and, if she suspects anything, very angry. The image fades after a moment though – the two rooms and their contrasts too compelling in the present to ignore. She looks at one, then the other, turning around.

"It's my great privilege," Ruth says, laughing, "to have *two* work rooms – one completely neat and organized, one for the chaos I always create when I'm in the midst of any work. You see? I can't even offer you a place to sit. We could walk in the garden." She points to an old double door that must once have been the entrance to the house. "The rain has stopped, but it's probably still too damp."

They walk back through the newer part of the house into the

kitchen where Ruth heats water for more tea.

"Your home is beautiful," Ami says, and after a moment of tense silence in which each woman feels the presence of Belle, of Samuel, of the memoir they have not spoken of, she adds, "Your memoir about your father – I've been reading and rereading it all summer. It's a wonderful book."

An expression of uncertainty, or suspicion, crosses Ruth's face, causing Ami to add more honestly, "I had trouble reading it, the early sections – where the first Samuel is killed. Your descriptions of the brutality are – almost overwhelming. I had to skip some parts." Ami hears her own apologetic tone, looks up at Ruth again and says, "The story of your father's life, here in Norwalk, is inspiring. He must have been a brilliant man."

"Oh yes," Ruth says, clearly pleased. "And I have no trouble seeing *his* face reflected in Ashaki's." She takes the photograph of her daughters from the shelf and places it before them on the table, pointing to the young woman on the left. "But then, I see her all the time. My other one lives in Ghana. I hardly ever see her – maybe once a year at the most. I have to stare at her more closely to remember the nuances of her expressions."

Ami recognizes the maternal pain, and compliments Ruth's daughters, the one she sees and the one far away.

The two women share some general information about their children and grandchildren. Ruth has two girls from the daughter who lives nearby, in New York – "Willa, after her grandfather, and Nelsa, after Mandela," - and one grandson - "the fourth Samuel," who lives in Ghana with his mother.

Ami nods respectfully after Ruth finishes speaking their names.

"And your name?" Ruth continues. "It's beautiful. How did you get it?"

Ami repeats the history she imparted recently to Hannah and long ago to Samantha.

"I have an Israeli friend," Ruth says. "You know what your name sounds like backwards? The Hebrew word for mother – Ema. But not only that. It means *my people.* A good name."

How wonderful, Ami thinks, to talk to someone whose

pleasure in words is so like her own – pleasure in turning them around, seeing their undersides, separating meaning from sound and then connecting them again. "Samantha," she says, taking her turn at naming, "is my granddaughter," and she describes her, and her father, Jake, awkwardly crossing the hump of racial identification. "Jake is black. His father, my husband, was black. He died some years ago."

"I'm sorry," Ruth murmurs, thinking of William who is away just now for a week on business, how she misses his voice, his body moving around the house, the safe feeling of his presence. Lately, since she passed her sixty-ninth birthday, when he is gone even for a day, she is never completely free of her fear of his death.

"And my granddaughter, Samantha?" Ami is saying. "Her mother was Jewish – the granddaughter of Hannah Sokolov – the woman I came to see you about. Well, only part of the reason. Samantha is the real reason, I suppose. Your father's story – or part of it – was told over three generations of Samantha's family. It was a fragment, of course, and most likely distorted - but my granddaughter – Sam, we call her – was – well, it turns out she was named for him." Ami looks down, suddenly aware of her presumption. Then she returns to her own story. "Now, she wants me to write about my life – about being white and married to a black man, about having an inter-racial son." As she speaks the awkward hyphenated word, she hears Jake's loud critique and sees her granddaughter's disapproving frown.

"You've never written about that?" Ruth knits her eyebrows closely together and smiles in surprise. Her writing has always been about framing and shaping stories from her actual life. Before the book about her father, there was another one, little known but equally precious to her, about her own girlhood right here in Norwalk. It ended with her departure for Boston. Writing has been a tool for her, like a garden spade to dig into the wet earth, or sometimes like a pickax, or at times only her own exhausted fingers, each section of life sifted and examined with words, digging and describing, digging and describing, trying to figure out – as Virginia Woolf once put it – what

276

belongs to what.

"No, I've never written about it, not until now," Ami admits. The tone of confession in her voice annoys her. " I've tried to stay away from the actual facts of my life in my work. I've wanted my life to be separate from my work. I can't really tell you why – fear of exposure is part of it, I suppose, but also a feeling that I can get closer to the truth of things when I'm creating a story whose sources are unknown to me. And then – afraid to hurt people with my work. There's that, too." She feels Ruth's eyes pressing her, an intensely curious stare.

Ruth is thinking about Samuel and Belle, about Samuel and this woman Hannah, about Hannah and Belle, imagining the haircut that took place in the back room. It may be the very story she needs, because what she sees in it is her mother's vulnerability. Imagine – she is cutting the hair of a woman she must suspect is somehow carrying on with her husband, even an occasional and casual flirtation not only treacherous but possibly life-threatening. A white woman. A beautiful woman, perhaps. A beautiful white woman. Belle is holding a scissors in her hand. Ruth feels the temptation, then the rigid self-restraint her mother must have felt, the disciplining of desire drummed into her since she was a child. She will have to return to Belle's ledger, Ruth thinks, to her mother's own words, stories full of pain for a daughter, but – she tries to keep hope from clouding her judgment, then stalling her again with disappointment – maybe if she rewrites her mother's words in her own handwriting she can feel even more of Belle's emotions. She will have to do some imagining, she sees, because so much has been left out and will never be known. Yet, what does she have left except her own limited ability to intuit the truth of things? What else can she do?

"True stories" – Ruth stops herself, begins again. "For me, true stories are ... well, the thing itself. What I have to comprehend. I can't separate my life so neatly from my work. It's – well, it's just a version of me. I send my daughters everything I write hoping somehow it will give them a clue. I want them to see me in the work. But fear of exposure? Yes, I know about that."

"For me..." Ami begins, but cannot finish, her own confusion building in the last weeks to this shifting, unnamed movement inside her that might easily spill out in a flood of unintended questions and private conflicts. Fearing she might behave inappropriately and offend her hostess, she sips her tea.

"Tell me more about Hannah Sokolov," Ruth says. "I feel this story might be just what I need for *my* problem."

Relieved by this gracious rebalancing of scales, Ami pulls together the story she heard from Hannah and the additional pieces provided by Sam. Adding what she herself has surmised, she tells the story of what seems to have happened in Norwalk all those years before, ending with Hannah's final words about rearranging to Corinne, calling her Belle. "As I said in my letter, I'm certain there was no – well, no affair," Ami says. "But some powerful attraction, at least on Hannah's side. And some strong feeling for your mother as well. What has become the issue for my granddaughter is the name and what it symbolizes about her life, about who she feels she is. As I said – her name is Samantha, Samantha Reed. Your father's story, or Hannah's version of it, was used as a kind of inspiration for – for many things. Sam feels a sense of connection. She's read your book, of course."

Ruth is touched by the unexpected continuation of her father's story, his legacy branching out into a surprising place. "Samantha Reed," she says. "Sam. I'd like to meet her sometime."

"Did you ever put up a stone for your great-grandfather, the first Samuel, when you took the trip down to Saint Elizabeth where he was killed?" Ami recalls the description of the land, the majestic Chesapeake, the old Summers house, now a restaurant and an inn where Ruth Hughes found herself unable to stay. Instead, she had chosen a hotel in the larger town nearby, had made that her home base while she searched for information and researched history.

But something is wrong, and Ruth says tactfully, "You probably don't remember. I said at the end of that chapter that he would never have a gravestone. His body was dismembered

– thrown – or scattered – who knows where. It would have seemed a cruel denial of reality to erect a stone, as if – as if we knew where he was. No, as I wrote then, I hope my book may serve as one modest eulogy – for him and for all the other bodies desecrated and lost."

Her sorrow and anger at history, as well as her irritation at Ami's failure, are palpable. Apologetic again, Ami looks down.

" I know it was brutally described," Ruth says, "but that's because it was brutal. How else to describe it?"

Ami remembers the vision of the slave ships on the water, hundreds of ships over three hundred years, millions of bodies, millions of lives, how terrible the vision was, how she tried to extinguish the sight. She remembers Sam's words about the shark patterns changing as they followed the trail of blood. "I'm sorry. I am truly sorry. No, I haven't read it carefully. You're right. I . . . I couldn't. Look, I don't want to tire you – take up your whole day. But may I return tomorrow for another visit? I was wrong not to have read your book closely before I came. I want to do that tonight, and – well – might we talk again?"

Ruth does feel fatigued by the dull repetitive specter of white timidity, but she agrees to a second meeting and suggests a nice inn in the historical district where Ami might spend the night. Her disappointment and irritation will pass quickly, she knows, leaving a well of familiar sadness, but even the sadness is already mitigated by the desire to know more from Ami Reed – a phrase, a gesture, an old memory of Hannah Sokolov's that may have seemed trivial to Ami, but for Ruth Hughes, intent now on her mother's story and the belief that she can tell it, it may mean all the world.

As she drives back down Knight Street, while she stops in the museum and with the help of a knowledgeable archivist finds out about the old graveyard on Cemetery Road, while she walks among the graves crowded within a circular stone wall, Ami feels she has forgotten something else of equal importance, an omission that would be even more offensive to Ruth than her failure to read carefully the brutal details of the first Samuel's death. Whatever it is nags at her as she searches for and finds the gravestones of Samuel and Belle Waterman. The gracefully curved marble is only knee high, and Ami kneels down, presses her fingers into the names so she can tell Sam she's done so, traces the first three letters of Samuel's name many times. She stands up again, looks around, as if she is waiting for something.

Outside the old stone wall is a commercial avenue – a laundry mat, an appliance store, a gas station, a supermarket. Ami takes in the details of what she sees – large plate glass windows, a sign advertising lean cuts of steak, an ATM – and the scattered life around the stores – two young black men in thick down jackets laughing out loud at something while they wait for their laundry to be done, a white woman pushing a shopping cart full of groceries to her car, a girl – she can't be much older than Sam – the brown skin of her face contrasting dramatically with the brilliant white of her hat – filling her car with gas. For a moment, it is as if everything is perfectly still. Nothing moves. Outside the stone wall life is held within a frame, silent as the graves within the wall. Ami herself is still, waiting and listening. Then everything returns to normal. The young men laugh and slap high fives. The woman lifts her packages into her car and pushes the empty cart onto the sidewalk. The girl gets into her car and drives away. Ami is certain she has forgotten something important. She recognizes the feeling she had the day she was driving Hannah to the Sound, the feeling that came with the summer, with Sam's letter, with her first reading of Ruth's book.

Chapter 37

If I were to choose one word to describe your mother, it would be exuberant. Everything seemed to excite her – and I suppose the negative or darker side of that quality is a tendency to suffer more acutely than someone of a more even disposition might. If Jake got angry at her, for example, even about the smallest thing, she would become sullen, lash out at him almost like a child, and it would always turn out, once they made up, that his anger had caused her so much pain she couldn't face it without becoming furious herself. I know this because she was not only my daughter-in-law. She was my friend. We talked, had dinner alone at times. I loved her – not, perhaps, like the daughter I never had, more like a beloved niece, without any of the usual maternal knots. And I liked her, too, especially her bravery. Once she felt she saw something clearly, or understood some complexity, she was unwavering in her faith in the truth of what she had seen. Perhaps your need for "the truth" is some-thing like hers, Samantha. When she went after it – some truth she suspected or intuited in experience – she seemed happy – I mean happy in its deepest sense – joyful – unselfconsciously her most essential self. Your father fell in love with this quality, I believe, and so did I. They argued about the race issue, because Maya insisted they must make it not matter to you, and I – well, I needed her vehemence, I think. Why? I am not sure I know, Samantha. To support my own doubt, I suppose.

You see – I am leaving in my hesitations, the self-analysis I would usually reserve for my journals, because. . . .

Because without these interruptions I am not sure I could

281

resist my long-standing attraction to shaping things. It's a discipline I worked hard for, a discipline that has gotten me through. But you want the truth, Samantha my dear, and I see now that to give you that – in the way that you mean it– I will have to proceed in this other way, mapless, so to speak. Lately, I feel very unsettled, fragile almost, because much of what I felt to be the story of my life is shifting, so I don't know how all this will read in the end – if there is ever an "end" in the sense I have meant that word. I don't like uncertainty any more than your mother did. I like pattern, and meaning, and a sense that I know where I belong.

Now, intending to describe Maya to you, as you asked, I've begun to describe myself, the very thing about memoir that unnerves me. Where is the suggestive mask of fiction, the controlled ambiguities of poetry in all this self-conscious prose?

Maya was a vibrant and dramatic young woman. She wore her long brown hair in a thick braid and always had gold hoops in her pierced ears – small ones for everyday, larger and thicker ones for evenings when she'd wind the braid around her head like a crown. An old-fashioned, exotic look to me – one that emphasized her Semitic heritage despite her fair, peaches-and-cream skin. She had a long narrow nose which she hated, always flirted with the idea of "fixing" it, but Jake wouldn't hear of it. He adored her face. He adored her in a way, and perhaps that is not the most reliable form of love.

Frankly, Samantha my dearest, I do not know if their marriage would have lasted if tragedy had not brought it to an end. But I do think you would have liked your mother, continued to find her enchanting as you did when you were a little girl, even if you fought with her about many things, as all mothers and daughters do. I know you worry about not having enough memories. But perhaps you have remembered her in part by becoming like her in many ways. You have her exuberance, her quickness to anger, and her bravery, I think, as well.

As to your other question – how she would have felt about you. You were her passion, I think as much as your father was. I remember how every year at Hanukah she'd let you light the candles, holding your fingers so you wouldn't burn yourself, from the time you were only two. She'd tell you of the miracle of light, but it was the idea of Jewish freedom fighters she was really interested in. And she'd continue the story at Passover every year, when you went to your cousin's for a Seder. I was invited several times, and – just now I remember her talking about the similarities between black and Jewish freedom from slavery. She might even have mentioned the story of Samuel and how you got your name – extraordinary, that I don't remember – yes, she must have done. And I was probably allowing my mind to wander, always impatient with religious rituals of any kind, staring into the candlelight or nibbling on matzoh while she talked. She wanted you to love everything you were, Sam. She wanted you to believe nothing in the world could make you question that love.

And I remember something else. When she had her mind on something – she was unstoppable. Like her insistence on her version of the Passover story. Like the day she went for her last swim.

She is trying to remember all she can of that Seder as she waits for the train from New York. The platform is large and crowded, and she leans against a broad pillar, sipping a container of hot coffee, a bagel with cream cheese wrapped in tin foil in her large purse in case Sam hasn't eaten yet. She is disobeying her son's instructions to bring fruit and avoid bread, believing that making an issue of food is the worst thing they can do for Samantha's "very slight" (she has emphasized to Jake) overweight. She knew as soon as she left the graves last night that she had to call, tell them where she was, who she'd been visiting, that Samantha had the right to come with her to the second meeting. She had called to get Ruth's permission first, then she tried to quell her anxiety about calling them.

Her room at the inn had been charming, the second meal of oysters in one day a luxurious treat. The bed was wide and comfortable, the bathroom sparkling with white porcelain and new dark red tile. A soft white terrycloth robe hung in the closet, and after a hot bath Ami cuddled into it. Although she'd had two glasses of wine with dinner, she poured herself another as she opened Ruth's book again. Now she knew why she had avoided a careful reading of the part about the killing, and she was prepared to reread that chapter closely, slowly, even it if meant she would not sleep all night. First, however, she had to make arrangements with Sam and Jake, and for the moment, that felt more intimidating than any book could be.

"Hey, Mom." He responded to her hello with a greeting she'd heard for so many years it seemed as long as her life – though of course, there had been a time when she did not know Jake, when Jake did not exist, but that seemed impossible at the moment, and the *hey, Mom,* was suddenly shocking rather than familiar. She felt the sensation of slipping, and was silent while she held on.

"Mom?" His voice again, so like his father's in tone, yet something in his pronunciation of words had always evoked Nicky's voice, and his rhythms of speech her own father's, as well.

"Yes," she said quickly. "Yes. I'm here, Jake." Another silence threatened and she made an effort to break into it. "I'm in a lovely room, a lovely little hotel in the historical district of Norwalk. Norwalk, Connecticut. I've been to visit Ruth Hughes, and I'm staying overnight so I can visit her again tomorrow. I'm calling to let Sam know I'm here. I did what she asked, and I think she should take the train here in the morning, Jake. I think – I think coming back with me tomorrow will – might help."

She was imagining him in his favorite chair, his long legs crossed at the knees – he might be cradling the phone between his neck and his shoulder – she could almost see his graceful feet, slightly pigeon-toed, his long narrow fingers, his delicate ear pressed against the receiver. Her own words felt as extraordinary as his calling her name – *Mom* – so direct, without preface or explanation – and she heard her voice crack, as if she were about to cry. She sipped her wine.

"Mom?" he said. "Are you all right? Why didn't you tell us

284

you were going? Sam's been – seems – better, ever since the funeral, and she misses you. Why haven't you come over lately? Is it because of the last discussion? What's going on?"

"Yes, no. I'm fine." She had begun to sound better now, she could hear her tone, more normal. "I don't know why I didn't tell you. I just felt I had to do this alone. But now I called to say – to tell you about my meeting with Ruth Hughes. It was fascinating, only it's hard to know what to ask – what I have a right to ask." Comfortable with description, she began to search for any detail that might interest him, but she asked herself, what had really happened? She felt ashamed for having stayed away – punishing them, punishing herself too, but the shame was too great for this small, personal failure, even for failing to read the woman's book carefully. The other thing nagging at her returned.

"Mom!" Jake raised his voice. "Are you there?! What's wrong with you?!"

"I'm sorry, darling. Nothing. I'm sorry."

"What are you sorry for? Maybe I should drive up and get you."

She must come out of this state, she knew, must stop worrying about what she'd forgotten. It would come to her. She must reassure him, or he wouldn't let Sam come. "Can you put Samantha on the line too?" She forced a stronger voice. "I'll tell you both together."

When Sam picked up the extension, said, "Myami – hi!" sounding pleased, she felt relieved, she breathed more evenly, and began to tell them about the visit, remembering from decades of practice how to sound calm and in control when she was frightened and on edge, how to seem steady when the edges were precarious. As she talked on, she heard her son calm down. He asked questions, responded with appreciative laughs and sounds. Once he called to Corinne, "my Mom says . . . , " and proudly he repeated her very words for his wife.

It had been simple all along. Obvious and simple. No elaborate structures or supposedly secret, hidden messages were effective against it. The eyestrain, the clogged sinuses – all of it was what it always seemed to be. She was worried about Sam, so worried she sometimes lost her voice. Her eyes ached from the strain of trying to see impending danger, warding it off, and at times she had been so afraid she could hardly breathe. She wanted to make up for Maya's death, for the loneliness and conflicts of childhood, for racial injustice. She wanted to protect her granddaughter, as she wanted to protect Jake – *the lovely angularity of his jaw* - and as she had even wanted to protect Jacob – *his hesitant hands, his body moving over her, within her, his large chest, his thick shoulders.* She could not bear to see them excluded, unwanted, unloved. That was the shame that stalked her. She was afraid she could not bear it – as a mother, as a wife – to witness it. Worse, if it were her, her own body in her own skin, could she have survived, as her son had done, as her granddaughter had to do? And if she made her true story known, with all its crevices and secret places, all its open softness and out-of-control need and desire, its violent rage and shameful terror, wouldn't she be showing them how weak she was? How much she needed *them* to help *her*? How would she protect them if she did that?

She kept talking about her day, and after telling them everything she could think of, she finally sighed and said, "Oh, Jake." With his name the feeling of extraordinary time came again, its stillness and its swift passing. The parts and stages of her own child's life: his infancy, his childhood, his child's birth, the terrible loss of his father, the two women he has loved; her son – a man of incomparable generosity and fierce conviction; his lifelong love for her.

"You sound tired, Mom – do you – "

"I'm definitely coming, Myami. Right, Dad?" Sam, unstoppable when she was following a trail.

"Okay," he said, but after a long pause, hesitant and concerned . . . "But Mom? Are you sure you're . . . . "

"It'll be fine, Jake dear, I'm fine." She assumed a lighter, stronger voice again, this time more easily. "Sam? There's a 9:05 from Grand Central. Or you can get it at 9:20 from 125th Street. It gets in at 10:30. I'll be waiting for you at the station."

"Come here on your way home then," Jake said. "That's an

order. We'll all have dinner. You can tell us about it."

"Wonderful," she said, meaning it, only the tone of her voice felt wrong – as if her son had extended an ordinary invitation, as if it would be a simple pleasure for her to stop by his home on her way to her own, as if she could ever fully comprehend the idea that the two *homes* were not the same. "Give my love to Corinne," she said.

"Bye, Myami. See you at ten-thirty then," and Sam hung up the phone.

"Good night then, darling. I love you, Jake," she said.

When she heard his reply – "Good night, Mom, and I love you too," a thousand such refrains echoed and multiplied, and she didn't want to slip again. She held on to Sam's voice, heard her shout that summer day, naming her, *Myami! Myami!* Calling it across the water to the seagulls, as if they would confirm her new reality by diving through the air and swallowing her name, just like they dived for and swallowed fish.

As soon as she clicked off the phone she felt the shift. It came in a more intense breathlessness than before, a tightening in her chest. Just as she was about to become concerned, it passed, and she inhaled through her nose, then her mouth, until she was filled up with air, holding it, cradling her breath. Something opened. Their bodies filled her vision – their absolute particularity, of color, of shape; her eyes closed from the strain. She would have to become large enough to encompass it all– that she is white and yet not white; that she is not black and yet somewhere inside black like them, that she is so alone without Jacob who, in some way that makes no rational sense at all, bequeathed her *mixedness,* not only through their son but in herself.

He had taken her in. And it had taken all this time for her to understand the burden and weight of the second gift right behind the first, hidden in Samuel's death scene if it were read with full attention. The nightmare gift, the eye-opening, mind-opening, nightmare gift. It is not *those people* who were enslaved, not the mothers and fathers and grandparents of *those people* who were enslaved, it is her people, her own people, right here in her own

287

country, in her world. And so it is herself, her body dismembered, her legs and arms striped with scars and dark with brands, her feet and hands cut off, her neck shackled, her sex invaded, her child, her Jake, sold away, her Samantha who is lost to her forever. Like Ruth's son and grandson. Like Louisa's child. To know this, and at the very same time to know the opposite – that none of it is her. Her body is whole, her child safe, her grandchild loved and strong. She would not have been the one who suffered most, just as Louisa was not. She would have been spared. There is the relief, and the shame.

But even that was not the end of it; the opening kept on, door after door, and when she tried to cry what came out was something so loud she had to hold the pillow over her mouth, because it didn't stop, it kept coming, a loud, furious call of terror, as if it were her lover, her child, her very own body, the history hers, her own.

She remembered every line of Jacob's body, the smell of his sweat, the way his mouth tightened slightly when he was angry, the way he'd jut his head forward on his shoulders, how his lips stretched and narrowed when he was pleased, how he leaned forward, his hands hanging loose between his knees. His body. His body. His skin. He was there in the room, as she wrote in her notebook for Samantha, as she opened Ruth's book to begin reading it again, he was feeling the shift, shaking along with her, protecting her, leaning in close.

The train is pulling into the South Norwalk station, coming to a slow stop. Samantha is the first one to appear in the opened doorway, and the conductor jumps down to give her a hand. As always, she looks lovely to her grandmother; going through a slightly awkward stage – who doesn't? – belly curving out more than usual from her tight black T-shirt. But her skin shines with youthful health. Her eyes light up when she sees Ami, and, long braids flying, she runs into her arms. Ami holds Sam tight – too tight, she realizes – and, hiding her eyes for a moment, she reaches into her purse for the bagel, holds it out to Sam.

"Thanks, Myami," she says. She unwraps the thin tin foil, its narrow creases sparkling in the morning light. She licks the creamy cheese oozing from between the slices and takes a large piece of bread into her lovely mouth. In that moment, Ami knows what she has forgotten, and what she must somehow find the right moment, the right words, to say to Ruth Hughes.

Chapter 38

I had never heard my grandmother sound like that – nervous and hesitant, like a young child required to speak before an audience for the first time. The light in the kitchen was incandescent, as can happen after a long rain. Myami had placed Ruth's book on the table, and now she kept one hand on the cover, the other holding my hand beneath the table. She had not slept at all, she'd told me, but watching the night, then the dawn, then the full morning had energized her. Her eyes were wide as she completed her recitation.

"He was cut to pieces, kept alive as long as possible so they could see him suffer. His feet, his hands, his sex, all cut off. He must have passed into unconsciousness by then, one can only hope. The parts of his body were scattered for the animals to eat or discard. His child was kept long enough to reach his maximum price and then he was sold away. That was what finally killed Ruth, broke her even though she had held on for so long. And a year later, Mr. Henry. Died before Emancipation – loading stacks of tobacco onto the wagon like he'd been doing for over fifty years. You looked up the weather – it was an unusually hot spring. He must have died from heat exhaustion, you said, and from a broken heart. Everyone he loved gone or dead or lost. He'd helped almost two hundred people to escape. In front of the flat rock with the words *Henry, slave of John Summers* scratched across it, you erected a marble tombstone, and you inscribed it properly – *Mr. Henry, Teacher and Freedom Fighter, 1784 – 1859, Remembered Always.* Your heart must nearly have broken, going down there, walking the actual land, writing it all down. Facing it. Your grandfather – that child in the wagon. Your great-great-grandmother – all lost.

"And the first Samuel – a young boy really, not more than twenty years old, foolish and brave, probably calling for his mother as he died."

Ruth was silent, but she met Myami's eyes with her own.

I was thinking about the other part of the story my grandmother had spoken about in the car on the way to Ruth's home. The part she had almost forgotten in her effort to suppress the terrible details of the first Samuel's death. We had both focused on the three Samuels because they were the center of the story as we'd heard it and read it, the ones whose name had been given to me, and because we had tried so hard to understand the loss in Hannah's life – a man she might have loved, all that she had buried when she buried her desire. A thick blinding storm of loss, so dense you might not find your way through it. That was the risk I was beginning to appreciate, why people loved silence, and forgetting. But there was more. Someone else.

"And her daughter." Myami breathed audibly. With the words outside her, she seemed to be taking them in. *"Ema,"* she whispered, *"my people."*

"What?" I tightened my grip on her hand, scared of her increasing distractions, her weakness, her suddenly apparent age.

But she continued in a clearer voice. "You wrote about her. Her daughter sold, too."

I looked from one woman to the other. I had not forgotten Lina whose real name was Melina. She had come to me one night in a dream, sold because she was mixed, a mulatto, a mongrel, a crossbreed, *inter*-racial, mixing up the nice neat family tree. Then I had dreamed her again. And again. Sold. Abandoned. A mother and a daughter torn apart, by a rolling cart, by a high tide ocean. I had woken screaming, in a sweat.

"Her daughter," Ruth said. "Yes."

"Louisa's sister," I added, loosening my grip on Myami's fingers. She looked at me steadily, eyes full of love and – I hoped – or saw – a kind of strength I had counted on in her from the start.

"Yes," Ruth told us, "according to the records of the sale of

291

Summerly slaves her name was Lina. She was only seven when she was sold to a farmer in North Carolina. But I lost track of her after that. They changed her name, and then they had some financial hard times soon after they bought her, and they sold all their slaves to a large plantation in Alabama. My own double great-great-aunt. Louisa knew. I found a diary she kept when she lived in Philadelphia. And she called her Melina. Melina Summers."

Ruth got up from the table and left the room, returning with a package in her hands. Carefully, she unwrapped plastic, then brown paper, and held an old blue-covered notebook out to Ami and me. "This is it," she said. "The record of her grief and her fears. Some coded entries about how she began to make contact with abolitionists through Mr. Henry. Many long passages quoted from the books she was studying, trying to educate herself, trying to face the enormity of what she had lived through, what she was continuing to live through, trying – trying, I think, not to shrink from the realities – though that seems the easiest thing for us human beings to do. And this bunch of folded, faded pages stuck to the back cover, all about her weaknesses, the fears and anxieties she was trying to overcome, the pages folded many times, as if she had wanted to discard them, but kept them in the end. She was a brave girl, really. And when she left to join her Aunt Emma in Philadelphia, after they had sold her child, after Ruth died – she took her journal with her, of course, and continued it there – though less regularly. So here it is, preserved in a library of Quaker manuscripts in Philadelphia and sold, after much proving and pleading, to her great-granddaughter – me. It includes her record of learning to become an activist, of her attempts to find her son and her half sister. She never saw her father again, nor her brother, did not even return to Saint Elizabeth when they died, her father from a debilitating disease that sounds like emphysema, her brother in the war. She married a fellow worker in the cause, and she spoke publicly about her black family, her son and her sister. She kept trying to find them both, but she never succeeded. She lived to be an old woman, and if he had known more about her she might have met her grandson, my father. But it was long after his death that I began my research, of course, long after both their deaths that I found out about Louisa. People don't keep track, and so much is lost."

"I want to say something to my granddaughter," Myami said, turning to Ruth, "if you don't mind?"

She turned to me and began to speak in that new way again, as if she were letting the words out without thinking, not trying to make any connections, as if she didn't know what she was going to say before she said it.

"Your mother – she wasn't religious – I've begun the description of her you want – but she felt – well 'very Jewish' – that's how she put it. And she was very moved by the story of the Danish Christians who – when the Nazis invaded? – how all the Danes wore the yellow star. We're all Jews, is what Maya felt they meant to say. So she'd say – and it would embarrass your father at times – I'm Black. I heard him ask her – numerous times, sometimes angrily – not to say it so often – with such certainty – not caring about who was around."

I rolled my eyes, casting a worried knowing glance to Ruth, whose eyebrows were raised.

Myami waited several moments, then said, "Yes, I know, I understand him, how he must have felt. But I understand her, too."

"It was pretty – presumptuous," I said, glancing up at Ruth again, but I thought, *and kind of brave.*

"You're smiling," Ruth said, smiling herself, "about your mother."

This is what I have been trying to tell Myami all this time, I remember thinking, noticing the look of recognition spreading over her face, *about the halves and the quarters not being the point, that it's the history that is in your flesh, in your body, in the skin you're living in – isn't that a poem? or a song?*

" Does all this make you – do you feel angry, at – at – " I looked at Ruth.

A silence then, moments too long for comfort, but no one broke it.

293

"At you?" Ruth finally said. "No, Samantha. Not at all. And not at your grandmother, or even at Louisa. Not personally. No – but we have to remember. To get past it, we have to remember together, out loud."

"It must have taken a great deal out of you, to write that book," Myami said.

"Yes, and it's gonna take a great deal more to write this next one." Ruth sighed and placed her hand on Myami's, resting on the book where it had remained all this time.

Short, neatly clipped nails, a tawny beige, smooth against dark brown fingers; and long, elegantly shaped nails polished crimson against fingers of a lighter tan, called white. Myami seemed to be relishing the touch of Ruth's skin, staring at her large knuckles deeply creased from age, an image she might already be putting into words. She's writing, and it's just like fiction, I thought – the same noticing, the same layers of meaning, and a small part of me couldn't wait to be home, alone in my room with my history notebooks, now three of them, filled with the notes and stories Nicky had told me to write down.

They withdrew their hands at almost the same moment and smiled sadly at each other.

"It takes a lot of hatred to hate another body that much." Myami was speaking, but they were Ruth's words, a line from her book.

"Come," Ruth said. "I want to show you something."

Under a large old apple tree, its tightly closed white blossoms just beginning to bud out of their brown-leaf enclosures, a dark gray tombstone marked a slight incline in the earth. Only one name was cut into the stone.

"I was always told this was my uncle," Ruth said. "My mother's brother who died young. Much later I found out he was my brother. Henry Waterman. Their son, named for Mr. Henry, who my father never *ceased* talking about. I used to tease him I couldn't stand to hear his story one more time. Later, of course, I wished my father were around, telling that story and all the others to my girls. Anyway, the child was premature. He died when he was an infant, only two months old."

"So you weren't the child Belle was pregnant with when Hannah – when she – " I asked, and I bent down to touch the stone. Then I stood up straight again.

"No. I came later. This child is the one."

The women looked down at the grave. Ruth pulled up some weeds and an early Queen Anne's lace, twisting it around and around in her fingers. "I'd love to see some photographs of Hannah – especially when she was young, living here in Norwalk."

"I've saved everything," I said. "I have all her photographs in a book, and I've included other mementos, too – like a piece of her quilt cover, since she was always so particular about how everything looked – and my own notes, too, all I can remember from what she told me about that time in her life, how she met them – your parents – how I ended up getting my name – and the history, I'm studying that too."

"You're smart to do it. I'd be lost now if I didn't have my mother's ledger – and even so, I'll have to imagine a lot of it. When I wrote the book about my father and uncovered all the historical facts, I could hear his voice the whole time in my head, describing things, telling me the stories his father told him, stories I'd heard all my life. But my mother – Belle – she put most of what she felt into her writing, and the rest she kept to herself, at least when I knew her. I didn't really know her well, but – but – it's so obvious and I never saw it before. My mother was a writer, and I'm a writer too."

A different silence stretched after those words, perhaps beginning in a place I too had known this past year, moving through something to something new.

Something occurring long before you were born, like Henry's conception, his birth and his death, could change everything, Ruth would write, years later, in an Introduction to the memoir about her mother's life. *I realized this in a moment of silence standing near my brother's grave with two strangers who had suddenly, unpredictably, become part of my own story.*

It could smolder through years of time, fueling what seemed daring and new with old, even ancient, heat. I was young again, angry and in love. I had just announced I was going to Boston. My mother had left the room. I was leaning against the fireplace, stiff and righteous.

I remained standing there alone for some time, because my father had gone into the bedroom after my mother. When he came out again, I was in the same place. She loves you, Ruth, he said, clearly enough for me to hear as I stood near my brother's grave talking to a white woman I had only just met, and her black granddaughter who cared enough about the place where our histories joined to help me, though she did not know it at the time, with my own story. She loves you, he said again. Just don't know how to say it right – all her love of words – all seem to go into her stories – something changed in her a long time ago. Ain't no changing it back.

The precise words, the pauses between them, the near break in my father's husky voice, the way he always reverted to the syntax of his childhood when he was full of emotion he was afraid he couldn't control – perfectly preserved for all those years.

So it is just like childhood trauma, I saw: something in adult life, if it's disruptive enough, threatening enough, reverberating resonantly enough with disruptions in the past, can change everything. Belle could have gone on living with Samuel's passion for his father's history. She had grown used to it. She even shared it. And his ability to retell it, layering it with new knowledge gleaned from his reading and studying of the history they all shared, that precious capacity handed down to him through three generations, enchanted and inspired her even if it made her feel second at times. But all the rest? That Samuel had been disappointed in their child? In her? And the part about the white woman? And then her son's death? No. Some things were too much, and when her daughter was born, when I was born, the Ruth Samuel wanted more than . . . more than precisely what?

That I could not say, but I had finally entered my mother's

*point of view, a place I can never again choose to avoid, or
escape, for it just keeps coming to me now, sentence after
sentence, feeling after feeling, a rush of words.*

I reread those words many times, when the book had been
written and published, when I had also read Myami's hundred
pages of unformed memoir: "A Draft," she called it, underlining
the word *Draft* three times – a warning, the kind of mask she
loved.

In Ruth's yard that day the heavy spring rain had stopped,
but the smell enveloped us, its misty remnants dampening our
hair and skin and clothes. "Let's go in," Ruth said.

I walked ahead, leaving the two women to have the moment
alone I could see they wanted to share. When I reached the door
and turned, holding it open for them, I saw Myami take Ruth's
arm in a companionable way, but her body looked bent, folded
in by the weight of what she had not known, had just begun to
comprehend, and would now have to carry, and I was afraid of
the day when I would lose her. The lines in her face were deep
set, and dark, as if etched with a sharp pen.

Epilogue

On Narrow River Road, on the North Fork of Long Island, where I went almost every summer with my grandmother, the writer Ami Reed – though I hated the sea then and would never accompany her into the water – at the edge of Orient Village, once called Oyster Pond, there is a small graveyard. At one end are two large tombstones, one for Dr. Seth Tuthill, died May 30, 1850, at age sixty-six; one for his wife, Maria, died January 3, 1840, at the age of forty-eight. Surrounding them are twenty small, flat rocks dug deep into the ground. A sign at the entrance says these mark the graves of the former servants, once slaves, of Dr. Tuthill whom he wished to be buried near himself. Although slavery was abolished in 1830 in New York State, cemeteries were still segregated, and the only way Dr. Tuthill's former slaves could be buried with him was on his own private ground. The wish seems to be of affection, or at least connection, yet none of the small markers is inscribed with a name.

And that has become my task – to discover the names if at all possible, and inscribe them onto the stones, or at least list them on the sign. I will very likely be unsuccessful. Records have been lost, I am told, or were never kept. Some have expressed doubt that twenty bodies in fact lie beneath the stones. But I persist, pressed on to recover and write the story by two old women, both over ninety now, too old for the demands of writing, they say, but not too old to push me toward this labor they both loved and served over a lifetime, now bequeathed to me.

If you could see me as I write these words, any one of you might think you see a white woman. You would see a face the color of sand, dark brown hair, almost black, loose curls that

298

might be called waves. You would see full lips – but these might be the inheritance of many genetic pools. Dark eyes – like my broad mouth – might be Jewish, Italian, Spanish. Even those descended from full-blooded northern Europeans sometimes have dark eyes, broad features, olive skin. And yet – an edge of something not quite definable in my eyes – a flash of anger, a shadow of grief – might cause a spark of recognition, or suspicion, and one of you might look again and see a sign of the race mixing that has formed so many of us since this nation began.

Then you might hear the sound of my voice, you might even pay close attention to the meaning of my words. For my child, or your child, may ask some day, how did we all get here? What came before? What is still being written in our own lives? And either of us, you or I, might pull out these nearly forgotten pages and say, here's one story, and there are many, many more, if you care to read, or to listen, or to search for them. There are many more – yours for example– one of us might say to the child some day, for there is always the chance of seeing reality as it is, there will always be new ways of remembering this story, and there will always be someone promising never to forget.

Samantha Reed,
Orient, Long Island

Author's Note/Acknowledgements

This work, all the characters, and some of the places, including the town of Saint Elizabeth, are the products of my imagination.

All of the passages quoted from the works of abolitionists and references to historical events are taken from actual texts, listed below or identified in the novel itself.

The cemetery on Narrow River Road in Orient Village, Long Island, is real. Like Samantha Reed in the novel, I attempted to research the names of the individuals who lie beneath the unmarked stones, but like her, I have been told it is unlikely I will discover the information I seek. However, I plan to continue trying.

I have read and learned from many writers in my research for this novel. In particular I want to mention those works as being essential to my understanding of the history of slavery and American whiteness, and to my appreciation of the topography of some of the central places in the story:

Bordewich, Fergus M. *Bound for Canaan, The Underground Railroad and the War for the Soul of America.* New York: Amistad/Harper Collins, 2005.

David, Jay, Editor. *Growing Up Black.* New York: Avon Books, 1968.

Dybas, Cheryl Lyn. "Requiem for the Chesapeake."*Wildlife Conservation: Saving the Chesapeake.* April, 2005.

Gates, Henry Louis, Jr. *The Classic Slave Narratives*: *Narrative of the Life of Frederick Douglass.* New York: Mentor/Penguin, 1987.

Jacobs, Harriet. *Incidents in the Life of a Slave Girl, Written by Herself.* Yellin, Jean Fagan, Editor. Boston: Harvard University Press, 1987.

Peffer, Randall S. *Watermen.* Baltimore: Johns Hopkins University Press, 1979.

Perry, Mark. *Lift Up Thy Voice, the Grimke Family's Journey from Slaveholders to Civil Rights Leaders.* New York: The Viking Press, 2001.

Ray, Deborah Wing, and Stewart, Gloria P. *Norwalk: being an historical account of that Connecticut town.* Canan, New Hampshire: Phoenix Publishing, for the Norwalk Historical Society, 1979.

Roediger, David R., Editor. *Black on White: Black Writers on What It Means to Be White.* New York: Schocken, 1998.

Walker, David. *David Walker's Appeal, To The Coloured Citizens of the World.* Edited and Introduction by Peter P. Hinks. Pennsylvania: Pennsylvania State University Press, 2000.

Warner, William W. *Beautiful Swimmer: Watermen, Crabs and the Chesapeake Bay.* Boston, Toronto: Atlantic-Little Brown, 1976.

Wood, Marcus. *Blind Memory: Visual Representations of Slavery in England and America, 1780 – 1865.* New York: Routledge, 2000.

Woodward, C. Vann, Editor. *Mary Chestnut's Civil War.* New Haven and London: Yale University Press, 1981.

Zinn, Howard. *A People's History of the United States.* New York: Perennial Classics/Harper Collins, 2001.

The poem described by Samantha including the words "the skin you're living in" is by the late poet and performer Sekou Sundiata, included in his Spoken Word/Poetry CD, *The Blue Oneness of Dreams.*

I would also like to thank the librarians and curators of the Norwalk Historical Society Museum, for making many of the old city records available to me.

For many years I have studied and learned about the subjects and themes of this book from the great James Baldwin. "People are trapped in history, and history is trapped in them," he wrote in "Stranger in the Village" an essay in *Notes of a Native Son,* which says much of what can be said, and has been said, about the historical, political and psychological layers and meanings of whiteness.

Personal Acknowledgments

There are many people who helped me in many ways in the years it has taken to write and research this novel. I would like to pay tribute to them all, and if I have forgotten some, it is with apologies and no lack of appreciation.

Early readings and editorial help was given to me by the following writers: the late Sekou Sundiata, a great poet and teacher; Sara Ruddick, also sadly recently deceased, a brilliant voice about history, prose and character, about the nature of motherhood and grandmotherhood. Their deaths are a great loss to me, as writers, comrades and friends.

My wonderful writing group, Jan Clausen, Beverly Gologorsky, and Jocelyn Lieu helped me in numerous ways – reading, listening, discussing, pushing me forward from revision to revision, edit to edit, discouragement to faith.

I am especially indebted to Jan Clausen for her fine, close edit and copy edit which markedly improved the novel, both formally and technically.

Jill Giattino accomplished a careful and much needed proofread, given out of long standng love. I thank her for her work, and her friendship.

Jaime Manrique, a writer I admire deeply, read various versions of the novel over the years, offering critical response, belief in the work, and in me. Nancy Barnes, whose friendship has always included working with ideas in progress to precision and clarity, is a cherished reader and friend, as is Rachel Cowan, whose reading of the novel kept urging me onward.

I am indebted to Miryam Sivan who gave me important advice and response.

Carole Rosenthal and Lynda Schor read many versions of the manuscript. Their readings of my work, over the course of many years, has influenced and encouraged me, and, not least, supported me in publishing two novels with the wonderful press, *Hamilton Stone Editions.*

Special thanks goes to Meredith Sue Willis, for all her help in preparing the manuscript and for her leadership in the work of Hamilton Stone Editions, which publishes many fine books of fiction and poetry in this difficult time for serious literature; and to Lou Robinson, a wonderful artist, who designed the cover.

Ruth Charney is my oldest and most constant reader. I cannot thank her enough for her faith in me, and her brilliant, critical eye. My life and work would not be the same without her voice, her presence, her love; not to mention all I have learned from her about oysters and other life of the sea.

Jay Lord introduced me to skipjacks and the work of watermen on the Chesapeake. I thank him for his help.

Leona Ruggiero read the book and offered important responses based on her deep knowledge of the politics of race. Our many conversations as mothers and grandmothers, and her powerful love for her own grandchildren of so-called mixed race parentage: Liam, Satchel and Declan Hamilton, helped me clarify my thoughts and my insights.

Joanne Frye, teacher, writer and critic, gave me the benefit of a public reading at The College of Wooster in Ohio, in the series, "Memory, and Imagination: Self, Race and Motherhood." I am grateful for her close reading of the final version of the novel, providing appreciation and deep understanding of the work during a difficult time.

Professor Mary Cappello of the University of Rhode Island invited me to read from this and a previous novel in the Read/Write Series, presented by the English Department, co-directed by Peter Covino. It was an enriching and inspiring experience.

I am grateful to all the editors who published chapters of the novel before publication, both on line and in print, especially Yona Zeldis McDonough, and to the noted musicologist and composer, Tom Manoff, who interviewed me about my work, including work on this novel, and posted it on his website (www.tommanoff.com).

I thank Wendy Weil, and her assistant, Emma Patterson, for their efforts in behalf of the various versions of this work. Wendy Weil's editorial suggestions at a critical moment improved the structure of the novel in a crucial way.

Finally, I am always filled with gratitude and joy for the help and support in reading, commenting, and editing I am given by my sons, both excellent writers in their different genres: Adam Lazarre-White and Khary Lazarre-White, both of whom provided close readings and valuable suggestions. Adam's editorial brilliance and powerful sense of dramatic tension, due in part to his own work as actor, writer and teacher, in part to a long history of love of the spoken and written word, helped me during a difficult period of revision and made this a better book. Khary's understanding of social justice, American history and in particular American race history is expansive, detailed and astonishing in its depth, all from his work as a scholar and activist. I have learned more about this subject from him than from anyone else.

To my husband and dearest companion, Douglas H. White, who reads, listens, and loves without condition or apparent limit, and who teaches us all, in his daily life, the deepest meanings of blackness and of humanness, I can say only, thank you, with all my love.